Brendan Myers

*For Terry
Many blessings,
Brendan Myers*

Book One of The Fellwater Tales

Copyright © 2012 by Brendan Myers

All rights reserved.

For all enquiries, please contact the author through his web site:

http://brendanmyers.net

ISBN: 978-1-894981-34-7

Cover design by Jordan Stratford
http://jordanstratford.com

"Fellwater" is a work of fiction. Any character's resemblance to any actual person, living or dead, is purely coincidental.

Dedicated
to all those who see,
who love,
who protect,
and yes, even those who plot and conspire,
as these mere characters do.

~ 1 ~

Katie stood on her balcony, looking at the river of people flowing across the street below. Parents were bringing their children home from daycare. Teenagers were jostling each other as they got off their school buses. Pensioners were weeding their gardens and trimming their hedges. Newsboys went door to door with their carts and bicycles, delivering their papers and flyers. Katie felt as if at that moment she was witnessing the universal whirl of life, and that all things were playing out their parts just for her. How easy and beautiful it would be, she felt, to lean out from her balcony, fall into that river, and follow its flow to the end! A brief gust of wind brought the scent of lilac flowers from a nearby tree. They had just bloomed that very morning, for the first time that year. Katie closed her eyes to breathe the scent in as deeply as she could. Everything around her at that moment seemed like a great revelation, like a message from the world, confirming that tonight was The Night. The moment had come to go to Eric's house, tell him her true feelings, and ask him if he loved her. She was sure he would see things her way, and that he would say yes.

After a final deep breath, she turned from the edge of the balcony, gathered her purse and coat from inside her apartment, and then made for Eric's house. She walked with purpose, but did not hurry. There were strangers to smile to, and tree branches to caress on the way. But her heartbeat quickened when she arrived at the low-rise, yellow-brick building where Eric lived, and her fingers hesitated before turning her key in his door.

Inside his apartment, Eric Laflamme was sitting in his favourite reading chair, looking at the clock on his computer and a pile of books on his desk. He was trying to decide whether he should stay up later to get more research done, or else call it a day and go to bed. There wasn't much incentive for him to stay awake any longer. An essay had to be written within a few days, and he was in no danger of being late for it, but he wondered if sleeping off the rest of the day, and pulling an all-nighter tomorrow, might be worth it. He put his laptop on the floor and walked over to the window. A spotted Calico cat jumped on the windowsill next to him. Eric reached down and gave his pet a friendly scratch, and was rewarded with the sound of contented purring.

Just as he made up his mind to do some serious studying, Katie stepped over his threshold and into his realm, looking a little flustered yet bright-eyed and cheerful. She smiled a wide and beautiful smile to Eric, who answered it with a sheepish grin of his own, just before they warmly hugged and kissed each other.

"You look absolutely beautiful today, Eric", said Katie.

Eric smirked. "I'm a mess, and I know it." He had not been out of his apartment all day. He was dressed in a white T-shirt and a pair of coffee-stained jeans, cut off at the knees. In large black capital letters, his T-shirt proclaimed the slogan 'Choose Angst'. A pair of thick woolen socks warmed his feet. His shoulder-length blonde hair, although tied back and out of his face, had obviously not been brushed in the last three or four days. A few days worth of stubble textured his face.

"Homework taken priority over showering again?" teased Katie. Eric answered with an apologetic grin. Katie was still dressed in her work clothes: black high heeled shoes, a burgundy pencil skirt and white blouse, and a matching burgundy business jacket. Her red hair was neatly combed and parted, although its waves and curls were little bit unruly, as red hair can never be truly tamed.

"You, on the other hand, are wonderfully beautiful. I am not worthy to be in your presence," joked Eric in reply. Katie thanked him by sticking out her tongue at him. Eric picked a small stack of books and papers off the couch, nonchalantly dumped them on top of another stack of books and papers on his desk, and motioned for Katie to take a seat. Then he stepped into the kitchen and continued babbling, to cover the fact that he was caught unprepared for her visit.

"Oh, don't worry about the mess, or about me," Katie said, looking at Eric's research notes strewn on the floor. "But I've got something planned for us for tonight, so you better have a shower!"

Eric ran his fingers through his hair, and decided she was right. He gave her a quick peck on her cheek, apologized for his appearance one more time, and disappeared into the bathroom. As soon as he was out of sight, Katie sighed and bit her lip. She was slightly annoyed that Eric was unprepared for her arrival, despite the fact that she came by surprise. And she didn't want to put off her question much longer, in case she became afraid to ask it. To pass the time she sat at his desk and looked at the books spread out upon it. One of them was an old, hardcover art history text, open to a page that featured a photograph of an ancient hollow mound somewhere in Ireland. Beside it was a small gift-wrapped package with her name on it. She picked it up curiously, and glanced at the bathroom door. Deciding she had enough time to open it and then wrap it up again before Eric finished his shower, she carefully peeled the wrapping off. Inside she found two small picture frames, both holding the same photograph: a shot of the two of them together, leaning on opposite sides of a tall Gothic arched door at the university where Eric was a student. Both were grinning into the camera from ear to ear, clearly happy to be there. This picture, Katie recalled, was taken on the day they met each other. Katie smiled again, reliving the memory. On the back of one of the frames Eric had written the words '*To Katie, for our six month anniversary, from Eric.*'

     Katie bounced up from the chair and exclaimed out loud "He remembered!" She kicked off her shoes, dropped off all her clothes, and stepped into the shower beside her lover. Eric was about to object, but she silenced him with a hungry kiss, and wrapped her freckled arms around his body, and traced her fingernails along his neck and spine, until Eric felt no further need to protest.

~ 2 ~

     Upon the evening, Katie and Eric donned housecoats and drifted to the balcony to share a bottle of wine, and to watch the setting sun pull the up the evening from the west, to cover the world like a blanket. Three crows settled on top of a nearby tree, and Katie studied them intently, wondering if they had come to remind her to ask her question. She closed her eyes for a moment, and then began the speech she had rehearsed in her mind all day.

     "We've been seeing each other for almost six months now. It's been a lot of fun, and I'm having a good time, and—"

     "I think we're the perfect couple. Cheers!" interrupted Eric, as he clinked his glass with hers.

     "Eric, do you believe in soul-mates?" she blurted. She hadn't planned to ask him this way, but the question just came out by itself. She held her breath and looked at him with expectation.

Eric's smile changed into a more confused, inquisitive expression. "Soul mates?" he said, and looked across to the park.

"I had another of my dreams last night. You know, the ones that always seem so real? I dreamed that our lives together have a purpose, and that two people who really like each other and who are really good for each other, are actually bound together in some magical way, and always have been, and are meant to be together. I think the dream might have been about – you and me."

Eric smiled and said, "I was just thinking this morning how good everything has been going for both of us. I made the Dean's Honour List this term, and you've got a really good job at the bank now, and we both have a wonderful relationship, and everything in life is in order. No complains, no worries. Everything has come together perfectly."

Katie looked at the park. The shadows lengthened themselves just a little longer than they should, the tree branches drooped a little lower. The three crows flocked closer to the railing of the balcony and watched, with seeming intelligence.

"But in my dream, there was more," said Katie, struggling to explain her thoughts. "I'm twenty years old now, and I've almost nothing to show for it. I used to have all kinds of dreams, all the time, about what I would do with my life, and where I wanted to go, and then I suddenly asked myself, what happened to them? What have I done, really, to make them happen? Do you remember when you were a kid, and people asked you what you wanted to be when you grew up?"

Eric tried to reassure her. "I wanted to be a scientist. Actually, an astronomer. But we're both still young. It's not too late for you to go back to university and get your DVM. We both have lots of time."

"But maybe we *don't* have lots of time. I'm at the point now where I should be able to say: I've got the purpose of my life in hand, and I'm going where I want to go, I'm on my way. But it feels like I'm going nowhere. I feel as if I don't belong here, as if I'm living someone else's life."

"Once I wanted to be a scientist. Now I study history. It's different, but it's not so bad."

"Do you believe you are doing what you are supposed to be doing?" asked Katie.

"I don't know, I don't really think about such things. I just go with the flow."

Katie turned away from Eric, with downcast eyes, and looked at the flowing water of the nearby river, turning its eddy-currents and little round waves. After a breath, she turned around to him again, with a little bit more frustration. "But that exactly what seems wrong to me. I mean, can you imagine how your life would go if that's how you lived? Just going with the flow, all the time? You'd be blown around, you'd be a leaf in the wind, a leaf on the surface of a stream, just being carried away from one thing to another, with no reason for it. No sense of where you are going, or where you are supposed to go. How do you know that tomorrow you will still want to study history? How do you know that tomorrow, you will still love me?"

Eric looked at Katie over the top of his glasses, and perked one of his eyebrows.

Katie continued: "And your dreams would be like that too – they would blow around, with no direction, and no meaning, and you couldn't do anything to make them happen. Well I can't live like that. I believe that things happen for a purpose, that my dreams have meaning, and we're all here for a reason. I need to know that you and I are together for a reason. I really need to believe that. And I want to know what *your* feelings are. Don't you understand?"

After reminiscing for a while, Eric said. "Katie, I really like you. I'm very happy to be with you, and I'm very happy that you like me too. We've never had an argument and I was rather hoping that we never would. We're both having a good time. Isn't that by itself a good thing?"

"Well, yes," Katie was forced to agree. Then she took his hands, looked directly into his eyes, and asked, "But isn't it more than that too? Don't you feel as if it's natural that we are together, as if we've known each other for a hundred years? That's what I saw in my dream that other night, the one I told you about. Remember? I saw you, and I, together, in a magical forest. I saw our souls growing together, like two rivers that flow into one.

"A beautiful dream," said Eric.

"But it's the only one of my dreams that I can see right now, finally coming true. All my other dreams are fading away, they're disappearing. But this one. You and I – we have been here before, we have known each other maybe hundreds of years, and we are soul mates, together. I feel that very deeply. Do you feel it too?"

There, she thought. The Question has been asked. All my cards are on the table now. Katie looked into Eric's eyes as a small shudder of fear passed through her belly.

Eric's response was to look down to the grass and quietly whisper, "No."

A breeze from the north began to blow, stirring up dust in the parking lot. Clouds on the horizon began to thicken and darken.

"No?" she pleaded.

Eric tried to explain. "Well it makes more sense to me to believe that life is so big and complex there isn't one single explanation for all of it, and maybe there's no single explanation for any of it. And people can love lots of people at the same time, for lots of different reasons."

Eric had mentioned the 'L' word for the first time. It was suddenly a different conversation. Katie narrowed her eyes. "If there's another woman in your life, I need to know about her, right now," she declared.

"No!" said Eric adamantly. "Katie, I mean people like your parents, your sisters and brothers, maybe a favourite teacher when you were a child—"

This, for Katie, was all she could take of Eric's rationalizations. It was time for her to press to the important point. She rounded on him angrily. "Do you even know what love is? You don't. Because if you did you would know what I'm talking about, and you would have told me by now that you —loved me. But do you love me? Do you?"

"You asked me what my opinion was, and I told you. I don't understand what's wrong here. What more do you want."

Katie grasped his shoulders. "I want you to understand what I'm asking you. I want you to understand – me."

Eric's reply was calm but defiant. "I'm being honest with you. Isn't that worth something?"

"Well you were being honest. And I'm glad I asked you now, after only six months, so that six years from now I don't wake up and find myself married to someone who doesn't love me!"

"Katie!" Eric protested. He reached out to her, but Katie pushed his hand away.

"Don't touch me!" she ordered.

And with that Katie gathered her clothes and shoes in a bag and marched out of the apartment, and slammed the door loudly behind her.

Eric sat down in his chair again, feeling exhausted and confused. Ganga moved to the window sill and watched Katie exit the building and stomp across the parking lot. He pawed the window, as if to get her attention, or to wave goodbye on Eric's behalf. But Katie did not look back. She marched angrily off, still wearing Eric's borrowed bathrobe, into the swiftly falling night.

~ 3 ~

Katie pushed herself through her apartment door, closed it behind her and leaned on it, until she sank to the floor. She dropped her bag of clothes to one side and thanked some God somewhere that relatively few people saw her walking through the town centre wearing only a bathrobe. A siren from an ambulance howled somewhere, echoing off the walls. The window blinds were like steel jail cell bars, and with the street light shining through them they cast an oppressive shadow on her. Yet she did not turn on the light. In her mind she replayed the conversation with Eric, and repeated out loud some of the things she said to him, and wanted to say to him. "The day was supposed to be perfect! How could you spoil it like that!"

She went to the bedroom to sort her bag of clothes, and there she noticed that she had left her jacket behind. She cursed quietly, but decided not to retrieve it just yet. "It's a Friday and I don't have to work tomorrow. I'm going out. And I'm going to do something fun to forget about everything."

She opened her wardrobe and found a pair of blue jeans, a white blouse with an embroidered neck line, and a scarf for a belt. She pulled them on, then sat by her dresser to touch up her face and tied two ponytails into her hair. She wanted to go to a club and jump around and play like a child. But she was also a grown twenty-something and wanted everyone to know it, so she also pulled on a pair of black high heel boots, and tucked the legs of her jeans into them. She picked a casual jacket from the hall closet and headed out the door.

The Underground, the only nightclub in the little town of Fellwater, was only a short distance away, and had been the centre of her social life since high school. It was where she bought her first rum and coke, at least two years before she was legally old enough. And it was where she knew she would run into a few friends, returning home for the weekend from their jobs in neighbouring towns and cities. The front door of the club was a large and heavy affair, more like a wall than a door, and designed to be overlooked. It was painted black, with the name of the club spelled out in solid iron letters. Katie pushed it open and walked down the steps to the basement, where the bar was. Sure enough, the club was full of friends. A table full of them shrieked with delight when they saw her, and called her over. Someone ordered a drink for her. Someone else took her jacket and put it safely behind the bar, with a nod of approval from one of the bouncers. And then her friends began shouting some kind of gossip in her ear, all at once. Finally one of the girls noticed her downcast expression and the stream of a tear on her face.

"I broke up with Eric today."

Everyone dropped their jaws in surprise. But their silence lasted only an instant. Then the cacophony erupted again, and almost drowned out the music.

"You did? Broke up with him? You seemed so good together, and you were so happy. Why what happened? What did he do? Tell me everything!"

Katie tried to get in a word of her own. "Well I asked him if he believed in soul mates, and if he thought that he and I were meant to be together, and he said no".

The cacophony howled and approved of her break-up. Well obviously he doesn't love you. I think you totally did the right thing. What a loser! He was no good for you. He said that? Well obviously he was cheating on you. He didn't know a good thing when he had it. You go girl! Free and independent again! Time to move on. You ready to forget him and find another guy? I hear that the bouncer has a thing for you.

The last remark caught Katie's attention. "What, Paul Turner? I've known him since high school" Katie said.

"Exactly," said her friend. Katie looked over to him, and saw he was examining someone's driver's license at the door. He and Katie had always had fun together, although they were never more than acquaintances. He was tall, more muscular than Eric, and more outgoing. Once he entered his twenties, the line of his sandy-brown hair began to recede, and he developed a premature streak of grey. But he never acted self-conscious or vain about it. More often than not, he would joke about it. Katie smiled at the thought of letting him try to pick her up. He had tried often enough in the past, but never seemed serious about it.

Katie turned back to her friends. "I broke up with Eric only an hour ago. The last thing I want is a new man. Tonight I'm just going to dance, and drink, and have a good time," said Katie, in answer to all the questions at once. Katie gulped down half of her drink. "That's all I have to say. I'm going dancing now. It's Friday!" And with that she definitively thumped her drink on the table.

The Underground was not a large club. There were less than a dozen tables, a few pool tables and video game machines, and a dance floor no larger than Katie's apartment. But Katie thought of it as her second living room. It had just the right amount of darkness and mood lighting. There was a forest-green military camouflage net hanging from the ceiling. On one wall there was a painting of a woman passionately embracing a demonic creature with big leathery wings. On another wall there was a white projection screen. Tonight it was displaying scenes from a low-budget vampire movie made in the 70's. The dance floor was painted with a black and white spider-web. Katie swaggered to the centre of it, and started bouncing in time with the heavy pulse of the music. The music was hypnotic, and it surrounded her, enclosing her in a world of sound. The flashing coloured lights bore through her eyes and deep into her brain. And the sound pressed against her skin, and resonated with her bones. Soon she was spinning in a world of sound and light. To welcome that feeling she sang and howled along with the music, raised up her hands as if hearing the word of a preacher promising salvation, and allowed herself to be taken away.

Just for a moment, the night club faded away. The people became mere shadows, and the lights fuzzy and distant. Just for a moment they resolved themselves into the shape of a bonfire at night, in a forest clearing. Around the fire was a ring of people, dancing, jumping, twisting their arms and bodies in long, frenzied circles, to the rhythm of a group of drummers who stood to one side of the circle. Some of the people wore linen dresses or trousers, and some wore only a loincloth, and some wore nothing at all. Many had delicate spirals painted on their arms and legs, in blue and green. Some of the drummers were singing something in a foreign language, but there were a few words she could understand perfectly. One of them was certainly a name, and she wasn't sure if she had not heard it before.

Standing off to the side of the scene was a tall, olive skinned man with short-cropped dark curls, wearing a crimson cloak, leather sandal boots, and metal plate armour on his chest. In one of his hands he held what appeared to be a large scroll. He both belonged to the vision and yet did not belong, not just for his attire, but also his demeanor: he watched the circle dancers dispassionately, almost disapprovingly. A burst from the fire sent a glowing ember toward him, and he crushed it into the sand where it landed. When he was satisfied that it was extinguished, he looked up, and met Katie's eyes, and smiled.

The image faded. Katie was still in the dance floor in the Underground, where a crowd of Goths, rockers, and hipsters danced in a circle around the spiderweb on the floor. A round little man with a handlebar moustache was trying to stroke her back. Her friends, who by then had gathered around her, chased him off. As she watched them jumping with the music and squealing with delight, she noticed another man leaning against the railing of the stair chatting with a bouncer. He had a black suit jacket, with a black silk tie and a blood red shirt, or so it seemed in the moving lights of the dance floor. He seemed tall and strong-looking, perhaps a former bouncer himself, although with such an expensive looking suit he surely did not have a minimum wage security job. Katie made a mental note to ask the bouncer about the man in the suit. But when the man turned his head to say hello to someone else, she saw his curly brown hair, his neatly trimmed beard, his olive skin.

It was the same man from the vision of the fire.

~ 4 ~

Katie surprised some of her friends by standing still, nearly motionless, near the middle of the dance floor. The man by the stair was a little darker-skinned, and his hair was a bit thicker and more curly than the hair on the man she had seen in the vision. But the face and eyes were unmistakable. She stood motionless on the dance floor, her eyes fixed on him, wishing for him to fix his gaze back at her. But other dancers got in the way of her line of sight. She walked back to the table and sat down. Her cacophony of friends followed her there. One of them, a fair-skinned blonde girl who tonight was wearing cat-eye contact lenses and vampire fangs, slid onto a stool next to Katie and whispered in her ear. "What's wrong Katie? Don't let the thought of Eric get you down. He was a bastard, admit it. You are better off without him."

"Oh, Siobhan," said Katie, when she realized her friend was there. "That's not it. I just had another of those visions I was telling you about. But this time, I had it while wide awake, just now, on the dance floor."

Siobhan nodded gravely. "What did you see?"

"Him," said Katie, indicating the man at the door. "I've seen him before. The man in the suit talking to Paul the bouncer. I know it. But I can't quite think of where. And I saw him in my vision, just now."

"I don't think I know him. He's never been here before – oh but he's a class act, dressed like that down here. In fact he looks a little lost. I wonder what he'd do if I tried to bite him!" said Siobhan, and she licked her lips.

"No, don't, please," said Katie. "I think there's a reason he is here. You know, I was saying that to Eric today. We're all here for a reason. Maybe there's a reason it's his first time in our club, and a reason why I find him so familiar. I've got a feeling about this one."

Siobhan howled with delight. Whatever happened, it would be excellent gossip, and she could enjoy embarrassing Katie about it for ages.

"Go get him, before I do," said Siobhan. Someone passed Katie her jacket, and someone else gave her a big hug and wished her good hunting. Katie looked over at the man, and took a deep breath. "Please promise not to tell Eric?"

"We promise. We won't tell him. But we're going to tell everyone else!" And they cackled with glee and ran off to the dance floor.

Katie steadied herself and walked to the bottom of the stair where the man stood. She made it seem as if she was on her way out to another bar. As she passed, she smiled brightly to the door man. "Have a good night, Mister Turner."

"You only ever call me that when you're up to something," said Paul, with a laugh.

"What, sweet innocent little me? I'm a good little girl," giggled Katie. She was teasing Paul, but she also hoped the strange man in the suit was close enough to hear. As she passed him, she met his eyes and winked, inviting him to follow. But as she did so, she suddenly felt a wave of weakness. Something about the man's gaze made her feel not just that she knew him, but also that he knew her too. He did not gawk or leer at her: he simply observed her, but with a calculating eye, one which sees through all pretenses, and which analyzes the heart and soul. Katie's legs buckled beneath her a little, so she made herself look away. She reached for the banister to steady herself.

"You okay there?" said Paul.

"Fine, just thought I dropped something. Gotta go!" And she flashed her best smile, trying not to make eye contact, and hastened up the steps and out the door.

Once on the street, she gave herself a moment to breathe, and reminded herself of her plan. She started walking down towards another pub, which she hoped would be quieter and less crowded, where she and the olive skinned man could have a conversation, if he chose to follow her. Every few steps she looked behind her, to see if anyone emerged from the Underground. Sure enough, after only a minute, the heavy black door opened and out stepped the strange man. He took a moment to button up his jacket, check his watch, and examine the street. Then he began to walk in her direction with brisk, purposeful steps. Suddenly Katie thought that this was a very bad idea. She had no idea who he was, or what she expected to happen when she got to chat with him. She stepped into the recess of a storefront, out of his field of view. She could hear his footsteps approaching. For a second she wondered if she should go to Eric's house and make amends. Surely it was impulsive and foolish to end a good relationship over one argument. But then it was too late. The strange man passed by, and just for a second they were close enough to touch, if only she dared to reach out. Again she had to steady herself, and she buried her head in the corner of the wall, and held her breath.

If he saw her as he passed, he made no sign of it. When Katie caught her breath again and looked up, in time to see him from behind, walking away. As he passed beneath a neon shop sign, its light sputtered and died, leaving him shrouded in mystery again. She decided to follow him after all, but at a discreet distance, as she was painfully aware of the sound of her heels on the concrete footpath. He rounded a corner and she hurried up to it, peering around to see where he was going. At the next corner he crossed the street and went up to the door of another bar. Funny, she thought to herself, that was exactly where I was thinking of leading him. Perhaps he read my mind.

The man grasped the door handle and opened it, but as he did so he turned slightly, and Katie made eye contact with him again. She couldn't duck away this time. But the man made it easier for her by flashing a knowing smile as he stepped inside the bar. Katie suddenly realised that where she thought she was following him, she was actually being led by him. He wanted to talk to her too. She crossed the street, smiled sweetly at the doorman so that he would not ask for her identification, grasped the door handle and pulled it open.

The establishment was called The Carriage House, and it was said to be the oldest pub in Fellwater, founded in the same year the town itself was founded. Katie took a few steps inside and looked around. Not seeing the strange man she was following, she went to the bar and ordered a rum and coke. He knows I am here, she reasoned to herself. He knows I followed him this far. So I will make my stand here at the bar, and make him come to me.

She was half way through her glass when she found that the man was standing beside her, his jacket unbuttoned, his hand holding glass of red wine. She was momentarily startled, but regained her composure quickly. Now that she had him to herself, she had to be sure of what she was going to do. She raised her glass and was about to speak, but he spoke first.

"Katherine Corrigan. It's lovely to see you again. You are looking well, I cannot help but be impressed."

Katie was stunned. He knew her name!

"I'm sorry, I don't believe we've met before," said Katie.

"My name is Carlo. And yes, we have met before."

~ 5 ~

Katie dropped her jaw in shock.

"That has got to be absolutely the *worst* pick-up line I have *ever* heard," she stated, loud enough for anyone nearby to hear.

"As the opening move in a dating game, it is indeed most absurd," said Carlo, quite casually. "But as a statement of fact, it happens to be true."

That was an odd thing to say, Katie thought. It was time to take control again. "I have a boyfriend you know, and he's training for the Olympic track team. I'm sure he would not be happy to see you chatting me up like this." It was a long shot, but it sometimes worked to get rid of unwanted men. She looked around the room, partly to see if anyone was paying attention, but also to see if there was another place to sit down, preferably a table that had a few boys already sitting around it. Seeing one, she swung around in her seat, preparing to get up.

But Carlo gently put his hand on her arm. "I know all about Eric as well. He is studying history at the local university. If I am not mistaken, he is at home right now, writing an essay about the first French settlers in North America. When you met him, you were at the same university, studying zoology. But you did not finish because you ran out of money."

Katie sat down again, unsure of what to do. "How do you know all this about me?"

Carlo leaned forward a little. "But surely what you really want to know is why you think that you know *me*. Is it not so? The answer is that you and I have met before. You know me just as well as I know you. And what you really want to know is how that this can be possible."

Katie looked back at him, considering her next move. It looked as if the only way she could take back control of the situation would be to get up and leave. But the sight of him in her vision was still very much a force in her mind. Hearing his voice was hypnotic: she felt she could listen to it all evening, no matter what he said. Despite his forthright attitude and the frightening amount of knowledge he had of her life, she did want to know why she found him so familiar. And she wanted to know why she saw him in the vision, tending the fire at some kind of tribal ceremony. She sipped her drink again and decided that the best thing to do was to push him off and let him win her attention again.

"I swear I've never met you in my life. Never!", she replied, and then she turned her back on him.

"Well, we did meet under some unusual circumstances. Naturally, I don't expect that you realize who I am, at least not right away. But I do hope that you will. Very soon. You will."

Katie didn't know what to say. Carlo took another sip from his glass and continued. "Unless, that is, of course, unless —you are already happy with your life as it is, and you don't need to change anything?"

The words struck Katie like falling stones. Did Carlo know about the argument with Eric as well? Katie did not like where this conversation was going.

"I've got a decent job, lots of friends, a really nice apartment, and a boyfriend. If I need to change anything, I can do it myself."

"Eric is a very good man", Carlo interrupted. "In fact I do believe that he loves you. Has he said so yet?"

Katie said nothing, but kept her eyes fixed on him, partly fearful of what he knew, partly curious about what else he might know.

Carlo continued, "If you decide to spend this life with him, he will be good to you, and make you very happy, most of the time. He is intelligent, caring, and rather handsome when he chooses to take care of himself. The two of you may even be married some day."

This made her smile. But then Carlo leaned closer, and as he did so all the sounds from the rest of the bar seemed to dim almost to silence. Suddenly Carlo was the only other person in the room. He spoke again, and she did not so much hear his words as feel them in her bones.

"But I know you, Katie. I know your soul. You want something more, don't you? You don't want an ordinary love. You want a love that shines as bright as the sun. You want a love that will stand strong forever, even if all the world was destroyed and time itself came to an end. You want a soul mate."

"Okay, funny guy," she demanded. "What are you, some kind of stalker? How do you know so much about me?"

"Because, as I say," answered Carlo, "we have met before, and you told me these things yourself."

Katie narrowed her eyes at him and asked, "Where."

Carlo paused, as if assessing whether Katie was ready to hear his answer. "We met," he said, "in your dreams."

Katie flustered with annoyance. "My dreams? That's the second ridiculous pick up line from you tonight."

Carlo continued his explanation. "And the most recent dream we shared," Carlo continued, "was only ten minutes ago. I think I would have looked a little different to you then. A little more – military, perhaps?"

Now Carlo had Katie's full attention. "How did you—" she started to ask, but could not finish the question.

Carlo leaned forward. "And there are more people like us out there, Katie. You and I are not the only ones."

"There are more?" asked Katie, her wonderment obvious.

"There are. You are not alone. *We* are not alone." Then Carlo stood and began to button his jacket, preparing to leave.

"But this is not the right place to tell you the whole story. For tonight, it was enough for me to do no more than re-introduce myself. That re-introduction is now accomplished. And I'm afraid I have some guests arriving at my home shortly, and I must be ready for them. So, I must depart. We will see each other again soon." Carlo stepped past her towards the door.

Katie turned in her seat to face him. None of her questions were answered; none of her plans fulfilled. The thought of leaving things as they were, before she could say or do anything, was simply unacceptable. She called out, "How will I find you again?"

Carlo smiled. "I almost forgot. You can usually find me at home." With a flick of his wrist, a business card appeared in his hand, which he presented to Katie. Then he swept out the door and out of sight.

Katie watched the door close after him. Her heart was still beating a hundred times faster than it should. Only that afternoon she was sure that her future lay with Eric. Now Eric's complete lack of sensitivity to her feelings had spoiled her whole image of him. And a new man, Carlo, had entered her life like a ray of sunshine through dark clouds. She still had many questions and a great deal of confusion. But in her hand she held a key that might unlock at least some of them. She looked down at the card.

Carlo Maliguida
Patrician of House DiAngelo
for All Ontario

On the back there were two postal addresses and a telephone number for each of them. One was not far away, in an older part of Fellwater. The other address was a post-office box in Rome, Italy. The card created some new questions in her mind. It appeared that Carlo was a man of some importance. But she had no idea what was meant by 'House DiAngelo'. And she had no idea what a 'Patrician' was. Eric would probably know. But Katie wasn't going to ask him.

There was someone else she could ask: Carlo himself. She quickly finished her wine, got up from the bar stool, and headed for the door.

~ 6 ~

Eric lay in his bed, and held up his copy of the photograph he had framed for Katie, and tried to understand what had just happened. This was only our first fight, he thought, so it surely means we haven't already broken up. Didn't the 'argument' start off when she tried to express some deep and heartfelt feelings for him? Surely those feelings would not be gone and forgotten in the space of four hours. But perhaps they could be. It is not easy to make analytic statements about feelings, or about how they work. Indeed Eric was unsure about his own feelings just at that moment. He was feeling hurt, of course. But he was also, perhaps strangely, feeling calm, as if a part of him was refusing to believe the situation had even happened.

Eventually he put the picture down on his bedside table, and turned off the light. He felt sure that he would see her again tomorrow, and that everything would be made clear. To rest his mind, he counted the lights from passing cars as they crossed his ceiling.

He had just about fallen asleep in his bed when his peace was shattered by an alarming noise. It was Katie's mobile phone, in her jacket pocket, left behind on Eric's couch. For a moment he wasn't sure where the sound was coming from. He thought to ignore it and let it go to voice mail, but it kept ringing and didn't stop. He turned over in his bed and plugged his ears with a pillow. The phone still rang. He got up, found the phone, turned it off, and went back to bed.

But a moment later, the phone rang again. Eric sat up in bed, and looked around, as if there were others with whom he could share his puzzlement. He got up and shut it off again, and then buried it under the cushions of his couch. Yet a third time, less than a minute later, the phone rang again. The caller report on the screen said "Unknown".

Eric clicked the Answer button and raised the phone to his ear. The voice on the other end of the line spoke first. It sounded urgent, and its message took him completely by surprise.

"Miss Corrigan. Listen carefully. Your life is in danger."

~ 7 ~

The street outside of the Carriage House was filling up with weekend party-goers on the crawl. Katie asked the doorman to point to where Carlo went, and the doorman indicated a large black luxury car across the road. Carlo was just closing the driver's door and starting up the engine. Katie took a deep breath, clutched her purse close. The feeling of something she knew was hers helped her feel a little more secure. Then she strode purposefully across the road, and stood in the path of Carlo's vehicle just as he was about to pull away. So he stopped, and stepped out, and gazed carefully into her eyes.

"You need to answer some questions, Mister DiAngelo", said Katie, trying to sound stern and in command. Carlo simply loomed his head toward her, inquiringly, as an amused teacher might do to an impertinent child. "I need to know why you are following me, or else I'll call the police and have you arrested for stalking."

An impish grin grew on Carlo's face, but he said nothing.

"I've a witness right over there," insisted Katie, indicating the doorman at the pub. Carlo tilted his head to observe the doorman casually smoking a cigarette and looking in the complete opposite direction.

"Shall I assume," said Carlo, after a breath, "that by standing in my way like this, you have made your choice?"

"What choice?" asked Katie.

"To no longer take the world as it is given to you, without trying to change anything. But rather, instead, to follow your dreams, and see if they can come true."

Katie looked away, in the direction of the road leading to her apartment.

"Or," Carlo continued gravely, "instead, you can just go home, and live the life you would have lived anyway. I will not trouble you ever again if that is what you want. But think about what is waiting for you there."

Katie thought about the stack of unwashed dishes in her sink, the empty pizza boxes stacked in the corner of the kitchen, the dusty CD's strewn about the floor, the unmatched second-hand furniture, and the framed photo which Eric had given to her earlier in the day. The only thing missing was the white picket fence.

But when her thoughts returned to the here and now, Carlo had driven away.

~ 8 ~

"Who the hell is this?" Eric howled into Katie's mobile phone.

The caller, whoever it was, must have been surprised to hear Eric's voice instead of Katie's. He looked at the screen to see who it was, but the word "Unknown" still scrolled across it. He put the phone back to his ear again and shouted angrily, "Is this some kind of sick joke?"

"It is vital that I speak to Miss Corrigan. Please put her on", said the mysterious voice again. It was a deep voice, but Eric could not tell if it was male or female. He could hear the sound of white noise in the background, like the sound of river rapids, or high winds.

"You've got the wrong number," he hissed, and he hung up. But a moment later, the phone rang again. Eric stuffed it in the couch again and stormed off into the bedroom, hoping that the caller would simply give up. But before long, with the phone still ringing, Eric lost patience first. He pulled the phone out of the couch again, opened up the case and tore out the battery. The phone immediately went silent and dead. "That's enough of that", he declared, as if the caller could hear.

Then Eric sat in his reading chair and gazed out his living room window, to the green space on the other side of the parking lot. In the darkness, he could discern the outline of the old stone bridge over the river. It was the last original one-lane bridge over the river that survived from the time the town was founded. All of the other original bridges had long since been replaced by modern steel and concrete, wide enough for modern cars and multiple lanes. But this bridge was kept as a heritage monument. The original iron lamp posts on its four corners were fitted with electric bulbs. One of them was flickering as if there was a fault in the wires. Eric contemplated the flickering for a short while, and then slowly moped into his kitchen to get a cup of water. But he froze in mid step when he heard the impossible sound of Katie's mobile phone, ringing, again.

Eric's grip on his water glass tightened, and his fingers turned white. He stared at the phone for a moment, and then reached for it, but withdrew his fingers just before touching it. The screen was lit, with the words "Unknown" scrolling across it, just as before. Soon curiosity overcame fear, and he turned it over in his hands. The case was still open, revealing the empty slot where the battery should be. Immediately he dropped it on the floor and stepped back from it. For a moment he thought about crushing it under a hammer. But then he thought of the message the caller was trying to deliver. Timidly, he picked it up again, pressed the Answer button, and held it to his ear.

"It is vital that I deliver a warning to Miss Corrigan," said the voice, calm but authoritative.

Eric could no longer argue with the caller. But he still hesitated. The caller surely would not like his answer. "I can't", he said, and hoped the caller could hear the honesty. "She really isn't here, I wasn't lying."

"To whom am I speaking?" asked the voice.

"My name is Eric," he answered. Out of nervousness, he added, "I'm the boyfriend."

There was a pause before the voice continued. "Eric, if you care about your woman, you may be able to help. You must find her as soon as possible. Then you must take her somewhere safe. Not her house, not yours. Her life may depend on it."

"You don't understand," said Eric, more frustrated than angry, "Katie and I had an argument today. And she probably doesn't want to see me. Why, what's happening to her? What's going on?"

"We cannot explain everything to you at this time," said the voice. "Miss Corrigan is in need of protection and it may already be too late."

Eric looked out his window, and contemplated where Katie might be, or whether the caller might be able to see him.

"Look, if she's in some kind of danger," Eric explained, "then I don't know what kind of help I could be. It's not like I have some way to protect her, or anything like that. I don't even have a car."

The caller's voice remained calm. "Master Laflamme, I realise I have not given you much information. I also understand that you have no vehicle and no weapons. Nonetheless, you still have you choices."

The caller's words made Eric stop, and momentarily put the phone down. He noticed that the lamp post over the bridge was no longer flickering.

"What choices. I don't have any choices. What do you need me for?" said Eric.

"We need you to find Katie, wherever she is, and persuade her to go somewhere safe with you. She is in great danger right now, and we are coming to protect her, but we may arrive too late. Your other alternative is to stay at home and do nothing. But if you do, it is likely that Katie will come to great harm. So we need you to decide what your priorities are. That is all I have time to tell you right now. We will contact you shortly. You will recognize us by the sign of the tree." With those words, the phone abruptly went dead again.

Eric picked up the battery from the floor and examined it. Nothing seemed unusual about it. A few difficult philosophical questions entered his mind, as he searched for an explanation. But he was roused from such thoughts by the site of his cat nudging his shoes.

There's nothing for it, thought Eric, but to put those shoes on, and start running to the place she is most likely to have gone: the Underground.

~ 9 ~

Katie held Carlo's card tight in her hand as she walked to the address noted upon it. It was not far from downtown, in one of Fellwater's older, heritage neighbourhoods. She had no idea exactly what to expect, and she was a little afraid, but she tried not to show it. Most of the houses in Carlo's neighbourhood were nineteenth century manors and villas, built by the prominent businessmen of the time, Tall ancient oak and maple trees lined the boulevards, obscuring the street lamps and making each street seem more like a cave. When she came to Carlo's street she found it silent and still. No people strayed on the sidewalk, no cats or dogs alerted to her presence, and no squirrels or birds darted off. Less than a hundred yards past the corner, she came to a property surrounded by a low stone wall with an arched wrought-iron gate, sparingly lit by the spots of a street lamp shining through the branches of the trees. A brass plaque fixed to one side of the arch indicated the street address: #4 Julian Court. She regarded the boundary closely before crossing it. Two stone eagles on either side of the arch, their claws grasping spherical stone perches, seemed to regard her in return. When she gingerly touched the gate it swung open almost of its own accord.

The house itself was one of the older and larger

buildings on the street: a three-story red-brick manor house with heavy timbre frames and round arched windows. In the dim light, the timbres looked black. The roof was an imposing arrangement of peaks and turrets and gables, some of which had stained-glass portals reflecting strange muted colours into Katie's eyes. On the veranda, four limestone pillars supported a triangular portico, like the façade of classical temple. Each pillar had four little carved cherubs looking down from its capital. A great double door was set in the centre of the arrangement, and above it loomed a stained-glass window, lit from behind. It depicted a large wolf suckling two human infants. On either side of the door stood two stone statues, which in the patchwork light from the street lamps looked as if they were carved out of the finest white marble. One was female and the other male, and both leaned on lengthy broadswords, like vigilant sentries on watch.

As Katie approached the doors she turned back to face the street again, as if to reassure herself that the way home was still there. Yes, there it is, she told herself, between the two eagle statues. She vaguely recalled that when she arrived the eagles were facing outward, toward the street. Now they were facing the house, toward her. She hugged her breasts protectively, and turned back to the door, to avoid making eye contact with them, even though they were nothing more than concrete casts.

Katie held her breath and raised her hand to knock on the door, but it opened before she could touch it. Carlo stood in the hall, his tie loosened and his collar button undone, as if awaiting her arrival.

"It's very bold of you to come here alone," he mused.

Katie tried to be brave. "Eric doesn't want me, so I'll go hang out with a man who does."

Carlo smiled in return, and extended his hand to invite her into his home. When she took it, Carlo squeezed it gently and affectionately in both hands. They met each other's eyes, unblinking for a breath, until Katie suddenly needed to break the ice.

"I love the statues by the door," she said, trying to stay casual.

"I had them brought over from the old country," Carlo replied. "They are quite ancient. It was said of them, that they move in the middle of the night, and that only the very virtuous, or the very wicked, can see them do it."

Katie regarded the statues with this new knowledge. Thinking it might lighten her mood, she asked "Have *you* ever seen them move?"

Carlo chuckled softly, as a father might chuckle at something a child might ask, but he said nothing. The silence did nothing to help reassure her. But Carlo gently drew her into the hall, into the light and warmth of his world. He gently stroked her spine as she crossed his threshold, sending a shudder rippling through Katie's body.

She found herself in a long carpeted hallway, with similar columns in the door frames and foliate mouldings in the arches. There was a high staircase at the far end, and a wide gallery allowed a good view of the floor above. Antique light fixtures hung from the walls between the doors. The carpet was intricately weaved, and she felt a twinge of guilt at the sight of a patch of dirt in the shape of her heeled footprints. Through barely open double doors Katie saw a glimpse of the dining room, with its well set table and ornate chandelier. Nearly a dozen well tailored, serious looking men sat around the table, some old and some young, some smoking cigars and some drinking wine, and some speaking to each other in low voices and measured words.

"As you can see, I have other guests here this evening," Carlo explained. "And I'm afraid I cannot introduce them to you just now. But they can take care of themselves without me for a while. Perhaps you would like to see a little more of the house?"

Katie nodded, and Carlo guided her into a darkened room that had the pleasant smell of old leather and fireplace smoke. He reached out and turned the switch of a table lamp, revealing that the room was lined with heavy oak book cases on every wall. Every shelf was filled with the spines of old leather and canvass hardcovers. Between each bookcase stood a different feature: a window, a painting, a display table, a fireplace. But dust and cobwebs covered both books and displays, making the room feel more like a museum than a library. A writing table occupied the centre of the room, surrounded by several chairs. A reading lamp hung from the ceiling directly above it. By the window there was a comfortable reading chair, and a small table with a decanter of wine. Katie walked in and held out her hands, as if to absorb all the knowledge of the books and artifacts in the room through her skin. When she had made a full tour of the room, she turned

again to Carlo, gushing with genuine amazement.
"This is—such—an incredible house!", she exclaimed, quite at a loss for words.
"We call it the *studiolo*, after the Renaissance tradition. I am glad to see you already feel at home. Welcome to House DiAngelo".

~ 10 ~

Eric stuffed Katie's coat and mobile phone into a backpack, and then trudged out his apartment door and down the hall to the exit, feeling curious, but also troubled. When he pushed open the building's front door, he found himself flanked by two shadowy men in long coats. The beams of two flashlights shined into his face and momentarily blinded him.
"Who the hell are you?" demanded Eric.
One of the shadow-men lifted a radio to his mouth and spoke into it. His rumbling voice said, "He's here. We got him."
Eric immediately bolted back into the building, and the two men followed him. He ran for his apartment and locked the door behind him, to slow his pursuers down a little. With only half a second to consider his options, he made for his balcony, jumped down to the ground, and ran for the bridge. A quick glance over his shoulder as he ran showed him that the beams of his pursuer's flashlights were searching his apartment. Eric ran for the bridge, and found a small corner in the riverbank where he could hide. There he crouched down, and reached into his backpack he retrieved Katie's mobile phone and its battery, and quickly put them back together. He switched it on, and waited impatiently for it to register on the network, shaking it as if that would accelerate the process. As soon as it was ready, he found the record of recent incoming calls and selected the unknown caller who rang him only moments ago. Putting it to his ear, he heard an automated message tell him that the number is not in service.
Then Eric heard the sound of his balcony door opening again. He carefully peeked around and saw the men were following his trail, jumping to the ground from the balcony just as he had done. He saw the beams of their flashlights sweeping the area, searching for him. He knew that if he crossed the bridge to safety, he would be seen instantly. The other choice was to find a new place to hide. Eric waited until the right

moment, when most of the men seemed to be looking the other way, and then dashed to the road, into the back garden of a nearby house. But by the shouts of the men behind him, and the beams of the flashlights through the air, Eric knew he had been seen. Eric heard a series of popping noises, like balloons being burst with needles, and he knew that the men were carrying more than just flashlights. Eric threw himself over a garden wall to find a new place to hide. The fence was a rickety wooden structure covered with vines, and would not stop any bullets, so he crawled on all fours to the corner of the house, out of the line of fire.

When he felt safe, he risked a peek around the corner. He could see three men surrounding a large black vehicle, one apparently talking on a cellphone, the others searching the area with their flashlights. Although he was safely hidden for the moment, he knew he could not stay there all night.

~ 11 ~

On the writing table in Carlo's library lay a pile of books, some of which were very old, with fragile leather bindings and cracking yellow pages. The first one on the pile was family tree of some kind, with hand-written numbers in linear columns, and a long list of names. The date on the last page was already thirty years old. The second was a history text describing the birth of the Renaissance in northern Italy. It was already open to a page which depicted a painting of the Oracle of Delphi.

"I suppose my appearance in your life was a little unexpected," said Carlo. Katie smiled. "You are something of a surprise to me too," he continued, as he handed her a glass of wine from the decanter on the side table. "I did not expect you to confront me as you did, at my car, nor come to accept my hospitality so soon."

"I'm breaking out of my comfort zone," she quoted, as she explored the room. "I'm not going to be one of those reluctant types. I'm saying 'yes' to my journey. I'm manifesting my reality, attracting positive energy, I'm going forward with life." Then she twirled around in a circle, and smiled her best smile for Carlo, her freckles shining like stars.

Carlo laughed happily. "And now the adventure has begun!"

"And so it begins," Katie sang back.

"You must have a great many questions?", said Carlo, stepping closer.

"Well to start with," said Katie, as she playfully swung her hips back and forth, "you say that you and I met each other in our dreams. So, what did I look like?"

Carlo laughed again. "Your hair was a little longer," he said.

"And you," Katie continued, as she came around the table, "I think you were a little darker, but it was night time, and hard to see."

"There was a fire, and a tribe of Celtic warriors dancing around it, to the sound of pipes, and heavy drums."

Katie stopped and looked at Carlo, remembering her vision. "How is this possible?" she asked.

"Let me tell you a story," he said. He turned the pages of one of the books on the table until he came to a series of cave paintings. "In ancient times, some people were a little bit more in touch with the great mysteries of the universe. In almost every other respect they were ordinary people, like you and I. They had to eat and sleep, they grew old, and died, the same way we do. But they discovered something, and it made them a little different from other people. They learned that they possessed within themselves an immortal soul."

"Lots of people believe that today," said Katie.

"I know", said Carlo. "Lots of people believed it back then as well. The idea that we have a soul is not the secret. The secret is the true and full significance of that fact. You have a soul, Katie. Shouldn't the very idea overwhelm you with wonder?"

Katie smiled at the thought. She stroked the edges of Carlo's book until her fingers came to his hand.

"Tell me more," said Katie.

"When ancient people discovered this truth," Carlo continued, as he too began to stroke Katie's hand, "some used that knowledge to make themselves stronger, and they became great warriors. Some learned to be more far-seeing and perceptive, and they became great artists, or great leaders. Some learned to extend their lives by a hundred and fifty years. Some learned to see the future or the past, like you can. People began to tell stories of the amazing things that they could do. In time, those stories became the mythologies of every ancient civilization, although exaggerated and changed over time until they became the stories, not of men, but of gods."

Katie's fingers made their way up Carlo's arm to his neck, and she began to idly unravel his tie. Carlo took her hand and placed it over her heart, and said, "But the real discovery is here, within the soul itself. You have something inside you that knows all the knowledge of the universe, lives forever, and shines as bright as the sun. Shouldn't you feel constantly amazed by that? Most people do not, even those who believe. And the reason is because few understand what it really means to have an immortal soul."

Katie held Carlo's hand over her heart for a moment, and then asked: "If this secret is so simple, then why doesn't everyone know it?"

"Because," said Carlo, "most people actually *prefer* not to know. Imagine that someone discovered the truth about her own soul, only to find that it is the soul of a kitchen maid, or a ditch digger. Imagine you could see the future, but all you could see was your best friend dying of cancer, slowly, painfully. Most people are perfectly happy *not* to know the truth about themselves. But I believe that you, Katie, are an exception. You are like one of those ancient masters who discovered her immortal soul and knew it for the wonder of the world that it is. That, Katie, is the secret."

"Is that how you knew me, and how you could see me in your dreams?" asked Katie, as her fingers made their way back to Carlo's shoulders, and played with the buttons on his shirt.

"An awakened soul knows another," Carlo confirmed. "Your present life, as the fine attractive woman you are now, with these strong shoulders, these wide beautiful eyes – this is not all that you are. I have seen you before, the same way that you have seen me." With these words Carlo caressed Katie's cheek with his finger. Katie froze for a moment with the electricity of his touch. She looked up at him, and tried to see the face of the man she saw in her vision.

Carlo gently let fall his hand to her shoulder and said, "That is why you came to me tonight, isn't it?"

Katie looked down for a moment, since she suddenly had no answer. But then she put her head on Carlo's breast, to listen to his heartbeat. "When I was a child I used to see things before they happened. I thought it was normal, I thought everyone can do that. It was simple things at first. I knew about what grades my friends would get on their report cards. I knew who was going to win the soccer game, before we even started playing. But when I tried to talk about what I knew, and when I turned out to be right most of the time, people got scared. My mother asked me not to talk about it. But secretly, I still saw things. Once I tried to see the bigger future, not just the future of next week, but the future of the world, of everything. And I saw that everything has a purpose, that even the world itself has a purpose. History is taking us somewhere, even though I don't know where. I've always believed that. I don't understand, but I know it's true. Then today, some things happened—that made me think that I might have been wrong—that the way of things isn't what I thought it was, or that maybe there isn't a reason for things after all—"

"If I may ask," interrupted Carlo, "why is it important for you to believe this?"

"It's just what I've always believed. I know this sounds stupid, I'm sorry if I seem like a silly girl, wasting your time—"

"On the contrary, my lady, I take this very seriously," reassured Carlo. "Please do continue."

"Well I mean, I went to Eric's house to tell him something—" but Katie interrupted herself here, having suddenly decided not to tell Carlo about the argument. "And then after that, I went to the Underground to go dancing, and then all the lights and music changed, and I felt transported to another place, with the fire, and the drums. And I saw you there. And after the vision passed and I was back in the real world again, then I saw you again, and I felt as if, I felt that—"

"That you already knew me?" said Carlo, calmly.

Katie whispered her answer: "Yes."

Carlo turned her face toward his with a light touch of his finger, and studied her eyes for a moment, as if looking for something within her. Then he moved to the window and gazed outside, and stroked his chin, thoughtfully. Katie waited with trembling arms. She touched his neck from behind, and tried to take his hand, but he only closed his eyes, apparently deep in thought, and did not move.

Katie sighed, and dropped her hand. "I'm sorry, I'm a idiot. I thought I wanted something here tonight but I guess it's not what you want, and I've wasted your time, I should go home." she said, and moved to the library door. But Carlo stopped her with two words.

"Sit down," he commanded. To Katie's surprise, she obeyed.

Carlo paused before he spoke. "You came here this evening because you wanted to know the truth about who you are, and why you can see the things you can see. And you have shown such enthusiasm, such – initiative. It's very interesting. It might be too soon to tell you everything, but perhaps I can tell you a little more." Then he turned to her and continued, more seriously. "This world of ours is so troubled, so full of sadness and suffering, so full of – trivialities. It needs the right kind of people to lead it back to the light. But such people are rare today. Rare and precious and special. They often have no idea just how powerful they are. That is why it is so important that I found you. You are one of those rare and special people, Katie. You are one of us. And we have work to do together. That is why you are here."

Katie paused, to try and decide whether she believed what she was hearing. A question burst from her, almost against her will: "Who are you?"

Carlo turned another page in his book, until he came to a picture of an ancient Greek temple. "We are the descendants of those first people to discover the truth about the soul. We are the living human descendants – of the gods."

~ 12 ~

Katie looked at Carlo with indignation, and a bit of disbelief. "That's quite the amazing story," she chortled.

"You don't believe me, do you?" Carlo enquired.

"Of course I do," Katie lied, as she got up again and strode to the door. "I've always known that I'm a goddess. And you are a fine gentleman, who seems to know just what to say to impress a goddess like me. But I have places I need to be in the morning, a universe to run. It's hard work being a goddess. And it's been a lovely evening but I must be off. Ta ta, and cheerio, and all that. Good night."

Carlo reached behind one of the bookshelves and clicked a hidden mechanism. A nearby bookshelf swung open, into the wall, like a door. Behind it was a stairway leading down. The sight of it made Katie stop.

"It often happens that people like us sometimes need a little bit of help to awaken the soul. The DiAngelo family has refined several techniques to – shall I say, assist this process. I'd like to show you one of them. I wasn't planning to do this tonight, but you have shown such initiative, you might be ready after all." Then Carlo leaned close to Katie's ear, almost brushing it with his lips, and said, "But this moment is your last chance to turn back and go home."

Katie slowly turned to look at him, and nodded.

"In that case," said Carlo, with a smile and a wave of his hand, "ladies first."

Katie stepped into the passage and looked down the stairs. Carlo stood behind her, close enough for her to feel his breath on her neck. The walls of the passage were of unfinished bricks, and the stairs of cracked wooden slats. It was dark, although there was a glimmer of light at the bottom. There was a strange smell in the air, combining the mustiness of old dust with the sharpness of some kind of incense. Katie felt both curious and afraid. But she continued on. Carlo was close behind her, blocking her exit; the time for backing out was long past. At the bottom of the stair there was a rickety wooden door. She pushed it open, and found a low-ceiling cellar room with no windows, lit by candles on side tables. The wall across from the door was painted with a mural, depicting three angelic figures floating in the sky above a group of scrambling, astounded witnesses. Among the scrambling people was one woman who appeared calm and in control: she was pointing to the angels above, as if heralding their arrival. The walls of the room were hung with embroidered curtains, and between them hung dozens of masks. Most were Venetian carnival masks of varying shapes, colours, and sizes, although there were also a few Greek theatrical masks and Egyptian funeral masks among them. And there were modern masks as well, of men and women of all walks of life, which were so very life-like that Katie found herself unnerved by the unblinking stare of their empty eyes.

"This is our private chapel," explained Carlo.

At the centre of the room stood a small table, draped with a red cloth, on which sat a large antique wooden box flanked by candles. Carlo gestured toward the box on the table in the centre of the room, and said, "Open it."

Katie obeyed again. Inside the box she found a small glass bottle, stopped with a simple cork. The liquid inside seemed to be moving, like the waves on the surface of the sea. Carlo gently took the bottle from her hand, caressing her wrists and fingers as he did so. He opened it, took a drink, and handed it back to her.

"Drink," said Carlo.

Katie asked "What is it?"

"Water," he answered. "Water from a very special well, not far from here. And a few spices. It will help you see things a little more clearly."

Katie looked at the bottle, and at Carlo. Then she put the bottle back on the table and said, "Before I do this, I want you to do something for me."

Carlo raised an eyebrow.

"I want you," said Katie, "to kiss me." Then without allowing Carlo to hesitate or to pull away, she grasped his head in her hands and pushed his lips upon her own.

~ 13 ~

"You still have your choices. Some choices!" Eric exclaimed to himself. Then he covered his mouth, lest he accidentally give his position away.

Eric tensed his muscles as the footsteps approached. He could hear that one of his pursuers was coming toward him. The other, then, was either still in the car or else coming around the other side of the house. It looked as if the only way out was over the fence into the next back garden, which would expose him to their bullets.

A window near Eric suddenly filled with light, and he realised that the residents of the house were alarmed by the sound of the gunshots. Eric carefully peeked around the house and checked the front door. One of the men was standing on the front porch, talking with someone inside the house. Eric saw the man pull a wallet from his coat pocket and flash it open to the person in the house. Although he could not see clearly, it appeared to hold an official badge of some kind. Shaking, Eric crept around to his hiding place again.

But then he noticed the car. It was empty, the engine was running, and the driver side door was open. The other men were searching the grounds near the foot of the bridge. An idea dawned in Eric's mind. He counted to ten, and then raced for the open door of the car. Checking to see if he had been seen, he got into the driver's seat, put the car in gear, and drove away.

He didn't get far. The other shooter came out from

beside the house and opened fire. Eric ducked to avoid getting hit. The shooter next took aim for the tires, and Eric suddenly found himself careening out of control. He stood on the breaks and the car crashed to a halt in front of a driveway. He pulled the keys from the ignition, leapt out of the car, and started running again. He threw the keys to the car into the river. Another bullet flew past him and Eric felt it rip through his flesh in his upper thigh. He howled in pain: he had never been shot before. He fell down behind the cedar hedge and had a look. It was only a flesh wound, but he was bleeding and the pain made it hard to walk. As best he could, he crawled to the end of the hedge, hoping to hide again.

But the shooter came no further. Two police cars, with their sirens blaring, raced into the scene, and one of them stopped at the abandoned black car. Eric peered as best as he could through the hedge, and saw an officer get out and start to question the shooter, who displayed a badge in his wallet. The policemen in the second cruiser began searching the hedge. Eric tried his best to scramble away, but the police were alerted by his noise. They ran to him, grabbed his ankles and pulled him out.

"All right, who are you!" demanded one of the officers.

"My name is Eric Laflamme, and those men over there —"

"Never mind them," interrupted the officer. "We got a report that someone was–"

"I've been shot!", Eric shouted back.

The officer grimaced, and motioned to a colleague to get a first aid kit. "We just received a call about a B and E, and an auto theft, and that the suspect was fired upon lawfully while resisting arrest."

"What, in the last ten seconds!" Eric exclaimed. "Look, I was at home just now, then there were these two guys at the door who tried to abduct me, and they chased me and shot at me —"

"Tell it to your lawyer. I'm placing you under arrest."

"It's my apartment!" Eric protested. "I can prove it to you, I've the keys right here. I'll show you."

But the officer paid no attention. He pulled out his handcuffs and clamped them heavily over Eric's wrists, and then began to read him his rights.

~ 14 ~

In the morning, Katie awakened with a driving, pulsing headache. Turning her head even the slightest bit was dizzying. When she opened her eyes the light of the morning was painful. She tried to sit up, but fell back into the bed again. Memories of the previous night were stirring in her mind. When she was able to look around without too much discomfort, she found herself in a small bed with metal railings all around it, surrounded by curtains. When she drew the curtains the light invaded her eyes again, and she squinted painfully.

She found herself in a hospital room, about the size of her apartment bedroom. On one side of the room there was a window, on another there was a sink next to an equipment cupboard. Katie slowly sat up in the bed. Above the sink there was a small mirror, and Katie looked at herself in its reflection. For a moment she thought the room reflected in the mirror was a dark, clay and timbre-frame house, with round walls, and smoke stains on the rafters.

A voice from across the room interrupted the vision. In a chair by the window sat a strong and matronly woman, apparently in her middle years. She was tall and silver eyed, and her grey-streaked brown hair was tied in a tight bun that made her look older than she probably was. She wore a dark, conservative trouser suit, and sported large pearls on her fingers, ears, and necklace.

"I trust you slept well?" said the woman. Her voice reminded Katie of a stern schoolteacher from her childhood.

"Who are you," Katie groaned.

"My name is Emma DiAngelo. I was asked by Carlo to bring you here, and to see that you recovered. You are safe, you are in a local hospital."

Katie looked at the hospital identification band on her wrist, and pulled on it a little to see if it would come off.

Emma got up and pulled her chair closer to the edge of the bed. "What is the last thing that you remember before waking up here?" She pronounced the strange question as if it was the most ordinary thing in the world to ask.

Katie looked into the mirror again and saw herself reflected just as she was: a twenty-something young woman, with tangled and knotted red hair, wearing a lime-green hospital nightgown.

"Carlo took me down to a room in his basement. And he was telling me about your family and things, and then he kissed me, and then I woke up here."

Emma studied Katie's face with expectation. "And?"

"That's all," Katie finished. "He kissed me, and I think we started making out, and that's all. Listen, why am I here in this hospital?"

Emma's face became stern. "You were in our private chapel, about to undertake a little ritual we call the Awakening. It's quite normal for people of our, shall we say, our history, to enter trance or become disoriented for a while when they have tasted Fellwater for the first time. We wanted you to wake up in a safe place, just in case."

"That's what was in the bottle? I don't remember drinking it."

Emma studied Katie coldly for a moment. Then she indicated a suitcase next to the chair. "Your clothes are in here. And I also brought something more suitable for a matron of House DiAngelo."

"A matron of House DiAngelo?" asked Katie.

"Did Carlo not explain it to you? In this world there are about four hundred or so families descended from the great souls of ancient times. Our family, House DiAngelo, is one of them."

Emma fell silent for a moment, as if remembering something. Then she turned back to Katie. "You can stay here as long as you need to. For most of us the Awakening takes a few days, and it can be painful. But we will be here for you, through it all. You might need to do it for one of us next time." Emma smiled, then stood and opened the suitcase and began to lay out an expensive looking dress for Katie to wear. She asked, conversationally, "How much do you remember of my boy?"

"I saw him, yes. I do know him. But—"

Emma continued, apparently oblivious. "Well then you must remember the time you were his portrait model. In one of our mansions in the old country we have the last remaining canvas of his, and I think you would appreciate seeing it, since an ancestor of yours sat for it. He was quite a fine artist."

"That's not where I saw him," said Katie. "I think it was Ireland, or maybe Scotland."

Emma looked at Katie, confused. "House DiAngelo did not have a presence in Ireland until after their little revolution in 1916. You could not have seen him there."

"But I know what I saw," Katie retorted.

Emma gazed at Katie with the kind of gaze a grandmother gives to an impertinent child. But a second later, she simply shrugged. "I am sure it will all come back to you soon enough. Carlo is one of the eldest of our house. If he says that you are to be the matron of House DiAngelo then that is good enough for me."

Katie reached for the dress and examined it, without getting out from under the covers. It was a navy blue gown, made of shimmering silk, with gold embroidered angels meshed with precious stones along the neckline.

"I see you would like some privacy to get dressed," said Emma. "I'll inform the nurses that you have, well, awakened, and I'll see you for breakfast as soon as you are ready. Food will do you good. I'm sure this dress will fit you and that you will look absolutely lovely. And I'm sure that your bond with the family will come back to you in time." Emma smiled her grandmother smile, and left Katie on her own.

Katie now felt almost as puzzled as she felt sick. She stood up from the bed and her head began to spin again. She dragged herself from the bed, wrapping herself in one of the bed sheets. The dress Emma had picked for her fell to the floor, but Katie took no notice. She went into the sink, but had to clutch at the railing on the bed to balance herself as she walked. She felt as if at any minute she would fall over. She leaned on the sink counter and looked at herself in the mirror. Her face was pale and her eyes bloodshot. The pigtails had been pulled out of her hair, something she did not remember doing. Her muscles were trembling. She opened the blanket a little bit and examined her breasts. There was a round bite-mark on her flesh above one of them. She also found bruises on both of her arms. Her skin everywhere was pale, making her freckles stand out more than usual. She touched her nipples and found that it hurt to do so. She filled a glass with water and drank deeply, and tried to think back to the previous night. When could anyone have given me that much alcohol, she wondered, and when could anyone have poisoned me? The most vivid memories were of the series of visions which came to her of the crowd of half-naked, blue-painted people dancing around a fire. She looked into the mirror again, and in the glare of the lights it became like a window, opening to another image. This time she saw the private chapel in Carlo's basement. There Carlo lay naked on the floor, and a naked, red-haired and freckled woman lay on top of him. She held his face in her hands, and whispered something into his ear. Then she sat up, took a small bottle from a nearby table, and tasted the liquid inside.

Katie had to look away. A sense of powerlessness overwhelmed her, and she shivered involuntarily. On her hands and knees she crawled back into the bed, wrapped herself in the blankets up to her neck, and tried to hide from the world.

~ 15 ~

Eric spent the night in a police station holding cell. The previous evening he had been photographed, fingerprinted, medically examined, shouted at, accused of being a terrorist, and deprived of sleep. It left him feeling exhausted and humiliated. In the morning he woke up to the sound of the door of the cell opening and someone walking in.

"Good morning Eric," said the intruder, as if nothing was amiss. "How are you today?"

Eric looked up and saw a tall man in a black suit which looked a little the worse for wear, carrying a weather-beaten brown leather document case, and casually leaning on the door frame.

"I spent the night in here. You tell me," said Eric, groggily.

"I'm Nicholas, and I've been appointed by the court to plead your case. And I must say, what an extraordinary case it is. Both personally and professionally, I'm going to enjoy it. I've read the police report. So you say that your house was burgled. But that business about the theft of the car, and the damage you caused by crashing it - very tricky. The prosecution will probably argue that you didn't need to do that in order to chase the burglars out of your house."

"But they were shooting at me!"

"Yes, and I will argue that you were desperate to save your life and had to do something to get away from them. I will argue that you felt you could not hide since you had attempted to hide several times and they found you every time. So you did what anyone with a healthy sense of self-preservation would do. Sound good? Did you know that it was an unmarked police vehicle you took? That's why they were so mad at you. Did you know?"

Eric blinked with surprise. "No, I had no idea. I just saw a way to get to safety and I took it."

"Good. And did you know where you wanted to drive it?"

"To the police station."

"Excellent. That's exactly what I want to hear you say on the stand."

"It's the truth. What else would I say?" said Eric, beginning to think that this lawyer was something of a hack. Nicholas only laughed. After a moment, Eric asked, "Did they find the guys who were chasing me?"

"Well they did, oddly enough," answered Nicholas. "And this is going to be the really interesting part of the case. They turned out to be police officers themselves. They were off duty, working as security guys on the side. Rent-a-cops, really. Any idea what they wanted?"

Eric couldn't believe the question. "Isn't it obvious?"

"To kill you, for sure, but have you any idea why?"

"No," said Eric. "None at all."

"Well the officer who spoke with them said they identified themselves as police officers from another division, privately contracted to protect the life of one Katie Corrigan. Do you know anyone by that name?"

Eric blinked again. "She's my girlfriend. Why would she need police protection?"

Nicholas continued in a matter-of-fact way. "According to the report she is the fiancée of a rather wealthy foreign business man."

Eric was shocked. "No she's not!"

"And that they were protecting her from you."

"From me?"

"Yes, from you. Apparently the fiancée believed that you might try to do something to prevent the engagement. And by the way, the prosecution is adding the charges of attempted murder and uttering death threats to your case."

Eric started shaking. "Attempted murder! Death threats! That's insane! Katie and I have been dating for six months. Death threats? We've never even had an argument, not once."

"Not even once?" said Nicholas, with a strangely knowing look.

"Okay, just once. Yesterday," Eric admitted, reluctantly.

"And in this argument, did you utter death threats or try

to harm her?"

"No, I would never do that. I'm not even angry with her about it. Just confused. It makes no sense."

"My theory, Eric, is that she had been keeping her engagement a secret from you. She was having a last minute fling with you before the marriage, and used your argument yesterday as a convenient way to break it off. And then the paranoid fiancée's bodyguards got a little bit too enthusiastic about the job and tried to scare you away. How does that sound?"

Eric trembled. "Maybe, but I don't know."

"The trouble is, the bodyguards are policemen themselves so getting to them to confirm this theory might be tricky. I'll be honest, Eric. You're going to need a better lawyer than the court services can afford, and probably a private detective as well, if you want to get off totally free. And you're going to have to forget about Katie. I know it will be hard for you. But for the sake of the case, you had better leave her. I can plea-bargain for you to get the sentence reduced, but it would take a miracle to get you totally out of here. You can make things easier for both of us by never seeing her again. Not even to say goodbye."

At that precise moment, a police officer entered the cell. "Eric Laflamme?" he enquired.

"Yes, that's me", said Eric.

"Your cousin just paid your bail. You can go home."

Both Eric and Nicholas were startled. Nicholas asked, "Who paid it?"

"Like I said, his cousin," the officer answered. "Said her name was Brigand."

"You have a cousin?" Nicholas snorted, with a tone of voice that seemed to say, I know you haven't got a cousin. But Eric he knew to take advantage of the opportunity.

"Yes I do," he said quickly. "On my mother's side. Brigand – that's my mother's maiden name."

The lawyer looked at Eric with something resembling disapproval. He could tell that Eric was lying, and Eric knew it. But Eric also knew that Nicholas would have to play along.

"All right, let's get you out of the drunk tank." Nicholas finally said, with his smile back on his face. "And let's go to my office, to finish planning for your trial. Then I'll take you home."

As the three of them walked down the hall together, Eric tried to make conversation to cover up his growing fear. "It's funny that my cousin should make bail for me, right at the moment you said it would take a miracle to get me out of here."

"Yes, funny indeed," said the lawyer, not really paying attention.

"Why don't you want me to see Katie before the trial?"

"You want those rent-a-cops on your tail again?"

The officer opened the door to the visitor's foyer, and Eric and the lawyer walked through. Standing front and centre was Eric's 'cousin': a strong-looking woman in her late thirties or perhaps early forties, a little shorter than Eric but with a sturdier build. She had shoulder-length reddish-blonde hair, held out of her face with two braids at her temples. She wore khaki trousers with cargo pockets, a yellow blouse, and an olive coloured sleeveless jacket covered in pockets. She looked as if on her way to go mountain climbing. She was chatting with the desk clerk, although her smile faltered for a second when she saw Nicholas. But when she saw Eric she rushed straight to him, apparently delighted to see him safe, and tried to hug him. Eric went along with the appearance.

"Eric! I'm so glad you're all right! Let's get out of here," she said. She had a crisp Scottish accent.

"Just a moment," interrupted Nicholas. "You're the cousin of his who made his bail?"

"Aye," said the woman. "And we've got to go. The family is expecting us."

"What side of his family are you on?"

The woman knew that Nicholas was trying to trap her, but she would not be baited. "The good side, of course. And what side are you on?"

"I'm Eric's lawyer, Nicholas DiAngelo." The name was obviously familiar to the woman, and she frowned. Eric looked at her quizzically.

"Miranda Brigand. A pleasure to meet you." Neither one offered the other a hand to shake.

Nicholas continued. "Eric and I are not yet done planning trial strategy, so we are going to my office to continue. He will be home before dinner."

"We are expected home sooner than that," said Miranda. "Everyone in the family is dying with worry."

"The family," sneered Nicholas. But then he turned his

smile on Eric again. "Come, Eric, it's important that we do this as soon as possible. It won't take long."

Miranda held Eric's arm. "Perhaps we should ask Eric where *he* wants to go. After all, he still has his choices."

Nicholas and Miranda glared at each other, as if each was psychically willing the other to concede defeat. Other people in the waiting area had fallen silent to watch the contest. Even the police officer who escorted Eric and Nicholas was apprehensive. Eric was just as confused, as he had no idea who this woman was, or which of the two people now apparently fighting over him could be trusted. But then he remembered that the voice on the phone who sent him to find Katie also said something about having choices. He looked at Miranda, while in his mind he compared her voice to the voice on the phone. As he thought about her, he noticed a blue and green tattoo on her right arm, in the shape of a tree, with a wide trunk, a dozen branches all intertwining together, and a triple spiral in the roots. Eric decided it was the sign he needed to see to know who to trust. His words floated across the room, expressing a wish that flowed straight to what mattered most to him: "I want to find Katie."

Nicholas slapped Eric's ear. "Haven't you been listening to me? And what in the world makes you think Katie wants to be with you, after what you did?" The statement was calculated to make the police staff in the room think he was guilty of more serious charges. A nearby officer got his handcuffs ready, in case it might be necessary to detain someone. Nicholas stepped in front of Eric, between him and Miranda, and said, "You and Katie must never see each other again. Trust me Eric. If you agree to this, you are sure to win your case and you will be free. I can guarantee it. But if not—" His voice trailed off, letting the unspoken threat hang in the air.

"If everything you say about her is true," said Eric, carefully choosing his words, "then I want to hear it directly from her."

"After the events of last night, I think he deserves that much, don't you?" interjected Miranda.

Nicholas sniffed. "You will" Then he strode quickly out the door. A cloud of darkness seemed to form around him as he went.

Miranda breathed a sigh of relief, but then turned to Eric with a determined pose. "All right, Eric, I'll take you to her, but now we have to get to her before *they* do."

~ 16 ~

Miranda and Eric burst out the door of the police station just in time to see a black car speeding away. Eric recognised it instantly from the bullet hole in the back.

"That was the same car!" Eric exclaimed.

"I know," answered Miranda.

"Who are these people?" Eric howled.

"They are very bad people, Eric. Trust me, you don't want to know the rest."

"All right then, who are *you*?"

"That will take some explaining, and right now we don't have time. We have to get to the hospital. Katie was checked in there last night."

"How do you know? What happened to her?"

"Let's find out. Can you drive a stick shift?"

"Well I haven't got a license—", Eric stuttered.

"Well you're driving anyway," said Miranda. She tossed to him a ring of keys and indicated a forest-green range rover. Eric squeezed himself behind the wheel and Miranda jumped into the front passenger seat. As soon as they drove out of sight of the police station, Miranda reached into the seat behind her and retrieved a long wooden pole of dark oil-cured wood, almost black in its grains, with two metallic end-caps.

"What's that?" Eric asked.

"A mediaeval English Longbow," said Miranda. She bent the pole with apparent ease, bracing one end with her foot, and she looped the lose end of the string on the other side.

"Used in the Battle of Falkirk, this one was," she said conversationally, which Eric found absurd given the situation.

"Didn't the Scottish lose that battle?" shouted Eric over the noise of the road.

Miranda chuckled. "Yes, because the English had these bows. But don't worry. This one was in the Battle of Agincourt as well."

As soon as they were on the road, the black car appeared in the land rover's rear view mirror. "You see them?" said Miranda.

"Yes, I see them. What the hell do they want?"

"They probably want to invite us over for tea. What do

you think!"

Eric smirked at the stupidity of his question. "The lawyer said he doesn't want me to see Katie ever again. Why not?"

"Because they are trying to recruit her into their family."

"What family!"

"*Their* family."

Eric swerved the range rover to avoid being rammed from behind by the black car. He could see the outlines of two men sitting in it, and the driver looked like it could be Nicholas, the lawyer. But Eric could not be sure. And his mind was also trying to work out the meaning of Miranda's last statement.

"Why, what do they want with her?" he asked.

The black car slammed into the range rover from behind, forcing it on to the boulevard, but Eric managed to twist it back on to the road again.

"Shut up and drive, will you!" shouted Miranda.

Eric pushed the gas pedal down to the floor, and swerved around the cars ahead of him. As he did, the man in the passenger seat of the black car leaned out and opened fire on the range rover. Eric and Miranda ducked out of the way. Then she stood up through the sunroof with her bow and shot at the chasing car. In mid flight, the arrow shone brightly, like a streaking meteor. It struck one of the side view mirrors, and knocked it right off. Where it hit the ground, it caught fire.

"Are all English longbows like that?" shouted Eric, impressed.

"No, just this one!" answered Miranda.

Her second shot missed as the black car swerved to avoid it just in time. It struck a public rubbish bin, which was forced back as if it had been struck by a sledgehammer, and it too caught fire. Pedestrians on the footpath ducked as well, and ran for cover. Eric rounded a corner and narrowly missed being side-swiped by a motorcycle. The black car followed. Eric tried rounding another corner, and Miranda got a clear shot at the black car but missed as it jumped into the oncoming lane. Her arrow struck a post box and sent it flying all the way across the road. Within moments it too was aflame.

"I'm going to try letting them overshoot us. Hold on!" warned Eric. He turned on to a long straight road, watched as the black came was close behind, and then swerved into the boulevard and screeched the land rover to a sudden stop. The black car shot past the passenger side, and Miranda managed a shot before it stopped and the occupants returned fire. Miranda's arrow smashed through a window and started a small fire in the car's interior. Eric ducked and put his foot down on the gas again, sending the land rover on a collision course with the black car. The driver in the black car was genuinely surprised and rushed to pull his vehicle out of the way, giving Miranda a chance to fire off two more arrows. Now the pursuer had become the pursued.

"Brilliant driving there Eric!" Miranda said.

"It was fun, too!" answered Eric, laughing. Then he turned his attention to the black car again, which was speeding far ahead of him. Eric pushed the gas pedal down hard, trying to close the distance.

"Keep it steady, I think I can get a shot at the tires now", ordered Miranda. She selected an arrow with a comet-shaped arrowhead and carefully took aim. The black car began to swerve wildly, making it hard for her, as if the driver knew what she was planning to do. And the passenger leaned out the window, taking aim with his own weapon.

"Hold on!" shouted Eric, and he collided the range rover into the back of the black car. The passenger knocked his head off the side of the window, and his shot went high into the air. Miranda seized the chance. Her arrow became a streak of bright yellow-orange flame the instant it was released from the bow. It swerved in mid air, following the movements of its target, and flew through the rear windshield where it struck one of the back seats. An explosion ensued, filling the interior with flames for a second. The car veered off to the side of the road and the occupants jumped out as fast as they could. Eric wheeled the range rover around and sped off into the distance, as the black car fell off the road. He saw one man raise his gun, but another gave the order to lower it.

Eric and Miranda cheered and clasped hands to congratulate each other. "We're on our way now!" Eric cheered.

"And you said you've never driven before," laughed Miranda.

"I didn't say that. I just said I don't have a license!"

At that moment, Eric heard the sound of Katie's phone, in his pocket, ringing. He reached for it and saw the caller's name on the screen, and the sight made him flush with relief.

"It's Katie," he told Miranda, as he answered it. "She's at home, she's not at the hospital."

Miranda grabbed the phone from him and threw it out the window. "That's what they want you to think!" she shouted. Then with more sensitivity, she said, "I'm sorry Eric, but they will do nearly anything now to throw you off the trail. If you had believed that man really was your lawyer and if you had gone with him, he would have killed you. You know that."

"Yes", Eric admitted. "But if all that you have said is true, then you might be one of them too."

"I told you last night," said Miranda, "look for me by the sign of the tree." And she touched her tattoo.

"That was you? On the phone?" A brief shudder of unease rippled up his spine. Looking at Miranda, he saw her in a different light. But he also saw the desperation and sincerity in her face. Reasoning that she could not know about those calls unless she herself made them, he decided to trust her. "If that's so", he said with a grin, "then you're going to have to get Katie a new phone."

Miranda smiled.

"By the way," asked Eric, "how did you do that?"

Miranda giggled like a little girl with a secret. "If I told you, I'd have to kill you."

~ 17 ~

In the hospital room, Katie tried to fight back the tears and think of what to do. If I had known what would happen, I certainly would not have made the same choices, she said to herself. So perhaps this situation is partly my own doing. Yet if that is true, it might mean the situation is partly my fault. I chose this, but I chose blindly. But did that mean I chose wrongly?

Katie pulled the suitcase to herself, and opened it. All of her clothes were there, folded neatly along with her jacket and boots, and after a little more searching she also found her handbag, with all of its contents still there. She looked at the floor where the fancy dress had fallen. Katie felt as if putting it on would be like moving one step closer to being more like them. She fingered the embroidery, then put it down, then picked it up again, and then finally stuffed it into the suitcase as if it was an old towel. Then she got up, slowly, dressed herself in a hospital nightgown, and went in search of the nurses station. She was still unsure of everything that had happened to her, and wanted to know what the hospital staff were thinking, and what they had decided her condition was. She stepped out of the door of her room and looked around, timidly, as if not wanting to be seen. At one end of the hall was a set of frosted glass doors, headed by a glowing Exit sign. At the other was another pair of frosted glass doors leading to another hall. She could see the shadows of people walking past through the glass, but strangely her own wing was deserted. The nurses station in the middle of the wing was empty. She walked behind its counter and looked around. In the CCTV monitors she saw that none of the other patient rooms were occupied. She started opening drawers and cupboards, looking for her file. Eventually finding it, she started to read.

> *Name: Corrigan, Katherine.*
> *Home Address: 4 Julian Court*

This already alarmed her: the address was Carlo's house, not her own. She read the record of what had happened when she was admitted to the hospital.

> *0235 hrs. Patient was delirious and anxious, apparently hallucinating. Resisted treatment. Bruises discovered on right breast, both arms and on upper left thigh. Speech was incoherent. Shaking as if cold; unable to stop. Heart rate averaging 90 beats/min.*
>
> *0250 hrs: Blood sample taken for lab testing. A sedative administered. Patient asleep. Remains under observation.*
>
> *0330 hrs: Lab reports presence of an unidentified substance in patient's bloodstream.*

Katie let the file slip from her fingers, where it fell in a heap on the floor. The feeling of weakness began to flood back into her veins. Pulling up her hospital gown, she saw the large round bruise on her left leg which the report mentioned. She hobbled back to her room and looked around, feeling a need to do something or to somehow escape. There was a telephone on a bedside table, old-fashioned to her eyes with its large keypad and its separate handset, and she thought of who she might call. If she could not explain everything that happened, and even if no one was able to come immediately, then at least she would hear the voice of someone who was part of her normal life. She climbed on to the bed, pulling the blankets with her, and dialed for Eric. He might not believe the story of last night, she thought, but I don't have to tell him everything. All I have to tell him is that I need to see him. As soon as Katie thought that, she remembered the reasons she was angry with him. Our argument last night was too stupid an issue to break up over. But he was so insensitive! Didn't he understand I was trying to tell him I loved him? Does he love me? Does he even want to hear from me?

But all these things, while still weighing on her mind, were overcome by the need to see him nonetheless. Katie was still feeling hurt and scared, and needed a familiar face to talk too, a familiar hand to hold. She dialed Eric's number. But all she got was his answering machine. The tears surfaced on her eyes again. She sobbed a message for him. "Eric, where are you? Never mind about last night, we can talk about that later, I really need you to come here as soon as you can. I'm in the hospital. Something happened last night and I need someone to be here for me. I'll tell you when you get here. Please get this message and come here, right away, I think I'm in a lot of trouble.."

She dropped the phone, missing its cradle, and had to pull it up by the cord to hang it up properly. Then she said, as if still leaving her message, "I think I need a friend."

Then she heard a sound from outside her room. There were footsteps approaching. She saw the shadow of a man walk past her door, then stop. The shadow's arm reached down and turned the handle.

~ 18 ~

"Someone will almost certainly be waiting for us at the hospital. We have to be ready."

Miranda had taken over the driving once they were out of danger, and Eric sat in the passenger seat. They were still headed for the hospital but had a lot of ground to cover before they got there.

Eric sighed. "All this cloak and dagger stuff. I don't

like being kept in the dark. If someone is going to shoot at me again, I need to know."

Miranda sensed his frustration. "You're doing very well Eric. I promise I will tell you everything soon. Right now we have a job to do, so let's do it and be done with it."

Eric nodded his assent, although he wasn't completely happy with being made to wait longer still.

A few minutes later, they arrived at the hospital. Miranda did not notice anything unusual, so she told Eric she would drop him off, then patrol the neighbourhood and come back for him. Eric didn't like it but decided that protesting would do him no good. Miranda appeared to be the kind of woman who didn't like to change her mind once she made a decision. He watched Miranda drive away before entering the hospital, and mused at how adventurous his life had suddenly become. Although he had many questions and few answers, he knew he wanted to find Katie, and that Miranda was at least helping him find her. That much was something he was certain of. He walked into the hospital doors and whispered, "I'm coming, Katie. I'm coming."

Eric found out where Katie was by going to the childbirth ward and pretending to be lost. A friendly nurse searched a computer record, and then directed him to a privatized area, where patients had to pay out of pocket to stay and be treated. It had fancier décor than much of the rest of the hospital, with its polished brass light fixtures and framed oil paintings on the walls. Still, he noted to himself, it smelled like a hospital. The hallway was about thirty meters long, with a nursing station near the middle on one side, and small social area across from it. But what surprised him the most was its emptiness. No one was there; not even a nurse on duty. Thinking it rather odd for a hospital ward, especially a 'first class' area, to be empty, he started to walk slowly, trying not to let his footfalls make a sound. The door closed behind him with only a soft thump. For a minute, he thought to put his head out the door again to ask what room Katie was in. But just as he was about to do so, he could see the vague shape of a guard through the frosted glass of the door to the ward, apparently speaking to a hand radio. He could hear the muffled sound of the guard saying something like "He's here."

~ 19 ~

Katie pulled the blankets around her again, like a protective shield. The door handle turned, the shadow stepped into the room, and Katie saw someone she did not expect to see.

It was Eric. Relief flooded through them when they saw each other. Katie was especially happy: she knew he could not possibly have received the message she left for him in so short a time, so he must have come of his own free will. She threw the sheet off herself and sat up, as quickly as the dizziness would allow. Eric ran forward and fell into the bed next to her, and wrapped his arms around her. They kissed, mixing their laughter with sorrow, and kissed again, glad to be together, and kissed again, glad to be alive, and kissed again.

Finally Katie had to break off the passion and speak. "Eric, something happened last night, I think I'm in a lot of trouble. I met some people last night, and something happened, and I ended up here, and I'm sorry, Eric, so sorry."

"I went looking for you last night, and I think I ran into some of the same people."

"You met Carlo and Emma too?"

"I don't know what their names were, but they chased me around the city, and they gave me this." Eric showed Katie his new scar on his leg.

"Oh my God, a bullet wound?" said Katie, with worry.

Eric nodded. "I don't know who it was who shot at me, but I do know they had some connection to the people you met last night."

"How do you know?"

"I talked with one of them at the police station this morning. He said he was my court-appointed lawyer – "

"You were arrested?" said Katie, with alarm.

"Well yes, and the lawyer told me never to see you anymore. But then there was this other woman who bailed me out, and who told me that you were in some kind of danger."

"I don't understand, Eric", said Katie. "Why would anyone say that?"

Katie sighed. "Well I was in danger, but I suppose I walked into it." Eric looked at her quizzically, but Katie just looked down,

Eric gave her a moment of silence, and then said, "I need to ask a difficult question."

Katie looked up again. "Okay."

"The lawyer also said that you were engaged to be married to someone."

This new piece of information surprised Katie, and frightened her a little more. Only one word could escape her lips: "Carlo?"

This made Eric more confused, and he stepped back from her. "That's his name? Is it true? *Are you* engaged to another man?"

"That must have been what Emma meant, when she said I was to become a member of her house."

"Katie", pleaded Eric. "I need to know."

Katie looked into the eyes of her lover of six months. Eric was clearly desperate, "It's not true, Eric," she Katie, as the memory flashed briefly before her mind's eye again. "They gave me something weird to drink, and I woke up here and I don't know how I got here, and—" her words got lost in a burst of uncontrollable sobbing.

Eric hugged her again, trying to be warm and caring. But from outside the window came the sound of a police siren, and several fast-moving cars screeching to a halt in the parking lot.

"I want you to tell me everything, Katie," said Eric, "but first I think we need to get out of here."

"Let's go," Katie agreed without hesitation.

Eric jumped to his feet. "Thank god!" he said. He squeezed her again as hard as he could, then got down to business. "This is our situation. I think there is a guard at the door of this ward. And I just heard the sound of more of them arriving outside. So no matter which way we get out, we're going to have to run. But I brought help."

"What kind of help?"

"Those people we met last night have enemies who want to help us. I'll tell you everything once we're safe."

"Let's take the stairwell. There might be a fire exit at the bottom."

Eric agreed, and gave her his shoulder to lean on as she hobbled to the exit. True to Katie's guess, there was a fire escape at the bottom. Eric pushed the crash-bar open. Instantly, an ear-splitting racket immediately destroyed their hope for an undetected getaway.

"The exit had an alarm!" said Katie.

"Now they know exactly where we are. We're going to have to leave this behind," said Eric, indicating the suitcase, "and run."

Katie picked her handbag out of the suitcase, drew its strap over her shoulder, and dropped everything else to one side. Then they both threw the doors wide open and ran as fast as they could. Katie fell behind Eric quickly, as she was still dizzy, and was running with bare feet. Eric fell back and picked her up to carry her in his arms. Their desperate escape was noticed by a policeman sitting in his cruiser near the hospital's front doors. He swerved toward them and parked across their path, so Eric stopped running and put Katie down.

"Did I mention I was arrested last night?" said Eric.

"I'm sorry," said Katie, breathlessly.

The officer emerged from the cruiser and approaching them, his hand on his gun, and asked for their identification. While Katie searched her handbag for her wallet, two men wearing dark red trench coats emerged from the same fire escape that Eric and Katie had ran from a moment before. They took positions on either side of Eric and Katie, framing them in a triangle with the policeman. Eric leaned over to her and whispered: "Katie, if I never see you again, I want you to know —"

But his words were cut off by the sound of Miranda's range rover crashing over the gardens between the road and the parking lot. It was a sight Eric was more than happy to see.

Miranda stepped out and shouted at Eric and Katie. "Get in!"

"Who the hell—" exclaimed Katie.

"It's okay, we can trust her," said Eric.

Miranda, meanwhile, turned her attention to the policeman and the two mysterious men flanking him. "Officer you can stand down," she said with authority.

"Who the hell are you to give me orders!", said the policeman.

But one of the other men stepped forward and cut him off. "Cartimandua," he spat.

Miranda addressed the man in the coat. "These people are under the protection of the Brigantia. You cannot touch them."

"House DiAngelo has already claimed that one," he said, pointing at Katie. "And this city is our territory."

The policeman balked. "I thought you said you were undercover Mounties?"

"We're from the S.P.Q.R.," said the other man.

"What the hell is that?"

"Stand down, officer," ordered Miranda again. "I'm warning you."

One of the two men stepped forward, pushing the policeman aside as he approached Miranda. "You have no authority here, Brigand," said the first man. "And these people are not yours to claim. The girl came to House DiAngelo last night of her own free will. And the boy was born in our domain, not yours."

"Give them back to us," said the second man, "and we will forget this little incident."

"This might be your territory but these are *my* people," said Miranda, sternly.

Eric and Katie watched this stand-off through the windows of the range rover. Just as the two men in the long coats rushed at Miranda, it suddenly seemed to Katie as if Miranda's image shifted and changed. It was subtle at first. Her bare arms appeared to swirl with spiral tattoos of blue and green. Then it seemed as if her whole appearance was transformed. Her hair became longer, more wild, and moved as if blowing in an unfelt wind. Her trousers became a thicker, more like a wrap of fur and leather tied in place with straps. Her sleeveless jacket became a heavy linen dress with a thick leather belt, and thick leather bracers covered her arms. In her hands she held a long spear. The two men facing her down threw off their coats and revealed iron breast plates, leg-guards, and helmets. From scabbards at their sides they drew wide short swords. They lunged at the Celtic warrior woman before them, but she deftly defended herself. The flash and clang of metal on metal startled Katie, and she involuntarily hugged Eric. Miranda struck and parried the soldier's sword blows, ably fending them off. Although they kept coming on to the attack, none of them could get through to land a blow. The policeman, watching all this, stepped out of the way of the flashing iron and steel, and staggered backwards to his cruiser, apparently in a daze.

Finally, as she side-stepped one soldier's attack, Miranda brought the blunt end of her spear down on the back of the other man's head, forcing him to flail and drop to the ground. The next attacker was stopped as she spun around and slammed the shaft of her spear across his brow, and then the tip into the muscles of his leg. He dropped to the ground instantly. Two more in red trench coats ran out of the hospital toward the melee, but they slowed their pace when they saw their two fellows on the ground, and the tip of a Celtic spear pointed at them. One grimaced and drew his gun. But Miranda leaped high into the air, flashing almost too fast to be seen, and landed on top of the men. She knocked away the gun with her spear as she landed, and then with a swift spinning kick she sent the shooter flailing back into the fire doors. The last man, his shoulders perked for an attack, decided to step back instead.

"This will not go unpunished," hissed the man.

"I did not kill them," declared Miranda, "so our peace treaty is still intact." The man made a growling sound in reply.

"Now tell your patrician," she continued, "these people are under the protection of the Brigantia." The man nodded, understanding the message, although clearly not happy to hear it.

As Katie blinked in the sunlight, the men sprawled on the asphalt had their long red coats and modern suits again. Miranda stood over them, once more in the guise of a modern mountaineer, with her arms folded, apparently satisfied with her work. Then she turned to Eric and Katie.

"Let's get you somewhere safe."

~ 20 ~

Katie sat on a couch in Miranda's living room, and sipped a strange but pleasant tasting tea from a hand-made ceramic cup large enough to be a bowl. She was wearing a pair of blue jeans and a warm flannel jumper borrowed from Miranda. The house was one of the town's original log cabins, but with two modern extensions built on either side. The floor was of hardwood but a shaggy throw rug covered it in the sitting area. All the available space along the walls was occupied with shelves that followed the contours of the logs in the walls. They held books, potted plants, decorative objects of all kinds, and framed photographs. There were a few strange masks among them, Katie noted with a shudder, as they reminded her of Carlo's secret room. Long, heavy embroidered curtains of earthy colours hung beside the windows and doors, "to keep the drafts down" as Miranda had explained, although they lent an atmosphere of time and history to the room. Half of the original cabin's space was open to a high ceiling, and the other half had a kitchen below and a bedroom in a loft above, accessed by a wrought iron spiral stair in the centre of the room. The ironwork in the railing resembled tree branches and creeping vines. A wide French door in the middle of one of the walls led to a back garden. And against the end wall sat an iron wood-burning stove with a glass front plate, from which a small fire warmed the room. Some of the stones it sat on were carved with long spirals, lines, and zig-zags. On the beam just beneath the ridgepole of the ceiling, there was a face of an old man carved into the wood. He seemed to smile and brood at the same time, with the deep clefts in his forehead and chin, and his beard and hair trailed off into a clutch of oak leaves. He looked down on the couch in front of the wood burner where Katie sipped her tea. Eric sat in a chair next to her, with his own bowl of tea. He was telling Katie about his own adventure from the previous night, but Katie was not really listening. Her eyes were fixed on the fire, mesmerized by the flickering light. When Eric mentioned the bullet wound on his leg, Katie squeezed her arms to see if the bruises were still there, and found that they were, and that they were still painful. She told herself not to show them to Eric.

Miranda emerged from the kitchen, carrying a cutting board full of cheese and sliced meats, and a basket of bread rolls, which she set down on a coffee table and offered to her guests.

"Now that you are comfortable," she began, "I suppose both of you want an explanation for last night, and for this morning."

Both Katie and Eric nodded, but said nothing. Their questions were written on the expectant look on their faces.

"Eric, you are a smart guy, getting your fancy education, let me start by asking you this," began Miranda. "Do you believe that your life has a purpose?"

Eric raised his eyebrows. "Katie asked me the same question last night."

"And your answer was stupid," Katie interjected.

Miranda looked at Eric for the story.

"I told her I hadn't thought about it much," Eric admitted.

"Think about it now." Miranda's voice was calm but authoritative. Katie's gaze told him that she too wanted to know. Although their reunion at the hospital was happy, there were still unanswered questions. Eric massaged his brow and temples for a moment before speaking.

"In the last twenty-four hours, some amazing things happened," Eric began, addressing himself mainly to Katie. "I saw some things that I thought were impossible. My gut is telling me to pretend it didn't happen. But I also can't ignore another feeling. When those men were chasing me, my reason to get away from them was not just to save my own life. It was to see Katie again. I had a purpose last night."

Katie held Eric's hand.

Miranda continued questioning him. "And what about today?"

Eric spoke as if each word was a hard-won battle. "Well I—if I can believe that last night actually happened, with the phone ringing, and your longbow, and those men who you were fighting – if I can believe that even after everything that happened I am sitting here with you, and with Katie beside me, in your house, then I could believe almost anything. But up until last night, it never struck me as an important question. I'm telling the truth when I say I never thought about it. And now I honestly don't know where to begin."

Katie asked, "Could you imagine that the purpose of your life is just to be with me? Just like you felt last night? Wouldn't that be good enough?"

"I—still want—to be with you, I'm still very sure of that", said Eric, as he squeezed her hand with affection. But Katie withdrew her hand reflexively.

"But yesterday you were being all brainy about everything and you just didn't get it. It's not about the big issues. It's just about you and me. You really pissed me off."

"But Katie," said Miranda, "there *is* a larger force at work."

Katie looked at Miranda quizzically.

"Your purpose, Eric," explained Miranda, "and yours, Katie, at this moment, probably is to be with each other. But what if I told you that your connection to each other is only one of the ways that a deeper, more ancient purpose expresses itself? And that this purpose is older than the both of you, older than me, older than the stones in the wall, older than the Earth itself?"

Katie interjected here, thinking she knew what it was. "But each of us has our own purpose, as individuals."

Miranda smiled. "That sounds like Carlo talking."

"What do you say it is then," asked Katie.

"Carlo is partly right," Miranda admitted. "But there is more to it. This spirit that gives you your purpose – it dwells not only within you. It also dwells everywhere. Those ancient mystics who first discovered the spirit within themselves also discovered the same spirit at work all around them. They found it in all things that move, live, breathe, and change. The energy that keeps my heart beating is kin to the energy that makes the tree grow, and helps the birds fly, and the animals run. It's the same in the songbirds in the morning and in the crickets at night. It's in the wind, the river, the moss that covers that tree. It's in viruses and parasites. Everything that lives produces it and shares it with every other living thing on earth. That's the secret of the soul, Katie. It's not just that you have one. It's that your soul is spread out on the land, the sea, and the sky. You can find it everywhere, everywhere! The greater purpose that it gives to all things, even to the two of you, is that we should all come together, see each other for who we really are, and see how beautiful life is."

"What does this have to do with last night?" asked Eric.

"The descendants of those original people who first discovered the spirit of the world are still alive among us now. There are about four hundred families of us, all settled in different countries. The people you met last night, Katie, and those men who were chasing after you, Eric, belong to a family called the House DiAngelo. I belong to another one, called Clann Brigantia. Most of these families get along with each other just fine. But the DiAngelo have been fighting my family since the time of the Roman occupation of Britain. And now, for whatever reason, the two of you are caught up in our problems."

Eric and Katie sat in silence for a moment, looking at Miranda, evidently unsure of what to make of the story.

"And I'm sorry for it," said Miranda, finishing her explanation. "For now that you are in, it will be very hard to get out again. It is one of the basic truths we have learned, that once an adventure has begun, you cannot go home again until it is over."

After a moment, Eric offered an alternative explanation. "Or, perhaps the explanation for last night is just that Katie had a one-night stand with a member of the local mafia, who impulsively fell in love with her and is trying to get rid of me in order to have Katie all to himself."

Katie glared at Eric coldly and punched his arm.

"The DiAngelo are not the *cosa nostra*," Miranda explained. "But they *are* dangerous nonetheless. They want you for something, Katie. And whatever it is, they also think that Eric is in the way."

Katie was still uncertain. "Carlo wants nothing. He was the perfect gentleman", she said.

"Yet you woke up this morning in a hospital bed," replied Miranda, "with some unexplained injuries."

Katie was a little bit afraid now.

"You're not the only one who can see things at a distance," Miranda explained with a smile.

Katie tried to digest this knowledge. "Why are you fighting each other?" she asked.

"The short version of the story is that they think that we swore an oath of fealty to them, many centuries ago. They think we owe them allegiance," said Miranda.

"I take it you think you don't," Eric guessed.

"No, absolutely we do not!" Miranda chortled with ire.

"What's the long version?"

Miranda thought for a moment. "Let me put it this way. When you were younger, did you ever believe in magic?"

"Of course," Katie answered, "but that was a long time ago."

"What kind of magic?" asked Miranda.

Katie let out an embarrassed laugh, and said, "It's silly."

"Go on," Miranda encouraged, "Don't be afraid."

Katie breathed deeply and said, "There was a big climbing tree in my best friend's back yard, and I used to imagine that it was an old woman, and that she would hide me in her branches so that no one would see me when wanted to be alone, and that no matter what was happening she was there, and she always loved me. It's kid's stuff, I know," she apologised, and twitched her nose as if the idea itself had a sour smell to it.

"Step out into the back garden, and have a look at the biggest of the oak trees there," Miranda suggested. Katie thought the idea strange, but looked out the doors anyway. Eric could not see what she was seeing, but could see her face. At first it was skeptical. But then a creaking sound could be heard from outside, and Katie's face changed to surprise, and pure joy. Eric followed Katie outside see what she was seeing. Then just like her, he too was overcome with wonder. The lower trunk of the largest of the great oak trees in the garden bore the shape of the head of an old bearded man. Its skin was formed of bark and its beard was of moss and leaves. Its brow came as high as the lower branches of the tree, which sprouted from his head like unkempt hair in the wind. Its eyes were closed, but its face was warmly smiling, as if in the midst of a wonderful dream.

"His name is Stephen Hobb," Miranda explained. "He was once the most reckless and dangerous of the warriors in our clann. He was fearless and strong, he could do anything, but he was wild, and had too much love for war. When the battle fury took him, he could not tell friend from foe. But when we arrived here, the beauty of this land overwhelmed him so much that he sat down to just gaze upon it, and he never got up again. His soul became so close to the soul of the land that after a while he simply took root. And now, he sits here still, overlooking his valley, though it holds a village now. And he is perfectly at peace."

Eric absorbed the sight of the tree man with intense curiosity. His mind was moving from one explanation to another. Katie, similarly, was fascinated. The look on her face was the look of someone who just had the floor pulled out from under her and yet found herself still standing up.

"You wanted to know what our fighting is all about," said Miranda. "We are here to protect people like Old Hobb, and the places where they dwell. If they were to be lost to the world, the loss would be forever."

~ 21 ~

As the springtime sun crossed the sky, the morning became the afternoon, and then became the evening. Outside Miranda's cottage, a moderate spring storm began to stir up, and the battering of the rain and wind made the cottage seem very fragile. Old timbres creaked and old windows rattled. Inside the cottage, the only illumination came from the fire in the stove and a few candles on the walls. Katie and Eric curled up together on a futon beside the wood burner, beneath a quilt embroidered with the same strange spirals of the stonework and the curtains. Miranda had asked them to stay for the night, "for your protection" as she put it. Then she went off to another room in the modern part of the house, saying she had to get in touch with other members of her family.

"What do you think of Miranda's story? Do you believe her?" asked Katie.

"I haven't decided yet," said Eric.

"It explains everything: the visions I was having, the amazing things those people can do, and old Hobb, everything."

"Not everything. We still don't know what they want with you, or why they wanted to kill me, or even who 'they' are, really."

"You sound like you're afraid," said Katie.

"With reason!" exclaimed Eric, showing off the bandaged bullet wound.

Katie softened. "I'm sorry Eric."

Eric relaxed. "Anyway, it's not so bad. I didn't have to go to the hospital for it."

"No, just to jail," said Katie, jokingly.

Eric giggled and cuddled her closer. "We're together again, that's what matters," he said. They held each other close and quietly for a while, until Katie raised her question again.

"Well *I,* for one, believe her story, even if you don't." Katie continued. "Because Carlo told me a similar story last night. So there's extra proof for you."

"If you ask me, and I'm studying history at the university now –" Katie grimaced at his attempt to pull rank on her "—here's what I would say is what happened to the gods. The ancient people she was talking about, their religion was animism. They believed that everything had a spirit or a soul. Their rituals were based on they way people got their food: hunting, gathering, or farming. People prayed to the gods so that they could eat, so that the rain would fall and the crops would grow. Then when the first big kingdoms and empires came along, there were all kinds of advances in science, engineering, art, and so on, along with big new problems like population pressure, and warfare. If something like a famine happened, it might mean that the gods were angry, or the priests did the ritual wrong, or even worse, that the gods couldn't deliver the goods anymore. So then some reformer comes along and says that the chief god of the pantheon is actually the only god that there is. And the priests of the new chief god promise to deliver the goods in the afterlife instead of the here and now. That way, people could feel their problems in this life were only temporary, that things would be better in the next world. And a famine wouldn't make them lose their faith. Then the ruling classes discover that they can use religion to become politically powerful. In the 4th century Emperor Constantine the Great made Christianity the state religion of the Roman Empire. Then about two hundred years later the Emperor Justinian closed Plato's academy, and ordered all the non-Christians to convert or else leave the empire. So it's quite simple, really. People converted when the old religions couldn't feed them anymore, and the new religions could."

"Or else when their overlords forced them to convert," Katie added.

"That's more or less the accepted historical opinion," Eric confirmed.

"But what if some of the old gods are still around?"

"I don't know. I mean, should we all start worshipping them again?"

Katie was disappointed in Eric again. "Why are you so incapable of seeing anything magical or wonderful in the world, even when someone props it up right in front of you?"

"But that's what I'm trying to tell you Katie. Isn't the world wonderful and beautiful enough? Just as it is? Does a tree have to be a fairy tree before we will say it is beautiful? That's what I see. Despite all that's happened, to us, to everybody, to the world, there are still some beautiful places around, and some wonderful things happening. Beauty doesn't have to be a big spectacle. It can be very simple. For example: take — well, take us."

"Us?" said Katie, unconvinced by Eric's reply.

Eric did his best to sound sincere. "Isn't it magical enough that you and I found each other? And after what's been going on, that we are still together? Maybe all it takes to make the whole world beautiful is two people in it who love each other. Like you and I. Isn't it?"

Katie was about to say 'yes' but somehow the words got caught in her throat and didn't quite come out. All she could do was make an inarticulate sound that might have been the beginning of an answer. The image of Carlo rose in her mind. She saw him as he was when they first met, a handsome and powerful man. He was there for her the very moment she needed a man like him, as if given to her by the gods. Eric's words were straight and true, but she was not sure whether it was love for him, or for Carlo, that she was feeling. Tears began to well up in her eyes, and she turned away, lest Eric see them.

"I should go home," said Katie, trying to brush off his question. "I need to get some clean clothes and things, and I won't sleep right if I'm not in my own bed. Anyway I have to work tomorrow. Missing work twice in the same week, for no good reason, that's got to be bad," Katie was babbling as she put on a coat and shoes Miranda lent to her.

"Please stay, Katie. It might not be safe," said Eric.

"Well you're the doubting Thomas, why should you be worried?"

Eric indicated his bullet wound again. Katie had to concede he had a genuine reason to stay out of sight. "Oh right," she said. "But don't worry. I'll just get that suitcase we left behind at the hospital. I don't want to wear Miranda's things for the rest of the week. Then I'll come right back here. How dangerous can it be?"

"Katie, they staked out my home. They knew where I lived. What if they are waiting for you?"

"Then I'll kick their ass!" It was only a façade of bravery, and she giggled. But Eric knew it was a sign that Katie had made up her mind. Eric sighed, resigned to let her go.

"I suppose I can't stop you," he sighed.

Katie nodded, and headed for the door.

"Katie, do you—" said Eric, knowing what he wanted to ask but not knowing how to ask it.

Katie turned to look at him. She had one foot in the room, one foot out, one hand on the doorknob and one hand almost reaching to him.

"Oh Eric, I'm all over the place right now," she said, her voice nearly breaking with emotion. She stepped out of the room, steeling herself not to look back as she went.

When Katie closed the door, Eric felt his muscles weakening and his heart beating a little harder. He moved to the window and watched her get into her car. But he couldn't bear to see her drive away. He had to lean on the wall to hold himself steady. Recalling the circumstances of the last time they parted, Eric began to wonder if he made a mistake in letting her go, or not going with her. He sat for a moment in front of the fire. His gaze was drawn upward, following the line of the chimney pipe, then the line of the stones and timbre frames of the wall, to the apex of the ceiling where the carved face looked down on him.

~ 22 ~

Eric went looking for Miranda. There was a door in the corner of the kitchen which lead to one of the modern extensions of the house. Through it Eric found a small laundry room with three other doors. One of which drew his attention right away: It was heavy, made from reddish-brown wood, and bore the image of a tree, carved from top to bottom in raised relief. Animals of all kinds, from small birds and squirrels to deer and horses, played in the branches. A sun and a moon floated on either side of its crown. Entwined in the roots of the tree was an intricate three-armed spiral.

The door was slightly ajar, but Eric knocked anyway, softly, hoping to be unobtrusive. No one answered, but the door swung open a little further, revealing a dark room, with a flickering of light in the centre, and a layer of sweet smelling smoke, and the sound of the rain on the roof. He opened the door a little further and took a step into the room, his head peering around the door. When his eyes adjusted to the darkness he saw a large, circular room, with upright timbres supporting the ceiling, each carved to look as if covered in vines. At the pinnacle of each pillar was a carved human face, some of men and women, some of children, some of elderly characters, some half hidden in a veil of leaves and branches. Between each pillar was a window, open to the trees in the yard, giving the room the feeling of a gazebo in a forest. At the apex of the cone-shaped, timbre frame ceiling there was a little roof-box, where the smoke drifted up and outside through little shutters. The floor was made of flat polished flagstones, with some furry mats scattered around it. In the centre of the floor a little fire burned, and Miranda sat cross-legged beside it, her back to Eric and the door. She was naked as far as Eric could see: her clothes were folded neatly to one side. Eric took a step back, out of modesty. But Miranda didn't seem to notice he was there. Eric watched as Miranda withdrew some feathers from a pouch beside her and whispered something into it. Then she dropped them into the fire. A burst of flame brightened the room for a brief moment, and a new cloud of smoke wafted upwards to the roof-box above. It seemed to Eric for a moment that he saw in the smoke the shape of a bird, flying up and out of the fire, through the chimney, and away.

Eric stepped slowly backward, away from the door,

trying to be as silent as possible. He retreated back to the sitting room, sat on the couch, and tried to think. All was not what it seemed with this woman, he said to himself. I hope she really is on my side, as she says she is. He looked around the main room again, mainly in the hope of finding something reassuringly normal. On one shelf behind some of the trinkets were two dusty framed certificates. One was an army officer's commission, signed by the Queen, for the rank of Captain in the Highland Black Watch regiment of the British army. The year on the certificate was 1965. The other certificate, with a much more recent date, was for completion of an apprenticeship course in midwifery. Most of the shelves held ornaments and keepsakes. There was a small plastic figurine of a female Catholic saint, in something like a yellow nun's habit, holding a bishop's staff. Beside it was a plaster model of a hill with terraced sides and a square tower on the top. On other shelves there were numerous small candles, cups and chalices of different materials and shapes, figures and masks of mythological deities and heroes from different cultures around the world, little copper kettles and brass cauldrons, little brown shoes with green laces, corn dollies and dried flowers, iron knives with strange symbols carved into their black wooden handles.

    A book on the lives of early Scottish settlers in Canada caught his attention. With its cracked spine and well-thumbed pages Eric guessed that Miranda had read it numerous times. He was about to start reading it himself when Miranda emerged from the other side of the house. She was fully clothed again, and smiling as if she did not know Eric saw her in the round room, or as if there was nothing unusual about what he saw there.

    "I have just been talking with some friends of mine," she said. "They have agreed that the two of you shall come under the protection of our house, and a few of them will be coming over tonight to help." Then she looked around, and with a puzzled expression asked, "Where is Katie?"

    "She just went back to her apartment to get a few things," said Eric, trying to be nonchalant.

    The smile vanished from Miranda's face instantly. "You blooming idiot!" she howled. "Why did you let her go?"

    "She said she needed some clothes—" he said, but Miranda angrily interrupted him.

    "Are you completely, unforgivably daft? The Romans

are still looking for her!"

~ 23 ~

Katie strode purposefully down the street, heading toward her home. The rain was not heavy, but in less than a city block she was drenched in it. She pulled the collar of Miranda's jumper up to her neck and chin, in a useless effort to keep warm. Any sudden noise, a squeal of car tires, a roll of distant thunder, caused her to jump and to breathe a little faster, until she could reassure herself that she was in no danger. Lilac trees and little marigolds that only yesterday coloured her world with joy were today muted and grey, offering no comfort, nor did any sun show itself behind the low and heavy rainclouds to light her way. At a crossroads a car waited for its green light, with a cheerful pop song about falling in love blasting from its radio as loud as the thunder above. Katie recognized it as one of the songs she often danced to in the Underground, but this afternoon its rhythm and message felt false: it only reminded her of what she had lost. She shouted at the driver to turn it down; the driver only sneered back, and drove away. Katie ran after it for a few strides, but soon gave up. The next passing car splashed her from a roadside puddle, and she shrieked with surprise and anger.

    The shortest way home took her past the Old Bridge Road, which as Katie well knew would take her past Eric's house. She decided to hike as quickly as possible without looking at his building, in case it took her mind back to Eric. But when she got close enough, she couldn't help herself. In the grey light of the overcast sky, the building looked bleak, as if abandoned entirely. The sight filled her mind with conflict. Eric had told me he loved me, at last, she thought to herself. But it didn't happen the way I wanted it to happen. The circumstances were all wrong. And he still doesn't see the ancient soul bond that we have. What if he's incapable of seeing it? If he can't do the one thing I really need him to do, even if it isn't his fault, then could I still love him? Never mind that for now. Stick to the road, girl, get home safely, get washed and changed, and then decide what to do.

    When she finally arrived at the door of her own building, she gave herself a moment to lean on a wall and congratulate herself for getting there safely. "Mission accomplished!" she exclaimed to herself. Then she climbed the stairs to her own door, fumbled with the key for a while with her cold and unsteady hands, flung her door open and slammed it behind her, and locked it too.

Then she looked around and saw her kitchen table, thrown upside-down, its chairs thrown in a pile on top of it. Her couch was stood on its end and shoved into a corner. A knife had slashed it and the stuffing was spread all over the floor. All the pictures on the wall were knocked off or broken. The blinds were pulled off the window. Her coat closet was open and all her coats and shoes and boots were thrown aside. Katie dropped everything in her hands, and ran from room to room, finding everything in the same chaotic disarray. In the kitchen, all the cupboards were open and some of the dishes were smashed into fragments on the floor. The fridge was open and much of the food had been thrown out, and some was splashed on the walls as well. In the bathroom, her cabinet had been emptied and the shower curtain rod was bent in half. And in the bedroom, the bed and blankets were ripped and shredded, her clothing was strewn about, some of it ripped as well. The drawers from her dresser were pulled out from the frame and thrown aside. One of them was broken into three pieces. And her bedroom mirror had been smashed with her bedside table lamp.

Katie poked through the ruins of her home, gingerly and carefully, as if any sharp point might cut her open. A thunderclap from the rainstorm outside caused her to involuntarily shriek out loud, and freeze in place for a moment. With shaking hands, she cleared a little space on the floor to sit down. The discovery of her home phone, ripped from the wall and broken as if battered with a hammer, instilled in her another tremor of fear – whoever had done this, she reasoned, didn't want me to call for help. But Eric had returned her cellphone back at Miranda's house, so she used it to call the police. Then she slumped herself against a wall. From that angle, she caught a glimpse of her reflection in the largest surviving fragment of a broken mirror: her knotted hair, her pale skin, her red-rimmed eyes.

"Once the adventure begins, you can't go home again until it is over," she mused to herself out loud. She crawled on to her bed and pulled her knees up to her breasts and cradled them in her arms, and stopped fighting the tears for a while.

She might have stayed there all night, but the clunk of a footstep in the hall and the rap of a knock on her door. She shook herself to alertness again, quickly threw on some nearby clothes, and opened the door, but let chain lock catch it. There she saw a well dressed man carrying an umbrella, and brandishing some kind of identification badge.

"Miss Corrigan?", he enquired.

"Yes," she confirmed, a little skeptical.

The man smiled and introduced himself. "My name is Detective Nicholas DiAngelo, I'm with the local police. May I come in?"

~ 24 ~

"Typical academic," muttered Miranda. "Knows all the book knowledge there is to know, but nothing about what *really* matters." She was rummaging in her store room, looking for something. Eric stood beside her, plaintively trying to explain himself.

"I had to let her go, I didn't have a choice," he said.

Miranda grumbled. "Oh I don't believe that, and neither do you."

"I told her that I loved her," Eric blurted.

"You thought that just saying the words 'I love you' would make everything okay?" she scowled. But seeing the look on his face, she softened a little. "We'll find her, don't worry. But don't just stand there feeling sorry for yourself. Get ready to leave."

Eric crossed the cottage to the other side, to put on his coat and shoes. When he was ready, he saw Miranda return from the store room. She was dressed for action: to her cargo pants and yellow shirt she added army boots, leather gloves, and a military jacket with the sleeves rolled up to her elbows. In one of her boots Eric saw the handle of a knife. In one hand she held her longbow, and in the other navy blue coat.

"You look ready for a war,"

"That's what this is," said Miranda. Then, throwing the trench coat to him, she announced, "Put this on. It might help protect you."

"From what? From magic exploding arrows?"

"From the rain!"

The two made their way out the front of the cottage toward Miranda's range rover. Without breaking stride, Miranda gestured at it and spoke a command word that Eric didn't understand. Instantly the headlights sprang on, the engine ignited, and the doors opened. Eric gave Miranda an incredulous look, but she did not notice. She jumped in the driver's seat. So Eric got in the passenger seat. Before he had his seatbelt on, Miranda launched the range rover on to the road.

~ 25 ~

Hearing the name 'DiAngelo' made Katie tense for a second.

"You reported a break-in, and some kind of property damage?" said the detective. Katie stared at him through the door for a moment.

"Look," he continued, "I'm here to help. It's best if you let me come in and look around." He flashed his police badge. Katie decided to let him in.

Nicholas made a little gasp under his breath when he saw the mess in the apartment. "That's quite the modern design you have in here", he remarked.

"Well I was not the decorator", Katie answered.

Nicholas started examining the room more methodically, moving from one broken item to the next, while questioning Katie at the same time. "When did you arrive here?" he asked.

"A few minutes before I called you."

"And did you see anyone coming or going at the time?"

"No."

"When did you leave your house last?"

"Yesterday night."

"So this must have happened some time in the last twenty four hours."

"Yes."

"Have you noticed if anything is missing?"

"I don't know, I haven't searched the place yet."

"Good," said Nicholas. "This is a crime scene, and we don't want it contaminated. Don't touch anything."

Finished his tour, Nicholas began to photograph everything. He photographed the broken kitchenware, the smashed table and chairs, the torn couch, the shattered glass picture frames. In the bedroom he photographed her ripped-up clothes, including her underwear, which made Katie a little uneasy. After he was through, he picked up the photo of Eric and Katie together, which Eric had given her. It was broken, and the photo itself ripped.

"Who is this in the picture with you?"

"His name is Eric Laflamme."

"What relation to you?"

Katie had to think about it for a moment. Did she still love him? If not, then there was no way should say he was her boyfriend. But neither could she lie to a police detective. It might make him suspicious if he ever found out.

"He's my boyfriend," she answered after all.

"You're a lovely couple. Have you had any problems, any arguments recently?"

"Yes," said Katie, "but it was nothing, just ordinary relationship stuff."

"Where can I find him?"

It seemed an odd question to Katie. "He didn't do this. He's not that kind of guy."

"But it seems to me that whoever vandalized your flat was particularly interested in this picture. It is as if by ripping it down the middle like this, he was trying to send you a message. I'd like to question him."

"He couldn't have done it."

"Was he with you last night?"

"No, he was—" Again, Katie stopped to think. Eric spent the night in jail, so this police detective might have seen him there. That was his alibi. "He was in jail."

"In jail?" said the detective, raising an eyebrow. "Well that doesn't cross him off my list of suspects."

"But he told me what happened to him. Some people were chasing him—"

"Suppose I read his file, and I find out he was booked for burglary right here."

Katie was about to protest when the detective's mobile phone rang. He held up a finger to silence her, and wandered into the bedroom to answer the call. From behind Katie could see him examining some of her underwear with his free hand, smelling one piece, and pocketing it. She was about to shout at him to drop it, but then she distinctly heard him tell the caller, "Yes, I intercepted the call, and I got here first. Are you coming? How soon? Very good sir, I'll keep her here until you arrive."

Katie now seriously suspected that Nicholas was not who he said he was. She began to creep quietly down hall, to try and hear more of Nicholas' phone conversation, but her heart began beating faster, and she stopped in case its sound might alert Nicholas of her eavesdropping.

Nicholas emerged a little sooner than Katie expected, started rummaging through the debris in the main room again. As he did so, he said, "I've a few more questions for you."

"I have some questions for you, actually, if that's okay", she stammered, as she tried to think of what to ask.

"Go ahead," said Nicholas, as he stepped on some books to get closer to the centre of the debris.

"If you're a police detective, can I see your badge again? I've never really seen one up close before."

Nicholas tossed his answer casually over his shoulder: "No, I cannot surrender that to anyone but my captain."

That did not really answer Katie's question. Katie moved to examine the books that Nicholas stepped on. She noticed that Nicholas moved too, apparently to examine a box of empty wine cooler bottles. But he had positioned himself between her and the door. Katie experimented by moving to a different part of the room, pretending to look for something. Nicholas shifted himself slightly, again keeping himself between her and the door. The suspicion in her mind grew again.

"I was thinking," she said, "this is a crime scene, right? Maybe I shouldn't touch anything. I think I'll go crash at a friend's house for a few days, until you're done here."

"Don't worry too much about that," said Nicholas. "A forensics team is on its way, but they will be done quickly. You should stay and watch, actually. Might be educational."

Katie's heart beat a little heavier again. "I don't really know much about police work," she chose her words carefully, "But aren't you supposed to keep people out of a crime scene, even if it's their own home?"

Nicholas laughed gently. "This is an ordinary ten-forty-one. It's not a big deal. We'll even help you clean up afterwards."

But this made Katie feel more skeptical. Her mind raced to think of what to do. She was still feeling a little weak from whatever illness had gripped her last night, so there was no point in trying to force him out of the apartment. She could try to run away, but if he chased her, she may not get far.

Her next step trod upon the leg of her kitchen table, where it had been pulled from its bolts and tossed aside. It suddenly occurred to her that she might be able to wound

Nicholas long enough to make an escape. She turned her back to him, crouched down, and pretended to be very interested in something else.

"Hey! I think I found something that might be important," she announced, trying to sound convincing.

Nicholas ambled over to her, curiously. When he was in just the right position, she jumped around and clubbed him in the forehead with the table leg. He stumbled back, more from surprise than from injury, and promptly tripped on Katie's recycling bin. As he fell into a heap of broken kitchen wares, Katie darted for her apartment door, threw it open, and ran down the hall. She was sure she could reach her car before Nicholas could catch up with her. She had not yet decided where to go, but at least she knew she could get away.

But when she flung open the front door of her building, she found a black luxury car parked in front of it, blocking her escape. Between her door and the car stood Carlo Maliguida.

~ 26 ~

Eric sat in the passenger seat of Miranda's range rover as they sped across the town, far faster than was surely legal. They raced past his apartment building where he saw his cat standing in the window, like a sentry on guard. The arch of the old bridge made the range rover become momentarily airborne, and when it thudded back to earth Eric had a death-grip on the safety handle above the door. When they came within sight of Katie's apartment building, they could see lights on in Katie's window. Miranda slowed down to a more inconspicuous speed, and then parked in front of a neighbouring house.

"Let's go in, and see if she's at home," suggested Eric.

"Not yet," said Miranda. She indicated a grey sedan parked nearby and said, "See that car over there? It belongs to Nicholas DiAngelo."

"That's the lawyer from the police station!" exclaimed Eric.

"The very man", Miranda confirmed. "He's an enforcer for the DiAngelo family. And I doubt he's really a lawyer."

Eric studied the car for a moment, and then looked up to Katie's window. Shadows on the ceiling told him that Katie was not alone.

"I still think we should do *something*. It makes no sense

to have raced here so fast, only to just sit and watch Katie's front door."

"Not yet, not yet," insisted Miranda. "They haven't spotted us yet."

Eric folded his arms.

"We need intel," Miranda reminded him. "You can't fight without good intel."

They did not have to wait long. A black luxury car arrived, and parked in front of the building's front door. Miranda made a gasp, barely audible, but enough to catch Eric's attention.

"I know that car," Miranda whispered.

A tall and sharply dressed man with curly black hair stepped out of the car, and approached Katie's front door.

"That man," explained Miranda, "is the head of the DiAngelo family for all of Ontario. He answers directly to their leader, someone they call *El Duce*. His presence here is – not good. He's got to be the one who poisoned Katie last night."

Eric looked at her. "You are sure of it?"

"If he didn't do it himself, he surely gave the order," she concluded.

Eric set his jaw firmly. "I'm going in there," he said, and he opened his door.

"No you are not," said Miranda, gripping his arm. "These are the people who tried to kill you last night. You want to risk your life again?"

Eric was growing more impatient. "Then what do you say we do?" he growled.

"If they go anywhere, we follow them. If they try to hurt Katie, we stop them. But until they make their move, we watch them. That's all," was Miranda's definitive answer. Eric wasn't happy with this, but he also knew she was essentially right. So he fixed his eyes on the man at Katie's door, and waited for something to happen.

~ 27 ~

"My lady, to see you again is a great honour," began Carlo, bowing smartly and kissing Katie's hand. His manner was gentlemanly and his voice was smooth, but his grip was painfully strong. He was smiling broadly, with the kind of smile that young boys have when they throw stones at stray cats. It suddenly occurred to Katie that Carlo was the man who Nicholas was speaking to on the phone, when she was eavesdropping on him.

"What are you doing here," she demanded.

"I have a few associates in the law enforcement community," explained Carlo, "and so I learned that your home was recently invaded. I would be most honoured if you came to stay with me, until the forensics team is finished examining the crime scene. In fact my mother has arrived, and she has been hard at work preparing the house, so you will feel at home."

"I've already made other arrangements," declared Katie, although it wasn't true. She was no longer sure she could trust Carlo anymore. She tried to step away, but Carlo did not let go of her hand.

"I was terribly worried about you, when I heard you left the hospital," continued Carlo, in a casual way. "But I'm very happy to see that you are well."

"Let go of me," Katie demanded.

"We would also like to know," he continued, pretending he was not gripping her hand, "where you have been all day."

"It's none of your business."

Carlo scowled. "You went to see someone. Who was it."

As Carlo spoke, Nicholas arrived on the scene. He had a large bruise on his forehead, and a very angry look on his face. He took position just behind Katie, and made sure she knew he was there. Katie decided that she no longer had any chance of escaping.

"Someone named Miranda Brigand. She said she knows you," she answered.

"Oh yes, I know her," Carlo was clearly unhappy to hear Miranda's name, but kept his composure. "She makes excellent homemade beer. But otherwise I would not trust her. Now are you coming with me? We have some work that we left unfinished last night, and you have promises to fulfill."

"I made no promises to you, never!" Katie retorted.

"But you did," asserted Carlo, the first trace of anger entering his voice. "You came to my house of your own free will. You followed me down to the family chapel. Everything that has happened to you has been *your* choice. And now everything is in motion. Your destiny is resolving itself here, now, on this sidewalk, on this rainy night. It is everything you wanted."

"This is *not* what I wanted!" argued Katie.

But Carlo was insistent. "You asked me to give you a new life. Did you think you could try before you buy?"

Katie dodged the question. "I will go no further with you. I don't trust you anymore."

As Katie spoke, Nicholas emerged from the building and took position just behind Katie, and made sure she knew he was there. He had a large bruise on his forehead and an angry expression on his face. He nodded to Carlo, indicating his readiness to act. Carlo acknowledged the signal with a nod of his own, then turned back to Katie and narrowed his eyes.

"I'm sorry to have to say this, but you already had your last chance to turn back. It is too late now to change your mind. Tonight we finish the work."

With horror, Katie realised Carlo was not offering her any more choices. She took another step back and prepared to run, but Nicholas was right behind her, and his tight grasp on her shoulders guided her back into Carlo's reach. Carlo reached one arm around Katie's waist and firmly guided her toward his car. She tried to struggle and squirm away, but the strong hands of the two tall men would not let go. Carlo easily forced her into the back bench of his car and then slid himself in beside her. Katie tried to open the opposite door but it would not budge for her. Nicholas took the driver's seat, and he drove the three of them away.

~ 28 ~

Eric and Miranda could not hear the exchange between Katie and Carlo. They could see it through the rain-drenched windshield of the range rover, but only as a blur. For all that Eric knew, Katie and Carlo were reconciling, and that Katie might have not been fully honest about what happened to her when she visited the DiAngelo mansion. He compared Carlo's stylish suit to his own coffee-stained shirt, borrowed trenchcoat, and second-hand jeans. He contemplated Katie's flowing red curls, and her creamy freckled skin. He called to mind the pencil skirts, designer jackets, and high heeled shoes that she wore to work at the bank. He thought of a few of the highlights of their six-month relationship: the tour of Niagara's wineries, the illegal camping in a northern conservation park, the live bands at the university hall, and the day he tried to comb her ungovernable hair. He thought of some of the little games they played with each other, such as the way she would kiss him to stop him from reading out loud from his history books, knowing full well he was doing it because he wanted to be kissed by her. He remembered the way she sometimes shed small tears of happiness when she found one of the little love-notes he hid around her house. And he thought of the smell of her skin, and the brightness of her smile, and the trust in her eyes, and the warmth of her body as she slept in his arms after a night of delicate lovemaking. And he suddenly saw himself as one of a billion ordinary nobodies, a perpetual student always on the brink of poverty, unexceptional, invisible, and undeserving of anyone's love. Only twenty-four hours ago he had made up his mind and heart to love this woman, and had told her so, after weeks of raising the courage to do so, only to find her already a thousand miles beyond his grasp.

Eric emerged from his reverie when he saw Katie appear fall into Carlo's arms and stumble into his car. He jumped out of Miranda's vehicle and jogged toward her, calling her name. But she did not see him. Nor did Carlo, or if he did, then he made no sign of it. Nicholas, by contrast, smiled at Eric and touched his hat in a mock gentleman's greeting. The message was simple: We have her, and you don't. We have won, you have lost. Eric understood perfectly, and stood still.

Miranda came up to him and tugged his arm "We'll follow them. I think I know where they are going," she implored.

But Eric wanted none of it anymore. "There's no point. Nicholas was right."

"Right about what?"

"He told me that Katie is engaged to some rich European guy, and she has to get rid of me before they can get married. Now I've seen it for myself. So that's it."

"I don't believe it," declared Miranda definitively. "I think this whole thing was staged to put you off. Think about it. Katie met Carlo only yesterday, she wouldn't already be engaged to him."

"But maybe she didn't meet him only yesterday. Maybe she has known him for years, and I was just her last fling as a free woman before she marries this guy."

"You don't really believe that, Eric," implored Miranda.

"You're telling me not to believe my own eyes! I just saw my girlfriend get in a car with another man, clearly a much better man. It proves that what Nicholas told me this morning was right. The adventure's over, for me, and I'm going home." He started walking away.

"Use your head, Eric!" Miranda ordered. "It isn't true!"

Eric turned to her, a new kind of question in his eyes. "Why are you doing this?"

"What do you mean?"

"I mean, why are you trying to help me? What's it to you?"

Miranda was taken aback. "Isn't it obvious? You and Katie are in danger—"

Eric interrupted her. "Yes, you told me all about your ancient war, but your story just doesn't add up. It doesn't explain what Katie and I have to do with it. So why are you helping me find her? What's in it for you?"

Miranda was taken aback by Eric's vehemence, and could not immediately give him a reply. So Eric gave up in exasperation. "That's what I thought," he said, and started walking home.

Miranda's reply finally came to her. "She's one of us!" she shouted.

Eric stopped and turned. "What the hell?"

"I've been trying to tell you. Her family is in the line of the old Celtic gods. She's a Corrigan, a sister tribe to mine. She is one of us."

Eric stopped walking and started thinking. This new revelation might possibly explain a little more of what was going on. But Eric was running out of endurance for new surprises. He gave her this one last chance to explain.

"She doesn't know it yet," Miranda tried to continue. "But she's about to find out. And if *that* man is the one who tells her—"

"I get it," Eric interrupted. "You want her for *your* side."

"There's more than that," Miranda protested.

"No there's *not*, Miranda! If all you say is true then either that guy takes her away from me or else you do, and in either case I still end up alone."

"Eric!" shouted Miranda, with some real desperation in her voice.

"You once said I always have my choices," Eric argued back. "You also said that I can't go home until the adventure is over. But this is not an adventure anymore. It's a fool's errand, a wild goose chase. There's no dragon to slay. And I'm no hero. And the damsel in distress does not want to be rescued! So I'm choosing to go home. You can have your coat back too. I'm going home."

With those angry words, Eric tossed Miranda's coat back to her and turned down the road toward his house. The route took him beneath the canopy of the forest park, over the old bridge with its flickering lamp, and then into his shattered, unrecognizable apartment. As he crossed the bridge, he regarded its flickering lamp on the corner. Bridges are special places. They cross boundaries and bring people and places together. But Eric stopped in the middle of the bridge, neither one side nor another, to look upon the river. Sticks and branches and other bits of flotsam were meandering along beneath him, carried by a current neither strong nor fast, but nonetheless impossible to hold back.

~ 29 ~

Nicholas and Carlo brought Katie back to the DiAngelo mansion, Each held a heavy hand on one of her shoulders as they walked her past the eagles at the gate and the caryatids by the front door. They brought her into a sitting room, invited her to "make yourself comfortable while we make preparations", and closed the door behind her.

The room was one of the most opulent she had ever seen. All the furniture was antique and custom made, in a neo-baroque, Second Empire style. There was a fireplace with a polished marble apron and arch, easily as wide as Katie's outstretched arms, and half the height of the wall. Paintings occupied nearly every available space. Most of them were portraits, but there were a few paintings of famous buildings and monuments of Italian cities. The space above the fireplace was held by a large gold-framed mirror. There was a bay window on one end of the room draped with silk curtains. At the other end was an archway. Two wooden posts carved to resemble Corinthian columns framed an entrance to the other half of the room: a dining area, with a large oval dinner table, with a meticulously embroidered table-cloth, and a dozen hand-carved wooden chairs. A crystal chandelier hung from the ceiling directly above the table. A pair of double French doors were the only obvious exit, but she found they were locked. At the other end of the room, a smaller door in the corner apparently led to a kitchen. It too was locked. These two spaces together, Katie decided, made up the most decadent space she had ever entered. Nonetheless, it was a prison.

Katie explored the room to see if she could find anything to help her escape. Her shoes made clear footprints in the groomed carpet with every step. On a sideboard in the dining room end, she found a row of framed black-and-white photographs of various people. Each frame had a little brass plaque in which was engraved the name of the person depicted there. Carlo was among them, but she did not recognize anyone else. Then her breath caught in her throat. The sense of fear that had struck her when Carlo kissed her hand suddenly struck her again. Beside the framed photograph of Carlo, right where one would expect a photo of his wife, was a framed photo of herself. The picture depicted her smiling and happy, as if in the midst of an enjoyable conversation. The background was dim and slightly out of focus, but she could tell by the general shape of the shadows, and by the business jacket and blouse she was wearing in it, that the photo was taken during her work hours at the bank. She picked the frame off the wall and turned it around, and found a manufacturer's mark on the photo backing, which included a date. It was only a month in the past.

Katie took up a poker from the fireplace and tried to break a window, but it would not crack in the least. In fact she heard the faint sound of a musical bell each time she struck the glass. So she tried to break off the knobs of the double doors, but they too resisted her, and after several attempts she noticed that like the glass, they too remained unscratched. The knob of the kitchen door resisted her attack just as inexplicably. In frustration she took her iron poker to the dining room table, smashing all the plates and glasses. Finally she hammered on the door with her fists and demanded to be let out, as loudly as she could. But it was not until she had screamed herself almost hoarse, and had nearly given up, that she heard click of footsteps from outside the room. It suddenly occurred to her that anyone who opened the door might not necessarily be coming to let her out. She picked up the fire poker again and hid it behind her back.

The hall doors opened to reveal Emma DiAngelo standing there.

"Delighted to see you again!," she said. "I heard a little disturbance down here, is everything all right?"

Katie darted past her and ran for the front door. But she did not get far: Carlo, emerging from behind Emma, blocked her path. He clamped his iron hand down on Katie's shoulder with one hand, and twisted the fire poker free with the other.

"You know," he said, "I had hoped that an hour in my sitting room would have calmed you down. I suppose you will have to wait in there a little longer." With those words, he moved toward her, clearly intending to manhandle her back into the sitting room. She looked to Emma, pleading for help with her eyes, but Emma only sighed and rolled her eyes, as one might do to a silly little girl who brought her own trouble on herself.. Katie decided that fighting them would be futile. Carlo guided her back into the sitting room and pushed her down into a chaise-longue, and then turned to leave.

"Why are you doing this to me?" Katie demanded.

"Where shall I start? You have the utter gall to run like a fugitive from the hospital where I arranged for you to recover from your awakening as safely as possible. You then consorted with Miranda Brigand and her gang of backward ruffians, although I can forgive you for that since you don't know who they really are. But then you physically assaulted a member of my family. You should be grateful that I did not lock you in a *dungeon*, rather than my own house."

"You took my life away. I want it back," retorted Katie, tired but still defiant.

"Your life before we found you was an empty and ridiculous sham. All you did was work a mindless job all day, and then by night drink and dance your hard earned money away with that circle of sycophants you call friends. You had no direction and no purpose, and you knew it. We gave you a chance to be a part of something that really matters."

Carlo was raising his voice by the end of this tirade, which Katie realized he had never done to her before. But she had her counter-argument ready for him.

"Well now I have a new pack to run with, and I can still be part of something that really matters, and I don't need you anymore."

"You should think about those new Celtic friends of

yours, the Brigantians," snapped Carlo. "They have been watching you and your Eric almost as long as I have been. And think of the name 'Brigand', for a moment. The word means an outlaw, you know. Think of what kind stock they come from with a name like that!"

Then Carlo softened his demeanor, took Katie's hands, and drew her to her feet to look into her eyes as he continued. "Last night you wanted me to take you to the world of wonder that you've always dreamed of, and that's exactly what I did. We re-built an ancient bond between us, a bond that is many thousands of years old, and very powerful. I can only explain it by saying that you and I are old souls, meant for great things. Ordinary people, like that boy you are fond of, well they may still be good people, but they will never be all that *you* can be. I know that part of you still clings to your old life. But another part of you wants to move on from it, and put it behind you. Last night you committed yourself to the path. There is only a little further to go."

Katie gazed into Carlo's face, and saw the gentle nobility that attracted her the first moment she saw him. She reached up and tentatively touched his shoulder, almost as if reassuring herself that this man was not a dream. Then Katie suddenly winced. Carlo's stroking hands touched one of her bruises. It was as if he knew they were there. They were just the right size for his fingers. She backed away from him, and moved behind one of the chairs by the fireplace, so that there would be something between her and Carlo.

Emma sighed, and turned to Carlo. "She resists you because she does not know your larger project. Perhaps now is a good time to tell her, especially if you want her to play an important role in it."

Carlo glared at Emma coldly, as if annoyed that she dared to offer him advice. But her reasoning prevailed in him, and his next words were spoken in a kinder tone. "I have never lied to you, bambina. Never. But my mother is correct to say I have not told you everything."

"Let's hear it then," said Katie, as she folded her arms and prepared to be unimpressed.

Carlo began with a deep breath. "I suppose you see me as some kind of Machiavellian power monger, recruiting people like yourself for some mysterious purpose. But this is not about me. This is not even about the DiAngelo family. I am only doing what must be done to lift the world back to greatness again."

"That is your plan?" said Katie, annoyed.

Carlo continued unabated. He drew Katie to her feet with a gentle gesture of his hands, and guided her to the windows. "Look at the world, Katie. Do you not see the poverty, the corruption, the violence? Do you not see the criminals everywhere, in the streets and back alleys of this very town, and in the highest halls of power, running your banks and government and corporations? Do you not see the thousands protesting and rallying for justice in every important city in the world? And what about the apathy and resignation of good men? It may surprise you to hear me say it, but I am a spiritual man. The suffering of the world pulls hard at my soul the same as it pulls on yours. And who is there to give the world any real guidance? Politicians? No one believes in politicians anymore. They always fail to deliver the perfect world that they promise. Or else they just make us fear something, in order to stay in power. What about religion? Those silly fundamentalists with all their pompous moralizing, they know nothing about God. What each of them really wants is to be worshipped like the next Messiah. And those liberal intellectuals with all their political correctness and their talk of human rights – they have it all wrong too. Even Christ said that the poor will always be with us."

"I know all that," Katie interjected. "But what can any of us do about it?"

"My purpose, any decent human being's purpose," Carlo explained, "is the edification of man. Civilization has fallen low again. Surely you see this yourself? There is great wealth and technological power here, great military glory, yes, but such limited imagination. And so this age has no Michelangelo, no Botticelli, no Da Vinci of its own. Instead it has manufactured celebrities, who care more about being popular than being wise. It has avante-guard postmodernists, setting up comic book panels in art galleries and calling it art. And the people waste their lives in jobs they hate, just like you do. This is not life as it ought to be. This is life thrown by the wayside, thrown to the gutter, like so much rubbish, like the wrappings of fast food. The people who should be leading us all back to glory are like beggar men warming themselves by a fire that has long since gone cold. Surely you can see that this age needs a new *rinaschimento*. What is the word in English? A new

– Renaissance. Surely you can hear the people crying out for a real purpose in life, just as you did! My purpose – our purpose – is to give them one."

"Why choose me, then," Katie asked. "Why me instead of anyone else in the world who you could have chosen?"

"Because I have seen into your heart, Katie. You call out in the middle of the night for something beautiful and real to believe in. You're like that little wooden boy, Pinnochio, petitioning the blue faerie to make you into a real human child. That call comes not just from you, but from the empty spirit of this age."

"I never called for *you*", Katie countered.

Carlo's next words floated out with casual cruelty. "People cry out to God for help in the dark times of their life. And then, to their shock and surprise, the cry is heard – by someone like me."

Katie stood motionless, listening, and cradling her belly with her hand.

Carlo opened a liquour cabinet and retrieved a cloudy glass bottle, not unlike the one in the secret chapel from the night before. As he continued speaking, he uncorked it and poured its contents into a crystal wine glass. "I have been traveling around the world recruiting artists, writers, thinkers, intellectuals, poets, all the creative people. I've been recruiting investors and men of business too. We have bought television and radio stations, web sites, and newspapers. We're going to be controlling the message very soon. We have placed the right kind of people in the police, in social services. We have musicians and songwriters and record companies ready to make anyone we choose into a star. And you can be one of them. This world of magic of ours, we are going to show it to everyone, very soon. We're going to open the last secret door, unlock the vaults, pull back the curtains. There will be no more hidden houses, no more secret people. Everyone will know the truth. But the last kind of person I need, the one position that remains to be filled, is a prophet for the new age. I need someone who sees what you can see, to announce the new beginning like an angel announcing a new immaculate conception. You shall be that angel, Katie. You are the new Oracle of Delphi, the new Sibyl for a new Aeneas, the new Lady Liberty leading the people. Despite your doubts and misgivings, I still believe in you, Katie, and I still love you."

Carlo placed the glass with the strange potion into Katie's hands, and stroked her fingers as he did so. "Drink this," he said. "to open your mind, complete your awakening, and join us."

~ 30 ~

In Eric's sitting room, Ganga the cat turned from the windowsill, where he had been watching the world that his ancestors once ruled, and trotted off to a basket beneath Eric's computer desk. There he curled himself into a comfortable ball and closed his eyes. But just as he was about to sleep, the blond-haired human who fed him arrived, dripping wet from the rain and clearly unhappy. Ganga meowed to draw attention, but Eric brushes him off with a dismissive tone of voice that Ganga had never heard coming from him before. How irksome!

Eric hung his wet clothes on the radiators, and had a shower. Afterwards, he put on a clean shirt and a pair of cargo pants, telephoned his landlord to report the damage to the unit, and collapsed into his chair at his desk. He reached down to pick up Ganga, but the unruly cat resisted, and scampered away at the first chance.

"All right, I know you haven't been fed, I'll do it now," said Eric, and he went to the kitchen. "It's the little things in life like this that get you in the end," said Eric as he prepared Ganga's food and water.

Within reach of his arm was the photo of himself and Katie together, that he framed for them both not a few days earlier. Eric picked it up and gazed at it wistfully for a while. A wave of sadness weakened his body. The walls of the room faded away and dissolved, and suddenly he was back at the time and place the photo was taken, able to watch himself like in a dream. There was the front portal of the old university building, its ancient tower above, its wards and windows on either side. There he and Katie stood, leaning on the door-posts, hand in hand. Paul was behind the camera. He urged them to kiss and let him photograph them kissing. Eric smiled again, as he smiled on that day. They did indeed kiss, and they kissed close and warm, wrapping their arms around each other, their faces drowned in each other's hair. Then for no apparent reason, they both started to laugh. It began as a quiet chuckle. Each asked the other, "What are you laughing about?" perfectly simultaneously, and then they both burst out in helpless childish giggling. Within moments Katie's legs started to weaken and Eric had to hold her. Paul put the camera down. No picture in the world, he said later, could truly capture that moment.

Eric's reverie was disturbed by the sound of a car door slamming shut in the parking lot outside his building. The room swiftly re-materialized around him, and all was just as it was before, although his door was swinging on its hinges. As there was no latch anymore to hold it closed, there was nothing to prevent anyone from entering the flat. Eric looked out the window in the direction of the sound. He saw four men emerging from a black vehicle. They were not dressed in suits, but in cloaks, and the hoods covered their heads. Nevertheless he knew who they were.

"Here we go again," said Eric to Ganga, with some resignation.

Eric reassessed what he thought he knew about these people from the events of the day. He believed that Katie was engaged to another man, and that this man had hired security guards to protect her, some of whom were off-duty policemen. He also believed they were trying to kill him. Perhaps as a result of these beliefs, as well as the strange, emotionally charged state he was in, a novel thought crossed his mind. If everything he had been told about Katie was true, and if these men were who he thought they were, and if they had come to do what he thought they had come to do, then there would be no delaying them or stopping them. Eric sensed a little of what Katie had meant by purpose. Something in the stride and posture of the men approaching his home spoke to him of inevitability.

"Let's get this over with."

Eric summoned as much of his courage as he could. He put on a coat and pushed aside his swinging door. With fast steps he strode down the hall. He arrived at his building's front door at the same time as the four men. As calmly as possible, he stepped out to meet them directly.

"Well, here I am," he announced to them.

The men surrounding Eric looked at each other for a moment. One of them shrugged his shoulders, and gestured that they should carry on. Then with professionally-trained aggression, two of the men took Eric by the arms and lead him to a car. They were not rough with him, but they were firm. They thrust him in the back seat and thrust a canvas bag over his head.

The engine started, and the car drove off.

~ 31 ~

Katie spoke in the most sincere tone of voice she could muster. "Can I have – a moment to myself? Just – put the cup down somewhere, and – I'll drink it when I'm ready."

Emma nodded to Carlo, indicating her approval of Katie's request.

"Very well," said Carlo. He dutifully placed the glass on the mantelpiece, and smiled to her. "You might find its effects a little – disorienting – for a while. Call me when you have taken it."

Katie nodded. Carlo smiled, and added "I'm glad you are with us. Truly."

As Carlo swept out of the room, Katie pointed at Emma and silently mouthed the word *Stay*. Emma saw her signal, and arranged herself so that Carlo would exit to the hallway before her. Then she closed the doors, and approached Katie with motherly concern.

Katie looked her in the eye. "I know everything that happened to me last night."

Emma grinned. "Wonderful!" she exclaimed.

Katie whispered to her, "No, it's not like that. Last night – Carlo — he hurt me."

Emma was dismissive. "Nonsense, my son would never harm you, he has chosen you for the Sybil of our house."

"What if I don't want to be the sybil of your house?"

"Oh don't be foolish, you will have everything you could ever want," Emma scolded.

"But at what price!" Katie sobbed, with eyes beginning to tear. "When I first met him, I thought he was perfect, but I should have known, I should have known better. No one can be as perfect as that. Maybe I deserve what I got for being so naïve."

Emma could see that Katie was upset, and her tone softened, and she placed her hands gently on Katie's arms. "I know it's hard," she said. "The awakening is never an easy time for any of us."

Katie interrupted her. "You don't understand. There's more. Carlo—he took me to that room in your basement and he —then he—took my clothes off and he—"

"Yes, I could hear the two of you happily making love last night," Emma countered. "That was foolish of you both. But if you try to soothe your guilty conscious by accusing him of something rash, then we have a problem."

"Yes it was foolish," Katie admitted quickly, "but is it fair to punish me like this? Bringing me here against my will? Locking me up in this room? And who are you people anyway, and why is there a picture of me over there? Emma - Mrs. DiAngelo - I'm really scared of Carlo now. I need to get out, and I need your help."

Emma slowly articulated her response through gritted teeth. "My son is a patrician of House DiAngelo, I cannot go against his wishes. And if you tried to run away, I would have to stop you."

Katie and Emma regarded each other closely, but briefly, just long enough to acknowledge that each was about to do what they felt they had to do. Then Emma turned away and said, "I'm sorry."

Katie thought the apology a little hollow. "I'm going now," was all she said in reply. Then in quick long strides she made for the door.

Emma raised the alarm by shouting Carlo's name.

Carlo was leaning on a wall in the hallway, near the stairs, chatting casually with Nicholas and two other men. When he heard Emma's shout and saw Katie dart out of the sitting room, a grimace of anger crossed his face. Katie made for the front doors, but found them just as rock-solid as the doorknobs in the dining room once were. Carlo snapped his fingers, and instantly Nicholas and the other two men fell upon Katie, and dragged her away from the doors and threw her to the floor at Carlo's feet.

Carlo folded his arms "Needed some time to yourself, did you?"

"Let go of me!" Katie demanded.

Carlo addressed his henchmen. "Take her to the family chapel, and don't let her out until she is ready to co-operate."

As Nicholas and the men hauled Katie toward the library and the passage to the basement room, Carlo clarified, "Nicholas – the *other* family chapel."

"Yes sir," confirmed Nicholas. Then with the help of the other two men, he dragged a viciously kicking and struggling Katie out of the house and shut her into the trunk of his car.

~ 32 ~

The car drove around, turning, stopping, starting again, bumping uncomfortably, swerving left and right, and winding its way to its destination. Locked in the trunk, Katie lost track of time and place.

Eventually the car did stop somewhere. Katie heard the engine die and she felt relief that the waiting was now over, but her relief was mixed with fear of what may happen next. When the trunk was opened, she was pulled out, and the two men who had wrestled her into the trunk of the car now held her arms on either side. She was able to look around, but not move.

It was night-time. The rain had stopped, but the sky was still overcast and glowing faintly orange, reflecting the magnesium street lights of town. Looking around, Katie found herself in a cemetery. On the side of the road where the car was parked, there was the façade of a building resembling a classical temple half-buried in the side of an embankment. It had large black doors of iron, held closed with latches and locked with chains and a padlock. On either side of the door there were two niches, each large enough for a statue, although they were empty. Fixed to the door, made of the same black iron, was a relief image of the DiAngelo family heraldic device: an angel holding an hourglass.

"This," explained Nicholas, "Is the DiAngelo family's 'other' chapel." He withdrew a large black key and opened the padlock. The chains fell to the side with a clang.

"You can't do this to me!" Katie demanded.

"Why not?" sneered Nicholas.

"I'll scream!" shouted Katie.

"Who will hear you?" was Nicholas' rhetorical answer.

Katie began to feel desperate. "What do you want!"

Nicholas indicated the bruise on his forehead. "For my part, I owe you something in return for this."

With a nod from Nicholas, the two men who were holding Katie pushed her back up against the gate of the crypt. Katie twisted and kicked and pushed as much as possible, but there was not much she could do. She stamped her feet and tried to slide to the ground, letting her body fall like a dead weight. But the men held her up. Nicholas undid his tie, wound it around Katie's neck, and secured it tightly with a knot. Katie continued to writhe and twist as much as possible but she was helplessly pinned to the gate by the strong arms of Carlo's men, and the knot that Nicholas tied around her neck constricted her breath.

"So," said Nicholas, addressing his two companions, "what shall we do with her?" The two men laughed softly.

"Well we can't kill her, the boss won't like that," said one of the men.

"And we can't leave any scars," said the other.

"But otherwise," said Nicholas, and he let the sentence go unfinished. His two companions chuckled. He caressed her chin again in a mockery of affection.

"Anything to say to me? 'Sorry', perhaps?" mocked Nicholas.

"Let—me—go", rasped Katie, as best as she could.

"All you have to do is apologize to me, and then we can all go home," said Nicholas.

Katie spat at him.

Nicholas wiped his face with a handkerchief from his pocket.

"I think that says it all, don't you agree lads?" The boys snickered. Nicholas turned back to Katie again. "You can stay here until you are ready to be more respectful."

Katie began to slip down, trying to avoid Nicholas's touch, but could not escape it, more from lack of air than from the strength of his grasp. She was beginning to pass out. Her eyes began to lose focus, and the strength began to drain out of her legs. She vaguely saw the men close in on her, heard the creak of the door opening, and felt her body being carried inside. The shadows began to lengthen and the orange light of the sky retreated to the distance. Then the sound of the iron gate clattering shut jolted her ears. The sound of chains shackling the gates scratched on her skull. And then the silence of the night enclosed her.

~ 33 ~

In the stone crypt where Katie lay, the only sources of light came through three slit-shaped windows above the gate. From Katie's perspective, as she lay on the stone floor of the little room, they looked as if they were a thousand miles away.

As best as she was able, she tried to loosen the tie that Nicholas knotted around her neck. She could not undo the knot, but she could hold it out a little and breathe easier. When she felt a little stronger, she tried to feel her surroundings. The floor was stone, and she could find the grooves between the slabs, but she could not find the walls.

Strangely, one of the lights shining into the chamber seemed vaguely to move. It was slowly bobbing up and down. And it was approaching her. Then another little light appeared beside it, moving like the first. Katie blinked, and tried her best to sit upright. But there was no wall she could find by which to prop herself up. A third moving light joined the first. They were level with her eyes now, rather than above her, but still apparently many miles away. The distant sound of drums reached her, resonating with the beating of her heart.

A new thought entered her mind. I am becoming delirious. Here in this cellar, on this stone floor, I may be about to die. She tried to shout to the men outside, but her voice was cracked and faltering.

A shadow passed in front of the lights. Katie tried to see what caused it. It passed again, and through her tear-filled eyes it vaguely resembled the shape of someone's head. It put Katie into a memory of the chapel in Carlo's undercroft, with its walls covered in masks. As Katie blinked the image resolved itself. She tried to call out to it but her voice was weak, and she could not draw much breath.

Katherine Corrigan, said the shape. It was the voice of Carlo.

Katie's heart sped up.

Your awakening is underway, Carlo's voice said again.

I'm in shock, Katie said to herself.

Yes you are.

You can hear me? Who are you?

You already know.

I'm not hearing this. You are not really here.

Yes I am.

You're not real!

I am real, and I am here with you.

Katie closed her eyes, but Carlo's mesmerizing voice would not go away.

It seems I do owe you an apology after all, said the voice, as calmly and as hypnotically as in the real flesh.

Let me hear you say it then, Katie told the voice.

I'm sorry you feel the way you do about me.

That's not a real apology.

What else can I say. I do not decide people's destines. I only fulfill them.

I think you are insane!

You also think I am not really here. And yet here we are, having a conversation.

I won't listen to you anymore.

Yes you will. We have been bound together, right from the beginning.

Go away.

I am a part of you even now.

Go away!

And we will always be together, even to the end.

Katie screamed as much as her strained voice would allow.

There now, said Carlo's voice after a pause. That did not change anything. It did not even make you feel any better.

If you know so much about destiny, then tell me if this is the way I am supposed to die.

Do you want to die?

If it will make you go away.

Mia bambina, the voice chuckled, you do me too much honour.

Just tell me.

You will find out soon enough.

Tell me!

I can tell you this much, the voice conceded, with a sigh of resignation. Katie, it said, the fates tell me that you will die alone.

Alone? Why?

Because that is how you have lived your life so far.

Nonsense. I've got my parents, a few friends, and I've got Eric.

You hardly listen to your parents anymore. They don't listen to you either. Your friends spend time with you only because you pay for their drinks at your dance club. And as for Eric, well, you were quick to give up on him yesterday, weren't you?

I don't want to die alone.

What do you want.

I don't know!

That's obvious, said the voice more angrily. You called

out for help during a dark patch of your life and so I came. I offered you everything you asked for. Now you have decided that you don't want it anymore. Well isn't that the story of your life!

     I want you to leave me alone.

     That's not what you wanted yesterday.

     Well it is what I want today.

     You don't know what you want today!

     Yes I do!

     No, Katie! I know the truth! Look at your self. Look seriously. Look honestly. Have you ever really known what you wanted to make of your life?

     I had dreams, Katie asserted. And I had plans. They were good plans.

     And what became of them? Do you even remember what they were?

     Of course I do!

     Let's hear one of them then.

     I was going to work with animals. I was going to be a veterinarian, or maybe train animals for movies, or something.

     And where is that dream now?

     Katie didn't have an answer.

     That's about what I thought, the voice declared.

     I can find it again, said Katie. I'll find all of them again. I'll make new ones. And I won't die alone. I will prove you wrong.

     Who are you to decide your own destiny?

     Katie sat up, pulled together the remains of her dignity, and spoke an answer that echoed in the darkness: I am the one who will have to live with it.

     A moment of silence followed.

     So be it, said the voice.

     Now go away, and let me live.

     For now, for now, the voice conceded. But we will see each other again, much sooner than you might expect.

     The room was silent once again. Looking up, Katie saw almost a dozen of the little window lights approaching through the darkness. It seems as if they had converged to listen to the contest she just apparently won with the cold voice of the man she almost took for a mentor. The closest three lights were more visible to her now, and they vaguely resembled hand-held torches. They seemed to shine on to the faces of people who now surrounded her, but her tear-filled eyes were unable to see with clarity. Some held torches, and some leaned on great broadswords or on the shafts of long spears. Others played hand-drums and still others blew into strange bronze trumpets that curved up to a horn that resembled a horse's head. The trumpeters pumped the air through their mouths as if pumping a bellows, creating a continuous low sound that rumbled in Katie's bones. And through all this music and noise, she heard the singing of a name. It was a name she had heard once before, in a place just like this, but now she knew it to be her family's original name. Maeve of Cruachan. Great Queen of Ireland. Goddess of the Land.

There were three women who stood out from the rest, with faces that radiated light as warmly and kindly as the torches held by the people around them. They wore long yellow dresses of heavy linen, covered in Celtic knotwork embroidery and tied at the waist with a leather belt. Two had hooded cloaks of forest green, and thick black hair that waved like tall grass in the wind. The third, in the middle, resembled Miranda, although in the shifting, changing light it was impossible to tell. She wore a green and blue tartan shawl over her shoulders, embroidered with the tree and triple spiral of the clan Brigangia.. Her bright reddish-blonde hair seemed to flow out from her head in all directions, like a slow-burning fire. She stretched out her hand to Katie, offering to help her stand.

Katie stood. The woman with the flaming hair was carrying a chalice, and she offered it to Katie. She drank deeply. Strength flowed into her. Their eyes met when Katie put the chalice down, and Katie felt as if she was being acknowledged as an equal. The two attending women pulled at her clothing and it fell away from her body, as if nothing at all had been holding it on. Although Katie was fully naked, she felt no shame, even while surrounded by a small crowd. Their gazes projected admiration, respect, even awe. Some of them bent down on one knee. Then the two women dressed Katie a short but heavy linen dress of the deepest forest-green, embroidered with Celtic knotwork patterns on the seams. They drew a leather belt around her waist and clasped it with a fine gold buckle, and attached a knife in a leather sheath to it on her side. They pulled fur leggings on her feet and tied them with leather straps. They tied two braids into her hair, one on either side of her temples. Then a man approached her, wearing a white robe and a green cloak that looked as if made of leaves. He had numerous small sacks, feathers, stones, and shells, hanging from his belt and his cloak. A dagger also hung from his belt in a sheath. In his hands he carried a shirt of leather armour studded with metal rivets, which he helped Katie to put on. Embossed on the leather was a delicate knotwork pattern which picked out the shape of three ravens in flight. The man also helped her put a pair of leather bracers on both of her forearms, and then handed her a spear. Its long shaft was made of sturdy hardwood, and its rivets were polished flush. The spearhead itself was vaguely leaf-shaped, almost as long as a sword blade, and inscribed with an intricate knotwork design resembling the veins of a leaf. He then stood back to admire her. And Katie could not help but admire herself as well. The final touch was the most unusual and exquisite piece of jewelry she had ever seen: a solid metal crescent-shaped neck ring, as thick as one of her fingers, apparently made of spun and threaded gold. Its two ends were cast in the shape of horse heads. The woman with the flaming hair presented this to Katie, and then put it around her neck like a necklace. Katie stood herself up a little taller, raised her eyes from the floor to the level of the horizon, unclenched her fists, held her arms straight, and smiled.

    The trumpets blasted a long loud note, the fires of the torches flared, and the warriors waved their weapons aloft and roared. Then the crowd parted to make a path for her. Katie stepped forward, not entirely steady. The necktie that Nicholas used to choke her lay on the ground before her, still knotted. Katie kicked it to one side. The gate burst open before her with a wave of the hooded man's hand. The metal twisted part way off its hinges.

    Katie stepped into the field outside, where it seemed the whole world was spread out before her. She saw rolling hills and meandering valleys, towering mountains and crashing seas. She saw farms and villages and towns and cities, with great highways and high towers, and the busy movements of people within them. She could see the sun, moon, and stars presiding over everything from above. Once again the world revealed itself to her as a field of life in all of its beautiful diversity: its heights, its depths, its conflicts, and its loves. This Katie knew to be her domain, the field and the stage of her life, and that there was no place she could not go, and nothing she could not change.

Quickly her gaze fell upon a cemetery on the edge of a small town, surrounded on one side by forest and on the other by farmland. Her attention focused on three men sitting on headstones, laughing with each other and drinking from a flask that they shared between them. Without hearing their voices she knew they were talking about her. They gestured as if holding and measuring parts of her body. Katie became angry, and the feeling brought her back to where she was standing, in the portal of the DiAngelo family crypt with its front doors open and half-twisted out of shape.

One of the men looked toward her, as if noticing for the first time that she had escaped. As he turned toward her, Katie saw he was wearing a red tunic with a metal breastplate and leather bracers and greaves—the livery of a Roman centurion. He immediately gestured to his companions and they stood up. A second one was similarly armoured, and he drew a sword. The third, however, wore a modern suit jacket and trousers, but was missing his tie. The three of them ran toward her, brandishing their weapons, and shouting their war cries.

~ 34 ~

Eric was eventually taken out of the car, brought up a short flight of steps, along something like a hallway, and down a longer flight of steps, and finally seated in a chair. Only then was the bag taken off his head. He found himself in a dark room, lit with candles that sat in holders on the walls. Two of the hooded men stood on either side of him, with a hand on each of his shoulders. In the dim light he could not make out many details of where he was, but he could see he was in some kind of private chapel. The hands holding him in place pushed him into a chair that faced a wall of mottled shadows. In the dim light he could make out a mural painted on the wall that depicted, as far as Eric could see, the scene from the Bible in which Christ was transfigured before his apostles in glory next to the prophets Abraham and Elijah. With curiosity, Eric noted that the auras painted around the two prophets resembled great open wings, and that both of them were carrying hourglasses.

A moment later, a deep Italian voice spoke in the darkness and resonated off the walls. "Praetorians, you have done very well," it said. Then the speaker stepped in front of Eric, blocking the view of the mural. He was wearing a suit jacket, and had short and dark curly hair. It was the same dark-haired, Mediterranean gentleman with whom he had seen Katie not long before, and who Miranda had identified to him as Carlo Maliguida. Next to him stood another man, similarly dressed, although in the changing shadows Eric could not make out his face.

"Good evening Eric. I am told that you came willingly this time," said the unidentified man.

"You've already proven that I can't hide from you," answered Eric.

"I hope you will continue to cooperate with us."

"I know your voice. We've met before, somewhere. I'm sure of it." Eric wondered aloud.

The speaker ignored his comment. "We want to ask you some friendly questions. It won't take a moment of your time."

Eric shrugged. "Looks like I have no choice here," he said.

The interrogator dived straight into his questions. "First of all, I want to know everything that you know about Miranda Brigand."

This surprised Eric a little. "Why, what has she got to do with anything?"

"Just so you know, I will ask the questions here," gruffed the interrogator.

"Fine", Eric rolled his eyes.

"What do you know about Miranda Brigand?" the man asked again.

"Nothing much, really. I met her only this morning."

"So she is not a relation of yours after all?"

"No, she's not. Why are you asking about her?"

The interrogator signaled the other men with a wave of his finger, and one of them punched Eric in the stomach.

"I am asking the questions Eric. I shouldn't have to tell you twice."

When Eric regained his voice, he said, "She bailed me out of jail this morning and that was the first time I met her. She helped me find Katie at the hospital and then took us to her house. Then Katie left, and we followed. I saw her leave her apartment with you. Then I went home alone."

"Is that all?"

"I don't know anything else about her. Why is she so important?"

The interrogator signaled the men again, and a second heavy fist landed in Eric's stomach.

"That's three questions, Eric, after you were told you get none. Very disappointing."

"Sorry," said Eric, not really sorry at all.

"I need to know everything you know. Was today the first time you ever saw her?"

"Yes, I'm pretty sure I never met her before."

"Be absolutely sure," commanded the interrogator.

"What does it matter if I did?"

"It matters because I need to know!" growled the man, on the edge of losing his temper. Without waiting to be asked, a henchmen clubbed Eric in the stomach again. Eric had to catch his breath, but when he did he started to chuckle quietly.

"What's so funny." demanded the interrogator.

"You didn't want me to ask questions, but you answered that one anyway," said Eric.

Carlo frowned. The interrogator then leaned over Eric, close enough that Eric had to tilt his head back to avoid getting a nose-full of his breath.

"Why did you give yourself up to us." he asserted, quietly but deliberately. Eric said nothing. So the interrogator put on a little more pressure. "Did you think you could intimidate us, or show us that you're not afraid? Perhaps you think I need some kind of acknowledgement of my authority from you, and that you can fight me by refusing to give it? Understand this. Right now you are nothing more to me than a source of information that I require, and I will have it."

For the first time, Eric was genuinely scared. The interrogator looked Eric in the eyes. "I ask again. Why are you here."

"I *do* know you," said Eric. "From the Underground. You're one of the bouncers."

This time, the interrogator himself punched his fist into Eric's stomach. Eric wheezed and grasped for breath before he could speak again.

"I am here because I wanted to know why you wanted to kill me last night. I wanted to know if it was true what Nicholas said about Katie being engaged to another man without telling me."

Carlo stepped forward, tapped the interrogator on the shoulder, and took over the conversation. "And do you think you found your answer now?" he asked.

Eric cast his gaze down. After a pause, Carlo lightened his tone a little. Something resembling sympathy crossed his face. "I can see that you really did believe Katie loved you, and that she fooled you as much as she fooled me. I believe I can forgive you for that."

"I hope you won't hurt her."

With a little bit of ire, Carlo replied, "The DiAngelo are a cultivated race. Despite what all those gangster movies may make you think about my countrymen, Katie will come to no harm from me over this indiscretion. And from this moment on, neither will you." Carlo gestured to the two men holding Eric down, and they released him and left the room, as did the interrogator.

"Does that mean you will let me go?"

"There is still some more information I require. But I think we can talk in a more gentlemanly fashion now, would you agree?" As he spoke, he waved his hands in the direction of the walls. Candles and oil lamps all around the room suddenly flared to life, and Eric could see the space completely. There were narrow curtains hanging all along the walls, spaced between sections of stone wall where a variety of Venetian carnival masks hung on display. Carlo then opened a cabinet near the side of the entrance and from it produced a bottle of wine and two glasses, one of which he handed to Eric. He poured out a drink for them both, and sipped his own thoughtfully. Eric remembered Katie's story of meeting this man and accepting drinks from him, so he sniffed the wine but did not drink.

Then Carlo said, "I need to know what Miranda told you about me. I need to know what she knows."

"Not much," said Eric, standing and massaging his hands. "Something about a war between her family and yours. Apparently you believe her family owes some kind of loyalty to your family, but she won't give it."

Carlo's expression changed to a more curious one. "Well I wouldn't call it a war. More like a debt to be paid. Did she tell you how our little disagreement started?"

"She said it started with the Roman occupation of Britain."

Carlo chuckled a little bit. "That is all the Celts ever talk about anymore."

"There is some truth in it," offered Eric. "The Celts of

Britain and of continental Europe were defeated by the Romans. There was the Siege of the Island of Anglesey, and the Battle of Alesia. But the Romans eventually withdrew, when they had too many problems at home. Then Britain was colonized by Saxons, Vikings, Normans, practically everybody."

Carlo smiled. "I had forgotten that you were reading history. But even you must understand that what you are taught as 'history' is only ever half of the truth."

"History is written by the winners, I know that," said Eric.

"It isn't the winners who write history. It's the people who show up."

Eric acknowledged this remark with a thoughtful nod.

"Nice to see you cooperating with me at last," smiled Carlo, as he sipped his wine again. "Now tell me, why did she want you and Katie to get involved?"

"I don't really know. She didn't give much explanation."

"Think harder," ordered Carlo. "Perhaps she did, but you don't realise it."

"I asked her once, but she didn't really give a straight answer. She said Katie was 'one of us'."

Carlo leaned forward. "One of 'us'? And did she say who she meant by 'us'?"

"She did, but you'll never believe me."

"Try me."

Eric hesitated before answering. "She said she was a member of a kind of secret society."

"A secret society? How very theatrical."

Eric looked at the mural dominating one wall of the room. He was now able to see more details, such as the three eagles which circled behind the Christ figure, and the crowd of amazed onlookers below them. On something like a ridge between the divine figures and the human witnesses, there were three bodies lying prone, apparently dead. One held a curved blade in his hand, the second carried a trident, and the third had a helmet and scepter.

"She said you were descendants of the Roman gods," Eric reluctantly answered.

Carlo repressed a smile that tugged at the side of his face. "And did you believe her?"

"Not really. It's too unlikely, too fantastic."

Carlo turned away from Eric for a moment, and studied one of the masks on the wall. When he turned back, he was a little friendlier.

"Katie is indeed one of 'us', but 'we' are just an ancient aristocratic family. We're what the Americans call 'old Europe'. Nothing more fantastic than that. We are arranging a dynastic marriage to reunite Miranda's branch of the family with mine."

Eric looked up. "So I really was just Katie's last fling?"

"These things happen," shrugged Carlo, nonchalantly. But seeing this did nothing to improve Eric's spirits, he added, "I am told that you were good man for her. You treated her well. I respect that. So unless you have any questions for *me*, you are free to go."

For Eric, this confirmed the story that Nicholas had told him earlier in the day, back at the police station. Eric felt safe enough to ask a question, to see if more of it could be confirmed. "Who were the men who chased me last night? Were they Katie's bodyguards?"

"You catch on quick," Carlo confirmed.

"Actually, the lawyer in the police station told me that's who they were."

"That would have been Nicholas, an associate of mine." Carlo opened a door behind Eric's chair, and called for his henchmen to return. When they came back, he told them, "Our guest has been very cooperative. We are finished here now. Take him home."

The men gestured for Eric to follow. They took him out of the room, up a dusty staircase that led into a library. Eric marveled at the books and artworks that were on display there. But the men did not let him linger. They ushered him forward, into a hallway and out of the house, where a car was waiting. Carlo followed Eric out to it, to see him off. He whispered something to the driver of the car, then turned to Eric.

"As an agreement of honour between gentlemen, I must ask you not to see Katie again. I hope you understand," said Carlo. Eric nodded, more from a sense of defeat than from agreement. Carlo offered his hand to shake, and Eric took it, although he kept his eyes downcast. Carlo kissed both of Eric's cheeks in the European style, which made Eric even more uncomfortable. Then Eric climbed in the back seat. The car drove north, out of the city, toward Eric's hometown. But it did not take the turn toward the Old Bridge Road. Instead, it kept going, through the downtown area and onward to the other side.

"This isn't the way to my house," Eric complained.

As soon as Eric said this, the man in the front passenger seat turned around and leveled a gun at Eric's eyes. In a low, monotonous voice, he said, "We know." And he threw a cloth bag at Eric and ordered him to put it over his head.

~ 35 ~

The three men were running at top speed toward Katie, who was calmly and purposefully stepping forward to meet them. The men looked as if they were coming on the attack, and so Katie steadied herself for a defense. She knew nothing about fighting. But she had a newfound sense of confidence and power. And that, she was sure, would give her some advantage. She stood her ground and pointed her spear directly at the oncoming soldiers.

As the men approached, Katie noticed something that seemed oddly out of place. She recognised that the third man racing up to the attack was Nicholas. The odd thing which she noticed was that he had not transformed into Roman armour as the other two had done. He was dressed in the same modern business attire he had been wearing before. But she quickly put aside that observation to contemplate later. The men had reached her, and they took positions around her with their swords pointing at her, ready to strike. Nicholas arrived only a few steps behind them. He looked her in the eye with a scowl.

"You should have ran, while you had the chance," he growled, clearly angry.

"You can't hurt me, you said so yourself" Katie replied defiantly.

"If they find your body with a sword wound on it" said Nicholas with a wry smile, "then my employer will know it was us who did it. On the other hand, if they find you with a bullet hole, then it could have been anyone," he said, and then he produced a gun from his jacket, pointed it at her, and let it speak for itself. Katie involuntarily pursed her lips.

At that instant, a flock of ravens and crows swooped down from the sky. They flew into the faces of the three men, scratching with their claws and flapping their wings in their eyes. Katie looked up, trying to see where they came from and how many of them there were. But in the near-darkness of midnight, it was impossible to tell. Nicholas fired his gun into the air at random, and the Roman centurions slashed their swords, but the only result was a few clipped wings and feathers. Soon blood began to stream from small cuts and wounds on their arms and faces.

"The Brigantians are here! We have to retreat!" shouted one of the soldiers.

"No, we have our orders!" Nicholas shouted back.

Katie was just as surprised by the sudden appearance of the crows as were the three men. She stood unhurt among them, marveling at their sudden appearance and her good luck. She didn't see, then, that Nicholas managed to fight his way through the crowd of crows and get close enough to grab hold of her spear. He had only one hand on it, as the other was uselessly protecting his face. But his grip was strong. Katie quickly grasped both hands on her spear and pulled it tight. This newfound gift was a treasure and she would not dishonour her benefactors, whoever they were, by losing it so soon. Nicholas threw his body weight against her, trying to wrest it from her by knocking her to the ground. But because of the birds attacking him, he could not see properly, and Katie was able to twist herself in just the right way to make him lose his balance. He fell to the ground. Katie was about to gloat over how easy it was to throw him, when one of the Romans was able to grab her from behind and drag her backwards. Katie held on to her spear, which Nicholas was still holding, to resist. But the soldier was forced to let go when one of the crows landed on Katie's shoulder and began pecking at his eyes. Nicholas, who still had a grip on Katie's spear, tried to pull her down to the ground with him. He too was forced to protect himself from the assaults of the thick flock of black birds, and eventually he let go of Katie's spear in order to protect himself. The third Roman was struggling with two birds that had landed on his shoulders to peck at his face, and were refusing to be thrown off.

From a short distance, the sound of a trumpet blast penetrated the disorder. On a nearby ridge, Katie saw the silhouette of three people. Two held aloft the same long bronze trumpets she had seen a moment ago. The third, between them, held aloft a long pole from which flapped a hanging banner. A tree, with a three-armed spiral in its roots, was depicted on it. This one waved at Katie to come over. Then, one by one, more figures appeared on the ridge, as if emerging from a retreating mist. Men and women, dressed in the garb of Celtic warriors, complete with swords, shields and spears, materialized from the mist.

Seeing that her three assailants were pinned down, Katie stepped lightly away from them, and tossed a cheeky smile at Nicholas from over her shoulder as she went. Nicholas shouted an obscenity back at her, but couldn't finish it as the birds were too persistent.

Arriving at the ridge, Katie saw that the woman who waved her over was Miranda. She was wearing a heavy linen dress, much like Katie's although longer, and with a hooded cloak instead of a armour. Her two companions with the trumpets, both male warriors, wore leather trousers and linen shirts open at the neck, with a pleated tartan thrown over one shoulder. Blue and green tattoos resembling plant foliage covered their arms. Swords hung from their belts in leather scabbards with polished gold bands. They both held their heads high to her, and stood upright and strong, as if proud to be in her presence. Miranda pulled back the hood from her face and smiled with admiration.

"Well done, well done!" exclaimed Miranda. Katie blushed, and turned her head down to hide her face in her hair.

One of the trumpet bearers nudged Miranda's side with his elbow, and so she adopted a more formal pose. She thumped the banner pole on the ground three times, and spoke.

"As clann chief of the Brigantia, and summoner of House De Dannan, it is my duty and pleasure to welcome you once again to your ancient and rightful place in our House, and to be the first to address you by your ancient name: Caitlin Ni Corrigan, descendent of the Great Queen of old Ireland. Hail and Welcome!"

The crowd of warriors repeated the last refrain: "Hail and Welcome!"

Katie was overwhelmed. She told Miranda, "Oh, no need for that." But it was false modesty. Underneath her hair, she was beaming.

"You finished your Awakening, you deserve a parade," said Miranda. She touched Katie's chin to lift her head. "Now in the ancient tradition, I am supposed to recite your genealogy to sixteen generations, and the traditional wisdom-speech on the qualities of the great kings and queens of old, but sure we can leave all that to later. You probably want to know what just happened to you?"

Katie touched the hem of her costume. "Yes, please."

"In the confinement of the crypt over there," Miranda explained, "you confronted the ancestral spirit of an ancient enemy, and you resisted him. And so your connection to the soul of the world was restored to you. Now all your potentials can be fulfilled, and you can be who you truly are."

"I really am one of you?" Katie asked.

Miranda smiled, "Strictly speaking, you are a Corrigan, not a Brigantian. But you may very well be the last of your clan. So we would like you to think of yourself as an honorary Brigantian, and you're welcome in our feasting hall in every way."

Katie smiled, but it was an unsure, unsteady smile. "If I am someone called Caitlin now," she asked, "What happened to who I was?"

Miranda noticed, and put her hand on Katie's shoulder. "Don't worry," said Miranda. "You are still Katie. You don't have to leave your old self behind. But now you can be so much more as well. Think of it like a secret super-hero identity."

"So Carlo was right," Katie marveled.

"Since you mentioned him," said Miranda, turning more serious, "you should know that he will still try to track you down, and now with more urgency than ever before."

Katie looked down to where she left Nicholas and his two henchmen. The birds had gone. One of the men was wrapping a bandage around a bloody wound on his upper arm. Nicholas was searching around with a flashlight, as if he did not know where Katie had gone.

"They can't see us right now," said Miranda. "I have raised a mist around us. It's a trick the old Druids used to do, that I learned back in the day."

Katie turned back to Miranda and said, "Thank you for sending the crows to protect me." The two honour guards laughed. Katie gave them a puzzled look.

"We did not do that," explained Miranda. "They came to protect you on their own."

"On their own?" asked Katie.

Miranda answered as if it was a well known, ordinary fact. "Because your purpose was clear and your will was strong. Because the soul of the world responds to such things. And because you are a descendent of the Morrigan."

~ 36 ~

"Where are you taking me!" shouted Eric.

"Shut up," ordered the man with the gun.

Eric did not have to wait long. The car pulled along the River Road, until it came to a modern concrete and steel bridge, where it stopped. This bridge was right on the town line, where the river under it flowed out of the town centre into a conservation area. The two men got out and roughly manhandled Eric along with them. They took him to the middle of the bridge, and pushed him against the railing. Looking down, through the bottom of the bag over his head, Eric could see the river as it rushed over shallow rapids at the bottom of a gorge some fifty meters below. The stone walls of the gorge amplified the sound of the rapids, drowning out all other sounds, and all other thoughts.

One of the men spoke into his ears: "This is what is going to happen. You will fall, and the river will carry your body miles away. If you try to run, the sound of the rapids will cover the sound of the gun. This is what you will get if you mess with the Boss or his woman ever again. You will not get a second warning."

The muzzle of the gun was pressed against the back of his head. He heard the click of the bullet being lodged in the chamber, ready to fire. Eric tensed his muscles, and waited for the end.

Then, nothing happened.

Eric relaxed his muscles a little. Nothing happened.

He slowly drew his hands around, and lifted the bottom of the bag on his head. Nothing happened.

He removed the bag entirely and turned around. Nothing happened.

The men were gone, the car was gone, and Eric was still alive. The water passed beneath the bridge as it always did. Nothing happened.

"It was just a warning," breathed Eric, greatly relieved. He started to walk in the direction of home. The River Road joined the Old Bridge road a short distance away. Home was not far: just through the forest, to the Old Bridge, and then across the parking lot. Eric held his arms outstretched and spun around in a circle, glad to be alive. "It's over!" he exclaimed. "It's over! I can go home! It's over!"

Eric started walking. The rain had long since stopped, but night had fallen and everything was blanketed in shadow, but for the little islands of orange light created by the magnesium street lamps, and the flickering reflections of various lights on the puddles. It was a gloomy picture. But to Eric it was beautiful.

As he began to walk, he tried to take stock of his situation. He asked himself, why did Carlo's goons not kill me? Was that my reward for having been nice to Katie? Well, no use looking a gift horse in the mouth. I'm alive, and that's a good thing. What if Miranda's story is true? Eric chuckled when he thought that interviewing the re-incarnation of one of the first settlers in this country first-hand would be a great benefit to his work as a university student. But his next thought was more down to earth. I couldn't do that—no one would believe me. Well, soon enough I'll be home. I'll have my books again, and my studies. I've got some exciting research prospects coming up. What else? I'll have my cat. Ganga will still be there. He's a good friend. Even if he sprays the place a bit too much and the neighbours get pissed off. I suppose I should get him neutered. What else? I'll have my email and my internet. I've got friends all over the country now. Maybe I should go on tour this summer, and visit some of them. Maybe I should go to Quebec and see if the feeling of the old town inspires my research somehow. Anyway I could do with a holiday. What else. I've got my apartment door to fix. The landlord might take a while before getting around to putting on a new lock. Well it's a safe neighbourhood, there's probably nothing to worry about. I'll go to the Carriage House tonight for a pint or two, and celebrate not being killed. There might be a live band tonight. Live music is my life. In a few days, everything will be settled again and back to normal. Everything is going to be fine.

"That's what I wanted. Isn't it?"

Eric stopped walking. Something, or rather someone, was missing from this portrait of the perfect life, the life he told Miranda he wanted. However much I might deny it, he realised, I am going home to an empty house. The adventure is over, but I have nothing to show for it. Only loss. Katie is gone. Love, it suddenly seems, is not part of a normal life. It is part of a life of adventure, a life of wonder and struggle and change. There is nothing ordinary about love. Or, there shouldn't be, if it is all that we imagine it to be. If love is sincere and genuine then it opens the gates to another person's soul, while at the same time the gates of my own soul open to another. And that is always an unfamiliar land. So love is dangerous. It requires taking risks. And the possibility of shipwreck and disaster is never far away. But in the same way, there is always a chance for new discovery as well. Love makes a life extraordinary. And here I am, walking away from it, back to the ordinary uneventfulness of how things used to be. Is that what I asked for? I got my old life back, but I had to give up Katie to get it. Is that really what I wanted?

If I go after Katie, then Carlo will probably try to have me killed. That is what the warning was all about. But if Katie has any love for me at all, that is what she would want me to do. And I, for my part, must take every last chance to avoid condemning myself to an ordinary life, whatever the danger might be.

When Eric rounded the path to the point where his apartment was in view, he saw that he saw the light of his sitting room was on, and he saw the shadow of someone waiting for him inside.

"Those bloody people won't leave me alone," he said to himself. He felt the pressure in the blood veins of his temples thicken and increase. But he also knew that he would have to deal with them if he wanted to be with Katie. Eric crossed the bridge and headed home, determined not to hide or run from whoever was waiting for him there. Once on the other side of the bridge, the broken lamp on the corner shone out steadily, lighting his way.

~ 37 ~

Katie stood on the ridge with Miranda and the warriors, watching Nicholas with his guards fruitlessly looking around.

"It seems a shame to keep them in the dark like this," she said. "What do you think?"

"They can stay in the dark, for all I care," muttered Katie, without hesitation.

"I know how you feel," Miranda replied. "I really do. But we need to show them that we are protecting you, or else they will never leave you alone."

"Then we should kill them or something," said Katie, remembering the bruises Carlo left on her body.

"Nothing so drastic. We just need them to know that you are with us now."

This comment made Katie feel a little like a pawn in some kind of game. She was about to protest, but Miranda was already half way to Nicholas and his men, and her warriors followed her. Speaking to her followers, but carrying on as if continuing the conversation with Katie, she said, "And I think some of the lads here are not too happy with all this standing around, isn't that right?"

The warriors cheered, and shook their weapons in the air. Katie shrugged it off, knowing there would be plenty of time for questions later. At any rate, she hoped that what was about to transpire might answer some of them. Miranda led her followers until they stood within a spear throw of where Nicholas and his two Romans were binding their wounds and conferring with each other. Then she addressed herself to Nicholas. "Praetorians!"

Katie presumed that was the moment the mist of invisibility was lifted. Nicholas looked up, and evidently he could suddenly see Miranda, Katie, and their retinue quite clearly. Surprise registered on his face, followed by anger. The two centurions produced their swords, ready to attack. But three of the Celtic warriors immediately converged around Katie, creating a shield barrier. Others drew their own swords, prepared to meet the attack. Nicholas gestured to his centurions to hold back and stand their ground.

"Cartimandua," said Nicholas, with undisguised hatred.

"You can tell your patrician that this one," said Miranda, referring to Katie, "is under the protection of the Brigantia."

"I will tell him," agreed Nicholas, seeing that he was enormously outnumbered. "But I'm sure my patrician would want me to remind you of your unfulfilled bargain."

Katie looked at Miranda, puzzled. There was definitely more going on than had so far been revealed to her.

"That is not to be resolved by you," countered Miranda.

"Not by me, no," said Nicholas. "But you still owe him, nonetheless."

Katie interjected here. "And Eric Laflamme is under our protection too. You leave him alone."

Miranda looked at Katie, both surprised and pleased.

But Nicholas was annoyed. "I do not take orders from

you, little girl," he said.

Miranda stood up for Katie. "This woman is an honorary shield maiden of the Brigantia! She stands above you now. You will treat her with respect."

Nicholas only grimaced. Addressing Miranda, and ignoring Katie, he said, "You can claim to protect whomever you want. It changes nothing. You still owe us."

Miranda smiled back at him. "Enough with the veiled threats, Nicholas. Make good on them right now, or else get out of here." The band of Celtic warriors behind Miranda started to shout roars and threats of their own, and thump their swords and spears on their shields. The men with the trumpets began intoning the long, low sound of what was clearly a battle-call. Katie felt quite invigorated, knowing that this big display of bravado was for her benefit. Otherwise, she would think it was all very silly.

Nicholas watched the display for a moment, and then turned to his two companions. "Damn Celts always said they never knew defeat. Even when we had the half of them chained in our prisons. Screw them! Let's go." Then he spat on the ground and turned toward his car. The band of warriors cheered and started bashing each other with their weapons in a noisy show of self-congratulation. Even Miranda joined in the celebration, cheerfully smacking her banner-pole against the shields and spears of her warriors. Katie saw that as the two centurions passed behind the trees and headstones of the cemetery, their armour disappeared and normal, modern long coats adorned them again. It was as if they changed during the split second that Katie blinked her eyes. The wheels of the car splashed in a puddle, and took them away.

Miranda turned to the rowdy band of warriors who were still whooping and hollering in delight at their 'victory'.

"Lads, let's carry our new sister home and give her a right royal welcome!" she announced. Immediately, from behind the ridge a chariot pulled by two horses drew up. Miranda guided Katie into it, and her smile dispelled any worries Katie had about controlling or steering it. Once she had a grip on the railing, it started to run toward the ridge, with all the warriors running behind and around it. The chariot shook and jolted on the rough ground, and Katie gripped the edge until her knuckles turned white. Miranda led the chariot up and to edge of the ridge, then over it and right into the air, as if a solid invisible bridge supported them. The flock of crows re-appeared, flying and diving and racing in and around the wild merry band as they ran into the sky. They ran much faster in the air than mere mortals run on the ground, and so it was not long before they were high enough for Katie to see most of the lay of the town below her. She picked out landmarks like her apartment, the Carriage House, the Old Bridge and Eric's flat. She saw people walking and driving about, coming in and out of houses and bars, oblivious to the wild ruckus presence above. She saw the black car that carried Nicholas and his two bodyguards racing along the main road, toward the DiAngelo mansion. She saw the fields and forests beyond the wards of the town, with the glow of little lights from farm houses and the occasional backyard bonfire. Katie held her arms above her in absolute delight of the moment. It was not the impossible magic of the sky race that made her feel such happiness. It was the sense of coming home, the sense of having found a family. Katie felt beautiful.

~ 38 ~

The race began to turn down toward the earth after a while, and Katie could soon see that their destination was somewhere in the conservation area that bordered Fellwater to the west. They spiraled in and down, and finally touched the earth in an open space just at the edge of the forest. Then they followed a path through the forest until coming to a thickly overgrown ridge. In the midst of the trees was a stone cairn of flat rectangular flagstones, roughly as high as Katie's shoulders, and as wide at the base as the stretch of her arms. Its stones were worn down by the weather and covered in moss on one side, and indeed it looked as if it should have fallen over ages ago, or been picked apart by tourists and hikers. From a wineskin hanging from her belt, Miranda poured a little bit of beer on to the stones.

"A little offering to the powers of this forest, which help us protect us and keep our secret garden safe," Miranda explained.

"What secret garden?" Katie asked.

As the beer trickled down the stones of the cairn, Katie had her answer. Some of the trees, rocks, and shrubs of the ridge rolled and twisted to one side, revealing a shallow rift in the ridge. Its ceiling was formed by an overhanging canopy of leaves, vines, and branches. The parade of Celtic warriors moved into it. Katie observed all sorts of strange plants and creatures: butterflies and mushrooms that glowed in the dark, rocky outcroppings that seemed to have human faces, and tree branches that moved out of her way. The air was occasionally punctuated with an otherworldly music of whistles, pipes and strings, little bells, clicks and knocks, and other strange calls, like hundreds of distant wind chimes, and the music of the flowers. It reverberated through the air, as if coming from everywhere and nowhere. It sounded to Katie's ears like what flowers would sound like if they could sing.

Emerging from the tunnel, she found herself in a wide valley, bordered on three sides by the ridge, and on the fourth side by the river. The ridge slope was steeper and higher on this side, and wild with cedars and raspberry bushes and wild sumac, although stone stairs and wooden boardwalks could be seen climbing among them. A dozen or so roundhouses with clay walls and pointed roofs sat in a cluster by the ridge on one side. Some of them had goldenrod and heather growing in the thatch. A fox peered out from behind one of them, and it nodded its head as if to welcome the new arrivals. Surrounding them lay garden patches and little yards, some blooming with tomatoes and corns talks and strawberries, some with spring tulips, and some with apple, cherry, and mulberry trees. Yet most of the valley was a wide great field, dotted here and there by maples and alders and red oaks, and carpeted with wild flowers and short grasses that sometimes moved in the wind like the waves of the sea. The breeze brought the pleasant smell of pine from the forest, that soon clung to the skin like a thin oil, and washed all one's tension away. Beneath Katie's feet a wide footpath paved with bricks and cobbles picked a meandering way from the entrance tunnel to the roundhouses. But no fence or ditch or bank contained its edges, or kept it apart from the fields upon which it lay, like a ribbon one could roll up and lay down elsewhere. It was a landscape you could go wandering in, and care not at all if you became lost.

"Fellwater", Miranda proudly declared. "Your town was named for the rapids and the cliffs over the river. But the river was named for this secret garden. We found something in the water here, that – well, I'm sure you'll find out."

But Katie was hardly listening. She walked ahead of her with her arms spreading out, as if to take in the whole sight, all at once. In the centre of the valley stood a wide ring of tall, wedge shaped standing stones, perhaps thirty in all, and as she came closer to them she saw that each was carved with a human figure, facing the inside, in a style that resembled an illustration in an ancient illuminated manuscript. When she came closer to it she saw that some had little niches carved in them where candles burned, and some had baskets of apples and fresh bread laid at their feet. Someone walking near to Katie was explaining that each figure represented a hero or a deity from Celtic mythology. But Katie was still only half listening. Her attention was drawn to one stone in particular, which bore the figure of a woman in armour holding two crossed spears, with three ravens in flight surrounding her head. The skull of some large animal lay at the stone's foot.

A fire blazed heartily in a dugout sandpit at the centre of the ring of stones. Some people were stoking up the flames, and hoisting a wooden tripod over it from which hung a pot-bellied cauldron. Others were setting up picnic tables and laying out food for a feast. At one of the tables two old men played at a board game that looked like it might be a variation of chess. At another, a cluster of musicians tuned their fiddles, guitars, and hand drums, and discussed the songs they wanted to play. Still other people nearby enjoyed some deep talk over a pitcher of wine, or some good natured roughhousing, as they gallivanted about on each other's shoulders.

Miranda took Katie around the party, to introduce her to everyone. People cheered at her arrival, raising cups and drinking-horns to toast her. She heard people addressing her with her 'new' name. And a sudden wave of remembrance reverberated through her. This was exactly as she saw it, in the vision of the ancient place, not two nights before. The faces, clothes, voices, music, and surroundings were all the same. As was the wonderful feeling of familiarity and love. People spontaneously hugged and kissed her, as if that, and not a handshake, was the standard greeting among them.

Looking around, Katie noticed that the horses and chariot which carried her were nowhere to be seen. She also noticed that although the area was spacious, she saw no stables or paddocks. She asked the nearest person where the horses were, and was directed to two men standing just off to the side of the entrance to the house. They were topless and had rough leather trousers. One was holding a horse mask under his arm, large enough to cover his whole head. The other man was at that moment removing a similar mask.

Miranda's trumpet bearers commanded the crowd's attention with a brief flourish. "Brigantians!" she addressed them, as she climbed on stool carved from a tree stump. "May I present Katherine Corrigan, newly emerged from the awakening, and better known to all of us as Caitlin of the clan Corrigan!" A cheer went up, which made Katie blush and hide her face in her hair again. Miranda acknowledged the cheers and encourage Katie to stand on one of the picnic tables where everyone could see her.

"Now Caitlin here, she had a pretty tough awakening. Twice in two days, she was caught by the DiAngelo." Miranda paused here for the boos and curses to die down. "The first time, we rescued her." This provoked a renewed round of cheers. Miranda whipped them up further. "And the second time, like the great warriors of old, she escaped on her own!" More and louder cheers erupted with this news, along with shouted promises to stand as Katie's personal champion, blood-oaths to kill Nicholas and Carlo, and even offers of marriage.

"And I think it's a sign," continued Miranda, quieting the crowd with her words, "that it will not be long before all our lost companions are returned to us. It is even possible that another one of us lives right in the centre of Fellwater, and will soon begin his own passage, and will feast by our fire before midsummer's day. But tonight, we celebrate the return of the daughter of our great queen!" The conclusion of Miranda's speech sparked the loudest wave of cheers, and the trumpeters joined in the noise with their own flourishes as well. She looked around at all the faces there, all perfect strangers who were suddenly as close to her heart as family.

"And now, honourable companions!" Miranda declared. "Now that our princess is returned to us, we shall feast like kings!"

The trumpets proclaimed themselves again. Miranda gestured to everyone to turn their attention to the fire, where several men were hefting the meat off of the spit and putting it on to a cutting board. Next to them, others were arriving bearing huge wooden beer kegs on their shoulders.

A cheer went up, and the crowd started partying again. The musicians struck up a set dance tune, and couples took each other in their arms to dance around the fire. Some even lined up to take a turn to jump over the fire. And the mead horn was filled again and passed from hand to hand. Miranda went around the circle, meeting people, shaking hands with some but embracing and kissing most. When Miranda came around to Katie, she hugged her tightly and kissed her forehead like a loving mother.

"The rest of the night is for dancing, feasting, singing, making music and love," said Miranda. "So relax, introduce yourself to everybody, and have fun."

More cheers followed Miranda's last words, and the musicians began to play again. Miranda waved one of her warriors to her side. "Donall," she told him, "bring my chalice."

A strong-looking man with long brownish hair and an unkempt goatee answered her request. From a niche in one of the standing stones he brought a reddish, hand-thrown clay chalice, adorned with a spiral design along its rim. Miranda presented it to Katie.

Katie took the chalice but hesitated, remembering that Carlo had offered her a glass of something strange earlier that evening.

"The mead cup is an ancient symbol of welcome and hospitality among our people," explained Miranda.

"Especially when offered by a red-haired queen," Donall added with a smirk.

"It's just," explained Katie, "Carlo wanted me to drink something too, and that's when everything started to go wrong."

"Oh, this stuff will surely put you down for the night," Miranda joked.

Katie tasted it gingerly with the tip of her tongue, and found it sweet and pleasant.

"What is it?" she asked.

"Mead!", said Donall. "Fermented honey! Nature's most perfect food. And most perfect drink!" Some nearby onlookers laughed loudly.

"And the particular cup you are drinking from," Miranda continued, "is quite the treasure, almost as old as our clan."

Katie sipped a bit more. "It's really nice," she said, not quite sure what to say.

"Want to try drinking from a horn?" asked Donall.

"A horn?"

Donall grinned impishly and thrust a hollow bullock horn into her hand, filled almost to the top with more mead. A few nearby onlookers cheered her on. The mead in the horn suddenly made a plopping noise and splattered her face. Waves of laughter rose from the crowd, along with cries of, "Hold it with the end pointing down!"

At another end of the stone circle a large painted wooden pole had been erected and about twenty or so ribbons hung from the top. Someone was standing at the top of a stepladder beside the pole, attempting to put a ring of leaves and flowers over the top of it. People applauded him when he succeeded. The musicians struck up a lively dance tune, and people took the ends of the ribbons in their hands. When they were all collected, they began to dance around, half going clockwise, the other half going counterclockwise. Katie had no trouble joining in. The dancers dipped around each other, over and under each other, so that the ribbons weaved and meshed seamlessly down the pole. The maypole dance finished when the ribbons were weaved so far down the pole it was impossible to continue and everyone became jumbled into a big happy hug. It was beautiful, and Katie once again knew the blessing of belonging.

~ 39 ~

At the end of the night, most people trotted off to find places to sleep if they had not already collapsed in a drunken stupor on the ground. Katie sought out Miranda. She found her playing a guitar with the musicians, and sitting on a beer keg.

"Katie! You enjoyed yourself I hope?" she asked.

"I feel like I came home," Katie answered enthusiastically.

"If you have any questions, just ask."

Katie looked around. Most everyone was either asleep, or engaged in a deep private conversation. A few couples were wandering off into the distance together, for private intimacies. It all seemed perfectly harmless, even innocent, except for the otherworldliness of the place, and the strange ceremony she had witnessed.

"Who built this place?" she asked.

"We did," said Miranda. "About two thousand years ago, more or less? Yes that's right. We were kind of homeless, and then the Ouendat people, they let us set up a camp here. In return we agreed to help fight for them, whenever they asked. It's a very good arrangement. Everyone gets what they want."

"It's perfect," mused Katie.

"Yeah, until the bloody Sassenach got here, gave them guns and whiskey and diseases and all kinds of things they didn't really want or need. Oh—and they knocked down our stone circle. They didn't want anyone to know that we got here first. We had to build it again."

Katie watched as a few of the warriors stumbled into one of the stones, laughing, and pouring the contents of their drinking horns over their own heads.

"Maybe that's how it fell down," she suggested.

"We Brigantians are not the clan that gets the most drunk," Miranda retorted. "We are the clan that drinks the most. There's a difference!"

A few nearby people who overheard Miranda's words toasted her enthusiastically.

"There used to be a lot of places in the world like this," said Miranda, suddenly growing melancholy. "There used to be a secret garden just outside every village in the world. Small ones, mostly. A little hillock, where roses grow in the winter. An old house, on the edge of town, bigger on the inside than on the out. A little clearing in the forest, where the animals could talk to you. We try to protect them, you know, the few that are left. We get the land zoned as a conservation park. Or we spread ghost stories about the place, to frighten people away. Sometimes we just buy the land outright, if we can. Every country in the world used to have these places. Some countries had hundreds of them. We were such beautiful people, then. We could do anything. But those days are almost gone now. This place is one of the few that nobody knows about. Maybe one of the last."

Donall, listening to Miranda from nearby, folded his arms and looked away.

Katie tried to be cheerful. "At least you still have it, at least this one is still here. It can't be all bad if this one at least, is still here."

"Anyway," sighed Miranda, as she finished the last drop in her horn, "The feast is almost over, for me. I can't stay up so late like I used to. You can stay in one of the roundhouses tonight, or else I can get someone to take you home."

Katie adopted a thoughtful look. "Actually, there's somewhere else I'd like to go instead."

~ 40 ~

Eric took a long route to his front door, to avoid being seen from his own apartment windows by whoever was in there. With a quick dash he made it to some bushes, where he watched the window through the branches. He could not see who the person was, but could tell when he or she was turned away from him, so he knew when the best chance to dash for the door would be. When the chance came, he made it to the door unseen. He squeezed through it, opening it as little as possible and gently closing it to make no sound. He picked up a fire extinguisher on his way up the stair, in case he needed a weapon. At the door he paused to listen, and to look through the hole where the handle used to be, to judge the best time to enter, hopefully with the intruder's back facing him. But when that chance came, he saw that the 'intruder' had distinctive long red hair.

She was seated on Eric's couch, playing with the cat. Eric knew exactly who she was. He put the fire extinguisher down, and leaned against the wall, to think of what to do next. The threat from the DiAngelo men still loomed on his mind. He also recalled the last time she visited him at home, and how that evening ended. Eventually he decided there was no point in standing in his own hallway, waiting for something to happen. He gently and quietly pushed open his door, letting himself be seen, letting her know he was there before entering. It suddenly felt as if he needed her permission to enter her presence, even though she was in his own home.

"Katie?" he said. He was almost afraid of how she might respond.

Katie turned and saw him. "Eric!" she exclaimed.

"I had another run-in with those men, and they told me that –" Eric started to say. But Katie pounced on him before he could finish, and kissed him hard enough to suffocate him. She pushed him on to the couch and climbed on top of him, wrapping her legs around his, and drowning his face in her hair.

"Who are *you*," Eric mused, jokingly.

"I'm the goddess," Katie giggled back. "And you are my champion, who rescued me from the evil hospital today."

Eric laughed, and pushed his fingers through her hair, to the back of her head, and pressed her face into his, to kiss her, possessively, yet lovingly.

"I have a heroic quest for you, my champion," Katie

announced. "But I need you to answer a question, honestly and truthfully, before I tell you what it is,"

Eric raised an eyebrow, curiously. "Okay," Eric agreed.

"Did you, or did you not, wreak my apartment yesterday?"

"What?" Eric stuttered in disbelief.

"When I got home this afternoon," Katie explained, "everything was broken. My furniture ripped with a knife, my plates and coffee cups were smashed, even some of my clothes were torn up."

"No, no, I didn't do that!" Eric exclaimed.

"But you are the only one with a key," Katie accused.

"I swear to you, Katie, I didn't even know about it until you told me just now!"

Katie got up and stood over him. "And I saw that picture of us that you gave me. I found it ripped right down the middle, like you were trying to send me a message. Did you do it?"

"No!" Eric repeated.

Katie analyzed him carefully, trying to decide whether she believed him.

"In fact, I need to know something from you," Eric asserted. Katie felt annoyed with his attempt to take control of the conversation.

"I had another run-in with those men I told you about, the ones who were trying to kill me, you remember? And today I met their boss, what was his name, DiAngelo."

Katie felt the hairs on her arm prickle at the mention of that name.

"He took me to his house, told me personally that you were engaged to marry to him, and that if I ever –"

"Engaged!" Katie burst out. "No! God, no."

"No? The lawyer at the police station told me the same thing. Apparently he was actually working for this DiAngelo guy, not for the courts. And they threatened to kill me if I ever saw you again."

"Well I absolutely assure you I am *not* engaged to Carlo DiAngelo," she declared.

"Why, then, would they tell me otherwise?"

"I don't know," she gruffed back.

Eric could think of no other way to answer but to say what he wanted. "I love you Katie. But I need to know where I stand in your world. I need to know what's really going on, before I agree to anything. At the very least, I need to know that being your boyfriend won't get me killed."

Katie giggled, but then her mind hit upon something that seemed important.

"Wait a minute – what did you say was the name of the lawyer who you met at the station this morning?"

"Nicholas DiAngelo."

Katie's train of thought led her to discover a common element to both of their stories. "He was the one who told me that you destroyed my apartment, and he showed me the torn photo."

"Interesting. Maybe he did it," Eric speculated.

"They want me for something. He has some kind of big political plan, and he wants me to be a part of it. It might be a good opportunity for me, except that –" and then Katie cut herself off. She was not yet ready to tell Eric everything. She turned away, and hid her face in her hair.

Eric moved to stand next to her after a moment, and put a compassionate hand on her arm, but Katie brushed it away.

"I'm not accusing you of anything," Eric persisted. "But a short while ago I was convinced I would never see you again. And not just because of those people who threatened me today. But also because, I thought after our argument yesterday that you didn't want me anymore. And just now, when I came home and saw you waiting for me, I became afraid. It suddenly seemed as if your presence made my house into a temple. And I was not worthy to enter, because I did not tell you I loved you until it was too late."

Katie stood motionless, absorbing Eric's words. She retreated into her own thoughts, trying to find where she stood in her own world. Eric laid his hand upon her arm again, but this time she fell into it, and pulled him closer.

"I believe you, Eric," she told him. "And as for Carlo, well I would never—I don't want to see him ever again."

"Thank you, Katie."

"And – I love you too."

Eric kissed her gently, and lay her head on his heart and winded his arms protectively around her.

Then Katie added, "And I need to move in with you."

Astonishment and puzzlement possessed Eric's face.

"Like I said, my apartment was broken into, and

trashed," Katie explained. "They even tore up my bed!"

Eric thought it best to agree without hesitation. "Yes, Katie, you can stay here with me."

"And I've another quest for you, my champion," Katie giggled. "I need you to be a historian for a while tomorrow."

Eric was a little surprised. "Wow, you've never taken much interest in my studies before."

"I know," she said, "but there are some names and places I want to know more about."

"I'll make a list," said Eric, and he reached for a pen and paper. In Eric's apartment, one was always within an arm's reach of a pen and paper.

"We can do that later," said Katie. "For right now, it's not the historian I need. It's the lover." Katie tossed his pen away, and started unbuttoning his shirt. Eric smiled, and fingered the strings of the blouse that Katie had borrowed from Miranda. Katie unbuckled Eric's belt and pulled it from its belt-loops, and used it to lasso him into the bedroom.

Once there, Eric gently guided Katie's blouse off her body. He and kissed her navel, and drew his hands up and down her spine, and along her side to caress each breast, and he kissed her neck from her shoulder to her ear, all the while seeking the places where his touch elicited from her a little moan of pleasure. He lay her on the bed and pulled her jeans up and over his own head playfully as he removed them. Katie giggled for the second that it covered his face. But once it was off, her expression changed to shock.

In Katie's mind's eye, she was suddenly transported to the chapel in the DiAngelo basement. The dark walls seemed to close in on her, and the masks on the wall gazed down in cold judgment. She shrieked and twisted herself away, and ran out of the room.

Eric called out for her. "Katie? What the hell?" He pulled his trousers back on, and threw on his shirt without bothering to button it up again, and went looking for her. He found her huddled in the bathroom.

"What happened?" he asked.

Katie's voice was shaking. "I don't know," she said.

Eric sat down beside her and tried to put his arm around her to comfort her. But Katie pushed it off.

"It's only me, Katie."

"I know," answered Katie. "But—you must think I'm

such a silly girl—but I just can't do it right now. Not tonight. I'm sorry. I just can't."

Eric sighed with frustration. "What did I do wrong?"

"Nothing."

"Are you still angry with me? What is it? Why the sudden change?"

Katie looked at him, trying to explain what even she did not understand. "It's not you, it's—It's just—I still can't tell you. It's still too close. I'm sorry. I have to go home."

"You just told me you wanted to stay here," Eric countered.

"I know but –" Katie began to say, but she could not finish.

Eric knew better than to assert himself when she was in this state. "All right," he said. Katie went to the bathroom and stared at the mirror. For a second in the reflected glass she saw an image of the DiAngelo mansion, partially on fire. She saw herself standing with Eric in the burning doorway, in a pose that parodied the photo of the two of them by the university building, Katie forced herself to look away. When she felt strong enough she stood up, gathered up her things and walked to the apartment door.

Eric had not finished putting his clothes back on when she began to leave, so he asked her, "Can I see you tomorrow?"

"I don't know," said Katie, without turning around.

When she was out the door, she started to run. She made her way to her own apartment, to the bathtub and turned on the shower. She covered the mirror with a towel, and then stripped off her clothes. Then she climbed in to the bathtub, found soap and a sponge, and started washing herself as aggressively as possible. She reached for a piece of coral on a windowsill and scrubbed herself with it until her fingers cramped and a little bit of blood started to flow.

~ 41 ~

By the following morning, time had resumed something resembling a normal course. For most of the next week, Katie felt as if she was sleepwalking. There was work at the bank for her to do. There were accounts to open, cheques to clear, coins to roll, bills to stack, payments to receive, statements to stamp, envelopes to seal, and everywhere people to smile at. From customers to colleagues, accountants to managers, everywhere there were people to smile at. This was all part of the job. Even when not on the job. Outside the bank there were car mechanics, parking lot attendants, shop keepers, friends from the Underground and the Carriage House, next-door neighbours, and it was still her duty to smile at them. Each day was a never-ending stream of people to smile at, broken only by nights of dreamless sleep.

One day, as she was about to leave the bank a few minutes after closing time, a customer in a black denim jacket and red T-shirt startled her. He was enquiring about something to do with interest rates for car loans. Katie politely answered his questions and tried to usher him along so that others waiting behind him could have their turn. Then he asked about job opportunities at the branch, and then he asked what her name was. Katie ran out of patience. She told him that the branch was about to close, but he would not be put off. The more he persisted, the more Katie began to hate him. Finally she switched off her station computer by unplugging it, and sternly told him to "Have a nice day." Collecting her jacket and her purse from the staff room, she left without saying goodbye to her colleagues. They watched her leave with mild curiosity, smiled at each other, and quickly forgot about it.

In the parking lot outside, the customer waited for her. Katie needed only to walk home, and she set off at a brisk pace, but the man followed. When she was a few yards from her own door, she turned on him, grabbed him by the neck, and pushed him against a shop window.

"Why are you following me," she growled at him.

"I'm not, I just happen to be going—" he protested.

"I don't believe you!" shouted Katie, and she pushed him roughly aside. He almost fell to the ground, and he had to flail his arms to regain his balance.

"Stupid bitch," he said, as he dusted himself off.

Katie might have left him there, but for that last remark. She took the man by the lapels of his jacket, and shouted at him for the benefit of others on the street. "Why do guys like you have to go chasing every pretty girl they see? Do you think we exist only for your benefit? Why can't I just be myself and be beautiful without being—a thing to whistle at!"

The man saw that he was suddenly the centre of a lot of public attention.

He tried to make a good show of it by smiling at her and petting her shoulders, as if they were friends having a playful scuffle. "Don't worry, she's just crazy," he told a passer-by.

But Katie would have none of it. She threw him off again. This time he sailed through the air and crashed into a bank of shrubbery on the other side of the road. He picked himself up, muttered something under his breath, smiled at the onlookers, and walked back to the parking lot by the bank. The onlookers were now watching Katie, and marveling at her apparently superhuman strength. Katie stormed into her apartment and slammed the door behind her. Through her windows she watched the man get into a car and drive away. Then when he was safely out of sight, she dropped herself on to her bed, kicked off her shoes, and tried to breathe.

It was two weeks since the destruction of her flat, and Katie had done almost nothing to clean it up. Little paths were cleared to allow her to walk from the hall to the door and the kitchen. But the fragments of wood, the smashed cups and plates, the shredded papers, and other broken things still lay everywhere. The bedroom too was a disaster: dirty clothes and unmatched shoes lay where they had been dropped, and ripped blankets and pillows were jumbled haphazardly on the bed. Katie did not seem to see any of it. The television controller was within arm's reach so she switched it on, and stared blankly at the passing, flashing images of people smiling at her.

~ 42 ~

Things were different for Eric, but no less strange. He spent all of his spare time in the library, working on his undergraduate thesis. He built stacks of books and articles gathered from wherever he could find them, until his rented study station began to resemble a fortification. On more than one occasion, library staff caught him at closing time asleep on a pile of books and notes. When he ran out of coins for the photocopier, he took to re-arranging some of the bookshelves so that other students wouldn't be able to find the books he was using. He hardly spoke to anyone, and his appearance grew ragged as he didn't shave nor change his clothing. The details of his appearance and health and hygiene were totally forgotten in his obsession with the research. Everything else became secondary to the task of chasing the big idea. As to what the big idea was, sometimes even he wasn't sure. All he was sure of was that it was big. And that it would take his mind off Katie.

This obsession also revealed itself in the seminars he attended, which became one of the few occasions where he actually spoke to anyone. Through most of his seminars, he frequently drifted off topic, something he was frequently warned not to do. In a tutorial on the French revolution he wanted to talk about the Renaissance in northern Italy and its effect on the architecture of Versailles. At another seminar on the situation of French colonies in Canada he turned to a report on the Irish potato famine. And on several occasions, he showed up late for tutorials he was assigned to lead, leaving the other students wondering what was happening, whether they had the right time and place, and whether Eric knew what he was doing. After the third late showing, Eric was summoned to his supervisor's office to explain himself.

He came out of the meeting feeling a little mortified. His supervisor had gently but sternly reprimanded him, then told him to take a break for a few days. So he went home, put on some music and simply sat in his chair. He tried to sit still and do nothing, but was too restless, so he started to clean up his desk instead. Among the things he found there was the photograph of him with Katie, together by the door. A wave of butterflies filled his stomach. Given the strange way things were between us the last time I saw her, how would it go the next time? She hasn't called in two weeks; does she even want to see me anymore?

But that thought works both ways, he suddenly realised. Neither have I called her in that time, so perhaps she thinks I'm the one neglecting her. So it's time to see her. At least that way I'll know a little better what is going on in her world.

"And, I wouldn't want her to see me or my room looking like this," he told Ganga. So he quickly finished picking up the mess. He showered, shaved, ironed the trousers and shirt he wanted to wear, and headed out. First he went to a convenience store where he bought a greeting card. In it he wrote an invitation to dinner. Then he bought three red carnations. These he took to Katie's bank, to give to her. A colleague of hers commented on her handsome boyfriend. And a customer promised to do the same for his own girlfriend. Katie, for her part, was a little embarrassed by this show of

romanticism in such a public place. But she agreed to come.
    When the appointed time came, Eric walked to her house. The plan was for Eric to summon a taxi to take her to an unknown destination. Katie let him in the building but made him wait in the hall, since she was not ready yet. Eric was annoyed, at first. But when he saw her step out, he forgave her instantly. She wore a white peasant's blouse with a green bodice, a black gypsy skirt that fell to her knees, and matching heel boots. Her hair was down, and held off from her face by two small butterfly clips. Her every step made it gently flow as if in a light evening breeze. Its colour matched the sunset. Eric all but melted with admiration. He took both her hands and tried to say hello, but couldn't. He could only smile and giggle like a child. And Katie was very satisfied with Eric's reaction. She planned her appearance hoping that it would have that very effect on him. It made her feel important, proud, and loved, that he should be so happy to see her.
    Eric had changed his clothes again before the date. His hair was neatly combed and tied back with a silk ribbon. He wore a white cotton poet's shirt, with frilly cuffs and loose neck strings, a crushed velvet waist coat in forest green, with silver buttons, and black leather trousers. He even polished his shoes. He completed his ensemble with a black top hat. It was a foppish combination, and when she first saw it she laughed out loud. But it made Katie feel loved that he should take some effort to look good for her. And they both giggled like children at how they had chosen similar colours, without planning it.
    "Well you look almost—not quite, but almost—as if on the way to court a lady," Katie giggled. She took his top hat and placed it on her own head. They walked arm in arm down to the street level, where Eric summoned a taxi and took her to dinner.
    The Mill was one of the tallest buildings in the town, and a surviving building from Fellwater's pioneer times. These days it was used as a hotel. It also hosted a rather upscale restaurant, and the bar had a section where floor-to-ceiling windows gave an impressive view of the rapids at the beginning of the gorge. Normally only businessmen and tourists stayed and ate there, since it was more expensive than the Carriage House and other local establishments. But locals would use it on special occasions like weddings and graduations. Eric decided that a date with Katie counted as a special occasion. A white baby-grand piano stood in the corner where a man played slow jazz

music, and a fire with a strange, heavy but pleasant smell burned in the fireplace. A waitress told them that the fire was burning turf bricks imported at great expense from Ireland. Katie found it nearly impossible to believe that earth could burn. Eric reminded her that she had recently asked him to believe some impossible things, and that he was doing the best he could.

"Why Eric, are you beginning to believe?" she asked, and smiled.

"Maybe," said Eric, with a self-conscious grin. Katie smiled back, knowingly, almost motherly, and Eric melted in his shoes again.

Over each course of the meal, they had a different subject to talk about. For the appetizer it was people at Katie's bank, students in Eric's lectures, old friends from high school, and where they had gone. For the main course they had their favourite movies from when they were children, and their favourite songs to sing in the shower. With a bottle of wine they talked of what part of the world they wanted to see some day, and who their personal heroes were, and why small town life is better than city life. These were trivialities, but they were the kind of trivialities that matter. It was, for both of them, a beautiful conversation. They were falling in love again.

While waiting for dessert, Eric turned the conversation to something he knew Katie would appreciate.

"I did the research you asked me to do," he said.

Katie leaned over the table. "What did you find out?" she asked.

"First of all, about Cartimandua," Eric began, as he withdrew some notes from his pocket. "She was a Celtic queen of a tribe called the Brigantia, from what is now Yorkshire and Northumbria, the whole northern part of England around the first century, right around the beginning of the Roman occupation of Britain. Her story's quite interesting. Apparently she had a row with her husband, Venutius, about whether to side with the Romans who were moving in, or to fight against them. Cartimandua wanted to ally with the Romans because they built bigger and nicer houses, and they brought wine, and spices, and that sort of thing. Venutius saw them as invaders. So Cartimandua divorced him and married his arms-bearer, a man named Vellocatus. And this Vellocatus became the new king."

"Wouldn't the first husband have still been the king?"

"No, because in lots of Celtic tribes, kingship passed on

the female line. Basically a man becomes king by marrying the queen, or marrying the daughter of the previous queen."

"Women rule!" said Katie, proudly.

"And that's not all. The reason for that was because the Brigantians saw their Queen as the incarnation of a goddess of the land. In the case of the Brigantia tribe, it was the goddess Brigid—hence the name of the tribe. So whoever marries the goddess gets to rule the tribe."

"Just like Miranda told us!" said Katie with glee.

"If Miranda is a descendant of Cartimandua, she would be the queen of the tribe and whoever she chooses to marry would become the king."

"What if she actually *is* Cartimandua?" asked Katie, bright-eyed with wonder.

"Well then she must be nearly two thousand years old," answered Eric. "I hope I look that good when I get to that age!"

Katie giggled. "What about the name 'Morrigan', did you find out anything there?" she asked.

"Yes," said Eric. "Similar story. It's the name of a Celtic goddess in ancient Ireland. The name means 'Great Queen' or 'Phantom Queen', depending on where you put the accent. She's a goddess of war, but also of sovereignty. The sources I found said that when you became the king of Ireland, you were married to this goddess as part of the coronation ceremony. In Irish mythology, the gods are fighting a race of monsters called the Fomorians. And one of the chief gods, a fellow named Dagda, has sex with her—" Eric paused his narrative here as Katie giggled "—so that he can gain her favour and win the war."

"What a way to do it! Make love not war!"

Eric smiled. "Well, the truth was probably that the contenders for the kingship had to fight everybody for it just like ancient kings everywhere else in the world. But this was their way of justifying their right to rule. It was the foundation of law and order in their society."

"So their coronations must have been a lot of fun," said Katie, her hand sliding across the table towards his. "What about the name 'DiAngelo'?"

"I couldn't find out much there," admitted Eric. "You said you thought it was the name of a banking family in Rome during the Renaissance. Well the Renaissance is all about the Medici's and the Borgia's. And it's all about Florence and Venice and the north of Italy. Rome and the Pope also support lots of artists but for the most part it just sort of tags along for the ride. But I found something else that was really interesting in Rome. Want to hear it?"

"Yes," said Katie, her fingers closing around his.

"Some of those ancient Roman emperors also believed in this same business about being the descendant of a deity. And some of the old emperors demanded to be treated as living gods. For example, take Caligula. He starts off rather well. As a child he grew up on the road with the army, so he understood the military life and the soldiers loved him. When he became emperor he built roads everywhere. Then he started to think he was Jupiter, the king of the gods. So he built an extension to his palace to connect it with a nearby temple, and then he would stand on the altar so that people could worship him."

"That's crazy," said Katie.

"He had huge feasts and festivals in his own honour all the time, too. So when his government began to run out of money, he started inventing all kinds of strange new taxes. He would order rich people to leave everything in their wills to him, and then he would have them killed. He opened up a brothel in the palace, and ordered the wives and daughters of senators and noblemen to become prostitutes. He raised his horse to the rank of Senator. He even made his own sister pregnant, and he killed both of them, and you don't want to know how."

"I can imagine it was terrible," said Katie, pulling her hand away.

"Well if you believe you have god on your side, or if you believe you *are* God himself, like he did, then you will also believe you can do no wrong. You will end up thinking that human morality doesn't apply to you."

"I hope he got what was coming to him," said Katie.

"Yes he did. He ruled for only four years, and his own generals got sick of the corruption and debauchery, and took him out."

Katie observed that Eric seemed to be enjoying this historical re-telling a bit too much. "You academics get excited by the strangest things, Eric," she said.

"I suppose we do," admitted Eric with a grin. "The really exciting thing for me is that this idea appears everywhere. I found some evidence that the Norse god Odin was a real man, a Germanic tribal chief, whose life story became part of the mythology of his people. And the pharaohs of Egypt used to say they were the living presence of a god named Horus, and the child of the goddess Isis. The emperors of China and Japan, and the kings of the Incas and the Aztecs, all claimed to be descended from the god of the sun. Really, Katie, I've got to thank you for asking me to do this research. It's fascinating stuff. I had no idea before."

"That proves that there must be some truth in what Miranda told us," said Katie, proudly.

"Well not yet," said Eric, as he returned Katie's affectionate finger stroking. "There's another explanation. If you think about it politically, well, you can quickly see that it makes for very good propaganda. If you're the queen of your tribe, and you tell the people you are the descendant of a god, well, what a great way to make the people follow you! It would make the social order look like a cosmic order, a divine order, eternal and perfect, impossible to challenge. If everybody believes that you are the great-grandchild of the god that created the world, then you get to have all the power and wealth that you want. And the regular people either love you or live in fear of you. Either way, they do what they are told, and they don't start rebellions."

"I suppose that's true," said Katie. "But on the other hand, isn't that what people believe about Jesus Christ?

Eric had a reply on his lips, but he held it back. He could see that Katie felt very charged up by the idea. Her hand was tightly holding his.

"Think about it," Katie continued. "What if that is just what all those gods and giants and monsters from ancient mythology really were? What if they were just people, the same as you and me? Only, they were a little stronger, a little faster, a little tougher, maybe a little wiser? And then the stories of their lives just got exaggerated and changed into legend?"

"Well maybe," conceded Eric.

"What if it's the same for him. What if Jesus was just a man, and people said he was God because he had so much more love than everybody else?"

After a thoughtful pause, Eric said, "I can't imagine any Christians agreeing with you. It's very important to them that their founder was not just a human being, not even a special human being, but the son of God."

"But this *is* a Christian idea," asserted Katie, now getting caught up with excitement over the idea as much as Eric was a moment ago. "Doesn't the Bible say Jesus was both God and Man?"

~ **43** ~

The next place where Eric took Katie on their date was to a park where a folk music festival was in progress. In a hidden pocket of his waistcoat, Eric managed to smuggle a bottle of red wine into the performance, which pleased Katie endlessly.

The park was fairly large, and an audience of about two hundred people were taking their seats, some spreading blankets on the grass, others unfolding lawn chairs. Katie and Eric took their seats near the back of the audience area, on one of the many picnic tables that lined the edge of the park. Their view of the stage was perfect, right over the heads of everyone in front of them.

"You said that you were suddenly interested in all things Celtic," said Eric. "So I thought, why not take you to a concert with a Celtic rock band."

Katie smiled and rested her head on his shoulder. This festival was Eric's way of telling her he loved her.

The night was warm and lit with the light of a nearly full moon. The trees which surrounded the concert area were tall old hardwoods, mostly maples and oaks. They filtered out the lights and noises of the traffic around the park. For the concert lights had been installed to illuminate them with slowly changing rainbow colours. It made the park seem as if it was an enclosed world all on its own, a world dedicated to music and to beauty.

While the stage crew was setting up, Katie and Eric started talking. After their break-up and reunion, they wanted to get to know each other again.

"When we were kids, the music festival was meant for rich people from the big cities around," said Katie.

"I remember," said Eric. "A lot has changed in our little town."

"The junior public school closed," said Katie.

"I went to the other school, it's still open," joked Eric.

Katie pushed him with her shoulder playfully. "That empty lot in front of your parent's house is developed now."

"Yeah, that really pissed me off, I used to play there all the time as a kid. They should have left it alone."

"Well, the conservation area is still here," said Katie. "But there's a fence all along the edge of the gorge now,.."

"That's okay with me. It stops drunk people from falling in, on the May Two-Four Weekend. So it's probably a good thing," Katie judged.

"I disagree. None of us locals are going to trash the place. The tourist industry is a lifeline of our town, we all want to take care of it. And the view of the river in its original, untouched perfection is worth a few out-of-towners dying every year."

Katie laughed.

"And I hate the new housing division on the east side," Eric continued. "All that plastic siding! The houses look like they don't belong."

"You know that old railway that used to go from here to Thistletown?" said Katie. "They flattened and widened it. I used to bike to high school on that track, and I used to like racing my friends on it while dodging the rocks and potholes and things the farmers built to stop the snowmobile drivers in the winter. It was great fun!"

"I did that too!" said Eric excitedly. "Now the woods and farmland is all ruined by new housing developments. I think it's a crime."

"It gets worse. They are building a greyhound race track next. It will have slot machines and a restaurant and everything."

"I heard about that," Eric nodded. "But it will be on the main county road, so hopefully we can ignore it."

Katie sat up. "God, we're talking like a pair of old people. Shouldn't we be talking about, oh I don't know, the movies, and bad hair days, that sort of thing?"

"I don't know," said Eric. "I'm twenty six, you're twenty five. Is that old?"

"Everything is changing so much, it's like you can't know what's going on one day to the next, and you don't know what will happen tomorrow, except that you will be one day older, and your dreams for life one day farther back in the past."

"Sometimes I think nothing changes," said Eric. "Just the names of the people involved. Otherwise it's for the same old reasons we build cities, or go to war, or whatever. It's like, whatever you set out to do, somebody has done it before.

Whatever your dreams, someone else has already dreamed them. And it makes me think, what's the point?"

Katie looked up to the sky. Eric's words resonated with something inside her, but she wasn't sure if she wanted to acknowledge it. She tried to pull the conversation back to the beginning. "They're even tearing down the war memorial, the big one downtown. Because no one goes to the Remembrance Day parades anymore."

Eric looked surprised. "Really?"

"No!" Katie laughed.

Eric bumped her shoulder again. "You had me worried there! My grandfather was in the French Resistance, you know."

Katie laughed. "Everybody says that about their grandfathers."

Eric giggled. "Well it's my family story, and I like it, so I'm keeping it."

Katie put her head into Eric's lap. "I'm glad to have you back, Eric."

Eric leaned down and kissed her. "Not half as glad as I am to have you again, Katie."

The next band to perform on the main stage was ready to start. Katie turned her head to see them.

"Just imagine that we're at a music concert from two thousand years ago," she said. "Wouldn't people have looked on the performers as being special people, doing something magical and powerful?"

"Of course," agreed Eric. "Theatre itself emerged from religious ritual."

"Well, yes," said Katie, "but that's not what I mean. Remember the concert where we met? Remember the man playing the Celtic tunes on the flute? He was such a presence, he had so much energy. The whole band had such powerful energy. Everybody could feel it. Maybe in ancient times it would have been said they were in touch with something divine."

"Yes, I suppose they would," agreed Eric again.

"That's what I mean. The old gods and heroes must have been people like that. And then stories about them continued to be told after they died, and got a little bigger and more exaggerated with each generation, until they became what we have today."

"Well there's nothing about that I would disagree with," said Eric, "except the idea that these people are still around. I mean, any one in this crowd here could be one of them. Any of them."

"But that's the beauty of it," said Katie, a sparkle shining from her eye. "Look, that women there, playing with her little girl, that's Demeter playing with Persephone. And that retired man over there, trying to fix his broken chair, that's Vulcan, the blacksmith of the gods. That teenager over there, dressed like a Goth and acting as if he's too cool to be here? He's Hades. And that hippy chick over there, with the little flappy stupidshoes and the long patchwork skirt. She's Gaia, the Earth Mother. The gods are everywhere. All you have to do is look at people the right kind of way. Think of the captain of the hockey team that won the Stanley Cup. That's Sir Galahad, holding up the Holy Grail. Think of that politician who wants to get tough on crime. That's Thor, on the warpath. The musicians up on stage tonight? Dionysus! Every one of them. Maybe that's who these people really are. Because like you say, the things they are always trying to do are the same, and its always the same story."

Eric felt himself being drawn into Katie's story in spite of his earlier misgivings. He smiled a child-like, almost embarrassed grin. "And you and I? Are we like Aphrodite and Adonis?"

Katie made a silly face. "I'm not Aphrodite. She never had enough personality for my liking."

"But you are a goddess, indeed," said Eric, trying to be romantic.

"That's right, Eric," said Katie. "I am the descendent of the Morrigan."

A twinge of fear momentarily passed through Eric's mind. This was the effect Katie was hoping to produce in him, so she smiled mischievously. With a little hesitation, Eric asked, "then who am I?"

Katie's impish smile changed to a more loving one, and she said, "You, mister Laflamme, are my champion. So come dance with me!" And she pulled him off his seat to join the growing crowd of people dancing in front of the stage.

The raucous, energetic music of the Celtic band on stage had created a small sea of teenagers and twenty-somethings in front of the stage, dancing and jumping and bouncing and howling along to the music. Katie led Eric right into the middle of it, and Eric was perfectly willing and happy to let her lead him there. In Eric's mind, it was their first date all over again. And in Katie's mind, it was their first date from many thousands of years ago.

   Looking about her, through the haze of moving bodies and waving arms, Katie was occasionally able to spot people who apparently were from the party at Miranda's house on the night of her passage. Not a short distance away, almost within arm's reach, men and women in kilts and tunics were dancing along with the rest, brandishing weapons as if psychologically working themselves up for battle, or holding drinking horns and liberally splashing their contents around. Some were playing along with the band with hand-held drums. These sightings were brief and fleeting, snatched only momentarily in the spaces between other dancers, like dreams glimpsed in the spaces between our waking lives. Even one of the performers, just for half a second glimpsed through the forest of waving hands, appeared in Highland dress, and then just as quickly again was in his modern shirt and jeans. She was about to point this out to Eric, but she could see that he was lost in the music himself as well. It was best to let him let his hair down, for he rarely ever did. She could always tell him about it later. But right at that moment, right in the here and now, what mattered to Katie most was that their presence made her feel as if she had a tribe to belong to, and so she felt safe, and protected, and free. She took Eric's hands and the two swung each other around in little spins, pirouettes and twists and spirals. They bounced and howled and laughed together as if it was once again that magical, ancient time when the lovemaking of the gods originally created the world.

~ 44 ~

Each performing soloist or group was on stage for about an hour and twenty minutes, and between them there was a gap as the stage hands set up the next act. During that time, storytellers, poets, and stand-up comics came up to entertain the crowd.

   "Time for a break," said Katie, as she dropped herself heavily on the bench. "Jumping around in heels is hard."

   "We'll both sit the next one out," said Eric, and he put her legs over his lap and massaged her feet.

   "This might be more pleasurable for me than for you", he said.

Katie laughed, and touched his arm with affection. Katie took a cup and thanked him for it, and had a little sip. As Katie's attention drifted away from the musicians on the stage, she looked over to the festival's food court, which was under a gazebo between the stage and the merchant's area. She noticed someone familiar enter it. Unsure of why her attention was drawn to him, she looked a little more intently, almost staring across the space. He was dressed in red and black, and he had short black hair, but she could see no other details. When the man turned and she saw his face, her demeanour instantly changed to worry and fear. He looked in her direction, smiled, and walked into the shadows of the trees behind the gazebo, and was gone.

Katie's muscles tensed, and her stomach tightened. Then she shook her head, and tried to put the man out of her mind. She smiled to Eric, gave him a little kiss, and poured out some more wine for the both of them in their little plastic cups. Strangely, this time the wine felt a little sour. She smelled it and her face twisted.

"What's wrong?" asked Eric, noticing her reaction.

"I don't know. Is this a new bottle?"

"No, it's the same one," Eric answered.

Katie took another sip, and it made her gag. She felt a strange, rumbling sensation in her belly, as if about to vomit.

"I have to go home," she blurted. Eric was confused.

"Why? There are two more bands to come tonight."

"I can't stay. Something's wrong. I have to go home."

And she stood up, a little unsteadily, and made for the exit.

Eric followed. "At least let me walk with you."

But Katie was suddenly gone. As far as Eric was able to tell, she had simply vanished, right from inside of his arms.

From Katie's point of view, she simply ducked into the first available place to hide, which was among the shrubs, trees, and bushes that skirted the edge of the festival area. She wanted to get away by the most direct route possible, regardless of obstacles. When her hair clip got caught on a low branch, she let it get pulled off rather than stop to untangle it. With her mind totally focused on making an unseen escape, she hadn't noticed that the shadows seemed to bend around her to help hide her, and the ferns and grasses of the ground made way for her. And as she walked the soil smoothed over her footprints, hiding her path.

~ 45 ~

When Katie disappeared, the first thing Eric did was look to see where she went. He also, somewhat ashamedly, looked to see if anyone else had noticed that she vanished. He got up and checked the bushes and trees, but saw nothing.

"Not even any footprints in the soft soil," he murmured to himself. Looking to the stage, he noted that the next band was about to begin its set. The security guards at the gate were preparing for the end of the night. Eric watched the crowd, looking for Katie, but saw only strangers. He walked all along the perimeter of the park, this time not restricting himself to the place he last saw her There was a children's playground, a horseshoe pit which the festival used for battle re-enactments, several side stages set up for the festival, and a former railroad station converted into a pub. Eric checked around all of them.

In a copse of shrubs behind the food court he saw that the orange plastic perimeter fence, set up by the festival to prevent people without tickets from getting in, had in one place been pushed over and hastily put back into position. He would have thought nothing of it except that when he passed it by, he heard a strange twisting, creaking sound, like tree branches being bent by a heavy wind. Looking closer, he saw that the ferns, tall grasses, overhanging branches, and shrubs were moving aside, making a path clear.

Eric said, "I wonder if I'll ever get used to this". He looked around to see if any of the security guards were watching, and saw that they were all intent on the band on stage and the crowd of teenagers in front of it. So he climbed over the barrier and followed the path. The end was still dark, and he was not long into it when darkness descended behind him as well. The music of the festival faded, until all that could be heard was the wind in the leaves, the crickets in the grass, and silence.

The path took him downhill. When he reached the edge of the thicket, the trees cleared for him again, and he found himself in front of a little fence facing a service lane. But there was no one to be seen. If Katie had been here, she was gone again. The only thing that seemed as if it indicated her presence was the hair clip, on the ground where it had fallen.

~ 46 ~

Katie made it to the park gate, where the security guards were packing up the ticket kiosk. She hid herself behind a merchant's tent, since for some reason she didn't want to be seen by anyone. All right, let's think this through, she said to herself. What's my situation? What can I do here? Carlo knows what happened now. But Miranda says I'm under her protection so I shouldn't worry about him. Why should I let him scare me? I've got everything I want now. I'm strong, I've got my sense of purpose. I know who I am. He can't touch me. Nobody can touch me.

Katie stepped out from her hidden corner, but as soon as she did, another tremor of pain swept through her belly. This one was a little harder to bear. She groaned loudly, and stopped. She stepped back into the shadow of the merchant's tent.

"Why did that happen?" she said out loud to no one. She touched her belly. She felt a slight tremor there, like a low rumbling vibration, which stopped as inexplicably as it started.

Looking back in the direction she came from, she realised that Eric was no longer at their table, and so probably looking for her. So she went to find him. She would apologise, and enjoy the rest of the night with him.

As soon as she stepped out again and became visible, she was sidetracked by Paul Turner, the bouncer from the Underground, who caught sight of her and jogged up to say hello.

"Katie! Nice to see you here!" he exclaimed.

"Paul!" Katie answered. "Yeah, Eric and I were on a date tonight. But I've lost him, did you see where he went?"

"Yes, this afternoon, while we were still setting up. Where is he now?"

"He's somewhere in the park, I got a little sidetracked by someone I wanted to avoid." she explained.

"I can have him thrown out if you like," Paul grinned.

Katie smiled. "No, don't worry about it. I just want to find my man and take him home with me."

"You better hurry," he said, and he lifted the rope that blocked the entrance gate.

"Mister Turner, you're a star," said Katie, and she jogged off in search of Eric again. Just as Katie was almost out of earshot, Paul shouted after her.

"That guy you said you wanted to avoid. Is he tall,

curly dark hair?"

Another tremor passed through Katie's belly. She turned around and answered. "Yes, he does."

"Think I know who you mean. He came by the Underground yesterday, asking about you. Said he was your fiancé.

"Well he's not, I can tell you that!" Katie retorted sharply.

"He said something else too. Is it true?"

Katie was puzzled, so she headed back to Paul. "Is what true?"

"That he's the father of your child?"

~ 47 ~

Eric picked up the hair clip. Although it was smeared with dirt, it was still intact. He brushed it off as gently as he could. He looked up to the sky, and for a moment watched the clouds, orange-lit from the streetlights, pass swiftly overhead, beneath a field of stars.

She has been here, thought Eric. And something made sure I came to this spot, probably to find her, but finding only this little treasure. From here she may have gone anywhere.

Emerging into the festival area, he saw that the concert was over and the security guards were busily ushering people away. Paul saw him almost immediately and went over to him.

"Katie was just here, looking for you."

"I'm looking for her too."

"Anyway, she's gone home now," said Paul. Then, with a grin he said, "Guess we won't be seeing much of you at the Underground anymore, eh?"

Eric was puzzled by this. "What do you mean?"

Paul's expression suddenly changed. "Oh, she didn't tell you?"

"I have to go," said Eric, and he started running off. Paul watched him go, shaking his head.

When Eric arrived at Katie's building he was exhausted. He leaned on the wall for a moment to catch his breath. When he was ready, he straightened his hair and his clothing. The building front door was left ajar so he let himself in, and climbed the stairs and knocked on Katie's door. After two knocks there was no answer, so he called out to her.

"Katie, it's Eric."

"Eric, go home," was the immediate answer.

"Why can't we talk?"

"It's a bad time."

"Can we talk tomorrow then?"

"No. Never. I can't see you ever again."

Eric flustered a little. "Never? Katie, I'm your boyfriend!"

Eric heard the sound of the door chain being slotted into place, and then Katie opened the door as far as the chain would allow.

"We can't see each other anymore," she said, as plainly as she could. Eric saw that her makeup was running a little bit, and her hair was disheveled. She was dressed only in a bathrobe.

Eric inhaled and exhaled, trying to think of what to say. "Well I think I deserve to know why," he said.

"Because pretty soon you're going to hate me, you're going to think I'm no good for you. Then you'll get bored of me or tired of me, and you'll find someone who is a little easier for you, and maybe smarter than me or better looking or whatever, and we should just end this now before that happens and it goes worse than it has to."

"Katie, that's crazy. I don't understand!"

"Well you don't have to understand. You just have to accept it and go. Thanks for everything, it's been a slice." With that last throwaway comment, Katie closed the door.

Eric paced up and down the hall a few times. He scratched his head and paced up and down the hall a few times more. Finally he knocked on Katie's door again.

"Go home!" said Katie. It was clear with the tone of her voice that she was crying.

Eric tried to be as compassionate as he could, as much as talking to someone through a door would allow. "Katie, please, what happened?"

"Just go home, Eric, please," sobbed Katie.

"If we are going to break up, then I want to give you a parting gift."

After a pause, the door opened, but again only as far as the length of the door chain. Katie did not let herself be seen by Eric. Instead she told him, "Just leave whatever it is here."

Eric bent down and carefully put her hair clip on the floor. He saw Katie's cream-white hand slowly reach over and carefully pick it up. She handled it as if it was made of glass. He could hear her sniffling, trying to stifle her tears.

Then he said, "All right, I'm going now."

Instead, Katie unlatched the chain from the door. Eric gingerly poked his head into her apartment, thinking that sudden movements might upset her. The apartment was still destroyed, and Eric marveled at the mess.

"I didn't know it was this bad," said Eric.

"How did you find my hair clip?" Katie asked.

"I went looking for you. I followed the sound of your voice, and found this."

Katie turned and slid into Eric's arms. "You must think I'm a horrible girl, always running away for no reason, and acting all strange."

"No, I don't think that at all," said Eric.

But Katie could tell he was just being diplomatic and conciliatory. "No, I am, I am. I've been terrible to you. Any other man would have given up on me already."

Eric just squeezed her affectionately, and kissed her forehead. He was, indeed, put off by some of her recent behaviour. But he thought to himself that it was probably not a good time to tell her that.

"You have said and done some things lately that really confuse me, Katie. But I have made up my mind to love you anyway."

Katie pulled herself out of his arms enough to be able to look him in the eye. She met his gaze and held it, and then asked herself why she suddenly felt the need to look into his eyes. *Maybe I'm looking to see how sincere he is. Maybe I'm trying to decide whether I love him too. Maybe I am imagining that I can read his mind. Or maybe its just because no one has looked at me like that in a long time.* Katie could feel a wellspring of weakness rising in her again. It was the first time that he had said those words to her. But she felt she had to stop him there. She pushed herself out of his arms as gently as possible.

"Well don't. You'll get hurt," she said.

"What do you mean?"

"Think about everything I've done to you recently. I mean, I didn't really have much compassion for you when those guys were chasing you. I walked out on you the first time you tried to tell me you loved me. I walked off again just when we were making out for the first time in ages, and then I ran away from you again tonight. Things are going to keep on going pear-shaped and one of these days you won't be able to take it anymore. You better go, before you start to hate me."

"I'll never hate you, Katie," said Eric.

"It's going to get worse. Something is happening to me, my life is going to change, I can't tell you how, but it will just make everything worse."

"You can tell me," said Eric, trying to be a safe confidant.

"No, I can't," said Katie. "It's too big, too terrible, and you will hate me, you'll think I'm a horrible woman, and you won't want to be with me."

Eric was adamant. "I'm not going. I love you, Katie, and I'm not going."

Katie again pulled herself out of his arms and said, "No, you better go. Go, please, just go, Eric. We can stay friends, or something"

Eric crossed his arms. "What do you mean, 'we can stay friends'? I know what that phrase really means. Its what you say to someone when you want to be rid of him, but don't want to be embarrassed if you accidentally meet again in a public place."

"See, I told you that you would hate me soon enough," said Katie.

"I don't hate you, Katie. But I don't understand you either."

"Just go, Eric, please. You're making it hard for me."

Eric tried a new tack. He sighed, and said, "I wish you would just tell me what is happening, and let me make my own decisions."

"Okay, just, let me, let me figure out the best way to say it." Katie turned away, and went back to the window. Unbeknownst to Eric, she had placed a home pregnancy testing device on the windowsill, and now enough time had passed for the result to be ready. Doing her best not to let Eric see what she was doing, she picked it up and looked.

When she saw the result, a new wave of fear and sadness arose from her belly and soon shook her arms and legs. She swallowed hard and fought it down. She turned to Eric and said, "No, I can't tell you, I can't tell you. You have to go."

Eric reached out with his hand. "Katie?"

Katie breathed deeply, summoned any remaining strength she had, and started to push him away. She punched his arms and chest, and shouted, "Go! Get out! Please! I can't do this anymore! Just leave me!"

The sudden transformation surprised Eric so much he was nearly thrown off balance. Katie slammed the door in his face, and left him in the hall. Eric hammered on the door, called on her to let him in again, but she did not answer. He waited a while and knocked again, but there was still no answer. When someone came out of another of the building's apartments and threatened to call the police, he went home. He pushed open his broken door and got a glass of water from his kitchen tap. For Eric, the night is now over, and the next day is too far away to think about. Ganga meowed about something but Eric ignored him. He picked up the picture of himself and Katie together and held it in his hands for a long time. Eventually, he fell asleep in his chair.

~ 48 ~

Time passed. The sun continued to rise and set, the face of the moon continued to change, and the winds continued to blow. People went to work, went home, went to work again. Dogs barked at strangers, cats prowled the alleys, birds and butterflies flitted about, and life continued to happen all over the world. Whether life happened for Katie and Eric, for a while even they did not know. Eric concentrated on his studies in order to have something other than Katie to think about. He hardly saw any of his friends or fellow students. And he spent more time than even he would normally approve of playing video games on his computer.

Katie joined the throngs who spent their time going to work, going home, and going to work again. Miranda visited her a few times and Katie was happy to see her, but the 'coming home' feeling she experienced in the grove was gone. The bank manager learned of her pregnancy and immediately transferred her to a desk job where she would not have to be seen by the public. Whether this was compassion or embarrassment, she could not tell. Her days were spent dealing with papers stacked on papers correlated with more papers. Her nights were spent in front of a television. So it was for Eric as well, until the early summertime. Life happened all over the world without either of them being aware of it, and without it being aware of them.

    Katie phoned the bank early one of these ordinary mornings to say that she was sick and would not be able to work that day. Then she ate some cold canned pasta directly from the can for her breakfast, and went back to sleep again. Around noon, when she awoke, she sat before her vanity mirror and began covering her freckles with foundation makeup, just as she would normally do on a normal morning. But after finishing, and simply looked at herself. She turned her cheek, left and right, and then decided to rub the foundation off with a shirt from her laundry hamper. Back at her mirror, she rested her head resting on her fists, her elbows on her table, and studied her freckles a little more closely. She stroked some of the bigger ones, to see if they felt different from her skin. She counted some of them, and then counted the ones on her shoulders. Then she stood up and stepped back, and held her belly. From the front, it didn't seem to her as if she was pregnant at all. But from the side, she saw the little bump of the first trimester. She told herself it was just a little bit of extra weight. Maybe the test was faulty, she thought, and I'm not actually pregnant. Maybe everything that has happened so far was just a strange, wonderful, horrible dream. But no, the apartment is still a mess. It happened. Everything happened. Why doesn't this apartment just clean itself up? It's such a big job, it looks like so much work. I don't feel like doing it today. I'll do it tomorrow. Yes, tomorrow. Yesterday I said I would do it today. The day before that I said I would do it yesterday. But this time I really will do it. Tomorrow.

    Katie put on a tee-shirt, jeans, and running shoes, the nearest clothes to hand, and then set out to a drop-in medical clinic for a second opinion. She did not have to wait in the lobby for long. A nurse escorted her to an examination room, and collected a small sample of her urine. Then she was told that the results would be ready in about an hour, and that she may as well go home and return later.

    While waiting Katie went outside, thinking to spend some time in the Carriage House. Beside the medical building was a playground, and about twenty kids were playing in three or four different groups, running around the space, climbing on the posts of a gazebo. Katie was about to call a friend on her mobile phone but her attention was drawn to the children in the park. Some were competing for time in a swing they had somehow determined to be the best one, even though there were five other identical swings in the same set. Others had built little private enclosures for themselves with lines of sticks and rocks on the ground, and would get upset whenever another child crossed over one of the lines. The parents were free-handed with them but watchful, and if any of the horseplay got too rough they would pull the guilty party out of the fray. Katie tried to ignore them and keep going to the pub, but could not tear her eyes away from the children. She watched one small boy steal a toy from another child then and scream at the top of his voice when the other child demanded it back. It filled Katie's stomach with revulsion. Will I have to put up with that for ten years or more! And what will that kid be like as a teenager? I don't want to know.

Two of the pre-teens were standing on the balance point of the see-saws. Each was trying to prevent the ends of his own see-saw from touching the ground, while at the same time attempting to force the other child to lose balance and touch the ground with his see-saw. It was a game which Katie remembered well from her own childhood. We called it 'Airplane', back then, she said to herself. I wonder if kids today still call it that?

Nearby, a little girl in the sandbox carefully lifted a bucket off a pile revealing the perfect sand castle. She smiled proudly and began decorating it with dandelion flowers and pine cones. She made a little draw-bridge over the moat with some popsicle sticks. The feeling in Katie's stomach churn with nostalgia, and hope. Maybe a child of mine will turn out like one of these ones, and will play the games I played as a child, and will grow up to do the things I wanted to do, and my little boy or girl will love me unconditionally. But there will still be years of feeding, cleaning diapers, late sleepless nights, and insanity before that happens.

Katie eventually tore her attention away from the playground and ran back into the health centre. It was no escape from the sight of happy children: there were three of them in the waiting room, playing with some toys in the corner. Another was peacefully asleep in her mother's arms. Katie's breathing became short and laboured. Suddenly she wanted to steal the child away so that it would sleep in her own arms. Or at least sit next to them and maybe stroke the child's little hands. She forced herself to look away. She walked up to the desk clerk and asked her, perhaps a little more aggressively than was necessary, if her results were ready yet. The clerk tried to politely brush her off, when the nurse passed through and said that she had just then finished. Katie was brought into the examination room again.

"The good news is that you are not carrying any STD's," said the nurse.

"That's a relief," said Katie, and she smiled a little bit.

"The other news is that yes, you are pregnant."

Katie shifted uncomfortably in her seat. Although she already knew this, to hear it from the nurse was another matter altogether.

"Would you like me to get you a cup of tea, while we discuss your options?" asked the nurse. "We should schedule an ultrasound soon. Then you might want to go shopping for a midwife. We can recommend one, if you like. Is this your first pregnancy?"

The nurse continued on, but Katie was not really listening. She was staring into the distance, thinking of all the children in the playground outside. When she tuned back to the nurse, she was finishing up a well rehearsed speech: "Well don't worry, we have lots of experience with that. We have a supportive and non-judgmental environment here. We have councilors you can talk to, and programs for things like diet and for exercise and what to expect. The father can take most of these courses with you."

This last remark made Katie very upset. She stood and started to walk out of the room. The nurse tried to encourage her to sit again, but Katie pushed her off. Despite the nurse's continuing protest, Katie half-ran, half-staggered out of the clinic, towards home.

~ 49 ~

For dinner that night, Katie ate more cold pasta from the can. Paul the Bouncer left a message for her on her voice mail, inviting her to come to the Underground that night. That's a good idea, she thought to herself. When the evening came, she showered and got dressed for going out. She put on a pair of flat soft-leather boots, a summer skirt, and a white flowery blouse. She pressed a star-shaped temporary tattoo on her cheek, the kind that children wear in Hallowe'en fairy costumes, and she put on a round yellow hat. Feeling ready to have fun, she stepped out the door and made swift strides for the club. For a moment she thought about calling Eric and asking him to come. But then she decided against it. Tonight should be a night just for me, she said to herself. Maybe this will be one of the last times that I can go out and have fun before the baby starts to show and I get too tired all the time. All right, it's settled. I'm going to dance and party as if none of this ever happened, because this might be the last chance I get to do so.

When she arrived at the club, she took a seat at the bar and ordered a rum and coke. Then she handed her jacket to the coat-check. When she returned to the bar, her friends surrounded her, and started talking all at once.

"Katie! Nice to see you. You're looking great! Like a mediaeval babe in the woods. Very sexy! No, seriously, It's very sexy. Haven't seen you much lately. Where've you been? How's Eric? Oh, who cares about Eric. How're you?"

Katie tried to answer them all at once. "I'm fine. I'm great, actually. Just fine."

The bartender came with Katie's rum and coke. She picked it up and was about to drink when Paul came over and put his hand on her wrist, to stop her from drinking it.

"I don't know if you should drink that. It might be bad for you."

Katie pushed his arm away with a grin, and drank half of it in one gulp. Then she said to him, "You used to buy me drinks all the time."

"But aren't you—" said Paul, then his voice trailed off, as he seemed unsure how to finish his thought.

"We heard the news," said the dark haired girl.

"We think it's great, honestly," said the girl with short blond hair.

"Paul told us," said the long blonde haired girl.

Katie looked at Paul accusingly. "What news?"

"That you are—you know," he said.

Katie knew. "And who told you that?" she demanded.

"The new boyfriend, of course," answered Paul. "Hey, I hear you're engaged as well!"

"No, I am not," Katie clarified, growing annoyed. "And I don't have a boyfriend."

The long blonde haired girls put on a sly smile. "So he's your sugar daddy then."

"No," she clarified again, a little angrier.

"But he is the father," said Paul. "He told me himself."

Katie looked at him, coldly.

"So it's true then?" said short blonde haired girl.

When Katie didn't answer, the dark haired one said, "Oh, Eric doesn't know, does he?"

"Well why should he," judged the short blonde one. "He's out of the picture now anyway."

"You could have him now, if you want him," Paul told the short blonde haired girl.

"He's a nerd. I wouldn't dare. But if our Katie is not engaged after all, then *you* could have her, Paul," she said.

"True, very true," Paul smiled. "But I don't know if I want to. Real soon now she's going to get all fat and horrible."

All the girls laughed. Katie snorted in disgust, and raised her middle finger to him.

Paul threw up his hands defensively. "I'm only kidding, Katie. Take a joke."

Katie stood up from her stool and faced Paul. Although Paul was almost a head taller, and a bouncer, he felt a little intimidated and took a step back. In her deepest, most authoritative voice she demanded, "How do you know Carlo."

"I sometimes work security in a building he owns. I've known him for years," Paul answered.

"What did he tell you."

"He told me the two of you were going to have a little girl together."

Katie began thumping his chest with her fist as she spoke. "Didn't you think this is my news to tell, not yours!"

"Look, I'm sorry, lay off okay!" Paul put his hands up in the air defensively.

The girls came to Paul's defense. "Yeah, cool it. Paul's a friend. And he's a bouncer here. He didn't mean anything. Don't overreact. Take a pill."

Katie rounded on the girls. "And have any of you ever been pregnant? Do any of you know what it's like *not to remember* how it happened? Did you ever think that this might happen to *you* some day, and you might want your friends to *support* you instead of tell you that you're 'overreacting'? What does that mean, anyway. Stop overreacting. I think what it really means is this: don't get angry about anything, ever, not even when someone takes a great big bucket of human shit and pours it on your head."

If any of the girls had a response, none put it into

words. Katie took her seat again and finished her rum and coke in a single gulp, and immediately ordered another one.

The dark haired girl tentatively broke the silence between them. "I'm having a party at my house, on Saturday. If you feel up for it. I mean, if it won't be a problem for you."

"Thanks," said Katie, without looking up. More silence followed.

The long blonde haired girl tugged Paul's arm. "Come on, Paul, dance with me."

"Siobhan, I'm working tonight," protested Paul, although he didn't hide the fact he was happy to dance with her. The girl dragged him by his arm to the centre of the dance floor.

"Aren't they cute together?" said one of the girls.

"Sure," answered Katie, "but it's the kind of cuteness that makes you want to throw a hand grenade."

The two girls put their drinks down on the table with a heavy clink. "Well I'm going dancing with them," said one of them.

Most of Katie's friends left her for the dance floor. In less than a minute, Paul and Siobhan were kissing each other. The other two girls were happily bouncing and shrieking along with the heavy thumping rhythms of the techno-music. Not so long ago, she thought to herself, I would have been among them. How quickly everything changes!

The more she watched the dance floor, the more she saw loving couples in each other's arms, playing with each other's hair, caressing each other's faces and bodies, and doing various other things normally done in private. She fingered the curls of her own hair, but with a downcast face. Within a distance of three or four seats at the bar, no one came near her. At a nearby table, several handsome young men were pointing to a girl at another nearby table, and giving each other high-fives. One looked in Katie's direction, and to his friends made an elaborate cry-baby impression. His friends laughed. Katie tried not to care.

Katie finished her drink and left the club. Instead of going straight for home she went for her car, and in it she circled the town a few times, with no particular destination in mind but *away.* If her foot pushed down the accelerator a little heavier than it should, she did not notice. She drove around the town with her mind reviewing the scene in the Underground instead of concentrating on her driving. After almost an hour she found herself waiting for a red light to change at the corner of the tree-lined road to the DiAngelo mansion. A horn from a car behind her brought her back to the present moment. So she turned her car down the corner of Carlo's street, parked it, and gazed down the tree-draped tunnel to the forecourt of Carlo's mansion. A few weeks earlier, Miranda had warned Katie not to go to the DiAngelo mansion again, which at the time she had no wish to do anyway. But sitting in her car, only a few hundred yards from the threshold where the trouble began, Katie imagined that the fates had brought her there again. A new scenario played out in her mind, in which she confronted Carlo and locked him in the crypt in the cemetery. She quickly dismissed it as fantasy, but the thought of confronting him to get some answers, and perhaps also some kind of justice, remained with her.

"Damn him," Katie heard herself say, as she marched down the road to the mansion. The stone eagles on the arch twisted their necks to regard her as she passed them, and one of them ruffled its wings. If Katie had seen this a few days earlier, that would have been enough to frighten her off. But this time she ignored them. Nor did she bother to knock and ask to be admitted. She simply put both her hands on the door and pulled with all her might. The latch and lock made a satisfying crunch as it broke. As the doors burst open, Katie almost fell backward with the momentum, but quickly regained her balance. The doors loudly bounced off the wall and rebounded, and one of them twisted out of the frame. Katie felt pleased by the sight of her handiwork.

Carlo's mother Emma ran into the hall from the kitchen. She began to swear angrily in Italian until she saw that the gatecrasher was Katie. Then she said, "Well, it's you. What was wrong with the knocker?"

"Where is Carlo," Katie demanded.

"You expect me to tell you after coming in like this?" Emma retorted.

Katie was not interested in pleasantries. She strode up to Emma aggressively. One of the light fixtures in the hall spontaneously burst into fragments of broken glass as she passed. Emma took a step back.

"Where," demanded Katie again.

"He is on a business trip to Italy," said Emma. "and will not be back for a few days."

"I don't believe you!" said Katie, as another light

fixture spontaneously shattered.

"No need for that!" Emma scolded angrily.

"No? Someone did the same thing to *my* house a little while ago. Was it you?" said Katie, almost enjoying herself.

"No!" replied Emma, as she took another step back.

"Was it that hired muscle head of yours? What's his name. Nicholas?" said Katie. Emma said nothing, so Katie said, "I'll take that as a yes. Any idea why he did that?"

Emma began to fear for her own safety as well as the safety of her house. She shook her head and tried to retreat into the kitchen again.

"I'll tell you why," said Katie, as another light broke into pieces. "So that I could come crying to you and Carlo, and he could say, Oh that boyfriend of yours was jealous and horrible to you, but don't worry we'll keep you safe. Well it doesn't work like that in my life."

"Then what are you doing here?" pleaded Emma.

Katie came right up to Emma, inches from her face, and said: "I am here to tell you that I'm not afraid of you, and I don't want you or your people interfering with my life anymore."

"Interfering with your life?" was Emma's careful reply.

"Because of Carlo, I am carrying your *grand child!*" shouted Katie.

Emma was momentarily speechless. A quick succession of conflicting emotions crossed her face. But she spoke sternly, to regain her ground.

"No," she asserted. "Not my son, not my Carlo. He is a good man. And you most brazen, coming here like this, breaking down my door, making such grand accusations! Do you know what an accusation like that will do to him?"

"I don't care!" shouted Katie. The next light fixture to break was directly above Katie's head, and she had to sidestep a shower of broken glass. Emma took that opportunity to get a little further away, and she moved to the door to the sitting room.

"You have no proof! No one will believe you."

Emma retrieved a cell phone from her pocket to call for help. She tried to duck into the sitting room to make the call, but Katie moved faster and had the phone wrestled out of her hands.

"And Carlo didn't have the courage to tell me himself. I found out about it from friends of mine at the bar! Face the reality, Grandma!"

"He's a good man. That is the reality," said Emma, but

her voice was shaking, perhaps from fear of what Katie might do next, but perhaps from the knowledge that what Katie was saying had some truth to it.

"No," said Katie, "I think you know exactly what kind of man Carlo is. I think you know the truth better than anyone. Now, you can help me, right now, and then you will never have to see me again. Or you can keep up this meaningless fantasy and see how long it takes to crash down around you."

Emma finally closed her eyes, and said nothing.

Katie decided that she wasn't going to get much better a response than that. So she said, "Let's start by you telling me what you people want from me."

~ 50 ~

That afternoon, Eric sat at his desk at home, supposedly studying. But he found it hard to stay motivated. On his computer he switched back and forth from his word processor to a video game. By about noon, he decided to pack it in for the day and do some practical things like grocery shopping and house cleaning. Although it is still early, he reasoned to himself, there is no point in continuing to try to work when I'm obviously not getting anything done.

As he gathered his things together, he noticed the book of art history which had been left on the desk ever since he bought it. The page was still open to the picture of the woman with the harp.

Ganga, who had been in another room doing whatever cats do when people aren't looking, came in and jumped on to the desk. He sat next to the open book and sniffed around it, as if reading it himself. A small involuntary laugh escaped Eric for a second, as he watched his cat behaving that way. Eric picked the book up and was about to put it away. But Ganga began complaining, as if he wanted to read it some more. Eric put it back for him while he went to clean up some other things. He sorted through some papers, closed and shelved a few other books, and then turned back to the book on art history.

Ganga, meanwhile, seemed to be intently studying one of the images on the open page.

"That picture," explained Eric, "is a painting by Raphael called 'The Transfiguration'. Here Jesus transforms into a divine being, and the prophets Moses and Abraham appear by his—wait a minute. Why are the two prophets holding hourglasses?"

Ganga looked up to Eric for an explanation.

"Wait—I think I've seen that before. Who was the artist?"

Eric picked the book up and read a little closer to the liner notes, scanning a few pages before and after as he searched. Finally he found it: "C. M. DiAngelo."

Eric almost dropped the book on his foot. "I know that name," he said. Then he reached to his bookshelf and pulled a few of his undergraduate textbooks, as well as the library books he borrowed earlier that day. In the index of one of them, he found the name 'DiAngelo' again. Turning to the page, Eric read out loud.

> *C. M. DiAngelo. Minor Renaissance nobleman and patron of the arts about whom little is known. History has not bequeathed to us the date of his birth, nor what his initials 'C' and 'M' stand for. Some scholars think the name 'DiAngelo' is only a pseudonym for Cosimo d'Medici. He is supposed to have been a prolific artist as well but his only surviving works are a few charcoal sketches, and a series of paintings, all of which are low-cost copies of more famous paintings by Renaissance masters, apparently intended for sale to the emerging middle class. The best preserved of these is a copy of Raphael's The Transfiguration, in which the artist replaced the Christian figures with Greek gods.*

Eric took Ganga by his jowls and kissed him on the nose, saying "Thanks for the help!" Ganga shook his head and dashed off.

Eric flipped through the book a little further, but could not find anything more. So he scanned and copied the textbook page that featured The Revelation, and stuck it to the wall near his desk with a thumbtack. Then he went to the university library to do more research. In the art history section he eventually found a book that contained photos of the charcoal sketches. Eric photocopied the pages for later reference. After a little more searching, he matched three of them with originals by other artists: Da Vinci's *Leda and the Swan*, Botticelli's *The Birth of Venus*, Mantegna's *Triumph of the Virtues*, and *The Oracle of Delphi*, from a fresco in the Sistene Chapel by Michelangelo. The DiAngelo copies were surprisingly similar to the originals, but changed in various details. And all of them featured an angel holding an hourglass somewhere in its composition.

'So this guy likes to copy other people's paintings and put his own stamp on them," Eric mused. "I suppose that's what you do when you're an art collector and you think you're just as good as the great masters. But usually angels hold banners or trumpets, like the heralds of a royal court, if they hold anything at all. Or they have swords, like the commanders in God's army. What kind of an angel holds an hourglass?"

~ 51 ~

Emma narrowed her eyebrows, as if the very question was an affront to her dignity. "We explained the plan to you already. We have been preparing to initiate a new renaissance, a second renaissance, to guide the world in its proper direction again. The world has become a circus of fools, and I'm proud that my son wants to do something about it. You should count yourself lucky to be included."

"It seems that all he wants is for me to be his trophy girl." Katie hissed back.

"No. Sweet Mother of God, we have explained this to you already! We require someone who can see what you can see, someone who can speak with the voice the gods."

"Well what if I don't want to do that!" Katie retorted. "What if I want to speak with *my own* voice?"

Emma looked around uncomfortably, and changed the subject. "Katie, I would like to offer you a bargain of my own. For my part, I shall see to it that Carlo lets you go. I will ensure you will never see him or hear from him again, if that is your wish. I'll send you back to your Eric if you want him, and you can spend your eternity with the Brigantians or the Anishnabe, or any of the other hidden houses that you want," she offered.

"You would do that for me?" said Katie, suspiciously.

"I like you, Caitlin of the clan Corrigan," explained Emma. "You are an old soul that has remained young. That's a special thing. So this is the least I can do."

Katie perked at the use of the name the Brigantians had

given her. But she was genuinely surprised and a little humbled by Emma's offer. Then with foreboding seriousness, Emma stated her terms. "But I want something from you in return. In exchange for my making sure that he leaves you alone, you will give custody of your child to me. "

~ 52 ~

"You want me to give away my child!"

Katie was on her feet.

"This is for the good of both of you," explained Emma, as she too rose to her feet. "You know yourself you aren't prepared for motherhood."

"Unprepared?" Katie retorted. "Were you prepared when your first child was born?"

"Yes I was," replied Emma, sternly. "I had my own mother there, and her sisters, right there with me. Orazio was there, my husband, may he rest in peace. Yes, when I became a mother I was ready. You have nothing like that kind of support in your life. You have not spoken to your parents in almost five years because your mother is an alcoholic and your father cares more for his three motorcycles than he cares about you. That is why you ran away when you were seventeen. You do not have the support you need to raise a child unless – unless you remain – with my son, and with me."

Katie leaned against the nearest wall, both shocked at what Emma knew about her family life, yet also painfully reminded of the truth of her words.

"How did you know about that," Katie growled.

"You will need help with everything between now and the birth," Emma continued, "and I know how to do all that needs to be done. Furthermore, your child will have all the toys and clothes and medical care and the best education, everything necessary for a happy childhood. We could even arrange for you to move into the house with us."

Katie looked away. "I wanted to fall in love with him, once," she said. "I thought he would be the man to take me away from it all."

Emma smiled.

Katie tried to finish the thought. "But now the thought of him – even the idea of him – makes me feel – like I am being used for something."

Emma looked upon Katie with a motherly compassion. "Just think of it this way. Carlo and I will be able to help you better than anyone. We will be able to understand the changes you are going through. We have lived for centuries in a world of magic you are just now discovering. And there is so much more of it to see, and it is so beautiful. I want you to discover it, and feel its power as we do. You will have everything you ever wanted. So will your child. And your place in the world will finally be clear to you."

Katie stood, and with her eyes explored the garden. She tried to imagine herself living in the house, visiting this garden every day. The thought was indeed appealing. But she still could not shake the feeling of dread.

"I have a vision of Carlo and all his men attacking me," she said, with a voice on the edge of faltering. "I see this grand house of yours on fire. I can't just wash it out of my mind. Every time I close my eyes it replays itself in front of me. I can't sleep. I'm useless at work. I can't even hold hands with Eric anymore. I just can't do it, not now."

Emma tried to be conciliatory. "Take a few days to think about it then. I am sure that some day you will see him as I do, and see the good man that he is."

Katie studied the floor thoughtfully.

"After all," Emma continued, "you are now carrying something that is of great value to the future of our world. Your child will almost certainly have the same gift for seeing the future that you have. And we all want to make sure that gift is protected."

Katie felt a flutter of suspicion in her belly, and steadied herself.

"Just think of it," Emma speculated. "A child prophet. So innocent. So new to the world. So untouched by the evils of this world. And you would be its mother."

Katie's muscles tensed, and she held her spear close to her again. "What do you mean, 'protected'?" she asked.

"Well you can't stay where you are," said Emma. "In the last few months of your pregnancy you will need someone to look after you. To say nothing of when the baby is born."

Katie looked up. "Eric can help me."

Emma chortled. "I think not."

"Yes he could," said Katie defiantly. "He's got a sister with some kids of her own. So he already knows what it's like to have kids around."

"Eric is not good enough for you!" asserted Emma, almost angrily. Then she regained her composure, and moved a little closer to Katie, as if about to explain something serious. "The spirit of an ancient goddess has been reborn in you. We began the process of waking it up, the first time you came here. And now you are one of the great bright lights of this world. Your Eric, now, he is many good things but he is an ordinary man. He is not like you. He is not like us. So he will never fully understand you, as we do."

"Yes he will," countered Katie. "I'll tell him everything."

"You can tell him what you like. But that will not make him a part of our world."

Then I'll stay with Miranda."

"That rabble," Emma seethed, "has not yet told you one of the hard truths of what it means to endure the Awakening."

"And what is that." snapped Katie.

Emma adopted a grave tone. "There is no turning back. There are certain thresholds which close forever once you cross them. Nothing will ever be the same for you again. And so everything in your life must be left behind. All your friends, your family, your home, your whole life. They are gone now. Completing the awakening means leaving them behind. Once the adventure is begun, you can never go home again."

Katie closed her eyes, and remembered something Miranda had once told her.

Emma continued to press her point. "I think you are just now beginning to realize this. It's hard, I know. But it is better for you to accept this truth now, than for the world to thrust it upon you later."

Katie looked around the hallway and tried to imagine living in it, and living in the house. It was a beautiful house, there was no denying that. But it still had all the terrible associations for her. There's the great salon, where I found a picture of myself framed as if I was already part of their family. They had me locked in the room for a while too. And beyond that, down the hall, is the library, and that passage to the basement. No, I cannot live here. But where else can I go?

"I think you are wrong about Eric," Katie said at last. "I think if I can be a part of your world, so can he."

Emma chuckled. "Don't be silly," she said. "His soul is

still asleep, he lives in the dark, he and his kind always will."

"You're wrong. I'll show the magic to him, I'll teach him how to see everything that I can see, and I'll show you."

"If you are right," said Emma with a touch of anger, "it will mean that anybody can be one of us."

"Would that be so bad?"

Emma folded her arms. "You're making a dangerous mistake," she warned.

"Then it will be my mistake, and not yours," said Katie, and she turned on her heel and left the house. When she was half way to her car, she clapped her hands again and the door opened for her and the engine started up of its own accord. So rushed was Katie to leave that she regarded this as normal. Then she simply got behind the wheel of her car and sped off, in the direction of Eric's house.

~ 53 ~

Library attendants eventually kicked Eric out of the building for making too much noise. So he caught the bus home, but got off the bus a few stops early in order to walk part of the way, and do some quieter thinking. As he passed through the park on the way to the old bridge and his home, he stepped off the path and walked to the river's edge. Here the riverbanks were held up by little stone walls, and Eric sat on one of them and dangled his legs over the side, where his toes were just a few inches above the level of the water. The reds and golds of the setting sun spread across the sky, behind the maroons and purples of cloud bands, and behind the dark silhouettes of trees in full summer green. Eric watched the flittering birds going from tree to tree, some settling into their nests for night time, others just then awakening. The stone bridge was a short distance away, and with the light of the evening sky behind it reflecting off the water below, it looked as if it was bridging a distance not over a river but over a boundary between worlds. A crow was standing on top of one of the lamps, standing guard over another crow which was scavenging the ground for food. Eric watched them for a long while.

"Katie and I used to look out for each other like that," Eric mumbled to himself. He picked up a handful of loose pebbles and threw them into the water, and then got up to walk the rest of the way home.

The crow on the lamp post saw Eric coming and cawed his warning to the other. Both of them flew off, and landed on trees just on the side of the path. When Eric came up to the spot, he noticed them again and stopped.

"Odd," he said to himself. "Crows don't normally let people get so close to them."

The birds regarded Eric carefully, as if measuring him up for some purpose.

"You're looking at me, aren't you?" he said. One of the crows cawed once, as if to say 'yes'. It made Eric step back in surprise.

"I don't suppose you are a friend of Miranda's are you?" he said. The crows stared at him blankly.

"This is stupid. Birds can't talk," said Eric at last, and he walked on. But he was not all the way across the bridge when one of the crows launched off of his perch and landed on the ground immediately in front of Eric.

"Crows were one of the animals sacred to that Celtic goddess that Katie was asking about," he said aloud. The crow cawed at him, in approval.

Eric looked around nervously, to see if anyone else was watching, or if he was being somehow set up. Seeing no one, he crouched down to be closer to the crow's own level.

In a quiet voice, he said, "I don't suppose you could get a message to Katie, could you?"

The crow nodded.

"Tell her," said Eric, and then he paused. "Tell her what? That I love her? But she doesn't love me. That I said hello? Too impersonal. That I'd like to see her? But I already know she doesn't want that."

The crow cocked his head, waiting for Eric to make up his mind.

"Tell her, if she ever wanted to talk to me again, it would be okay."

The bird then took off straight up in the air. The other one joined it and the two circled each other, and then swooped down, following the tunnel through the trees into the park behind him. When he turned to watch where they were flying, he saw into an almost different place. Streets and cars disappeared, houses vanished, the stone embankment on the riverside sank down, and all the sounds of the modern world fell to silence. Now there is only the life of the trees, tall as cathedral spires, and the gentle breeze flowing through it, the whispering of the water and the wind, and the bells and pipes and yearnings of the songs that flowers sing. The light of the sun poured into the cathedral from a horizon that had drawn close, and it poured upon everything through the shifting leafy canopy, gently and generously, shining like the truth. The shifting rays of light spotted upon Katie, and Eric saw her clearly, but not as he knew her. She appeared in the garb of the warrior woman whom she had come to embody. Her heavy forest-green linen dress adorned her, as did strong leather armour on her body and her forearms, warm leggings held on with leather strings, and a shining golden torc around her white neck. What Eric noticed most of all was her wild red hair, held off from her face by two braids at her temples. It billowed in an unfelt breeze, and framed a freckled face that Eric had lately seen only in photographs, and dreams. Perhaps the veil that covers the real world had momentarily been lifted, or perhaps a veil of dream-like illusion had descended. There was no way to tell, nor had Eric any way to know.

Then with the flapping of black wings and the changing light of the setting sun, the sounds and fixtures of the modern world returned. The revelation of the world of dreams lasted only an instant, less than an instant, but that mere instant was enough. Such things need only as much time as it takes to breath it in just once. It lasts only while the sun passes between two long clouds on a breezy day. Had it lasted even a second longer, it would have lost its power. All things around Eric returned to normal. Even Katie's appearance had resumed that of a modern woman. She started walking toward him, smiling more and more as she got closer and closer. Eric stood his ground, half disbelieving what he was seeing. When Katie was within an arm's reach, she stopped and reached out with her hands, as if offering to take Eric's hands and lead him somewhere.

Eric said nothing at first; he was rather unsure why she came to him. Slowly he reached up, and touched her fingers as if to reassure himself that they were real. Nothing remained of the vision, but the hope on Katie's face, and the wild red hair streaming around her, like a spiritual aura made visible.

"How did you—" Eric began to ask.

"Questions later, Eric," Katie interrupted. "I know you must have a hundred questions about what you just saw, but for right now what you have to know is that, well, the important thing is, just that, I'm sorry."

Eric turned back to her, not understanding. Had this show been put on by her just to soften the blow, in case he was angry with her? But he was indeed angry, and felt he had a right to be.

"Sorry?" he said, in an accusative tone. He threw his hands in the air. "First I find out you are engaged to marry another man. Then you tell me it was all a big mistake but after that you tell me you don't want to see me ever again. Now you are telling me you're sorry. But really, what am I supposed to think?"

"I'm sorry!" said Katie, plaintively. "I know what I did wrong. I pushed you out when I should have let you in. You were patient while I was going crazy, and I'm sorry. It's hard for me too, there's so much I wanted to tell you and so much I want you to understand, but I didn't know what was happening either and I didn't know how to tell you—"

Eric angrily interrupted her again. "This is crazy, Katie! Given the way you threw me out of your life, why should I let you back into mine."

"Because I'll die," Katie pleaded.

"Oh don't be ridiculous," said Eric, almost laughing.

Katie wanted to explain, although tears were beginning to swell in her eyes. "All my friends have turned away and even Paul thinks I've gone crazy, and I can't go back to Carlo because if I do then my life as I know it will be gone, he'll take it away. He will make me into something I don't want to be, and that's how I'll die. And then something else happened and I think I need help, but everyone abandoned me, there's almost no one left for me. No one is willing to help me."

"That's because you're unreliable!" Eric shot back.

But in reply to that, Katie shouted, "That's because I'm pregnant!"

Eric was immediately struck silent. His anger was suddenly replaced with complete surprise. He looked away from her, then back again. He paced a few steps around her. He let his rucksack slip from his shoulders and crash on the ground. Twice he began to say something in response but stopped himself before half a syllable escaped his lips. When he regained his composure after what looked to Katie like a monumental act of will, all he could say was, "Can you just—don't go anywhere—for a minute?"

Katie was confused by this response, but nodded.

Eric walked down to the river's edge, crouched down, and gazed at the passing water.

From a stone's throw away, Katie watched him, wondering what he was thinking, wondering how long it would be until he got up and said or did something. She thought to herself: I did not expect this. But that is perhaps my fault for not planning anything. What is Eric doing over there? Why is he taking so long? Never mind, give him his time, this is big news he has to deal with. Just my returning to him is got to be big news for him. Maybe I should just go. Maybe that's what he's hoping. He's over there by the river to give me a chance to go. That way I won't be laying any heavy choices on him. And haven't I put him through enough? Or maybe I should go for my own sake. If he doesn't want me back then I shouldn't go crawling after him. This is terrible! He's punishing me, that's it! But that would be unlike him. Oh, but what is he thinking?

Eric, sitting by the riverside, followed with his eyes the little twigs and leaves that floated along with the current, and studied the water striders delicately dashing across the surface. On his mind was just one question.

Time passes. To an observer it would appear that only a minute passed. For Katie and Eric, entire centuries went by. Eric eventually stood and walked back to her, his eyes level and alert, taking in the trees and leaves, the birds and squirrels, the shape of the clouds, the lay of the land, and finally Katie, who was pursing her lips with something resembling hope and shame.

"Please promise me that you will tell me everything that's going on?" he asked.

Katie blurted her answer out. "This time, this time, no more secrets, no more surprises, I'll tell you everything."

"Everything!"

"Everything."

Then Eric said, quite simply, "Okay."

"Okay what?" asked Katie.

"I mean, okay. If you want me back, then, okay, I am back." Eric answered.

Katie looked at him strangely. "Just like that?"

"Yes," said Eric.

Katie became a little flustered. "I wasn't expecting you to be so forgiving so quickly."

"But no more secrets," Eric asserted.

Katie was filled with pride. She hugged Eric tightly and

kissed him frantically. And Eric lifted her off the ground and spun her around, himself very happy to have her back. Katie kissed him a hundred thousand times, and in her world each kiss caused a flower to bloom somewhere. In Katie's world, all of nature celebrates a beautiful moment.

~ **54** ~

"You know," said Eric, when they had returned to his apartment, "we need to have a good long talk."

In an excited voice Katie answered, "I need to do more than that. I need to make it up to you. Come on. I want to show you something."

She stretched out her hand, inviting Eric to take it and follow, which he did. They walked together through the park, hand in hand. They followed the Old Bridge Road to a riverside path. From there they followed the path to a hidden entrance to the conservation area that local people frequently used. They climbed through the hole in the fence and were soon surrounded on all sides by the rustling pine trees of the old forest. A few steps further in, and all the car-engine sounds and other noises of the human world were drowned out by the wind in the cedar trees, the voices of crickets and night birds, and the rushing of the water in the river below. Some small animals and birds gathered along their path just ahead of them, as if they sensed their coming and were there to watch them pass.

When they came to the entrance to the grove, Eric touched the cairn and contemplated it with great curiosity.

"I think I've explored this trail thousands of times since I was eight years old. I wonder why I never saw this thing before," Eric observed.

"I think that there's a kind of aura that surrounds it, that keeps people's attention looking the other way," Katie theorized. "But maybe if you stay close to me, and hold my hand, you will see the way in."

Katie produced a flask from her purse, and from it poured a little bit of wine on to the cairn, as she had seen Miranda do before. Obediently, the trees, shrubs, and rocks twisted and rolled to either side, revealing the tunnel that led to the grove, glowing with the insects and mushrooms and other inexplicable lights that floated in its air. Eric did not speak, although the wonder and surprise on his face could not be disguised. Katie entered the mouth of the tunnel and gestured for him to follow. Two crows perched on the ridge above the tunnel entrance regarded Eric coolly, making Eric feel a bit like an outsider. For a moment he wondered if they were the same ones he encountered on the bridge earlier that evening.

With these thoughts in mind, he followed Katie into the passage. The strange glow of bio-luminescent plants and creatures in the tunnel walls and ceiling lit the way ahead. Eric could hear the clicks and whistles and faerie bells of the flowers and leaves, and walked slowly, in case his footsteps disturbed the music. Vines stretched and twisted around the walls, moving out of their way, opening the further reaches of the passage before them. A few smaller woodland animals like chipmunks and birds perched on these vines to watch them pass. Katie found the whole area absolutely delightful, and ran up and down the path, ahead and behind of Eric, and twirled around in a childlike dance, as if trying to absorb everything at once. Eric walked a little more hesitantly, although it was not long before he felt taken in by the faerieland beauty of the passage.

When they emerged into the secret garden, Katie excitedly pointed out various details to Eric: the stone circle, the workshop where the Brigantians baked their own bread, the tree where she saw the fox, the little path to a boat houses by the river. Only a few of the Brigantians were about; they waved a greeting to the newcomers but accorded them their privacy. Eric explored the scene with wide eyes. A cluster of beehives in a nearby garden patch buzzed with activity. A young man with long blonde hair and a green hooded cloak sat cross legged by the edge of a pond, apparently in deep meditation. A great blue heron passed overhead, and circled once around the visitors, before continuing to the riverside. Katie took Eric along a side path that led to a little pavilion, at the corner where the ridge met the river. Its stone platform was intricately designed with a mosaic labyrinth, and its pillars and capitals carved with leaves, flowers, and knotwork lines. Eric walked around it, and looked into the carved faces of men, women, and animals that gazed from the pavilion's corners and roof beams out to the world, and the foxglove and ginseng and jewelweed that peeked up from the grass, and the gentle mist rising from the warm water of the river.

"Strange place, this!" he remarked. "I've walked past the cairn by the entrance many times before without noticing anything out of the ordinary."

"They call it Fellwater Grove", explained Katie. "Miranda told me that this place was built almost two thousand years ago by Celtic Druids, who left Ireland around the time that Christianity took over. They wanted to build a place where they could preserve their way of life. Apparently there used to be many more of them, all over Canada, but they have grown smaller, some were taken over by other loggers or developers, and some simply faded away."

Eric smiled. "So is this the last one of its kind?"

"No, but it's one of the few," answered Katie. "But never mind that. What's important is that it's here. Look around, it's beautiful! And I want to share this world with you. I want you to see what I see. Eric it's so beautiful! Look at the clouds, the trees, the river, those birds, the setting sun, everything! It's life, it's everywhere, it's life as it was meant to be, and it's still all around us! It's important to me that this magic can be real, and that the world still has some mysteries and unexplored places."

"I know it is," was Eric's honest reply. He didn't want to be untruthful, but he also didn't want to start another row. "I want to appreciate it, but it's all very strange. So far most of what I've seen of this world of yours has tried to hurt me."

"You can feel safe here," Katie reassured him.

"It's not just that," said Eric. "The idea that the people who built this are still around, I mean, it seems as if it is *too* simple, too convenient. What more might there be to this story? What more have we not yet seen? And anyway, how could anyone find out whether this is all for real?"

"I think you would know it in your heart," Katie said, again with simple conviction.

"That's what everybody says. But there is more to it than that as well, you know? Because, what if your heart is mistaken?"

Katie was a little hurt by that comment. "When you say you love me, how do you know?"

Eric checked himself. "I see your point."

Katie pressed the point home. "I think we find the purpose of our lives the same way. I think we find it deep inside our hearts, if only we know how to look, it's all there."

"But what about people who have no heart? Let's not pretend that such people don't exist. If I was a racist, or a serial killer, should I do what feels right? If I believe deep in my heart that I'm better than everyone else around me, should I bring a gun to school and start shooting people for fun? And how do we know the people who built this place were not like that?"

"Eric, you're making me crazy!"

"Then help me to understand!" said Eric. He had to admit she could be right, but he still had his doubts. He cast his eyes downward and studied the ground.

"I'm struggling, Katie. I don't want to say that we could be deceived or mistaken about loving each other. That would be the most un-romantic thing in the world. But it seems to me that people are not perfect beings. We are fallible and fragile. We make mistakes, we hurt each other and hurt ourselves all the time. If the world is full of magic like you say, and if some of us have the blood of the gods in our veins, people would still be people. If we are made in the image of God, and yet we are such fallible, fragile, stupid creatures sometimes, then what does that say about us? And what does it say about God?"

Katie looked into her lover's eyes and saw that he really did want to understand, but just could not help himself from having doubts. It was time for her to reveal her most important belief.

"The heart cannot be wrong, Eric," said Katie, as calmly as she could. "Whatever other ways we make mistakes, at least the heart knows only love. And whatever knows only love cannot be wrong. That's the very deepest of my beliefs."

"I know it is, Katie," said Eric, equally calmly, taking her hands in his. "I wish it was as easy and clear for me as it is for you. I'm not trying to say you're wrong. I'm trying to say, I don't know what's right. I haven't got any answers. I've only got questions. And I think—if there is no purpose in life, if things can happen for no reason, if the heart can be tricked or mistaken, well, I'm not saying that that's the case. I'm saying – that's what I'm afraid of."

Katie put her head back on his breast, and pondered the thought. Eric wasn't trying to force his point of view on her, as another man might have done. He wasn't trying to say he knew better, or that he had all the answers. He was saying that he didn't know, and that he didn't understand. He was showing her a part of himself that he regarded as a weakness. He had the same need for purpose and meaning as she did. And although full of doubt, he was doing his best to reach out to her anyway.

She touched his face and raised his gaze to meet her own. She drew him close and whispered into his ear, "I think we understand each other at last."

Katie coiled her arms around Eric and closed his eyes with her kisses. She pulled him down to the grass and laid her body down beside him. The sounds and lights, the sunlight showering in rays through the clouds, and the scent of spearmint and clover on gentle breeze, and the whole life of the grove surrounded them both until it enclosed the whole of what they could see, hear, and feel. They left Nicholas and Carlo behind, they left Miranda behind, and all the bruises and scars of the adventure behind. They left behind the demands of work at the bank or classes at the university, the worries of bills and debts and the rent, the wear and tear of the ordinary. All these things they sent into the ground. They coiled their arms around each other to put away the streets and bridges of the village. They tickled each other's faces and played in each other's hair, to shut off clocks and empty calendars, to close down the shops and businesses, to set aside the flyers in the mailbox. They caressed each other's fingers and toes, to disconnect their computers and to let fall the square walls of their houses. They scratched little love marks into each other's flesh with their nails, and ignited every inch of each other until all other things were set aside. For one night, out of all nights, their lovemaking stripped all the world down to the bare essentials: the earth beneath them, the sky above them, and the love between them.

~ **55** ~

The autumn turned to winter, and the winter turned to spring. The deep freeze of winter was wearing down, and the snow banks on trees and roadsides were shrinking, and little wafers of ice formed where granules of sand protected thin wedges of snow from the sun. At such a time, Tara Corrigan was born. Miranda served as midwife, and in the weeks before the birth she insisted that Katie should come live with her, to be ready for the big day. In her meditation room she set up a special bathtub of water warmed to body temperature for Katie to sit in during labour. Eric had been in the habit of visiting the house every day in the middle of the afternoon during her last few weeks, to bring little gifts: clean towels, flowers, children's toys or clothes, some food, a storybook, and whatever he thought Katie would find useful or beautiful. When during one visit Katie started to go into labour, Miranda sent Eric out of the room. "Birthing is women's work," she told him. Eric was unhappy with this, but could see there was no point to arguing with her. So he went into the kitchen and washed the dishes. Katie was in labour for less than an hour, and afterward she described the experience as much less painful than she had been told to expect. Miranda gently placed the baby in her mother's arms, then left the room to give them a few moments alone. Katie's baby gripped on to her flesh with tight little fists and cried as loud as she could. And Katie cried too, between rounds of laughter, and little songs of welcome.

Let the first human words my baby hears be my own voice, introducing myself, thought Katie. So she propped the child's little head up to look her in the eye, and said hello. The baby stopped crying to listen, and when Katie was through she gurgled and stared open-mouthed. Katie took that to be her way of introducing herself in return and smiling back.

When Miranda emerged, Eric immediately dropped the dishcloth and went over to see her. Miranda shut the door before Eric could slip inside. But she smiled brightly and told him, "It's a girl!"

Eric hugged her happily. Then Miranda asked him to set up a place in the sitting room next to the fire for the new mother and baby be warm and comfortable. Eric, still anxious to see Katie, arranged some pillows and blankets on the couch as quickly as possible, while Miranda prepared some food and a pot of tea. Then the two re-entered the room to help Katie get out of the bath.

When Eric saw Katie and their child together for the first time, he felt a wave of weakness rise from his belly. He went first to Katie, and kissed her head, and tried to speak but found himself at a loss for words. The bundle of joy in Katie's arms continued crying noisily, pausing only long enough to look at Eric and register his face in her mind as someone new, but with a familiar voice. Then she carried on with her crying. Katie thought this response quite funny. Eric took Tara in his arms while Miranda helped Katie get out of the bath. While Katie dried herself off and put on a warm bathrobe, she prompted Eric to introduce himself to the baby just like Katie did, and to play with her. Eric gave his fingers to squeeze and his thumb to bite on, and his hair to pull. He took a coin from his pocket and put it in the baby's hands, saying "My father told me it's a family tradition."

Once Katie was comfortably established near the fire in the living room and the baby was returned to her arms, Miranda excused herself, to let the three of them have some private time together. Katie sang to her for a while, told her all about what a wonderful place the world can be, and some of the wonderful people in it who will become her family and friends, and what a wonderful life she has ahead of her. The baby cried all the way through it. Then Katie sang to her again, until she couldn't think of the words any more. So she simply hummed a wordless lullaby until she stopped crying and fell asleep. Not long after that, Katie fell asleep as well.

~ 56 ~

Around a month later, when Katie was feeling stronger, Miranda organised a party at her home in honour of Tara's birth. Most of Katie's friends from the Underground were invited, including Paul the Bouncer. Some of Eric's university friends also attended, as did many of the Brigantians from the hidden grove in the woods. The sitting room furniture had all been pushed to one side of the room or even taken out of the room altogether to make space. Several musicians set up their instruments in the loft above. Others Brigantians lined up for a Scottish set dance, and to rant and roar like proper warriors. Most of the rest of the guests did their best to give the impression that they thought this all perfectly normal. Katie and Eric sat on the couch together with the baby between them, surrounded by gifts. Katie watched the fun, beaming with happiness. Eric mostly attended to Tara, playing peek-a-boo with a toy over the edge of the couch, over Katie's shoulder, behind his back, and all around. At the end of the dance set, Miranda took up a position on the spiral staircase, to speak.

"Welcome to my home, all of you, welcome," she announced, mainly for the benefit of Eric and Katie's friends. "For those who are come to this house for the first time, welcome. My name is Miranda Brigand, chieftain of the clan Brigantia. We are the most honourable and heroic tribe of old Albion, and a mad band of righteous bastards too, aren't we lads?" People laughed out loud and toasted Miranda with their drinking horns. The newcomers looked at each other, unsure whether to join in the cheering or try to escape without being noticed.

"We are going to serve some food in the living room, in a moment," continued Miranda, "but before we do, there is a little tradition we have in our tribe which we would like to share with you. So if you will all gather around Katie and Eric there, in a little circle—" Miranda paused, as the people re-arranged themselves, "—and now hold up whatever you are drinking—and now if the happy mother and child will stand up."

Katie stood, using Eric as a crutch, and when she was up Eric returned Tara to her arms. One of the Brigantian musicians started tapping a gentle, comfortable rhythm on his drum, while the fiddlers and the guitarists laid down a minimalist melody. As they performed, Miranda came down from the stairs, and reached to a nearby side table where a clay bowl of water lay. She placed three drops of water from the bowl with her fingers on Tara's forehead, and recited a traditional Scottish baptism blessing with each drop.

"A little drop of the Three on your forehead, beloved one—"

Next she took a small green and blue sash from the side table and carefully placed it over Tara's shoulder and arm. Onlookers could see that the sash was embroidered with the tree of the Brigantians beside the three ravens of the Corrigans.

"To aid thee from the fays, to guard thee from the host —"

Finally, Miranda took the child in her arms and held her up for the whole gathered crowd to see. The musicians held the last note of their song for a moment, and then were silent. In a proud and clear voice, Miranda announced to everyone, "Let it be known to all the world, by land and sea and sky, that this child shall be named – Tara Corrigan!"

Everyone raised their drinks and repeated the name, and then gave a loud cheer. Miranda gave Tara back to Katie, as each of the Brigantians, obviously familiar with this little ritual, waited in line to introduce themselves to the new baby. Meanwhile, the musicians struck up a cheerful folk song again. Those who waited their turn tapped their feet along with the tune, chatted with each other, or got gifts ready to give to the new mother and child. Somewhere in all of this, Katie looked up, and saw the face of the tree-man in the ridgepole of the ceiling smiling down with pleasure and pride.

When all the 'introductions' were done, Miranda took Katie to one side, and said, "There's something I would like for you to do for me."

"Anything you like," answered Katie.

"Give Tara to Eric for a moment, and come along," said Miranda, and she took Katie out of the main space of the old cabin, and into the meditation room. They seated themselves on the floor together.

"Where shall I begin? You have been with us for about a year now. There have been a lot of changes in your life. How do you feel?

"I feel fine—My life is different of course, but it is almost back to normal, really. I still think about everything that happened, but sometimes it feels distant, as if it happened to someone else. Then once in a while I look into a mirror, or into a glass of water, or a window, and I see something that is about to happen. Sometimes it's something really big. I saw who was going to win the election, six months in advance. And I saw that winter storm we had this year, the really big one, in which all those power lines were down for a week. I see these things more often now, than ever before. And sometimes it's scary, when I see bad things about to happen. But it also reminds me of the first time I came to your sanctuary in the forest. So it's good.."

"I'm very happy to hear that," said Miranda.

"Why do you ask?"

"Just one last question," said Miranda. "Are you happy?"

Katie had to think about that question before answering. She breathed deeply and said, "I think so. My life is different, maybe a little harder than it was before, now that I have Tara to look after. But I still have Eric, and lots of new friends including you, so I think everything will be okay."

"I'm glad to hear you say it," said Miranda. "Now there is something I would like you to do for me."

Miranda went to a locked cabinet near the door and withdrew from it a small wooden box, perhaps only the size of a shoe box. Its entire surface was inlaid with intricate Celtic knotwork carvings on every surface, some of them in gold and silver thread. The lid had a carved human face, resembling a woman, in the centre.

"What is it?" Katie asked.

"It is one of the treasures of our tribe. It was made

about two hundred years ago, when this branch of the clan emigrated to Canada. The wood is Irish bog oak from Kildare, itself over six thousand years old."

Katie turned the box over in her hands, looking at every side. The wood was carved to perfection, and the face had the smoothness of real human flesh.

"The face looks a bit like yours," Katie marveled.

Miranda smiled wistfully and looked out a window towards Old Hobb, as if remembering something. "Well, the artist who made it is a good friend," she reminisced. Then she turned back to Katie and said, "We Brigantians are one of the last of our kind. Most of us just want to live our lives, the same way everybody else does. A few want to help people discover the things about the soul that we have discovered. Others think that only special people could become great souls, and that they had special responsibilities to teach and to help, to guide humanity forward. And still others want to use their knowledge and power to control people, live for hundreds of years, become rich or powerful, or even make ordinary people worship them like gods."

"That's not us, is it?" asked Katie.

"No, that's not us," said Miranda with a little smile. Then she continued. "But you must understand what I'm telling you. A delicate balance of power exists among the families that remain. For the most part we all stay out of each other's way. But sometimes conflicts rise up, and we get drawn into them whether we want to or not. It is then that we have to do our best to protect the things that are important to us." And she gazed out the window again.

"Why are you telling me these things?" said Katie.

"I have been the chieftain of this tribe for a very long time, doing my best to maintain that balance of power," said Miranda. "but I am almost finished here. I am much older than I look, Katie, and I am a product of an age that has been and gone."

"You're still young, Miranda," Katie consoled.

Miranda smiled. "Good clean living, good exercise and good food, and maybe a little bit of magic, to keep up appearances, that's all. But more and more each day I feel less and less at home in the world. It has changed so much, and so quickly. It's almost unrecognizable to me now. Do you want to know why I sought you out, why it was so important to protect you from House DiAngelo, and why I brought you into this room today?"

Katie looked to her with intense curiousity.

Miranda opened the box. Inside it was an object covered in a black cloth. She removed the object, placed it in Katie's hands, and let her uncover it. The object was a little chalice carved of a plain brownish wood. It looked as if carved by hand, and it exuded the smell of bees wax and honey from the thousands of servings of mead it had contained over time.

"This chalice," explained Miranda, "was used in our ceremonies of kingship, long ago. I would like to give it to you. Because when you are ready, I wish for you to replace me, as the chieftain of Clan Brigantia."

~ 57 ~

While Katie and Miranda were in the meditation room, Eric played with Tara, fed her some bottled milk, and talked with Paul and his friends. For the most part he stayed by the edge of the celebration, neither a part of it nor precisely a distant onlooker. He felt that the party was more for Katie and Tara than for him.

When Katie returned to the room, she looked as if she was staring at something a hundred miles away. When friends came up to congratulate her again and offer more gifts for Tara, she responded cheerfully but absently. She sat next to Eric, and closed her eyes. Eric held out Tara's arm as if Tara herself was waving.

"Hello," said Eric, playfully pretending that it was the baby speaking. "I'm Tara, How are you?"

Katie smiled a little, then said hello and held out her finger for Tara to shake. Tara grasped the finger and immediately put it in her mouth. Katie laughed, and sat back and idly reached for a sandwich.

"Aren't you having a good time, Katie?" Eric observed.

"Well, yes," said Katie, still distant.

"What did Miranda want?" Eric asked.

"Nothing," said Katie.

"No, really," Eric wondered. "You went in the room happy and smiling, you've come out seeming strange."

"Well," Katie began, but didn't finish.

At that moment, Paul looked over to them from across

the room.

"So," he said, "having a little lover's tiff, are we?"

"No, not at all," Katie admonished him.

"Yes you are," said Paul, as if this was a casual thing to say. "It's obvious. Not that it's a bad thing. Me and my other half, we disagree about everything."

"No we don't!" came a woman's voice from across the room. Paul made a rude gesture in the direction of the voice, then turned back to Katie and Eric to snicker.

"It's nothing to worry about, Paul," said Katie. "Eric's just being a wallflower."

"Well it's no wonder why," said Paul.

"What do you mean?" asked Eric.

"Well, buddy, look at Tara here," Paul told them, as he caressed Tara's face with his finger. "Your baby is beautiful, just like everyone says. She's got such big brown eyes, and a full head of curly black hair. Darkish olive skin. Very Mediterranean looking. Now look at Eric. He's blue eyed and blonde, almost Germanic really, for a guy who says his family is Quebecois. So put two and two together. I bet you *he* has already has—haven't you, Eric?"

Katie spoke with a scowl. "Eric is my man, and I am his woman, and Tara is our daughter, and that's all there is to it."

"No it's not," asserted Paul. "Look at Tara and think about it. If I didn't know better, I'd say that Eric is not the father."

~ 58 ~

Katie plopped Tara into a baby's car seat on the floor, and then stood up to face Paul. She grabbed the lapels of his shirt in her hands tightly, and snarled at him to "Get out!"

The music and dancing stopped instantly as everyone turned to watch. Paul's girlfriend Siobhan bounded over to come to his defense but was stopped by Miranda, who needed only to fold her arms and stand in the way to convince her to sit back down.

"What? Why is it wrong to speak the truth?" Paul protested.

"Because it's *not* the truth!" growled Katie.

"Yes it is," said Paul. He pointed to Tara and said, "look at her!"

Miranda put her hands on Katie's fists and attempted to lower them. "Let him go, Katie" she said. "This house is *nemeton*. There can be no violence here."

"What are you doing—didn't you hear what he said!" Katie snapped back.

"*I* heard," answered Eric, as he too rose to his feet.

Paul continued, with the air of someone who enjoys the attention. "I don't know how long you can keep the game up. This child is not your child, Eric. She doesn't look anything like you, as everyone can see but no one will say. This means, of course, that your girlfriend here is a liar and a cheat."

Silence fell upon the whole house. Some of the larger, more athletic Brigantians gathered round, just in case.

"I think it's time for you to leave", said Miranda, as politely as possible.

Paul glared at Eric. "Use your brain, Eric! Your girlfriend – none of these people – are what they seem."

"Katie is my girlfriend and the mother of my child. And this was Tara's naming party. Of all the times to drop a bomb like that one, Paul! Tara's naming!", answered Eric.

"Pull your head out of your ass, Eric!" continued Paul. "You are Katie's meal ticket. You're her walking wallet. She told you that you're the father because you have a scholarship at the university, so you have money. She will dump you the moment your scholarship runs out. Everyone could see that, but no one is saying anything. That's hypocrisy, buddy. So face the reality. Listen, we've known each other for a long time. We were in high school together. You're a lot like me—you cant stop yourself from wanting to protect a beautiful woman in trouble. But what are you getting out of it, really? A pretty girl on your arm to show off to your friends? A chance to get laid every day? You can find one of those at the Underground. In fact you can have Siobhan if you want her."

Across the room, Siobhan stood up.

"Katie loves me", retorted Eric.

"Hell, she probably does," Paul shot back. "Who wouldn't love someone who jumps at her every whim the way you do. But trust me, there's no honour in being loyal to a lost cause. Get rid of her before she drags you down."

"And who would take over as Tara's father. You?" Eric demanded.

Paul sighed heavily, then took a step closer to Eric. "I'll

give you a hint," he said. "He's tall, has dark curly hair just like Tara does, and he's already told you to stay away from Katie."

Miranda stepped between Eric and Paul, and spoke with authority: "It is time for you to go home." With a nod of her head, two of the Brigantian warriors clamped their heavy hands down on Paul's shoulder and ushered him out of the house.

"As you wish, my lady", said Paul, with a mock flourish. A third Brigantian pressed Paul's jacket into his hands and a fourth opened the door for him. A moment later, the headlights of a turning car swept the room and disappeared.

"I take it everybody here heard everything." said Eric.

"Everything", said the quiet voice of Siobhan, from near the window where she watched Paul drive away.

Katie was cradling Tara in her arms protectively, and rocking her slowly. Eric got down beside her, opened his hands, and asked with his eyes the question he could not formulate with words. Katie did her best to pretend he wasn't there.

"I should go," she announced. Then as quickly as possible, she gathered up her things and started to leave, carrying Tara with her. Eric tried to follow her, but she put him off.

"Just give me a bit of time to myself, please, do that for me?" she asked him.

"Very well," Eric agreed reluctantly.

"I'll see you at home later," she said tersely. In less than a minute, she was in her car and driving away.

~ 59 ~

Katie arrived at Eric's apartment, carrying Tara in her car seat. The apartment was not really large enough for a family, and so it was something of an organised disaster. Eric's books and papers messed up one side of the living room, Katie's television and her collection of movies and music CD's messed up the other side, and Tara's toys and diapers messed up the bedroom they all shared. Little paths were cleared from the hall to the kitchen and the front door. Unopened letters, mostly bills, were strewn in little piles in corners, on top of desks, and along the edges of the paths. The smell of stale food lingered in the air. Katie had grown accustomed to it and hardly noticed it anymore, but today, with Tara in hand, she smelled it again and rubbed her nose in disgust. This messy and smelly house is my life, she thought to herself. When Katie closed the door, the streetlight shone on her through the tarnished window blinds, like prison bars mangled after some botched attempt to escape.

Katie lingered in the half darkness for a while, her gaze going back and forth from the room to her baby in the little carrier on the floor. Tara stirred in her sleep a little, opened her eyes and looked around, apparently decided that there was nothing interesting or worthwhile to look at, and went back to sleep. Katie crouched down to her level and stroked her face. As if living in a prison isn't bad enough, she thought, now I have shackles on my ankle as well. No—don't think that way—Tara is not a shackle. She's my little girl. Mine and Eric's. And our house is not a prison. It is our home, our nest and our sanctuary. I must take a positive attitude, especially for the sake of Tara. That's what they say a mother is supposed to do.

I suppose I should start with cleaning up the place, she decided. If I am going to have a child, I may as well make my home child-friendly. And anyway, I'm tired of looking at the mess. The principal of my primary school once told me, 'Messy desk, messy mind'. I suppose the same applies to my home. Messy house, messy life. All right! It's time to sort out my life. Starting with my house.

Katie put some cheerful music on her stereo, and searched the kitchen cupboards for some big garbage bags. Finding a roll of them after a few minutes of searching through unwashed dishes, she opened one and started filling it. In about twenty minutes time she had three bags filled, and she dragged them down to a rubbish container behind the building. Then she returned to the apartment to start filling a fourth one. But the sight of the mess was still overwhelming. There were still smear-marks on the walls to be cleaned, a broken chair to be disposed of, and spoiled food to be composted. Various pieces of unwashed clothing hung on every corner, hook, and stick where a piece of clothing could conceivably hang. Three bags of rubbish filled, she said to herself, and it didn't seem to make a single peck of difference.

Katie went into the bedroom and sat by Tara's crib. She watched her baby sleeping for a little while. But her mind kept returning to the night at Carlo's house.

"Whenever I look at you, I see him," she told Tara.

A wave of melancholy was gathering in her belly and slowly rising. Soon she found herself involuntarily rocking back and forth. To distract herself, she started filling the rubbish bag with things lying around the bedroom that lay within arm's reach. But when her hand landed on a certain photograph in a broken picture frame, it became harder than ever to control her feelings. She pulled the photo out of the frame and wiped her tear-filling eyes, to see it better. Here was a piece of my life before it all changed and became unrecognisable, she thought. This one picture is all that remains of that time in my life. Now it is dominated by him. Everywhere I look, everywhere I go, everything I touch, he's there. In a way, he himself warned me that this would happen. Maybe I brought this all on myself. Maybe this is what I *asked* for. No, don't think that way. That's another mind-killer. But maybe if I hadn't been so eager for something different, so quick to jump up and follow his lead, then none of this would have happened. So in a way, this *is* my fault. And now everything has changed, there's no way of putting things back to the way they were. No going home again until the adventure is over. Would I want things back the way they were before? Life would have been easier. But that's an empty question. There's no way to know the answer. All I know is that I brought this on myself. He gave me the choice: he said that if I kept going on then there would soon come a point where there would be no turning back. And I chose to go on. But I didn't choose this! I didn't choose to be where I am right now, sitting in this bomb-crater of a bedroom. Even so, I'm living with the consequences of my ignorant choices. That little truth now stands highest above all the others. But how long must this go on? Where does it end? Does it ever end?

Katie's sense of resolve suddenly manifested itself. She gathered as many of Tara's clean diapers and clothes as she could find, folded them neatly, and put them where they belonged. She tucked the photo of herself with Eric under Tara's pillow, carefully, to avoid waking her. Finally, she bent down and gently kissed her baby on the cheek.

"Goodbye Tara," she said. The wave of weakness stirred in her stomach again. Better go now, she said, or I may not be able to go at all.

Katie strode purposefully out the door. She left it slightly ajar with a little brass candlestick. Then she headed out to the street, down toward the river, and then along the path that lead to the conservation area and the forest. Once she was out of sight of the main roads she broke into a run, afraid that if she dawdled then she might lose her resolve.

The air was cool, not quite winter but not yet spring, and patches of snow lay in clumps in the hollows and shallows. The air was full of fog from the evaporating snow, making the trees fade in and out of perception as one passed them by. In this heavy air the evergreen branches of the cedars and pines became like curtains, and the bare branches of the oaks and maples and birches became claws. There was an army of half-buried beasts here, all uniformed in shades of grey, reaching up to free themselves, or else to pull the living down to their subterranean world.

Eventually Katie came to a rocky promontory overlooking the place where two rivers flowed into one. A lookout platform had been built on it, with a little stone wall around its edge. It was not quite waist high and Katie had no trouble stepping over it. Ice made the footing especially treacherous, and she held on to the stones for support and balance. When she was steady, she looked down. On this ledge, Katie stood within a hair's breadth of the fifty meter drop to the rapids below. Here at last she let her feelings have full expression. Screams of fear and despair burst from her lungs, and tears of deep pain ran from her eyes like water flowing from cracks in a dam. The sound of her anguished soul echoed off the stone walls of the gorge, overpowering the sound of the rapids.

"Why did this have to happen to me!" she howled.

Her words reflected back to her from the distance, over and over again, as they traveled down the gorge.

"Why this! Why this!" she cried again.

But only her own voice returned to her. No answers, only her own questions, echoed off the austere stone walls.

"I had dreams for my life. I had plans, I had things I wanted to do. I had ideas. They were good ideas. So why take them all away from me!"

Only the flutter of birds, apparently frightened from their perches by the sound of her voice, gave any indication that her voice was being received by anything.

So in a final cry of desperation she screamed, "Anybody listening?"

Only her own echo, and the rushing water far below.

Katie looked down, and tentatively put one foot over the edge. The rock face was craggy and fragmented, but there was nothing like another ledge anywhere directly below. If she fell, she would fall the whole way down. At the bottom of the cliff was the river, its water level a little higher than usual, as it was carrying off the extra burden of the melting snow. Chunks of ice floated down with it, from some unknown place upstream. They came down in every shape and size, great and small, some still sharp-edged from a recent crack, others rounded with age. The river carried them all to the same destination, whatever their origin. They bobbed up and down and against each other and against the stone cliffs on either side, shattered into fragments over the rapids, and in the faint heat of the sun they melted into nothing. And the current of the river flowed on, slow and easy in some places, rough and treacherous in others, but always it flowed, indifferent, impersonal, and unrelenting.

The sound of light footsteps close by caught her attention. Katie turned her head and saw a little Calico cat, all spotted white, black, and orange, stepping along the edge of the stone wall. It stopped about a meter away from Katie, sat back, and regarded her. It made Katie think of Eric's cat, Ganga. Its gaze was dispassionate, as if judging not her actions but whether those actions were fully thought through. It made Katie think of those she was leaving behind.

"Ganga?" Katie asked the cat. But it did not move.

"What are you staring at?" she pleaded. Still it regarded her without blinking. Above her, the crow cried again, and sailed off down one branch of the gorge. Ganga looked down to the river below, then back up at her. Katie followed its gaze to the river, and began to imagine what would happen if she did fall.

There will be a few seconds of weightlessness, pure peaceful weightlessness. My hair will stream out from my head like flames, and it will be beautiful. Maybe I will even laugh with pleasure.

Then I will strike the river, splash in the white water and strike the rocks of the riverbed. The current will carry me away, down the river, down along the length of the gorge, with its high stone walls like a canyon cut deep into the earth. The chunks of ice from upstream will be my pall bearers, and the overhanging cedars will mourn me.

The current will take me to the mouth of the river, and throw me into the great Lake Erie, some two or three hundred kilometers away, however far it takes me. And then the lake will fall down the Niagara Falls and into Lake Ontario, then into the Saint Lawrence river, past thousands of little islands and harbours and holiday cottages, past rich people in their yachts, past smugglers and fishermen and adventurers in their canoes.

I will float by all the things of man, and enter the open Atlantic ocean. And there I will sink to the bottom, among the cast-offs, treasures, and wreaks of humanity. There I will lie on the sea floor like one of them, a remnant of the world, never to be found, never to change, never to be sad, never to know pain, never to fear or hunger or cry, never to sing, never to run in fields, never to climb trees in the fall, never to breathe, never to move, never to change.

Ganga was still staring at Katie, without blinking. The circling crow cried out one more time. She shivered a little at the sound of its voice. Its cries sounded eerily close to the sound of a small child, crying to be fed, or to be held, touched, and loved. It was snowing lightly, and she had not brought a coat with her, so in her mind she attributed this involuntary hesitation to the cold. But still her mind was brought back to her daughter.

If I fell from this ledge, Katie suddenly realised, Tara would never know me. She would grow up quickly and forget me, just as we all forget the first few years of our lives. She would be raised in some foster home, never know my voice, and never have a picture of my real face in her memory. She will only have a crumpled photograph of Eric and me. Perhaps she will have Eric, yes. I left her at home for Eric to find. But what if someone else finds her first? Then she will have a picture of a mother she never knew with a man who is not her father. And maybe they will take away even that.

No, I have to be there for Tara. And Tara will be my lifeline, my purpose, my very soul. I have to live so that she will know me.

Katie cautiously edged herself over the stone railing and stood again on firmer, safer ground. She looked one more time down to the rapids below. They said nothing they had not said before, and nothing did not say every second of every day, and yet Katie had her answer. And then she turned back towards home, and broke into a run. When she was back on the main streets of the town she continued running, caring not who turned to stare. Up the steps to the apartment she ran, and burst open the door. Tara was still there, and still asleep. Katie picked her up and threw the blanket over both of them together, and held her tightly.

"I'm back," she sobbed. And Tara opened her eyes.

~ 60 ~

At Miranda's house, Eric sat on the couch with hot a cup of tea in his hands. Tara's presents were spread in a little circle around him. Miranda had sent most of the party guests home, although a few lingered to help clean up. In the kitchen, Miranda was having a conversation with Paul's girlfriend, Siobhan. Eric knew her from among Katie's friends at the Underground, and although he was sitting within earshot of their conversation, he wasn't paying much attention. Eventually the two women came into the living room and sat near Eric.

"Eric", said Miranda, "Siobhan has just told me something very interesting, and I think you might like to know about it too."

"Go ahead," said Eric, although he wasn't really in the mood.

Siobhan hesitated before speaking. "Well I don't know what this has to do with anything," she began, "but Paul quit his job at the Underground a little while ago, and went to work for another guy. He says he's in some kind of security management. He makes a lot more money now, but his hours are all strange. Sometimes he stays at home for a week. Sometimes he gets called in to work in the middle of the night. Other times he's gone for days, and I've no idea where."

"What does this have to do with me," said Eric.

"Tell him what you heard his boss say," Miranda prodded.

"One time his boss came to see us at home. Paul sent me out of the room, but I wanted to know what was going on, so I listened from just outside. They were talking about some big new push his family was going to make. There was some talk about a great announcement they would make, and some politicians and reporters who were going to be part of it. And they also talked about an old debt to be repaid, and someone who had to be taken out of the picture. I couldn't hear everything clearly. But I definitely heard him say that someone who might get in the way was going to be removed."

"Paul's new boss, it would appear," Miranda speculated, "is Carlo DiAngelo. The ancient debt he referred to is the debt of fealty he says we owe him. But since Siobhan heard his plans, we have a chance to prepare, and perhaps get him off our backs for good."

"That's all this is about? An unpaid debt?"

"It's more complicated than that", said Miranda. "We have something that he wants. He's been holding this claim of loyalty over our heads in order to get it."

"So what does he want," Eric asked.

"Fellwater Grove," said Miranda. "He doesn't know where it is. But he knows it's close by. It's a place where the trees can hear you, and they will fight for you if you are brave. It's a place where the summers are never too hot, and the winters never too cold, and the stars always come out at night, and if you look into the water, the reflection always shows you the truth. A last remnant of a more magical, more heroic time, is our home. There aren't very many places like them left in the world anymore. And if he controlled enough of them, he could use their powers to do, well, to do anything."

"So you want to keep it for yourself," said Eric, cynically.

"It's not just that. It's our home!" Miranda exclaimed. "Our people built that grove ourselves, centuries ago. It's where we raise our children, where we belong, where we can be ourselves among our own kind. It's where we bury our dead. If we don't have our home, our own little part of the world, it would be like we never existed."

There was silence in the room for a moment. Most of the Brigantians nodded gravely to each other. But Siobhan looked to Miranda with something resembling annoyance.

"Okay, will someone please explain to me who the hell you people are, and what you're talking about?" she flustered.

"All I can tell you right now," said Miranda, "is that we are an old family with a few problems to sort out with another old family."

"A few problems!" Eric laughed. "Why don't you tell her who you *really* think you are. She won't believe you anyway. Go on, tell her."

Siobhan was expectant. She narrowed her eyes at Miranda, and waited to hear what she would say.

"All right," said Miranda. "We are a tribe of Celtic warriors from ancient Britain, one of the last, and our ancestors built a colony here more than a thousand years ago, and now it seems we have to defend it against one of the last Roman legions."

Siobhan eyed Miranda disdainfully. "You people can believe whatever you want," she said, and gathered her things to leave.

"Told you," said Eric, with a wink. Then he reached for his own winter coat and said, "Well, I'd love to help, but just a little while ago someone upset the mother of my child so badly that she ran home, so I'd like to see how she is doing."

"I appreciate your feelings, but this is very important to us and we could use your help—" Miranda began to say.

"I'm sure it is," said Eric, half-sarcastically, "but I've got problems of my own."

Eric moved toward the door, but Miranda stopped him. "We have trusted you with a lot of our secrets, so it is time you did something for us."

"You trust *Katie*, not me," said Eric, more strongly. "I am only *tolerated* by you, for Katie's sake. I know where I stand in your world."

Miranda ignored that. "You have been among us long enough to know what the stakes are. I'm convinced that the DiAngelo will try to attack the grove. They want to make sure we won't expose them for who they really are. I need as many people as possible to help bring in supplies and prepare the defenses."

Eric suddenly became thoughtful. "Actually, Miranda, I think that capture of your secret hideout is not his plan."

Miranda was annoyed. "What makes you think that?" she demanded.

"Let's take what Siobhan overheard what he said, and let's put it beside a few other things we already know," Eric reasoned. "For instance, we know that he has been recruiting people to help start some kind of political movement. He tried to recruit Katie for that same movement, because apparently he wants to use her ability to see things in the future. We also know that he thinks your family owes to his family some kind of debt. He told me so himself. Finally, you guys believe that Katie is descended from an old Irish goddess of sovereignty, and hence she's important to you as well. Now, if all these things are true, or at any rate if *he thinks* they are true, he will most likely do something simple and easy which will both force you to do what he wants, get you out of his way, and at the same time advance his other plans. He doesn't need to take your secret fortress from you if it will be easier instead to make you use it the way he wants it to be used. And the easiest way he can do that, which I can see, is the same way the ancient Romans used to enforce their contracts with the tribes of Britain and Gaul. He will take a hostage."

~ 61 ~

Katie had resumed the clean up effort in the apartment. She had filled two more bags of rubbish and was now starting on a third. She pinned notes on kitchen cupboards listing things she would need to buy or replace, and the list became quite long in a short amount of time. To amuse herself she arranged them in alphabetical order. And soon the collection of notes was spreading across the whole kitchen. The photo of herself and Eric, meanwhile, was taped back together and pressed into a different frame that somehow escaped being broken, and she hung it on the wall in the bedroom with pride.

Late in the evening, there was a knock on the door. Katie looked through the peep hole and saw a man and a woman in professional attire, and a police officer standing with them. The man had his back turned and was apparently leaning on a walking stick. Since a policeman was among them, Katie thought it best to let them in right away. She dried her eyes and calmed herself as quickly as possible, then opened the door.

"Miss Corrigan?" asked the woman.

"This is she," Katie confirmed.

"I am from the social services. We are here concerning the matter of the custody of your child."

Katie narrowed her eyes. "What's the problem?"

The man with his back to Katie then turned around. She instantly recognised Nicholas DiAngelo. He held an official looking paper, which he thrust into her hands, saying "This is a court order granting sole and exclusive custody of the infant child Tara Corrigan to her grandmother, Emma DiAngelo."

~ 62 ~

The atmosphere in the house suddenly became tense. Most of the tribesmen were quite impressed by Eric's detective work. Some of them nodded their heads knowingly, and voices of discontent could be heard among those who suddenly thought that the garrisoning of their sacred grove might not be necessary.

But Miranda was glaring at Eric coldly, her brow furrowed with annoyance.

"Very clever," Miranda conceded. "But there is more going on that you have not accounted for. The DiAngelo and almost all of his allies have been trying to take over all the hidden houses, all over the country, for centuries. Only five years ago he located a haven like ours belonging to one of our allies, just on the other side of Fellwater. It was a farming freehold, that never knew a blight or a drought, and its animals never knew disease. Now it's a suburb! That's the kind of people they are. We have been dealing with them for a very long time, we know how they work. Whatever they do, their ultimate purpose is to control every haven in the world. They don't rest, they don't negotiate, and they don't care about anyone but themselves."

Eric was still not convinced. "You told me a while ago that the DiAngelo claim you owe fealty to them. So I researched the life of your ancestor, Cartimandua. She *did* give her loyalty to the Romans, in order to win her civil war. The sources are very clear."

Murmurs rose quietly in the gathering circle. Discontent made itself known.

"Here is another possibility," Miranda retorted. "Cartimandua invited Roman auxiliaries to help her win the civil war. But after the victory, the Romans didn't leave. Instead they set up their own governor and threw her out. And the country was completely Roman for hundreds of years afterwards. They cheated and betrayed her, and she spent the rest of her days fighting them."

"That may be true," Eric agreed, "but I'm right about Carlo, aren't I? He thinks you owe him tribute, because he is descended from the Roman emperors who took your ancient lands. Suppose he tried to attack, as you think he will. He would have to take the grove in a fair fight. He might win, he might lose, you never know."

"He would never win!" shouted a few of the Brigantian warriors nearby.

Eric ignored them and continued. "Now suppose instead he takes Katie as his hostage. He wouldn't need a large force to do that. She is unprotected right now. And imagine the ransom demands he could make."

Miranda was thoughtful for a moment. Although she

was still cross, she gave a knowing look to Donall, who nodded gravely. Then she turned to Siobhan and asked, "When you were listening to Carlo's conversation, did he say anything to make you think his plan was to abduct someone?"

Siobhan had to think for a moment, and then answered, "No, I don't think so."

Miranda turned back to Eric, satisfied that she was right. "We go to defend the grove."

Siobhan added quickly, "But he said nothing about attacking anything either! He just said there was a treasure that would pay of some kind of debt."

"The treasure he referred to Fellwater grove," declared Miranda.

"The treasure he referred to is *my girlfriend!*" Eric protested.

"But you are not the chief of the clan, so you don't get to make that decision," Miranda replied. Then she turned to her people and began issuing orders.

"Right. I want Finnbarr and Maread to go to the grove right now and join the guard on the perimeter. Tell them what's happening too. Aeducan, I want you to get supplies. Parrafin oil and torches, building materials and tools, and food. And Donall, go to the DiAngelo mansion, hide there and watch for any movement."

The people she indicated bumped their fists together with Miranda in a parting salute. Then they ran out the doors to the back yard. Eric watched them race right into the air as if there was an invisible bridge at the back of the garden. In an instant they turned off to one side and were out of sight. He was about to ask Miranda how that could be possible, but she was busily giving out new orders.

"Síle, Claire, and Cillian, go to all the other havens held by our allies, Clann Gealeach and Teampall na Calleach, and go to the Algonquins as well. Tell them what's happening, and ask if they can lend any help. Afterwards, join the guards at the grove. And everyone, get as many weapons as you can find, even things you wouldn't think of as weapons like garden tools. Now go."

The rest saluted each other as the first group had done, and headed out the back door. They too ran straight into the air, and dispersed in various directions.

Siobhan, who had gone off to one side and was putting

her coat on to leave, noticed the warriors leaving in that impossible way, and stared open-mouthed with wonder. Her dismissive disdain disappeared, and she looked to Miranda with awe. She stepped tentatively back into the main space of the house.

She looked over to Miranda and said, "Are you people for real?"

Eric looked over to Miranda, daring her once again to tell Siobhan the truth.

Miranda grinned mischeviously. "It's the twenty-first century. Nobody knows what reality is anymore."

Then she tossed a ring of car keys to Eric. "And Eric, take my car and go and see if Katie is all right," she said.

"Thank you," said Eric, sincerely.

Miranda opened the back door and was about to go. Just before stepping across the threshold, she added, "Try to bring her back to the grove. She will be safer there."

Eric nodded. "I will."

With these parting words, Miranda ran down the back garden, and then into the sky and away. Eric and Siobhan watched her go, he shaking his head in bewildered amusement, and she staring at the treetops with something resembling sadness.

"How did you find these people?" asked Siobhan.

Eric sighed and answered, "Some of their enemies tried to kill me."

~ 63 ~

Nicholas pushed his way past Katie into the apartment, followed by the policeman and the social worker. He went straight to the laundry basket in which Tara was napping.

"She's right here," he told the social worker.

"Hey!" Katie screamed and ran to protect Tara. "You can't take her away from me!"

"I'm afraid we can," said the woman.

"But she is my baby! She was only just born! You can't do this!"

Nicholas poked at a pile of unopened letters lying on the floor. "I bet the notice of motion from the court is in here."

Katie appealed to the policeman. "This isn't fair, surely you can see that! Help me!"

The policeman acted as if he was indifferent to the whole situation. "I'm here to make sure things don't get out of hand," he said.

"Then arrest these people and get them out of my house!" Katie shouted at him.

The social worker ignored Katie's outburst and began a series of routine questions. "Is there anything about Tara's health we need to know? Is she on any medication, or a special diet? Has she any allergies you know about?"

"Don't you see that what you are doing is wrong!" Katie roared.

"Look, we don't like breaking families up either but in circumstances like yours—"

"Circumstances like mine!" Katie exclaimed.

Nicholas read from the court order. "The dwelling place is unsafe and unfit for a child, and there is prima-facia evidence of malnutrition and neglect. Furthermore, Emma DiAngelo has demonstrated to the court's satisfaction that she is much better able to provide a safe and supportive environment, where Tara will get the best possible start in life. So the court awarded custody."

"That's crazy! None of that is true! Look around!"

"I am looking around," said Nicholas with a patronizing glare. "And I'm seeing unwashed dishes in the kitchen, unwashed stains on the floor, things a child could swallow and choke on within easy reach, bags of garbage lying around, all sorts of reasons why the court's judgment was the right one. Anyway, the judgment gives you full visitation rights, so it's not so bad."

"I want my baby, not visitation!" argued Katie, but her argument fell on deaf ears. The social worker was gently wrestling Tara from Katie's arms, while Nicholas collected the diapers and clothes, along with Tara's car seat. Tara immediately started screaming at the top of her lungs. The social worker, apparently accustomed to doing this, carried on regardless. Katie struggled as much as possible, but the stone-faced glare of the policeman was enough to finally make her relinquish her grip on Tara. Then the social worker was out the door almost the same second she had Tara in her arms. Katie ran to the window to watch her take Tara away. By the time their car disappeared, Katie was completely in tears.

"That's it for me, then," said the policeman, and he

turned to leave.

Katie rushed over to him. "I want you to arrest him!" she demanded, pointing to Nicholas.

"What for?" said the policeman, puzzled.

"Last year he broke into my apartment and tore it up!"

The policeman turned to Nicholas. "Oh, this is the crazy girl you told me about."

The nonchalance with which the policeman said this made Katie take as step away.

The two men left the apartment. Katie stood frozen in her place, watching them leave. When she heard the sound of the building front door slamming closed, she was finally able to move. She gripped her belly, where Tara lived not so long ago, and went to the bedroom to sit on the floor beside Tara's crib. When her throat became too hoarse and her too lungs too exhausted to cry any more, she went to the kitchen. From the drawer, she withdrew the sharpest knife she can find. Then she went into the bathroom and looked at herself in the mirror. She removed her sweater and undershirt, and stood perfectly square to the mirror, with as perfectly blank a face as she could muster. Her reflection looked back at her. A splatter of freckles dotted the white surface of her shoulders like drops of rain, and the waterfall of red ringlets fell over her shoulders and down her back.

Katie brushed her hair for a little while, with gentleness and care. Then she braided it, tied it up at the top and bottom of the braid, and took up the knife again. She looked at her reflection in the eye, and raised the knife to the level of her neck.

~ 64 ~

In Miranda's range rover, Eric headed for his apartment, which he now shared with Katie. When he parked the car and turned the engine off, he sat alone in the car for a little while, thinking. Does it really, actually surprise me to hear that someone else might be Tara's father? Is that a statement about Carlo, or a statement about Katie? I remember people saying they were engaged. Maybe Katie knew about it, all this time, and didn't tell me. But then why tell me that I'm the father? What does she want from me? What do I want from her? What do I want—at all?

Well there is no putting this off. For the moment, the

thing to do is go up there and find out how she is feeling and what she wants to do. Then I can decide what to do.

Eric got out of the car and walked to his flat. He counted the steps up to the door, one through six, then the steps from the landing to his floor, seven to twelve. Finding the door unlocked, which struck him as unusual, he entered.

"Katie?" he called out. There was no answer.

"I hope you are all right, I'll go again if you still want to be alone for a while longer."

There was still no answer. He looked around the sitting room and found that it was a little tidier than he remembered it, except for a few places: a pile of letters had been disturbed, some other things were knocked over, and there were some large muddy footprints near the door. It appears that Katie had visitors. Perhaps she left with them as well? Perhaps I came too late to protect her from abduction? And why can't I hear Tara crying?

Eric went into the bathroom. Immediately he noticed that the sink was stained with a black substance that smelled like some kind of chemical. The rim of the bathtub was lined with little red hairs. In the little trash bin near the toilet was a long red braid, tied at both ends with little rubber bands. Eric picked it up and held it close to his face. If Katie had been taken, this braid of her hair would be all that he would have of her. He called out her name again, one more time.

An answer came from the bedroom. "I'm in here."

Eric followed the voice. Katie was standing with her back to Eric, wearing a bathrobe. A towel was draped over her shoulders, and a hair dryer was in her hands. She was intently studying her reflection in a dressing mirror. When Eric entered the room she slowly pulled the towel off and turned to face him.

"What happened!" Eric asked.

"I thought it was time for a change," said Katie. She had cut her hair, so it hung no lower than her jaw line, and dyed it completely black.

"I know you loved my hair," said Katie, "and I loved it too, but I just got curious to know what I would look like if it was different, and maybe if people would treat me different. Anyway, maybe this way Tara won't be pulling at it so much. What do you think? A new look, for a new stage of life."

Eric looked to the baby crib and asked, "Where is Tara?"

Katie smiled. "Oh, she's fine, she has gone to see her grandmother, she's going to be okay. Tell me honestly now. What do you think of trimming your own hair a little bit? Maybe adding some brown highlights? You have horrible split ends anyway. I could do it for you."

"Never mind that for a second, Katie. Why didn't you tell me your mother was coming here? I'd like to have met her."

"Well no, she was in a rush. But don't worry, Tara is fine, she's fine, she's going to be okay."

Eric looked puzzled. "Katie, you are not making much sense right now. What happened?"

Katie was determined to change the subject. She floated over to where Eric was standing and put her hands on his waist. "Just don't worry about it, everything is fine, we will go to see her tomorrow. But right now, how long has it been since we had some time to ourselves?"

"Not since before Tara was born," he admitted.

"Exactly," smiled Katie, and she drew him into her embrace. "So, what shall we do with our time? Would you like to go out? We haven't gone to the movies in ages. Or, shall we – stay in?" With these last words, Katie started to unbutton Eric's shirt.

Eric let himself submit to her seduction. It was not long before they were lying on the bed, she without her bathrobe, and he down to his boxers. Eric was enjoying himself but could not shake the feeling that something was wrong. Katie had pushed him on to the bed rather more aggressively than usual, and her kisses on his shoulders and pectorals felt a little more hurried, even desperate.

"You were in a completely different mood when you left Miranda's house today, what happened?" he asked.

"No more talking! Just sex!" was her answer. She climbed on top of him, picked up one of Tara's soothers and stuck it in Eric's mouth. She pinned his arms so he could not remove it, and laughed. She ground herself on his body aggressively, bit his shoulders and scratched his neck with her fingernails. When Eric tried to caress and stroke her in return she aggressively pinned his arm down again. So he tried biting her in the shoulder as she had done to him, and leaving love-marks there. Katie cried out in pain, but then pushed his mouth to the top of her breast, almost hard enough to smother him, and ordered him to do it again. She physically tore his boxers from his body while growling like an animal. Part of Eric's mind was puzzled by her attack, since it was not her usual style. But he was enjoying it enormously, and his body responded readily. When he felt himself aching for consummation, he reached for the condoms in the bedside table drawer. But Katie slammed it shut, almost catching his fingers in it.

"Eric, let's make another baby!"

A very startled Eric replied, "So soon?"

"Tara needs a playmate," she explained. She coiled her leg over him, and adopted a gentler demeanor. "The sooner we do this, the closer in age they will be, and the better it will be for them." She reached down with her finger and began tugging his boxers off.

"Shouldn't we wait until you aren't breastfeeding Tara any more?" asked Eric.

Katie climbed on top of Eric again. "No, we can't wait. I don't want to wait. Come on, why are you being so boring? It has to be now. I'll do anything you want me to do tonight. I'll put on my high heel boots, I know you love them. I'll let you tie me to the bed. I'll wear a mask and you can pretend I'm a different woman. I'll do whatever you want, I'll do it for you, if you do this for me. I want another baby."

Eric pulled himself up to a seating posture and said, "Why the urgency?"

Katie's smile faltered for a second. With a force of will she brought it back again, saying, "What, is it wrong to want another child? We just had a little girl, maybe you would like a little boy too? You could take him cliff diving in the quarry, and play hockey in the winter, and tell him stories about your grandfather in the war, and do all that father-and-son stuff. Would you like that?"

"I can do those things with Tara," Eric answered.

"But don't you want a son who is really yours—"

Eric put his hands on his forehead. "*That* is what this is about, really, isn't it? Katie, you can tell me, I won't be angry."

Katie's faltering smile finally broke. She collapsed on the bed beside him and buried her face in the pillow. New tears for old wounds surfaced in her eyes. Eric put his hand on her shoulder but she pushed it off as soon as she felt it. He got up from the bed and placed Katie's bathrobe over her. She pulled it on quickly, doing her best not to look at him. Eric pulled some of his clothes back on, and sat on the bed next to her. He reached out to touch her again but she recoiled again.

"Talk to me, Katie," he said.

"It's worse than you think," she replied in a low, unsteady voice.

"How could it be worse?"

"Go and check the garbage can in the kitchen, then. See what's in there."

Eric shrugged, and sauntered off to the kitchen. Light from the magnesium street lamps outside streamed in through the windows, diffused by the rolling fog rising from the remaining ice patches and snow drifts. It filled the room with a warm orange light, and drew long shadows from the furniture. In the garbage can he found a crumpled legal document. He unfurled it and read that it was a court order, granting lawful custody of Tara to someone named Emma DiAngelo, who the document described as Tara's paternal grandmother. Suddenly his legs became too weak to support his body. He closed his eyes and dropped the paper, and leaned on the wall, and slid down to the floor.

After a moment, Katie followed him, knowing what he would have found. She looked at him from across the sitting room, in silence. Eric sensed more than saw her presence. But he did not speak immediately. He spoke only when he was ready.

"How long have you known?" Eric asked.

"The court order came today," Katie answered.

"What about Carlo being the father, how long have you known about that?"

Katie sighed. "I suspected for a long time, but wasn't sure until after she was born."

Eric closed his eyes again. "Why didn't you tell me?"

"I was afraid you would leave me."

A twitch of anger momentarily possessed Eric. "It's *you* who keeps leaving *me*, Katie."

Katie was shaken a little bit by this remark, but said nothing.

Eric continued. "Whenever something bad happens in your life, big or small, the first thing you do is clam up. It's your worst habit. You push your friends and family away and bury yourself in the four walls of your room. It gets to the point where I wonder if I really know who you are at all."

Katie looked to her feet and curled her toes. "I didn't want to burden you more than I already have," she said apologetically.

"No. That's not it. What you wanted was to curl up into a little ball and hide from your problems, instead of doing something about them. But life can't be avoided like that. Life will break into your shell sooner or later. This—" he said, brandishing the court order, "—is a wonderful example."

"But I do burden you, I know it," said Katie. "And I'm sorry, I know I have not always been fair to you. Maybe I should move in with Miranda, or something, and make everything easier for you."

"You see, Katie, you are running away again," Eric said angrily. "And the amazing thing about this is – you went through that magical initiation with your weird new friends, and you say you are stronger now and that you can see the future, and all that. But none of your super-powers solved any of your *real* problems. They haven't made you any happier. And they didn't keep Tara safe!"

"Why don't you just leave me then, if I'm not good enough for you anymore," Katie hissed at him.

"Is that what you really want?" Eric hissed back.

Katie shouted defiantly at him. "What I want is to have my baby back!"

Eric was about to shout something else, when he suddenly stopped himself. He took a few breaths to calm down, and with as much love as he could express, he said, "So do I."

Katie's mouth sealed and her eyes closed seemingly involuntarily. Her ability to speak was momentarily taken away. A few breaths, and a drying of the eyes, and it returned, but only on the condition that her words should be kind.

"I was horrible to you tonight, wasn't I?" she asked.

"Well, we're past that now," Eric said.

Katie smiled at him. Just at this moment, it seemed that his love and trust was perfect. But it also puzzled her that it should be so. She drew closer to him and asked, "When I told you that I was pregnant, why did you take me back?"

Eric looked down to Katie's feet. "It's hard to say," he said.

"You were angry with me, back then, weren't you?"
"Very angry," he answered, honestly but calmly.
"But you took me back anyway."
"Yes, I did."

"Was it because you thought that was what you were supposed to do?"

"No."

"Were you afraid of what people might say if you didn't take me back?"

"No."

"Was it because you thought that Tara is yours?"

"Well," he answered, after half a moment of thought, "yes, but that wasn't everything."

"Did you want a child already, and just decided to pretend she was yours?"

"I don't think so. No."

"Then why?"

Eric was quiet again, thinking of just what the answer was. A hundred possible answers raised themselves up in his mind, and were dismissed just as quickly. For a moment he considered the possibility that there was no answer at all. Maybe people love each other for no reason, and that is precisely what sets love apart and makes it special.

When Eric finally spoke, he said simply, "I missed you."

Katie let the words sink into her mind. She began to see into Eric's heart a little deeper, and what she saw made her look upon him with renewed respect. When his words circulated fully through her body and came to rest on her heart, she moved to Eric's side, slid her arms inside his bathrobe, and squeezed his body warmly.

"I missed you too."

~ 65 ~

Outside of the window where Katie and Eric stood, the night was thick with a gently drifting mist. It slowly rose up from the ground, from the evaporating banks of snow and sheets of ice, from the mud patches and puddles on the road, from trees and gardens and little hollows in the rocks, and from the graves of the dead. It drifted through the village in waves like a procession of old ghosts. It changed colour is it passed, from silver and blue in the moon-washed fields of the countryside, to bright orange under the magnesium street lamps, to white in the headlights of cars and red in the tail lights, and to silvery white again in the open spaces of parks and darkened courtyards. Each house in the village had shut its doors and drawn its curtains closed for the night, protected from the rain and weather, and the prying of passer-bys. For the wild of the untracked forest begins but a few strides beyond the threshold of every door. Still, an occasional un-curtained window, or a door not fully shut, might attract the attention of a passing shadow, and its hooded head would turn to look. An argument in this house. A family dinner in that one. A retired couple sharing a glass of wine. A child at play with a dog. Another family gathered around the television A shadow might stop a moment to look a little closer, but most would continue on before long. An un-curtained window is not an open door.

We are all ghosts to each other, Eric thought, as he contemplated the passing shadows out his window, while Katie slept on his shoulder. We are as mysterious as the mist, but for the occasional glimpses of light through an un-curtained window, or the hint of sound through an opened door. Some people may pass by leaving not even footsteps in our lives. Some walk a short while with us together, sharing a few happy glances, finding momentary light in each other's faces. But then they venture forth in another way, perhaps to be seen again, perhaps not, and in any event, perhaps to do well. And some rare few stop to talk, and to invite each other to visit them at home. Suddenly a new flame is kindled in the hearth: a passionate love, a bitter hatred, a grand gesture of charity, a wretched act of cowardice, a happy bout of laughter, a long-awaited reunion. They, among all the rest, run the greatest risk of frustration and fear. Indeed they walk that much closer to the knife edge of murder, the cliff face of suicide, and the darkness of death. Here, this woman in my arms, my lover, my Katie, is still a mystery to me. But she is here, in my home. I let her in. Perhaps those who let each other into their homes like this, whatever they risk, have the best chance to know love.

The procession floated by the window where Katie and Eric held each other. A shape like an old storyteller noticed them there, and stopped to linger for a while. Eric looked up for a moment and saw the white shape watching him, so he raised a hand in greeting. The shape replied with the tip of a hat before drifting on its way. For a second it seemed that it took the hand of another shadow in the procession, as if taking the hand of a beloved companion. But in the space of a heartbeat it dissipated back into the mist from which it came.

~ 66 ~

The following morning was bright and clear, although cool and windy. Katie and Eric remained in bed almost as late as the crack of noon. Each lay awake for a while, assuming the other to be still asleep, and remained still so as not to disturb. But when they both moved at the same moment to kiss each other on the cheek before getting up, and got each other on the mouth instead, they laughed loudly and were fully awake.

When they were dressed and ready for the rest of the day, Eric remembered that he had been asked to bring Katie to the Brigantian Grove. They began gathering up some things that they thought the tribe might need, while Eric explained to Katie how Miranda came to believe the grove would come under siege.

While rummaging about the apartment he came across the photocopies of the DiAngelo sketches and paintings. He straightened out the creases and folds where they had been crumpled, and studied them anew. As he had not thought about it for months, a few new ideas about what the image meant began to suggest themselves in his mind. Katie noticed him apparently wasting time, and urged him to hurry.

"They need to know about what happened to Tara," she insisted.

"I think I have just discovered something," said Eric. He tapped his fingers on one of the pages and said, "I should have seen this before. Where is my brain!"

"What?" asked Katie.

"I'll tell you when we get there," he said. Then he put the copies into his backpack along with everything else they were taking with them.

They drove Miranda's range rover back to her house. Finding no one at home, they continued on foot to the forest, and onward to the grove. When they were within a stone's throw of the cairn near the entrance, four armed men in full highland warrior's gear jumped out from hiding places in the undergrowth. They brandished claymores and roared aggressively, ready to strike. Four more men holding throwing spears at the ready popped their heads and shoulders over the top of the ridge. When one of them recognised Katie, he shouted to the rest to stand down. They lowered their weapons and had a good laugh at themselves.

"We have been waiting all night for something to happen," one of them explained cheerfully.

"Well, something happened to us," said Eric. "We'll tell you about it inside."

The sentries became concerned, but Katie and Eric said no more. Katie took a canteen from out of Eric's backpack and poured a little wine from it on to the cairn. The entrance tunnel revealed itself, and she and Eric entered, followed close behind by the cold and tired sentries. Within the grove the air was warm and still, and the snow was gone. Some of the trees were beginning to bud, as if springtime was arriving here much sooner than to the rest of the country. There was a pile of winter coats off to one side, where people had cast them aside. A wooden catwalk had been constructed along the ridge, allowing the warriors to move around the ridge quickly without being seen from outside. A number of steps and ladders gave quick access to the catwalk level and the top of the ridge above it. Several warriors were perched in various hiding places, overlooking the approaches, and others were organising piles of weapons from swords and spears to wooden clubs and even large rocks. Katie marveled that they had been built in just one night, and was told that it had something to do with the passage of time being different inside the grove.

Miranda acknowledged their entry, but gave them no special welcome. "I hoped you would have come a little sooner," she gruffed.

"We had a problem last night," said Eric.

Miranda stopped and looked at them, expecting him to explain. It took her only a second to figure out the story by herself. But Katie could not contain herself.

"They took her!" she moaned.

Miranda looked at Katie with deep compassion. "Oh Katie, I'm so sorry."

Katie's knees buckled a little, and she leaned on one of the standing stones for support. "They came with a court order and some official people, and they took her. They took her! That's what they really wanted! And now she will get all the best toys and clothes and things I can't afford to give her, and she will grow up loving them more than me. I don't know if I'll ever see her again."

"You will," said Miranda, trying to be reassuring. "Anything we can do to help you, we'll do it," she promised.

Some of the nearby tribesmen stated an agreement. Then she looked to Eric and said, "You were right, yesterday."

"I'm not glad of it," Eric replied.

"Nevertheless I owe you an apology."

Eric nodded. "Thank you."

Miranda addressed both of them. "Best if you both stayed here for a while," she told them. "We have scouts watching them carefully, and once we have determined their movements and their plans we will decide what to do."

Eric was thoughtful. "I think I know what his plan is," he said.

"Let's hear it, then," Miranda sighed.

From his rucksack Eric withdrew his copies of the DiAngelo paintings and passed them around.

"A few hundred years ago," he explained, "someone by the name of C. M. DiAngelo made these pictures. I've been studying them on and off for the past few months, and I think they can tell us something of what's on the artist's mind. Take a look."

Miranda looked at one of the images with disdain. "What does art have to do with this?"

"This isn't art. This is military intelligence."

Katie smiled. If he was a nerd, at least he was *her* nerd.

Eric continued. "The biggest picture looks like a variation of a better known painting by Raphael called 'The Transfiguration'. I've a copy of the original here too. But this version has two angels instead of two prophets on either side of Christ, and they both hold hourglasses."

"The DiAngelo family crest," Miranda interjected.

"That's what that is!" said Eric. He reflected silently for a second at the various times and places he had seen the image before. Then he continued: "What is more, behind the Christ figure in the middle, the sky is mostly cloudy and dark, there is a lightning stroke hitting the ground, but above his head the sun is breaking through, in almost the right place for a halo. There are also three eagles circling around behind him. Those are not the symbols of the transfigured Christ. They are the symbols of Zeus, the high king of the Olympian gods."

Miranda studied the picture with greater interest. At the same time her respect for Eric was growing back again. After a moment, she asked, "Why do you think this picture represents Carlo's plan?"

"Because of these figures below", explained Eric. "In the rest of the picture, you find mostly the same crowd of amazed onlookers as in Raphael's original. But see among them, there are some interesting details. Look at these three men on the top of the little ridge there, just beneath the feet of the two angels. One of them is holding a little curved blade in his hand. That's Kronos, or Saturn, who was Jupiter's father, who Jupiter had to kill to assume the seat of the high king of the gods."

Katie asked, "What about the other two people lying beside him?"

"Jupiter's brothers. Poseidon, with the trident, and his other brother Hades, with the helmet. Notice how those two have shackles on their ankles."

"In the mythologies, did Jupiter enslave them?" asked Katie.

"No, he didn't," said Eric. "And that detail says a lot. *This* Jupiter wants more than just to get rid of his father. He also wants to control his brothers. And that's what I think his plan is."

"Then why did he chase Katie for so long, and why abduct Tara?" asked Miranda.

"I'm not completely sure, but I think that if Carlo wants to reveal himself as a new high king of the gods, he has to do some of the same things the old high king did. And more! Look at this image here, of a woman cradling a swan in her arms. That's Leda, one of the mortal women that Jupiter seduced."

Katie touched her belly. She asked, "She had a child, didn't she?"

Eric got excited. "Yes! Four children. Two sets of twins, hatched from those eggs there. One of them grew up to become Helen of Troy—" Then he cut himself off, suddenly realizing why Katie asked the question. "I'm sorry," he said.

"Go on," said Miranda, gently.

Eric squeezed Katie's hand apologetically, and continued. "The point is, these pictures tell the story of what Carlo thinks he must do, to become the king of the gods."

Katie's face suddenly became icy and pale. "That is his plan exactly," she said.

Eric and Miranda looked to her with interest.

Feeling the eyes of the tribe upon her, Katie spoke quietly. "He once told me in his own words what he wants. He wasn't very specific. I'm not sure how to explain it. He thinks the world has lost its purpose and direction, and he wants to do something about it."

Eric pointed to the copy of the Triumph of the Virtues. "See, here we have a goddess coming into this garden, driving out the evil people."

"What he wants from me is right here," said Katie. She pointed to another picture from Eric's collection.

Eric studied the image. "The Oracle of Delphi. The original was by Michelangelo, and it's in the Sistine Chapel. But instead of holding a scroll, like in the original, she holds an hourglass. That's because this oracle speaks on behalf of the DiAngelo interests, and so she makes it sound like the gods approve of what he's doing."

"He once told me that my place in his scheme would be something like that," Katie confirmed.

Miranda added a conclusion of her own. "Someone like you, Katie, descended from the Celtic gods, confirming the authority of a Roman patrician, now that would be a very powerful statement in our world."

Some of the nearest Brigantian warriors nodded in agreement.

"Did he tell you anything more?" she asked.

"Actually, yes," said Katie. Both Eric and Miranda looked to Katie with surprise. Katie spoke carefully here, as she could see that this last remark made her listeners suspicious.

"Let me be as honest as I can. I mean, he hurt me, I just can't forget what he did to me. But he has a plan, and perhaps it would be good for the world. When he described it, he made me think about my life, and what I was doing, and where I was going. I know so many people who do nothing but go shopping all day and watch TV by night, and it's what they say they want, but it doesn't seem to make them happy. Maybe I would have ended up the same way, if Carlo had not turned my head to show me that things could be different. He says he has a vision that he wants to bring to the world, to lift it back up on its feet. He says he wants to bring on a new Renaissance, and give people something to live for again."

As Katie contemplated this thought, her eyes looked up to the sky. Something resembling hope was reflected in them, and a dreamy smile played on her face.

Eric spoke softly. "You love him, don't you?"

Katie looked to the sky and thought about his question for a moment. "I admire his purpose."

Eric nodded, acknowledging her honesty, then looked down to the ground.

But Miranda stood and took her by the shoulders. "How can you say that! This man took away your child!"

Katie shook her head, and tried not to make eye contact with anyone. "I know, I know. But maybe he is right, maybe we need a new Renaissance."

"Concentrate, Katie!" said Miranda, nearly shouting at her. "I've seen his vision of the world. I know what will happen if he makes it a reality. It's not a garden of Eden. It's mediaeval feudalism! It's ruled by heartless men who think they are gods, and they'll sacrifice whole nations in the name of art. What he did to you, he will do to everyone. And he will do it so well they will think themselves lucky, and they will thank him for it. Is that the world you want to live in?"

"You just want to have some kind of revenge for something that happened thousands of years ago!" Katie retorted.

"Nonsense!" Miranda burst out angrily, shocking Katie into a surprised silence. Miranda saw this and let go of Katie's shoulders, took a breath, and tried to speak more rationally.

"What Carlo and the people like him do not understand is that this world does not belong to the gods anymore. It belongs to everyone and no one. The mythic age is over now. Carlo's vision might seem to be beautiful but it does not trust people to solve their own problems. So if the people need a new Renaissance, they have to create it on their own, or else they will be trading one spiritual poverty for another."

"Well why don't you start up your own Renaissance, and see if yours is any better!" Katie grumbled.

"That is exactly what we are doing here!" Miranda shouted again. Then she began to pace around the circle of stones as she spoke.

"The world turned its back on us a long time ago. We know that. In fact we accept that. Even we ourselves don't believe that dancing around the Maypole will make bad weather go away. But when the world left us behind, it also left so much more as well. The idea of the heroic life! Adventure, courage and strength. Generosity, friendship, and solidarity with your people. Where are those virtues now? What about the integrity of honour, the nobility of truth? Nowadays people say it's all relative, they only care about themselves, and they say there's no such thing as the truth. What about the pursuit of beauty for its own sake? Or even enlightenment? All practically forgotten. And what has the world embraced instead? Pop celebrities instead of heroes. Politicians instead of leaders. Mass production instead of craftsmanship. Hospitals that prolong life rather than promote health. Schools that reward conformity instead of intelligence. Law courts where justice goes to whoever has the best paid lawyer. And the people who work for change are ridiculed, ignored, sometimes attacked. Oh, we can see the nightfall of the earth, just as much as he can. But we are looking for the morning sunrise in the right place. That is what our whole community is about. That's what Fellwater Grove is about! We don't want to rule the world. We just want to live better lives. See that man over there, with the beard and the guitar? He's an office manager for a paralegal firm. The woman there, with the raven hair? She's a public health administrator, she works with native people up north. The woman next to her, with the blonde hair, works the front desk at a hotel. And that man over there, telling stories to the children, is a freelance technical writer. We are all just people, that's all, just people. But we are people who care about honour, and friendship, and courage, and true love, and all the things that really matter. We built this place to protect these things, and to make sure they don't die. The world might want them back some day."

~ 67 ~

A call went up from one of the sentries on the ridge, saying that the scouts had returned. Down from what seemed like the centre of the sky came a dozen or so Celtic warriors, running through the air, and on to the ground again. One latecomer, who Eric and Katie soon saw was Donall, fell to the ground in a painful-looking crash. Miranda ran over to him immediately.

"Did you find anyone from the other clanns?" she asked him.

"I did not," he reported breathlessly, as he brushed himself off. "I went to all the safe houses between here and Toronto, and no one was there."

Eric, overhearing this, tapped his finger on the picture of Zeus flanked by the angels. Miranda acknowledged him with a nod, then turned back to the scout.

"Thanks for trying, Donall" Miranda told him. "Now get some rest."

"One more thing," he said quickly. "I saw three Romans walking up to the gate right now."

Miranda was suddenly alarmed. "Brigantians, arm yourselves!" she roared. Instantly, all the warriors in the grove ran up to their stations along the top of the ridge, and arranged arrows and throwing spears in ready to reach places. Miranda herself strung her bow and knocked an arrow to it, and then took a position on the ridge directly above the entrance tunnel. Katie jumped up to a free place on the ridge, and grabbed an unclaimed throwing spear. Eric climbed up on the ridge near her, but kept his head low. As the only one there without a weapon, he thought it best to be careful.

Within a few moments, three shadows became visible in the mist, and as they drew closer they resolved themselves in the shape of three men. Two of them were in the armour of Roman centurions. One of these carried the eagle-topped standard of a legion commander. The third man, in the centre, with in a navy blue suit with a red and black striped tie, was Nicholas. He was still hobbling slowly on a walking stick, in obvious pain with each step, but managed to glower menacingly ahead of him nonetheless. When he was next to the cairn in front of the entrance, he stopped and drew himself to his full height as best as he was able.

"The Herald of House DiAngelo calls out the Chief of the Brigantia", hollered Nicholas as loud as he could.

Miranda stood on the ridge, and straightened herself to her full proud height and let herself be seen in the regalia of a Celtic warrior queen. Eric and Katie momentarily looked to her, impressed that she would let herself be seen, and perhaps easily shot at.

"Cut the ceremony, you wanker! You know my name!"

Nicholas smirked and continued with his official message. "My patrician hereby informs you that the plebian child known to you as Tara Corrigan is a born and natural member of House DiAngelo, through her father, and no one of any other house may claim her."

Katie could not contain her fury. She jumped on the ridge, her battle dress suddenly upon her, and screamed, "She is *my* child! You can't take her away from me!"

Nicholas ignored Katie and continued to address

Miranda. "You took one of ours, so it's only fair that we take one of yours."

Katie howled back before Miranda could reply. "There's nothing fair about it! I'm her mother, you can't do this!"

Miranda put a hand out to Katie, to signal her to calm down. Then she shouted, "You can tell your patrician that we don't recognise his claim. Tara is the daughter of one of ours, and has already been baptized according to our custom."

"That doesn't matter to us," said Nicholas. "Your whole barbarian tribe has a debt to pay to us anyway."

When the warriors of the Brigantia heard these words, they immediately started roaring angrily. They brandished their weapons and clanged them against their shields noisily. Warning shots were fired from bows and slings. Some challenged Nicholas to fight for his honour. Others swore oaths to kill Carlo. A few tried to rile him up with insults about his disability. Katie, for her part, only looked to Miranda to see if what Nicholas said was true. Miranda's face, looking at Nicholas, was grim and tight lipped.

"You can make as much ruckus as you like," said Nicholas, "but it changes nothing. You know the deal we made. Water from the well in your sanctuary, one hundred firkins every seven years, if you want us to leave you alone. And I hear you missed the last few shipments."

The warriors continued to shout defiantly back to Nicholas. When Miranda was able to quiet them down, she shouted back, "You tell that arrogant, in-bred, blue-blooded wolf's head that his empire collapsed centuries ago, and we are a freehold now, and we don't owe anything to anyone!"

This brought renewed shouts and cheers from the warriors. Nicholas had to holler at the top of his lungs to be heard.

"If that is your answer, I will take it back to my patrician, but you had better be prepared for war!"

Nicholas turned away again and started walking as quickly as his weakened leg and walking stick would allow. Just before he was out of range, Miranda shouted one last taunt at him. "Nicholas! How did you get promoted from chief enforcer to message boy?"

Nicholas paused in his step for a moment, but ignored the question. Soon his profile, with its bowed head and slumped shoulders, faded away in the mist.

~ 68 ~

Most of the warriors who were on the ridge during the stand-off with Nicholas climbed back down to the ground level, although a few sentries remained. They heartily congratulated each other for having chased Nicholas away, and smacked their spear shafts together and head-bashed each other playfully. A few were expressing outrage that the DiAngelo was still thinking of them as a vassal tribe. And some were mocking Nicholas for having been demoted. Donall openly wondered how long the DiAngelo knew the location of Fellwater grove, and reminded his companions to be vigilant. Miranda assigned sentry duty to a few of the warriors before coming down from the ramparts of the ridge. And Katie pushed her way into the conversation.

"We have to get Tara back," said Katie.

"The DiAngelo have claimed her," said Miranda, "so now she is under their protection just as you are under ours. There isn't much we can do."

"Yes there is!" Katie exclaimed. "We can rescue her!"

A number of nearby warriors started murmuring in agreement, including Donall. "We've been preparing for action all night, and didn't get any," he said.

Miranda said, "I don't know if we can do that."

"Well why in the world not!" Katie demanded.

"Your child is their hostage now," said Miranda. "As long as they hold her, they can do anything they want and we will not be able to lift a finger against them."

"All the more reason to steal her back!" Katie argued.

"I don't think you understand the risk here!" said Miranda, with genuine worry. "Even if you succeed, they will feel so humiliated they will track you down, no matter where on earth you go. Kidnapping won't be enough for them after a stunt like that. They will want blood! You will have to spend the rest of your days on the run."

"It's my child we're talking about. I need to take that chance," Katie pleaded.

"My child too," asserted Eric. "Why are you so reluctant to go after her? Is it that oath of allegiance thousands of years ago? Because, of all the stupid reasons not to do something –"

Miranda was stern. "You just don't get it!" she blurted.

"My child is stolen. What is there not to get!" retorted Eric.

Miranda realised his point, and sighed. She found a tree stump near the fire pit and sat herself heavily upon it.

"Let me tell you a story," she began. "It began when my first husband left me and started an insurrection. I was forced to choose between fighting the largest and most powerful military force in the world, or fighting my own people. No matter what I did, even if I chose to do nothing, it would have been the wrong choice. At the time I thought I did the best I could, by becoming an ally of the empire and using their legions to end the rebellion and bring unity to the tribe again."

The warriors surrounding the conversation listened in grim silence.

"So –" Katie started to say. "You are not just a descendent of the goddess Brigid – but you actually are –"

"Two thousand years old, yes," Miranda finished.

The budding historian in Eric suddenly saw Miranda with new eyes.

"Was Nicholas right about that oath of allegiance?" he eventually asked.

"No," answered Miranda. "I never gave the sovereignty of the tribe to them. As long as I was the chieftain, my people were always free. But I did make a deal with them."

"What deal was that?" asked Eric. A few others within earshot also wanted to know, and gathered closer to hear her answer.

"They put down the rebellion, and in return, I was not to interfere with them. I could do whatever I wanted, I could even remain the chief of the clan, as long as I stayed out of their way."

Miranda was getting emotional now, and Katie and Eric were both beginning to feel a little bit of sympathy.

With her voice cracking, Miranda continued. "We started out as warriors. We were brave and proud and strong. And we had the finest craftsmen and poets, and the wisest philosophers of our time. We shone like the sun, we roared like the sea, we thought ourselves as great as the ancient gods themselves. When the Romans arrived, you were right Eric, they brought luxuries and technology beyond anything we had ever seen before. But then we saw what a machine the empire really was, and what it was doing to our people. Our beautiful, noble people! We became complacent, dependent, greedy, like field mice who think they grasp great treasures when all they grasp are crumbs. Where once, before, someone made something beautiful, we would all be proud. But after, one of us would receive some trinket, some little thing, some pathetic honour, and we all felt envy, and we would stab each other in the back to get the next one. When I married my second husband, seven years after divorcing the first, I finally found a little bit of happiness for myself in this cloud-shadowed world. But they told everyone that I was a harlot and they turned my allies against me. Oh, they put down the rebellions, three of them, just like they promised. But then afterwards – they didn't go home. They stayed. They set up garrisons and trading posts everywhere, and they widened our roads so that more of them could come. And just to make sure I knew they were serious, they killed their prisoners in front of me. My own people! So I refused to pay their ransom money. So they burned our villages and fields, and salted the ground, so no good thing would grow again. They took so many of our finest young boys and girls, and sold them in the East as slaves. We had to retreat north, to the Highlands, to survive. We fought a guerilla war against them for a little while. But we were useless, worse than useless. Our pride was gone, we couldn't do anything."

"How long did you do that?" asked Eric.

"Hundreds of years, Eric, hundreds of years. We lived barely better than animals, until we lost our purpose, until all we knew was that we were fighting, and we forgot what we were fighting *for*. So some of us built leather ships, like the Irish used to build. We sailed to the west, in search of the islands where our stories say the gods live. Instead we came to this land, at a place now called Nova Scotia. We pressed on, further west, followed the great river to the great lakes, looking for a new home, and finally settled here. The local Ouendat Elders let us have this valley, and in return we agreed to help protect them from their enemies. Life was good like that for a while. But then the French arrived, and the English after them, and everything changed again."

"Did you never want to go back?"

"Oh, I did visit back many times," said Miranda. "I missed my old homeland. But there were fewer and fewer of us still there each time I returned. I haven't been back since the time of the Highland Clearances."

"This deal you made, not to interfere with them," Katie said, "It's obvious you are not benefiting from it so why continue to honour it?"

"On the contrary," said Miranda, her voice clearing a little. "It is probably the only reason Carlo sent his messenger now, instead of his whole army."

"But it's clear this deal of yours is no good to you anymore," Katie pressed. "What if he does all those things you are afraid he will do. Could you live with yourself if you did nothing to stop him? Could you live with yourself if he did something to Tara, and you just stood back and watched?"

Miranda was silent for a moment before answering. Donall, listening nearby, muttered something under his breath that sounded like agreement with Katie. Then with a deep breath, Miranda said, "This situation may seem terrible to you. But to me it is only one more terrible thing in a very long, *very* long litany of terrible things. You must understand: my time is passed. For many years now I have been hearing the call to go into the west. All the long centuries of fighting and running and hiding have wasted me. It will not be long now before I will have to answer that call. What remains for me to do, my one last task on this earth, is to find someone to take my place. These last few decades I have sought someone who had the spirit of the goddess of the land within her, as I once did. Katie, that is why you are so important. I think the spirit I am looking for is reborn in you. I wanted to give you the tribe. I would be giving you a never-ending battle against the DiAngelo and his allies along with it. But you will be able to fight that battle as I no longer can."

"I want my child back," said Katie. "I don't want to think about anything else until she is in my arms again."

"I know, Katie, I know," said Miranda, with all the honesty as she could muster. "If you go to rescue her, I will not stop you. But I will not be able to help you either. You will have to go alone."

~ 69 ~

Katie and Eric walked through the forest, away from the grove and toward home. They were not holding hands, as they normally did, but were a few meters apart, each occupied with their own thoughts. When they arrived home Eric went to the kitchen and started preparing some food for both of them, while Katie had a shower. Dinner was ready when she got out of the shower, and they ate together in silence. Afterwards, Eric sat down to his homework while Katie washed the dishes. This was their usual domestic arrangement, but tonight it was followed with dull monotony. Katie went to bed shortly after she was finished in the kitchen. When Eric followed her to bed a few hours later, he found her on the bed, but fully clothed and lying on top of the covers. He did his best to stay quiet in case she had fallen asleep. In fact she was wide awake, but turned away from him so he could not see her face. Eric spent a moment to look at her, wondering where she had gone in her mind, and rather wishing she could come back, or that she would take him with her.

When she sensed that she was being watched, she turned over and looked at him. Eric was a little startled to see that she was awake. They gazed at each other silently, as it was the first time they had made eye contact since leaving the grove in the early afternoon.

The first to speak was Eric. "Thinking about her?" he asked gently.

Katie sat up stiffly and said, "Thinking about those gutless pansies at the grove who call themselves warriors! There was a time when men would commit murder to defend the honour of their women. What is it with men these days, why are they all so gentle and sensitive now?"

Eric was taken aback, and didn't know how to reply.

"And Miranda is the worst of the lot," Katie ranted, ignoring Eric. "She harps on about honour and solidarity but when a chance to actually *do* something about it comes up, she just sits on a stump and says she's too old and tired!"

"Katie," said Eric, trying to calm her down.

"And you, Eric, you were such a deadbeat, you should have known what I was feeling! You should have stuck up for me when you had the chance!"

"Really, Katie, what could I have done!" Eric argued.

Katie's words tripped over themselves, as she wanted to say a hundred things but did not really know what she wanted to say at all. Eventually she blurted out, "You could have—should have—challenged Nicholas to a duel!"

Eric paused for a second, and then suddenly started

giggling.

"Shut up!" ordered Katie.

But this made Eric laugh a little louder. "What, pistols at high noon!"

"Yes," Katie roared. "You should have—gone up to Nicholas and told him—told him—stop laughing at me!"

"Do you have *any* idea how completely ridiculous you sound right now!" Eric said, between bursts of laughter.

"This is serious, Eric! I wanted you to—"

"—slap him in the face with a white glove?" said Eric, and he collapsed in the bed, now howling uncontrollably.

Katie stood up to Eric and tried to argue with him more, and even tried to slug him in the shoulder with her fists, until she too began to see the silliness of what she was saying. Then she too started to laugh, which made Eric laugh louder still. Then Eric accidentally snorted, which made Katie roar out loud with uncontrollable hysterics until the muscles in her sides ached with pain. The both of them soon had to bury their heads in the pillows. When all was quiet Katie looked over to him, but as soon as they made eye contact the laughter exploded from their lungs once again.

When they finally came to rest, Katie spoke quietly.

"The worst thing in the world is to be by yourself while surrounded by your friends."

"I know," said Eric, and he gently kissed her forehead.

~ 70 ~

The sharp sound of someone's knuckles rapping on the door interrupted their privacy.

"Who would be coming here at this hour?" Eric said.

Katie suddenly became fearful. "Don't go," she ordered him.

"Why not?" Eric asked.

"It's Nicholas," she said.

"Don't be silly, he wouldn't come here, not after the showing he gave today."

"I know it's him, don't ask me how I know it but I do. So don't answer the door."

The knocking was repeated, this time a little more rapidly. "I know you're in there!" shouted a voice.

"If it's Nicholas standing there, I'll tell him you're not

home."

"Okay," said Katie, and she flashed out of the room, barely touching the floor as she went.

Eric closed the chain on the door and then opened it just enough to see who was on the other side. Katie was correct. Eric was about to slam the door shut when he noticed that the visitor's clothing was unkempt and a wrinkled, his posture stooped, his tie loose and his top button undone, his face downcast, and weight supported by a walking stick.

"May I come in?" Nicholas asked.

Again, Eric was puzzled. Nicholas did not normally ask for anything. But Eric remembered Katie's fear.

"No, I think you better not," Eric answered, cautiously.

Nicholas looked down to the exit, then back to Eric and asked, "Can I speak with Katie?"

"She isn't here," said Eric, although he suspected that Nicholas could tell he was lying.

"Will you give her a message for me?" Nicholas asked. Eric nodded, so Nicholas said, "Tell her, if she wants to see her child again, well, all I can tell her is that Carlo will be out of the house this evening."

Katie came around the door to where Nicholas could see her.

"Why are you telling us this?" she asked suspiciously.

Nicholas trembled briefly when she appeared. "I just thought that if you were planning anything—I don't know. I shouldn't be here." he said, and then he turned to leave.

Eric looked at Katie, who nodded at him, and then he unchained the door. Nicholas, with a look of plain surprise, puffed himself up a little, as best as he was able while leaning on his walking stick, and tried to salvage his pride.

"I'm not doing this for your sake, in case you were wondering," said Nicholas.

"Why then?" Katie asked him.

Nicholas spoke gruffly. "It's just that he promised that awakening thing to *me*, and promised that I would join the house as a full member. I was going to be his right hand man. I was going to have a life that counted for something, finally, and something important to *do*, with my life. But he gave it to someone else."

"Paul Turner," said Katie and Eric in unison.

"The very man," Nicholas confirmed. "They even took

him to Italy, and they did everything in a Renaissance cathedral. That's the thanks I get for twelve years of dedicated professional service."

Eric folded his arms and said, "So essentially you want us to help you get some kind of revenge?"

"I wouldn't put it that way—" Nicholas answered, but was cut off by Eric.

"How would you put it?" he argued.

"Whatever way you want to think of it is fine, I don't care," he said in a faltering voice. "I'm getting out of this whole thing while I still can." He started to lumber toward the front exit of the building.

Katie leaned out the door, albeit carefully, and said, "Why should we trust you?"

"I suppose you shouldn't," said Nicholas, over his shoulder. "But if you got your child back, and everything turns out for you the way you want it to, maybe you will remember that I had some small part in helping you, and that for once in my life, I was an honest man."

Nicholas stepped gingerly though the door, and slowly headed away, in the direction of the old stone bridge.

~ 71 ~

Katie and Eric headed for the grove. Katie wanted to tell Miranda what Nicholas had said, in the hope it might convince her to change her mind and help. Although it was already completely dark, they had no trouble getting through the forest. When they arrived at the cairn, they found the entrance tunnel already open, and Donall the scout standing in it.

"I knew we would be seeing you again today," he said.

"What, do all of you have a magical sense of the future?" asked Katie, sarcastically.

"In your case, you're just predictable," he joked. Katie smiled back, but was too tired to laugh.

Then Donall said, "Look up there."

Katie and Eric did so, and saw hovering above them, about half as high as the tops of the trees, was a large boat, made of leather sheets stretched over a wooden frame and sealed with tar, and with bales of long grass thatched along its gunnels. Two oars stuck out from the sides, and a long rudder was attached to the stern. A short square sail was hoisted on a mast above it, and on it was painted the tree and triple spiral insignia of the Clann Brigantia. A rope from the deck dangled just above the ground in front of Katie.

"I thought you said you could not help us," Katie marveled.

"I don't know how this thing went missing from the docks," smiled Donall. "And I don't know how all those tools and weapons got in it either. I must have fallen asleep while I was on sentry duty." Then he flashed a knowing wink to her.

Katie winked back and said, "I hear you."

Then Donall's face became more serious, and he said, "I don't like all this standing around either. If I was chieftain, I would take fight back to our enemies. But I'm not the chieftain, so this is the best I can do. Now up you go."

Katie held on tightly to the rope, gave it a short tug, found it to be stable, and pulled herself up to the boat. Once she safely clambered over the side, she noticed there was no one there.

"Hey, how do you drive this thing?" Katie shouted down to Miranda.

"Just whisper into the mast the place where you want to go, and it will do the rest," Donall shouted back.

Katie threw down the rope for Eric, and he grappled his way to the top as well.

"Good luck!" shouted Donall.

Katie leaned into the sail and whispered, "The DiAngelo mansion, in Fellwater." The sail started to billow in the wind, and gently floated a little higher into the air. As soon as it was clear of the tops of the trees, it turned toward the town and picked up speed. Katie looked back and saw the grove from above. Donall was still standing by the entrance tunnel, watching them heading out. She could see a few people sitting around the fire pit inside the ring of stones. Then the grove was too far behind and below them to be clear. Soon they were high enough to see the complete layout of streets and laneways of the village, and just as soon it too was so far below them that it became a blurry patchwork of shadow and light.

"Amazing!" hollered Eric, from the front of the boat. Since Katie had already experienced the sky race, the flying boat was not a surprise, although she still found the experience wonderful. Eric, experiencing this impossible form of travel for the first time, was positively exhilarated. He leaned over the bow and marveled at the view, and the wind in his hair. And just to be silly, he shouted back to Katie: "Hey, I can see our house from here!" Katie giggled back, and warned him not to lean over too far.

The ground beneath them was speeding away quickly. The fields and wood lots of the township were like a quilt laid out on the earth, with the folds and ruffles taking the shape of hills and rounds and little valleys. The lights of more distant cities could be spotted on the horizon, steady against the blackness, although faint like distant candles. Wind lashed them, but not uncomfortably, and it made Eric's hair fly like a flag. Katie reached out and touched his hand, and he grasped it readily. Then the curragh swept closer to its destination, and the gridlines of its streets became more clear. Katie focused her mind on Tara, and tried to plan what to do.

~ 72 ~

The flying boat came to positioned itself just above the front courtyard of the DiAngelo mansion. Light from the rooms inside spilled through the windows and illuminated spots on the cobblestones, and on the gardens to either side of the mansion. Katie moved to the stern and took hold of the keel, and the boat drifted forward slowly.

"This must be how you steer this thing," she said.

"Well it's still a boat, even if it's a flying boat," laughed Eric.

Katie laughed, then admonished him to keep his voice down. By pushing the oars one way and then another, Eric quickly learned how to make the ship move left or right. Although it lurched clumsily at first, soon it glided smoothly where they wanted it to go. Katie directed it over the roof of the house, and then carefully positioned it right above an attic skylight. Eric realised what her intention was, and he threw down the rope.

"Got a plan?" Eric whispered to Katie.

"Not really," she admitted with a smile. "I just thought we could drop in, find Tara, pull her up here, then fly off back to the grove again."

"Well, let's do it," said Eric, and he threw one leg over the side. Katie released the handle of the rudder and the boat hovered steadily in place. Eric grasped the rope and gently lowered himself, hand over hand, down to the skylight.

"I'm really out of shape for this," he muttered. When he looked down and felt the instinctual fear of heights flutter in his belly, he added, "And probably out of my mind as well!"

When he was close enough, he reached for the skylight latch. It was unlocked, and he had no trouble swinging it open, although it creaked noisily. Both would-be rescuers cringed.

"Lower," Eric whispered to Katie. She took the rudder again and carefully let the boat drift down. Eric was passed through the skylight, and into the attic.

The attic was not well cared for. Its floorboards were still rough hewn, straight from the sawmill, and a few of them were missing or broken, revealing a bed of gravelly vermiculite insulation beneath. The ceiling was low and had no panels covering the skeletal structure of the roof joists. Boxes, chests, and old broken furniture lay about in no particular order, mostly against the sides to leave a centre aisle free, although a few stragglers lay in the middle of the space as if they had been hastily dropped there. There were wardrobes of Venetian carnival costumes, boxes of old shoes, piles of paintings leaning against things or stacked on top of each other, and a layer of dust over everything, just thick enough to show any footprints or fingerprints. The only light in the room came from what streamed in through the windows in the gables. The dust made the streams of light highly visible, like a network of spotlights. Some of the windows framed little squares of stained glass, creating patches of colour in various places. Most of all Eric was struck by the smell of must and mould. It reminded him of happy times as a child, playing in his parent's attic, which in turn reminded him of how far in the past those times now were.

When Eric touched the floor, he gave the rope a tug and it held steady. Good, thought Eric, she understood that she didn't have to lower the rope any further down. A moment later Katie lowered herself hand over hand and touched the floor beside him.

"I hope that was the hard part," she whispered.

"Me too," Eric agreed.

"Let's look for a trap door," suggested Katie. They tiptoed around the floor, carefully looking for a way down to the house below. Once they were out from beneath the skylight, the rope was suddenly pulled upward. Both Katie and Eric ran to grab it but neither was quick enough. They nearly ran into each other as they jumped for it. Through a window they saw the boat flying off into the distance, back in the direction from which they came.

"The getaway car!" exclaimed Eric.

Katie was crestfallen to see it go as well, but tried to be philosophical about it. "No going home until the adventure is over," she muttered.

"What?" asked Eric.

"Nothing," said Katie, shaking her head. "We just have to re-think the plan now."

"I guess we just search the house until we find Tara, then get the hell out."

"Easier said than done!"

"I know, but what else can we do?"

Katie saw his point, and shrugged. They looked around for a way down. Seeing nothing resembling a stairway, they both went in search of a trap door.

As they explored further, Katie found that the part of the attic over the front of the house was partitioned, and behind the partition was a storage space. A beam on one side of the space supported a long hangar bar from which hung more than a dozen old cloaks, robes, dresses, and carnival costumes. The other side held shelves for hats, shoes, and other accessories. Nearest the door, and facing Katie, was a skull with a black top hat. It momentarily startled her, but then she told herself there was nothing to fear from it, as it was only a toy, so she walked by. She examined the floor at the far end, looking for a trapdoor. A quiet scraping noise caught her attention and she looked back, but saw nothing unusual, and assumed it was only Eric moving something out of his way. She examined the floor underneath the rack of clothing, and heard the sound again. This time she turned toward the sound more sharply. She saw that the skull had turned to face her. She scurried out of the room as fast as possible, and found a corner where the skull couldn't see her, where she could catch her breath.

Eric, meanwhile, had just found the trapdoor. He opened it slowly, and found that it was a straight drop to the floor of the hallway below. Katie and Eric grimaced at each other. It was a long way down, and the noise of their jump was sure to alert anyone in the house of their presence.

"Old houses have such high ceilings," Eric lamented.

"No point just waiting around. Let's go!" ordered Katie.

She threw her legs over the ledge and dropped herself down. Eric followed.

Footsteps ascended a stair. Someone had been alerted to their presence. They quickly darted into the first available room and hid behind the door. The footsteps soon followed, hesitated for a moment near where Katie and Eric hid, and then moved to investigate the trap door.

"I left it open," Eric whispered.

Katie nodded, but held his fingers to his lips, signaling for silence.

After a moment of silence, there was a scraping noise like something heavy being dragged across the floor, followed by a low thud. Then there were footsteps again, accompanied by the creaks and groans of an old wooden structure. There was silence for a moment, and then the creaking footsteps resumed, followed by a slamming sound, a clicking sound, the footsteps again, and then the heavy scraping sound. Then the footsteps walked away quickly, and then Katie and Eric let out a long sigh of relief.

Looking around them at last, they found that they were in a nursery. There was quite a collection of antique toys arranged on shelves, along with larger items like doll houses, rocking horses, model trains, and treasure chests. It reminded both Katie and Eric of a child's nursery from a hundred years ago. The clouds and stars painted on the walls and ceilings certainly added to the antique flavour. But the room did not feel friendly. As the trees outside swayed in the light breeze, so the shadows on the walls moved like bony old fingers. And, oddly, the smell of linseed oil and mothballs permeated the air. The source of this smell was an artist's easel, and a little table beside it where a palette with some brushes rested. When Katie moved around to see what was on the canvass, she was alarmed.

"Tara was here, look at this!" said Katie. She turned one of the easels around to where Eric could see it. It held an unfinished canvass depicting a portrait of a child emerging from an eggshell.

"That's how the children of Jupiter and Leda were born," Eric remarked.

Eric checked the window. It was held closed with a small latch, so he unhooked it and carefully lifted the window up and peered outside. Directly beneath the window was a two-story drop.

"We won't be able to get out this way," he reported.

Katie had rushed back to the door. It seemed to her that every toy in the room, every teddy bear, every doll, every wooden soldier, every rocking horse, and every picture on the wall, was turning its head to stare straight at her.

"I think I'd like to pick a different room to hide in," she said, and gingerly opened the door.

The hallway was long and wide, more like a gallery than a hall, and like the attic above was illuminated by light from a streetlamp outside, coming in from the balcony door at the far end. There was a great space in the centre of the hall that was open to the ground floor below, and some of the light fixtures on the ground floor walls cast their long beams up to illuminate doors, portraits, and artworks from below. A railing ran around three sides of the space, and the stairs began on the fourth side, which was nearest to Katie and Eric. A great chandelier hung directly above the stairs, and the light from outside struck it and reflected off in various directions. All the doors, on both sides, were closed. Next to the nursery door where Katie and Eric tiptoed out, they saw that a wooden ladder was leaning against the wall near the attic trapdoor, and that the trapdoor itself had been closed and latched.

"There's another escape route we cannot use," Eric remarked.

They began checking every door in the hallway. Most opened to empty guest rooms, some of which looked as if they had not been used in months, or years. The last door in the hallway was a bedroom which they assumed to belong to Emma. There was a black and white photograph of her with three teenage boys on the bedside table nearest the door. These they took to be Emma with her sons when they were young. Emma looked no younger than she does now, Katie noted. And she had no trouble identifying which of the boys Carlo. He dressed in a respectable suit while his brothers wore casual clothes, and he was by far the tallest.

They were about to move to the next room when Katie saw a magnificent child's crib placed against one wall, built like a miniature four-post bed. A curtain hung from a fixture above it and draped down on either side, giving the crib the look of an altar. Its blankets were ruffled, and there was a pile of clothes and diapers next to it, along with some recently purchased stuffed animals, building blocks, and other toys.

"Tara slept here last night," Katie whimpered.

"We will find her, don't you worry," said Eric, trying to be encouraging.

Katie walked around the room. On the other bedside table, she noticed a mask. It was a female face, young but mature, and without expression, cast in a silvery metal in the style of some of the masks from the chapel in the basement of the house. It sat on a pile of neatly folded clothes.

"Look at this," said Katie.

Eric looked. "Weird thing to have in a bedroom," he said, without paying much attention.

"This is face of the woman who took Tara away!" Katie exclaimed.

Eric, who was investigating the window, came to have a look. He thought Katie was letting herself be distracted too easily, so he said, "It's just a mask, Katie."

"They have a room full of them in the basement. I swear this one looks just like the social worker who came to the house and took my baby away!"

Suddenly the smooth metallic skin of the mask twisted itself into a threatening, angry scream, and a voice seared out in a threatening howl. Katie was shocked so much that she screamed back and threw it across the room. It landed in the crib. Both of them were paralysed with fear for a moment.

"We've got to drown out the noise somehow!" shouted Katie. Eric wrapped it up with a blanket from the crib, and shoved it in his backpack. The sound was muffled, but it was too late; the warning had been raised. Within moments, they could hear someone below, running into the hall, and up the stairs.

~ 73 ~

"No point in sneaking around anymore," said Katie, and she ran into the hall to met whoever was coming up the stairs. The top of the stairs was now at the far end of the upper hall, and Katie was determined to get there first.

When Eric decided that muffling the mask was futile, he followed Katie out to the hall. There he saw her at the top of the stairs, her Celtic warrior armour upon her, and her spear in hand. She was pointing her spear down at a middle-aged woman in a nightgown who was glowering back with barely-contained contempt.

"Tell me where Tara is!" Katie commanded.

Emma turned to run back down the stairs, so Katie jumped after her, and made it to the bottom of the stairs first. Eric reached the top of the stairs at that time, and now Emma found herself trapped between them.

"Where is she!" Katie barked again.

"She is not your concern anymore," said Emma.

"Not my concern! My daughter!" Katie raged. She leapt up and pushed the shaft of her spear against Emma's throat. Emma had to grip the banister tightly to keep herself from falling backwards.

Eric was both impressed and frightened by Katie's capacity for violence.

"I'll search the house," he declared, and then ran past them. He searched every door on the ground level systematically, from the back of the hallway to the front. He paused momentarily in the sitting room when he came by the photo of Katie, which was still on the mantlepiece, but kept to his task at hand. Finally he came to the library. He recognized the room from the time that Carlo's men brought him here. On the reading chair he spotted one of Tara's blankets, along with a children's storybook that was open and face-down on the seat, and a milk bottle lying on its side on the floor. Milk slowly dribbled down from the nipple and made a little puddle.

"She was here, just moments ago," Eric muttered. He looked around for other clues. From somewhere inside the walls he could hear Tara crying. Frantically he searched the bookcase which concealed the secret stair to the room in the basement, trying to find the way to open it.

"I think that I found her!" he shouted. Katie entered the room, her face red with worry and fury. Emma was close behind.

"I think I can hear her, but I don't know where she is," Eric declared.

"She's in the secret room down here," said Katie. Then she rounded on Emma and commanded, "Open it."

"That's our private temple, you cannot go there," said Emma, and she put herself in the way.

"And that's my daughter down there!" roared Eric.

Katie smiled to hear Eric call Tara his daughter.

"I don't know who you are, but you are not Tara's father," Emma retorted. "She is the flesh and blood of *my* son, and you have no right to her."

Katie came to Eric's defense. "Yes he does," she said. "I don't care what Carlo thinks or believes, but I am Tara's mother, and I have *decided* who her father is!"

Emma was wild-eyed. "You can't just decide these things!" she cried. She gripped the book case behind her as if afraid of being pulled off it. Her demeanor was changing from defiant to plaintive, almost as if begging Katie to let her keep Tara. But Katie cracked the shaft of her spear against Emma's head, knocking her unconscious. Eric caught her before she hit the floor, and dragged her into the reading chair by the window. At the same time, Katie found the latch to the secret door to the temple below, and together they descended into the dusty darkness.

In the centre of the secret room, they found Tara lying on her belly on a little blanket on the floor. She was alert and awake, but crying loudly. Katie picked her up and kissed her and tried to console her.

"Am I ever happy to see you!" Katie told her. "Now let's take you home."

Before heading back up the stairs, Katie took one last look around. The room was illuminated only by a pair of oil lamps on either side of the mural of Jupiter. The masks that lined the walls were as empty-eyed yet life-like as before, and Katie noticed a spot where one of them was apparently missing.

"Let's get out of here before that woman wakes up," said Eric.

Katie's eyes were drawn to the mural. For some reason the image fascinated her, and she could not tear her eyes from it.

"What are you doing, Katie!" Eric hollered.

"This is the place where it happened—" Katie started to say.

Eric shook her shoulders. "But it's over now, it's in the past. We've got Tara, so let's get out of here!"

Eric's insistence broke her trance. She passed Tara over to him. Then she smashed one of the oil lamps on the floor beneath the mural. A small fire quickly ignited on the carpet, and spread toward the curtains. The flames licked up from below, and began consuming the lower half of the mural. Within seconds it appeared as if the transfigured divinity in the sky above was presiding over an inferno.

"*Now* it's in the past," she declared.

"All right. *Now* let's go!" Eric urged, and Katie wasted

no more time. They ran up the stairs, black and grey smoke following them, and slammed the secret door shut behind them. In the library, Emma was still slumped in the reading chair, but she had awakened, and was looking pale and red-eyed, as if she had just been crying. Blood trickled down her face from the injury Katie gave her. As quickly as he could, Eric took up the baby blanket, wrapped it around Tara, and pocketed the milk bottle. Katie leaned over Emma menacingly.

"Why did you take her," Katie demanded to know.

"I promised to keep Carlo away from you," Emma sobbed. "And you—agreed to give Tara to me in return."

"Is that true?" Eric asked.

"No!" said Katie, before Emma could speak. To Emma, she added, "You offered the deal but *I turned you down!* And you know it. Don't say you misunderstood me."

"It's just—" Emma croaked, "it's just that I thought—I know what kind of a man Carlo is. And I thought that if I had another child – maybe if I had a girl instead – then she would turn out better, and then –"

Katie thought she understood Emma now, although she did not feel particularly forgiving. She pursed her lips, stood up tall, and said, "Then you should have had a child of your own."

Emma put her head in her hands.

Smoke began to seep into the room from behind the bookcase that concealed the passage to the chapel. Eric tugged at Katie's sleeve, and they ran from the room. Katie smashed the front doors of the house right off of their hinges by punching the air in front of them. They fell flat on to the front porch, and the courtyard in front of the house was open to them. The light in the courtyard was dim, as it came only from streetlamps behind the trees and through the curtained windows of the house. Spots of light and dark shifted on the cobblestones as a breeze made the trees rustle and wave.

The escape route through the arch to the street was now before them. Katie and Eric stepped on to the front veranda, but then froze in place. Standing in the centre of the courtyard, with an almost dismissive attitude concerning the damage done to the doors, was Carlo. He wore a scarlet Roman toga, with gold embroidery on the seams, and carried himself like a man with wealth and power. Beside him, in the uniform of a legion commander, was Paul Turner. And behind them both stood a dozen men in full Roman armour.

~ 74 ~

Carlo stepped up closer and crooned, "Master Laflamme, we had a gentlemen's agreement, you and I. But you broke it the same day you made it. I feel within my rights to kill you."

"Get out of our way," shouted Katie.

Eric tightened his hold on Tara. "We know your plan, Carlo. I saw the painting you made, the Transfiguration, with Jupiter in the place of Christ."

"You think that image represented *me*?" Carlo laughed. "No, no. *El Duce* is still biding his time. I am only a voice that cries out in the desert, 'make way'."

Eric was aghast, and could not speak.

Carlo twisted his head to speak to his soldiers. "Praetorians!" he commanded. "Secure them."

Paul was the first of the Romans to unsheath his sword. "I'll say this much," he told Eric. "I did warn you to get rid of her."

The rest of the armoured men jumped forward, with swords raised, and ran to the attack. Eric ducked around and sought shelter behind one of the statues beside the door.

As the soldiers came on the attack, Katie transformed. Her hair grew long and red again, and suddenly ignited in flames. All the muscles in her legs and arms twisted beneath her skin, and tightened into great strong knots. Her mouth opened unnaturally wide, and from deep in her throat an otherworldly battle cry poured out. The soldiers closest to her were knocked over by the force of her voice alone. More soldiers leapt ahead to take their place, but were instantly repelled by Katie's furious spear fighting. One of them fell back with all the ribs on his left side broken. A second had his right knee shattered. A third was flung high into the air. He struck the trunk of a tree, fell to the ground, and did not get up again. And a fourth was flung through one of the windows of the house. Flames licked out through the broken glass. Katie jumped into the centre of the courtyard to engage the other soldiers. They bravely stepped up to replace those which fell, but each of them was thrown back by the blows of her unerring and now blood-stained spear.

At the sight of Katie transformed, Eric was wide-eyed with wonder and with fear. He held Tara's face close to his breast, so as not to let her see what her mother had become. Then through his back he felt warmth, followed by a painful heat. The curtains inside the window behind him were on fire. He looked around for a path to get away, but did not see any direction unguarded. Katie fought to protect them, but her protection was also pinning him with his back to the wall of the house.

    Carlo was watching the scene from near the arch by the road. He was shouting angrily into a mobile phone, apparently calling for more of his men. Eric could make out phrases like 'Get here immediately', but some of the conversation was in Italian, and some in Latin, and so unintelligible to him. Within moments, the sirens of emergency vehicles could be heard approaching. Three police vehicles screeched down the street, and around a dozen policemen spilled from them. They created a human chain between the courtyard and the street, preventing an escape.

    At that moment, Eric smelled smoke issuing from the front doors of the mansion behind him, and it gave him an idea. He shouted at Katie to follow him, and then ran in the direction he thought that Carlo's men would least expect: back into the house.

    Katie turned and saw him dart back into the mansion front doors, and quickly followed him. A dozen people followed after her. They ran down the main hall, and as they passed the door to the library Eric flung it open. A cloud of smoke poured out. Then he ran into the next available door, ushered Katie through it with him, and closed it behind them. With a finger to his mouth he signaled for quiet, and he crouched to the floor where the air was easier to breathe.

    As Katie calmed down, the muscles under her flesh reduced themselves to normal proportions, and the fire on her hair gently faded away. She and Eric, still cradling Tara, found themselves in a darkened kitchen.

    "You just brought us inside a house that's on fire. You better have a plan," Katie whispered.

    "The fire in the basement is the perfect distraction," Eric explained. "The smoke covered our hiding place here. And now they have to waste time putting out the fire. This might give us a chance to make a break for it out the back door."

    "To where?" asked Katie.

    "Did you notice those police cars?" asked Eric. "The

cops just ran out of them, they didn't close the doors or shut off the engines."

Katie thought back for a moment, then smiled and gave Eric a quick kiss. "You're a genius, did you know that?" she giggled.

The sound of hurried footsteps and shouting in the hall outside filled the air. Eric crept to what looked like a door to the back yard, opened it, and waved for Katie to follow. They tiptoed as swiftly as they could out of the house, taking care to shut the door quietly behind them. When they reached the front corner, Katie peeked around, and saw that very few people remained in the courtyard. Carlo was back on his cellphone, apparently calling the fire brigade. Katie made a deep breath, and before Eric could object, she leapt forward again, effortlessly knocked several unattentive policemen off their feet, and bolted for the gate. Eric followed, doing his best to not to jostle Tara too severely.

Carlo saw the action, and quickly stepped between them and the gate. With a snap of his fingers Paul put a sword in his hand.

"I would have made you the high priestess of a new order," he told Katie, almost lovingly.

"You want to talk about 'what could have been'?" asked Eric. "Or, do you want to see if your mother is still inside your burning house?"

"What!" Carlo exclaimed. And as his attention was suddenly diverted to the waves of smoke now flowing from his front door, Katie punched him in the forehead.

Carlo staggered back, more surprised than hurt, but his stagger gave Katie and Eric all the space they needed to race past him and out of the courtyard.

~ 75 ~

"Behind that!" shouted Eric, and he pointed at one of the police cars, parked on the other side of the road. He and Katie dived around behind it and jumped inside. The keys were still in the ignition and the engine was still running, so Eric dropped Tara into Katie's lap, put the car in gear and launched it on to the road.

"Lucky this thing was still on!" exclaimed Katie.

"With you around, I think luck had nothing to do with

it," said Eric.

They raced out of the neighbourhood at full tilt. It was not long before two police cruisers were following them. Katie switched on the vehicle's emergency siren, and other vehicles on the road instantly cleared a path for them.

"Now everyone will think we are on our way to a real emergency," Katie laughed.

"Did you know you were capable of transforming like that?" asked Eric.

"Like what?" said Katie. "All I knew was that I had to protect Tara and get both of you out of there. I just did what I had to do."

By the time they reached the outskirts of the town, the two police cruisers giving chase had been joined by two more. Loud pops of gunfire were heard over the blazing of the sirens, and the rear windshield and rear view mirror of their stolen vehicle was shattered by a bullet.

Katie ducked and tried to protect Tara. Ahead of them, Eric saw that the way was blocked by two more police cruisers parked sideways across the road.

"It's going to get bumpy for a minute," he warned Katie, and he veered through a farm gate and into a field. They lurched and bounced over the rigs and furrows until they came to the next field gate, on a crossing road behind the blockade.

"I didn't know you could drive!" Katie marveled.

"Neither did I," Eric replied, as he flung the range rover back on the road. The fleet of pursuing cars was momentarily held up as the blockade re-arranged itself out of the way. By the time they were moving again, a respectable distance had been created between pursuer and pursued.

"Where are you going anyway?" asked Katie.

"Back to the grove," Eric replied. Eric floored the gas pedal. It did not take long to arrive at the main gate of the conservation park in which the Brigantian grove was hidden.

Katie looked behind them, to see how close their pursuers were coming. Then her eyes suddenly bulged with wonder. As the first police car raced through the park gate, it was suddenly lifted off the ground and flung to one side by the branches of a great maple tree at the side of the road. Half a second later, the next police car was similarly tossed aside.

"The trees are protecting us!" shouted Katie. "It means we're on our own territory now!"

"Hang on!" Eric warned, and he smashed the vehicle through the closed gate barricade. Eric covered his eyes with his arm as it happened, and so his grip on the steering wheel faltered. The car came skidding down the entryway sideways, and slammed into a kiosk with enough force to knock it from its foundation.

The fleet of police cars pursuing them smashed through the trees just at that moment.

"Now let's get out of here," said Katie. They abandoned the vehicle and ran into the woods towards the grove as fast as their feet could run, with only the moonlight to show the way.

~ 76 ~

A path in the woods opened before Katie and Eric, as they ran. The undergrowth and shrubbery bent itself out of their way, making their flight a little easier. Then behind them the plants closed the path against their pursuers. Roots raised themselves to trip the roman soldiers, and low branches reached down to whip their faces. A few of the soldiers fell down, and found their ankles or wrists bound to the ground by vines. But by slashing with their swords at anything and everything that moved, most of the pursuers managed to at least always be within sight of their quarry. Katie and Eric arrived at the cairn before the entrance of the grove only a few heartbeats ahead of a score of centurions.

Donall was standing guard on top of the ridge that formed the outermost boundary of the grove and its defensive rampart. He was half asleep, leaning on his spear, when Katie's shouts of warning awakened him. When he understood what Katie was shouting about, he took up a hunting horn that hung on his belt and blew three long loud notes on it. By the time Katie and Eric made it to the cairn, there were a dozen warriors standing on the ridge, some armed with throwing spears and some with bows, looking out for whatever might arrive.

They did not have to wait long. In twos and threes, Roman soldiers emerged from the forest and took up positions behind trees and rocks. Once they were spotted, the Brigantian warriors on the ridge started shouting their war shouts and crying their battle cries and sounding their war trumpets. Katie and Eric sought shelter in the lee of the cairn, and nestled Tara as safely as they could between them.

Carlo appeared on the battlefield, just behind the line of his soldiers, dressed in a magnificent crimson toga, lined with gold braids on its edges and seams. Paul stood to his right hand, armed and armored. When he spoke his voice was powerful. It momentarily drowned out the noise the Celtic warriors were making, and echoed from all around.

"I am the Patrician of House DiAngelo for this province, and I demand that the chief of the Brigantia tribe come forth!".

A moment later one of the archers on the ridge pulled a hood off her head, and everyone could see that it was Miranda.

"This is our territory, Carlo! You cannot make demands here!" she replied angrily. As Carlo had done, her voice boomed across the field and echoed in the distance.

"My house has been burned, some of my people are dead, and a plebian under my protection was abducted by one of your people. I demand justice!" Carlo fumed.

"You had no right to claim Tara in the first place," said Miranda. "And as to the burning of your house, I am only sorry that it wasn't myself who did it!"

The Brigantians cheered for their chieftain, and blew their war trumpets and shouted their war shouts and cried their war cries until Carlo could barely be heard.

"We will shatter every stone in your grove and hang your bones from every tree, unless you return the child to us!"

When Katie heard this demand she stood and furiously shouted back to Carlo, "She is *my* child and you cannot have her!"

Carlo saw that Katie was standing in a very visible position. With a hand signal, he ordered his soldiers to attack. That same instant, the rest of the Brigantian warriors jumped off the ridge and formed a defensive ring around the cairn. From the flanks, two small teams of Brigantian fighters leaped down. Once they rolled to their feet and got their bearings, they unleashed their weapons and charged recklessly at the nests of Roman soldiers. They roared great battle cries which knocked some of the nearest Roman soldiers to their feet. Other Romans formed shield-walls in time to repel the attack. But a few were caught unprepared, and the roaring Celtic warriors dispatched them with laughter. Eric ventured a look around the side of the cairn and saw it happen. Quickly he ducked back out of the way.

"Can you get that entrance open?" Eric urged, shouting

above the din of battle.

"You have to pour an offering on the cairn here, like a cup of wine or something," she said.

Obviously, neither Eric nor Katie had any with them, so Eric said, "We're screwed, aren't we?"

"I have an idea," Katie said. She unsheathed a dagger from her belt and clenched a fist around the blade. Then she jerked it out of her hand. Her pain reflex made her yelp, but she bore it bravely, and when the blood started to run, she let some of it drip on the cairn. A heartbeat later, the stones and trees and shrubbery on the ridge started to rumble and twist out of the way, revealing the entrance tunnel.

"Don't move until I say it's clear", Donall shouted at them from above the entrance.

"Absolutely we're not moving!" Katie shouted back.

One of the Roman soldiers flew through the air and smashed against the stone of the ridge. Katie quickly glanced over her shoulder to see what happened, and saw that one of the trees had joined the fighting. It was picking the besiegers up with its lower branches, and tossing them away like toys.

Then Katie felt the cairn shudder, and some of its stones crumbled away. It had been struck by a soldier, thrown there by a tree. Katie risked another glance and saw that the Romans had built an effective shield wall, with the tips of their swords sticking out over the top of each shield, and they were advancing forward. The warriors on the top of the ridge flung heavy stones down on them. Some of the rocks forced one or two soldiers to stagger back, but the rest re-assembled the wall just as fast as it had been breached, and marched forward again. Soon they had built their shield wall so well that the trees could not reach them and the spears and stones from the ridge could not harm them, although those attacks made it hard for them to advance.

"Okay, run!" Donall ordered. Katie picked up Tara and obeyed without hesitation, and Eric was right beside her. The entrance was not far away, but they were running under fire, and had to keep their heads down.

A flying spear from an unseen direction struck the ground directly in front of Katie. It missed her but she tripped on it and flailed wildly. She twisted herself as she fell, in order to land on her back and keep the strongest hold on Tara that she could. She landed hard and heavily on a small cedar sapling.

Tara screamed even louder, but appeared unhurt, and Katie frantically apologised to her. She looked in the direction the spear came from, and found a hidden nest of three Roman soldiers that had not joined the shield wall. Their position gave them a perfect view of the run from the cairn to the grove entrance, and with that view a perfect shot at anyone who might try to make that run. The nearest place Katie could find shelter was at the cairn, so she tumbled back to it, while doing her best to protect Tara. Eric, for his part, had made it safely to the entrance and was sheltering in its mouth. He could see what happened to Katie and was encouraging her to try a second race to safety.

The Roman who hurled the spear that Katie tripped on signaled to Carlo that he could see where Katie was.

"Captain Turner! Take her," Carlo ordered. Paul saluted him and headed toward the cairn with his sword unsheathed. Miranda herself leaped down from the top of the ridge and stood in his way, and posed with her spear in a defensive stance. They stared each other down, as if trying to force each other back by willpower alone. Other nearby combatants from both sides stopped to watch them. Katie peered out from the side of the cairn to watch as well. Donall, still on the ridge, gestured to her to stay put, although his eyes were also on the clash of the titans about to erupt.

Both the Celtic heroine and the Roman captain leapt to the attack simultaneously. They fought ferociously, their two blades flashing in the torchlight from the ridge and the moonbeams from above. Miranda's hair flashed with red and yellow flames that singed the faces of those observers who got too close. Each of Paul's slashes and thrusts was an attempt to get past Miranda to where Katie was half-hiding behind the cairn, and each of Miranda's blocks and parries stopped him. Whenever Miranda saw a chance for an attacking blow of her own, she sent Paul staggering backwards. But he always regained his balance quickly. When he saw his first opportunity to strike a killing blow on Miranda, he charged. But a tree branch reached down and wrapped itself around his waist. He slashed at it with his sword and sliced it off.

"Chop it down," Carlo ordered his men. Meanwhile Paul threw himself at Miranda again with increased viciousness. A root bent itself upward and caught his ankle, and he crashed into the cairn, sending more of its precarious stones collapsing to the ground. He picked himself up easily and launched another attack on Miranda, but she was ready and waiting for him. As before, Paul and Miranda fought each other to a veritable stalemate.

Meanwhile, two of the Roman soldiers attacked the tree with hand axes, while two others protected them from the grasp of the branches. The trunk of the tree was severed after only a few blows, and they started pushing it down. It creaked precariously, and produced a groaning sound that strongly resembled a wail of pain. Some of its lower branches reached out to deal with the soldiers who were pulling on it, but with a few extra chops from the Roman axes it fell over with a deafening crash. Both Paul and Miranda had to jump out of the way as it landed between them.

But Katie did not see the tree falling soon enough. Its trunk landed squarely on the cairn and shattered it, and it trapped Katie from the waist down underneath a large mound of rubble.

All eyes were on her Katie now, and silence permeated the battlefield. Even Carlo lowered his sword. He assessed the situation quickly, and then with a gesture ordered his soldiers to break their shield wall and pull back.

A dozen Brigantian hands scrambled to Katie's side, to push the tree off the remains of the cairn and to clear the rubble away. Eric rushed to the spot and shoved two of the warriors out of the way in order to be the one to pull Katie to safety. Katie did her best to sit herself up and squeeze out from under the stones, but she was weakened badly, and Eric and Miranda had to pull her by her arms.

"Are you all right? Anything broken? Where does it hurt the most?" said Eric frantically.

Katie was confused, and on the cusp of concussion. "I think I'm okay, I don't feel anything broken, but my legs really hurt—"

As soon as Katie was free, Miranda prepared to resume her battle with Carlo, but was arrested by a blood-curdling scream of absolute mortal anguish.

"*Taraaaa!*"

The silent and still body of Katie's infant child was found crushed beneath the shattered stones of the cairn.

~ 77 ~

Eric picked up a fallen spear and ran for Carlo. He was roaring an incoherent jumble of curses and death wishes. Miranda herself intervened to stop him from his irrational rush, with a strong arm wrapped over his chest. Eventually he sat on the ground beside Katie, and was silent.

"Justice", declared Carlo, as he turned on his heel to walk away, followed by his soldiers. He did not look back.

Paul lingered a little while, as the crashing tree had dazed him. He tried to get close enough to see what happened to Tara, and genuine concern registered on his face. But Eric released a flood of profanities at him, and would not let him near. As far as Eric was concerned, Paul had sided with Carlo, and therefore lost the right to offer sympathy. Paul stepped back, turned around, and slowly followed Carlo away.

Miranda sent some of her people into the grove to get materials to treat everyone's wounds. Several of her Brigantians were bleeding badly, and at least five of them were not moving. She went to each of them one by one, checking their eyes for signs of life, and closing those that had none.

Katie rocked the body of her child slowly in her arms. She tried to sing a lullaby but could not find the words, nor the melody. It came out too much like tears. Eric helped her to her feet, and they staggered together, carrying Tara's limp form, into the entrance tunnel of the grove. Following them, the tribesmen carried the bodies of their fallen brothers and sisters in a procession.

The luminescent plants and creatures of the tunnel were still, and glowed with a somber blue light. They laid flowers on them and on the path before them, and hummed in low voices.

~ 78 ~

The following day was warm, dry, and still, but overcast and grey. Katie and Eric had spent the night in the grove, in one of the roundhouses. They ate a quiet breakfast of fruit and bread. Most of the Brigantians were still there. They took turns to go alone into the little roundhouse where the bodies of those who had fallen the night before had been placed. The rest of the time they clustered into little groups. They talked, cried, laughed, drank toasts, sang songs, ranted and roared, and celebrated the lives of their companions. Katie and Eric joined some of them, and were made welcome although there was a distance there which had not been there before. When they had a few moments to themselves, they went outside to sit by the remains of the cairn, where Tara had fallen. Katie walked with difficulty due to her injuries, and leaned on Eric for support.

"They say that when one door closes, another opens," she said wistfully.

"Do you believe them?" Eric asked.

Katie didn't answer. She picked up one of the stones and threw it as far as she could. "I just want to scream at everything and nothing, at everybody and nobody, at the sky, at Miranda, at you, at Carlo, at the whole world."

Eric shrugged and said, "Maybe it will help."

Katie stood and began shouting as loud as she could. "*Why did this happen! Why was my Tara taken away! What was the point of that! Why did it have to be her, instead of me! If everything happens for a reason then what in the name of all that's holy was the reason for her to die! Why! Answer me! Why!*"

There did not seem to be much of a response. Some nearby birds were disturbed and flew away, and from a distance the echo of her voice returned faintly to her.

She collapsed back on the ground and crawled into Eric's arms. "Well that was no help at all."

"Let me try," said Eric. He stood, but only looked around. He took a few breaths, to get ready to shout, but no words came to him. He sat back down again.

"You're right, it's useless," he said.

There was a long silence.

Katie sat up and asked, "Why are you so, I don't know, so nothing?"

"I don't know what you mean."

"You're so calm, so emotionless, like it never happened. How can you be that way?"

"I'm grieving, just like you," Eric replied. "I don't know what you're supposed to do when you grieve."

"Couldn't you just, I don't know, why don't you scream something? Why aren't you crying?"

Eric thought for a moment, and said, "I don't know."

"What are you feeling?"

"I feel like—I feel like—I don't really feel like

anything" he said.

"Well that much I can well understand," said Katie affectionately. She let Eric enfold her in his arms again, and they were silent together for a time.

"I wanted so much to believe these people. I wanted so much to believe everything they were telling me about who I was. Did you ever believe them too? Did you ever *want* to believe them? Or was it all just a silly game to you?"

Eric breathed a long sigh and tried to collect his thoughts.

"I had dreams, when I was younger, just like you did," he said. "But I'm not a child anymore, so I don't know if I can have the same dreams. Nowadays I'm used to dealing with things that I can figure out for myself. I'm used to doing my own homework. So when you met these people and they brought you into their world, and they fulfilled all of your dreams, I don't know, I felt like I didn't belong."

"I wanted you to be a part of it, Eric. I tried hard to let you in," Katie explained.

"Yes you did. But you didn't have to. All I really wanted was just to know that you loved me, and wanted me to be a part of your life."

Katie was pleased by this. But after a few heartbeats, she asked, "Wouldn't you like to find out some day if you have it in you?"

Eric hesitated before answering. "After last night, well, for all the magic in the world, I'm still just some ordinary guy. That's all I have ever been."

"That's not true, Eric," said Katie, sitting up again. "No one is 'just some guy'. Everyone is—" Then she stopped herself, as she suddenly realised she was about to repeat something that Carlo had once told her.

"Everyone is what?" asked Eric.

"Everyone is—" she began, but then lay down in his arms again and said, "Nothing."

~ 79 ~

That evening, the bodies of four of the Brigantians, two men and two women, were placed on the deck of the reed-and-leather boat that Katie and Eric had used the night before. Tara was wrapped in her baby blanket and placed in the bow. No one spoke, but a lone Highland piper on the ridge spoke on everyone's behalf with his long, lonesome dirge. When all the bodies were in place, the ship guided itself out to the centre of the river, then ascended elegantly into the air and departed in the direction of the setting sun.

Several tables had been set up at one end of the standing stone circle, and plates of food were being laid on it for a feast. Katie and Eric were invited to stay for it, but neither of them felt much in the mood for celebration.

"I'm going for a walk," Katie told Eric, when the ship was out of sight. "I need some time alone."

She walked toward the entrance, but half way there turned around and ran to Eric and hugged him and kissed him. He hugged her tightly and lovingly in return. Then in a soft, quiet voice, she said, "Goodbye," and kissed him for a long time.

Then she slid from his arms and floated away, out of the grove, past the rubble of the cairn, past the fallen tree, and into the moonlit woods. Eric thought this parting behaviour rather odd, but knowing her feelings, he decided not to question it. In silence he watched her go.

When she thought she was out of sight and earshot of the grove, she started to run. The curtains of cedar branches opened before her, and the fingers of bare deciduous trees held themselves upright respectfully. And in the time of a few heartbeats, she had come back to the promontory that overlooked the meeting place of two rivers. Once more, she swung her legs over the stone wall and stood on the very edge, a mere finger's width from the long drop to the rocky rapids below. The water no longer ran with chunks of ice, but was still high and fast-flowing. There was no wildlife that she could see, as there was the last time. All was still, in every direction. In the distance, echoing off the walls of the gorge, she could hear the lone piper at the grove, although the music was faint, and easily mistaken for the wind. And here, as once before, she finally felt safe enough to let her grief release itself completely. She called out the name of the child who blessed her life, and for a fleeting time gave her a sacred purpose. In her mind she recalled the little looks and glances, the wordless gurgles and sounds, the touches and strokes, and she weighs them up in her mind. She counted the long sleepless nights of endless crying and hungry tantrums. She recalled Eric, the man she chose to be Tara's father, and how they met, and kissed on their first date, and declared their eternal undying love before knowing even their birthdays. She recalled with pride the games and jokes they shared, the music and laughter, the long nights of lovemaking, and the late lie-ins the next day. She recalled with fondness even the arguments and break-ups, for they too were part of how they lived, and how they kept up each other's honesty and courage. In her mind she counted up all of these things and asked herself if they outweighed the despair of Tara's death.

One last time she screams out Tara's name, and as before no answering voice calls back to her but the echo of her own. She is gone. Life will have to go on without her. If it is to go on at all. And that, indeed, is the question Katie asks herself. Shall I go on? Will it be worth going on, without her? Never to hold and touch her, never to play in fields of long grass, or see her grow up? How will I ever face Eric again, knowing that every time I look into his eyes I will see *her* there, and the life she should have had. How can I ever return to the grove and the magical life that the tribe offered me, if every time I enter the passage I have to pass by the place where she died! Even if they rebuild that cairn, it will no longer be the signpost to the sacred place. It will be her grave. What if there came a time when the memory of her faded, and I walked past the place where she died without remembering. Would it dishonour her memory if some day I found that I was no longer grieving for her?

Katie gripped the rocks of the wall tightly and leaned her head over the edge. The churning white water of the rapids poured relentlessly on the rocks below. The quick way, the easy way, would be to fall, to release my hands and allow myself to fall. Let the rapids wash away my suffering like a second baptism, and give birth to me again where the river empties into the sea. Perhaps there I will see her again, perhaps that magical ship will take me to the place where it took her, and we can live again together.

Katie pulled herself back up again. There was a grim fascination in the idea of leaping out to join her daughter in death. But the part of her mind that spoke with Eric's voice would not let her do it. Leaping to your own death, she heard him say, will not bring you to the place where Tara is. And Eric, too, is grieving, she knew, and he too needs a shoulder to cry on. He loved my Tara as much as I did, and he still loved her even when he knew he was not the father. That is surely worth something. He may be suppressing his feelings right now, but I know he has them. Otherwise, he would not have stayed by me as long as he did. Let it be my purpose, now, to be something like a saviour to him, just as Tara was once for me. And in so doing, perhaps he will be something like a saviour to me, and will show me how to go on.

Katie thus resolved herself to return to the grove, to find Eric, and to go on with her life with him. She told the rocks and the river of this new-found purpose, in order to solidify it in her own mind.

The soil beneath her feet was weak from the melting snow and ice of winter. A few thin and half invisible patches of ice still clung to the ledge, just in a place of shadow, not yet reached by the vestigial warmth of the coming spring. Just as Katie turned to pull her leg up and over the wall, to safety, they gave way. She suddenly found herself precariously balancing with one ankle half-way over the wall, and one hand half-gripping a stone. Hanging by a hand, her heart half-stopped with surprise, she kicked around for a foothold, and howled for help. A heartbeat later, the stone under her hand slipped from its crevice in the wall and she—

~ 80 ~

Eric accepted some of the food from the feast, but ate it quietly by himself, at a distance from the rest. When Katie did not return he eventually gave up waiting for her, and asked Miranda to tell Katie that he went home. Once arrived at his apartment, he set the table and prepared a light meal for two, and waited. He lit candles and incense, and cleaned up around the apartment a little bit. When he came to Katie's clothes, he folded them with a little more care and attention to detail than usual. He arranged her shoes and boots neatly in pairs. With surreal curiosity, he put his foot into one of her high-heel boots, and found that it fit perfectly. For a second he imagined that doing so brought him closer to understanding her. Then he returned to the dining table, uncorked a bottle of wine, and waited. He waited while the hours ticked by, the candles sputtered themselves out, and the food he set out grew cold on the plate. The following morning, Miranda found him asleep on his living room couch.

"Wake up," she prodded him.

Eric groggily rubbed his eyes and scratched his head,

which scraggled his hair more than it already was. It took him a moment to realize who was speaking to him.

"Sorry I'm not more presentable this morning," he apologized.

"Don't worry about it," said Miranda, sympathetically. Miranda was dressed as Eric had never seen her before: a black sleeveless silk dress, long black gloves that reached up to her elbows, a black hat with a thin veil, and low-heeled black shoes.

"Where is Katie?" Eric asked in a rough voice.

"She is—we went looking for her—we were searching all night."

Eric sat up, although still not fully awake. "What happened? Did you find her?"

"There is only one way to say it, Eric. We found her body."

Eric did not move. He looked at Miranda for a long time, as if he had not fully comprehended what she said.

"There's a reception at the funeral home today," she said. "For Tara too. We told her family, and they insisted on a quick ceremony and burial."

Eric stood, and started to clean up the food and the plates which he had laid out the night before. But he walked as if still half asleep, as if in a trance, going through the motions of a normal life. Miranda stopped him by taking his hands and forcing him to look into her eyes.

"Do you understand me? Katie is dead!"

Eric stopped. Miranda had to stare unblinking into his eyes for a long while before Eric could acknowledge what she was saying. When his countenance finally relaxed, she explained further.

"We found her body, floating down the river."

His jaw tightened. "Carlo!" he growled.

"No," Miranda contradicted. "The DiAngelo had nothing to do with it this time. We searched the whole forest—none of them were about."

Eric tried a few more explanations of what happened, but could not articulate them with much clarity. Finally he asked where the funeral was to take place.

"There's only one funeral chapel in town," Miranda reminded him. "There's a reception there this afternoon, and a burial tomorrow."

"I will be there," he said.

~ 81 ~

Eric slept through the reception. But the following day he put on his best suit and went to the funeral home for the memorial ceremony. He shook hands with Katie's parents, and most of her friends. All of them had the same empty condolences for him, and he began to grow tired of thanking them for their concern. Miranda was there, dressed in her funeral best, as were most of the Brigantians whom Eric could recognize. Paul made an appearance at the funeral, and tried to lay a bouquet of carnations on the casket. But the Brigantians managed to eject him without drawing any unusual attention. Then the casket was loaded in a hearse and taken to the cemetery on the north side of the village for the burial.

"Let me walk with you," Miranda offered. "No one should be alone at a time like this."

They walked in silence most of the way. When they arrived at the burial site, most of the people who attended the funeral service were already there. With long, morose faces they watched the minister perform the Christian last rights upon her closed casket, in accord with the wishes of Katie's family.

"I wanted to tell you one more thing," said Miranda, after the service was over. "I'm leaving."

Eric was a little surprised by this. "Leaving?"

"It was once said of my kind that we are the people who live in that moment when the sun is about to set, or to rise, and it is neither night nor day, and neither this world nor the other. But I see what this world has become, and how little interest it has in sunsets, and other worlds. In the last few days I saw how I could not protect my people anymore. And I have looked into the water. I know who I am, and I know my time here is spent and done."

Eric tried to be encouraging. "There seemed to be a lot of you at the grove, last night. There must be more of you out there, and more places like your grove that need protection."

"Not as many as there once was, Eric," sighed Miranda. "And I feel it is no longer for me to look after them. I need someone to take my place, and when my successor is found, I shall be on my way."

Miranda opened her handbag and from it she withdrew a strange, roughly carved, brown wooden chalice, wrapped in a cloth cover.

"This treasure has been used in the selection of our chiefs since our clan was founded, many centuries ago. I'm giving it to you because I want you to be my arbiter of succession. No one knows that I'm giving it to you, and I don't want you to tell anyone you have it."

"Why not?"

"So that if anything happens to me before my successor is found, no one will be able to claim it. And if that happens, you will have to find the next Chief of the Brigantians without me. I know I'm asking a lot from you. But I need someone who reasons like you do, and who I can trust."

Eric nodded and accepted the chalice. His eyes then scanned the group of people assembled at the graveside.

"I think I know someone who might be perfect for you."

~ **82** ~

After the burial, Miranda and Eric waked together from the cemetery until they came to the Old Bridge Road.

"I've got to turn off this way to go home," said Eric.

"I know," said Miranda. "What will you do now?" she asked him.

"I don't know," Eric admitted. "But I don't want you to say 'You'll go on with your life', or 'Do what Katie would have wanted'. People have been saying that to me all day, and I'm tired of it."

"It is a bit of a cliché," Miranda agreed.

"Because I *don't know* how I will go on," said Eric. "She is gone, but everywhere I look, I can still see her. In these people leaving the funeral, she is in the sway of that woman's dress, walking down the road. I see her in that woman's red hair, blowing in the wind. She's in that other woman there, holding the hand of a little girl, taking her to the playground. I see her in that old lady there, cutting the hedge on her front yard. I see her in that tree, that lamp post, that squirrel, that crow. Wherever I look, I see is something that reminds me of her. It's like she is everywhere."

Miranda tightened her hands around his and smiled. "I think you are well on your way."

"Oh, I don't know what I'm saying," Eric flustered. "It

might just be some kind of nonsense to help me feel better."

"You will see her again. I believe that. I *promise* that," she declared.

"She is dead, Miranda," Eric insisted.

"Yes she is," Miranda agreed. "but her spirit lives on."

Eric raised his voice a notch. "That sounds a bit too much like another cliché. What the hell does it really mean!" he stammered.

"It means everything that *you* just said it means," Miranda chided him.

Eric looked away self-consciously. He paused, and then told her, "Maybe so, but I don't know. I mean, no, that's not what I mean. I know you're trying to help. And I appreciate it. But I just can't think straight right now."

Miranda could see his conflicting thoughts and repressed feelings, and decided it was best not to press the point. She hugged him tenderly for a while.

"I had better go home," said Eric, when she released him.

Miranda nodded. "I will visit you one last time before I leave for good," she offered.

"Please do," Eric replied.

They exchanged goodbyes and parted ways at the foot of the old stone bridge. Eric watched her go for a moment. For a longer while after that he gazed thoughtfully at the flickering of the lamp on the corner of the bridge. Ganga, the spotted Calico cat who lived with him, sat at its base, watching and waiting. And then Eric strode forward purposefully once again, toward home.

~ The end ~

~ Epilogue, some months later ~

As Eric left the festival and set himself in the direction of home, a figure stepped out to intercept him. He was taller than Eric by a head and a shoulder, and wore an eighteenth-century town crier's outfit, with loud clashing colours. He had long scraggly sideburns on his face, a black top hat, and a large rainbow coloured flower in his breast pocket. He would have looked ridiculous if not for the hundreds of ridiculously dressed festival goers in the park behind him. With his left hand he twirled a cane, and with his right he pointed at Eric, to get his attention.

"I know you. Is your name - I'm sure I know you - what's your name?"

Eric kept on walking. "I'm sorry I can't help you."

"That's a strange way to answer a man who asks you who you are. Maybe you don't know who you are!"

"I'm not going to go there right now. Goodnight," said Eric. And under his breath he muttered, "Weirdo."

The man jogged up beside Eric and matched strides with him. "Eric! That's it. You name is Eric. What's your last name? No wait, I know it. You're Eric La- wait don't tell me - it's La-something."

"Are you one of Miranda's people?" asked Eric.

"No, I'm not one of her people. I'm a friend of a friend of yours. We have a friend in common, that's who I am. And she and I are very close. And she asked me to say hello to you."

"Well, say hello back. And now I'm going home."

"And this mutual friend of ours, this friend of a friend," added the strange man, "Her name is Katie."

Eric stopped walking and glared at him coldly.

"Katie - Corrigan, yes that's it," the man finished.

"That's not possible," exclaimed Eric. "Katie Corrigan is dead."

"Yes, she is. She died a few months ago. And I saw her this afternoon, and she asked me to find you, and she asked me say hello."

Eric's adventures continue in "Hallowstone", Part Two of The Fellwater Tales.

ABOUT THE AUTHOR

Brendan Myers is a professional philosopher, specializing in environmentalism, ethics and social justice, game design, and spirituality. He has taught philosophy at six different institutions in Canada and in Europe, and provided policy research for government agencies, labour unions, game design studios, and various private clients. His work has been featured by environmental groups, interfaith groups, and humanist societies around the world. "Fellwater" is his first novel.

Originally from a small town in Ontario Canada, Brendan earned his Ph.D in philosophy from NUI Galway (Ireland). He serves as a junior professor of philosophy at CEGEP Heritage College, in Gatineau, Quebec.

Find him on the web at http://brendanmyers.net

Made in the USA
Charleston, SC
19 April 2013